Final Storm

The Conclusion

A. R. Vagnetti

Wicked Storm Publishing

Copyright

FINAL STORM... THE CONCLUSION
Copyright © 2022 by Wicked Storm Publishing
Written by A.R. Vagnetti
Edited by Haley Willens
Cover Design by Les at German Creative

Content Warning: If things like violence, blood, gore, references to rape, consensual BDSM play with explicit sexual scenes, menage play, graphic language, and demons are triggers for you, then move along; this is NOT the book for you. In fact, my entire Storm series is NOT for you. But if you laugh in the face of such things and take pleasure in them—you're my kind of person, and happy reading!

This final book in the Storm Series is dedicated to the multitude of Paranormal Romance readers across the globe. Without your craving for things that go bump in the night blended with your romance, authors like me would wither away to nothing. Essentially, you saved my life.

This final book in the Storm Series is dedicated to the multitude of Paranormal Romance readers across the globe. Without your craving for things that go bump in the night blended with your romance, authors like me would wither away to nothing. Essentially, you saved my life.

Chapter 1

Cellica

Being a werewolf is legit. Being a wolf, however, whose transition is way overdue, sucks balls.

People look at me with sympathy or horror because I haven't shifted yet. And while I realize my transformation is coming in just a matter of time, one I mentally scream to hurry the fuck up, this waiting is driving me insane. My hormones are out of control. One second, I'm happy as a Lark, the next I'm furious with the world, or bawling my eyes out for no apparent reason. But what really blows chunks? My libido only pulsates for a certain vampire who hates my guts. A goddamn vampire!

I can't get the Guardian Christoph Nox out of my mind. Since the first moment I laid eyes on him, after the fae attack at the ranch several months ago, those mismatched irises burned my insides, and I craved those full lips easing the flame down below. His handsome face and deep timber play like a projector behind my closed lids, getting me off practically every night. I swear I'm replacing the batteries on my vibrator weekly at this point.

The tall, muscular male stars in my dreams, my daydreams, hell, those eyes are in my coffee each morning. But anytime Nox is near, his scowl scorches through my skull, and his attitude is as cold as the arctic, matching his condescending remarks that make me feel like an insecure teenager. I grind my teeth every time he calls me *kid*. Obviously, at twenty-five, I'm not a damn kid.

Nox has no clue that his comments hurt because the second his razor-sharp words pummel my self-confidence, I retaliate. My anger overrides any common sense, and I say the stupidest, and yes, most immature, things to strike back and not allow him to see what a pathetic loser I am for him. Or how his mere presence gets my vagina all aflutter.

To make matters worse, Nox is best friends with my overbearing brother, Liam—the werewolf king. Liam, along with Josh, my other overprotective sibling, scare off every guy I've tried to date. Since the day I turned sixteen—nine freaking years ago—my siblings alienated me from the opposite sex, which wasn't hard to do living at the remote Wild Beast Ranch in Montana, miles from any town.

Don't get me wrong. I love them both to the moon and back. Liam had big shoes to fill when he inherited the crown after the former vampire king killed our dad in battle two years ago. Losing my father still tightens my chest. I miss him so much. Daddy was my everything. I never knew my mom. She died giving birth to me. My dad, Jimmy Scott, picked up the reigns of mother and father in addition to ruling the Werewolf Province, helping govern the Council of Unity, and being a business owner and rancher. Now those responsibilities rest on Liam's shoulders. Minus the actual parenting part. I no longer need to be parented as an adult, although my brothers would swiftly disagree. Not to mention, Liam's mated to a freaking Oracle—the seer of the immortal world.

I love my sister-in-law dearly, but in truth, she gives me the heebie-jeebies. I keep expecting those amber eyes to turn on me and accuse me of secretly panting after my vampire. Regardless, her knowing grins give me heart palpitations.

My brother's responsibilities run a mile wide, so I do everything to stay under the radar and not add to them. Thank goodness Josh stepped into Liam's old shoes as second in command, which leaves my sole responsibility, to graduate.

I get they are trying to protect me, be the pseudo parents they feel the necessity to be, but the minute a male werewolf learns my last name—they refuse to come within six feet of me. It's both of my brothers' faults that I'm a damn virgin at the ripe old age of twenty-five.

And my friends are no better. You'd think a girl could rely on her girlfriends to help her get laid. But no, the cowards are just as afraid of Liam as the spineless boys. So what's a wolf gotta do to get noticed? To rid herself of this barrier to womanhood. I fucking dyed my hair blue just so guys would pay attention. In all honesty, it was a welcome change from the mouse brown matching my equally boring eye color. I can't wait until my transition, and to see my irises light up to an awesome ice blue like Liam's.

"Hey, you coming out tonight?" my best friend Jessica asked the morning before I left, bumping shoulders with me as we walked through campus. "Please don't tell me you're heading to the ranch again. We never party on the weekends anymore."

"That's not true," I mumbled. The guilt from neglecting my friends pricked at my conscience. "And as much as I'd love to go drinking with you guys, I have a long drive ahead of me. Liam asked me to head up to the cabin in Idaho and check on the place. It will give me a chance to study for finals without distractions."

"Ugh. Why do you love that remote cabin so much? The thick woods have creeped me out the few times I've been there."

Because Nox's home is only a couple miles through those creepy woods and being near his retreat thrills me... but I couldn't say that. So instead, I gave her my standard response. "It's the one place I'm not being suffocated by the overabundance of male testosterone trying to control my every move," I answered.

In a few short months, I'll graduate with my Masters in Professional Accountancy with a Bachelor in Agricultural Business from Montana State University. Even though I've already been managing the books for the Wild Beast Ranch since I was eighteen, it's still a wild achievement to me.

Statistics fascinate me. Whole numbers, fractions, decimals, percentages, ratios, order of operations, exponents, and general algebra comfort me. Problem-solving gives me a rush. Using numbers and manipulating financial statements to paint a picture of the health of a company, organization, or individual, satisfies and completes me.

My friends think I'm sick in the head, but I can't explain this weird compulsion for figures. Even though the ranch is a four-and-a-half-hour drive from campus, I spend most weekends either balancing the books, moving herds, branding, or helping our on-site veterinarian whenever required. As a result, it alleviates Liam's workload. Plus, laboring outdoors with the animals keeps me grounded, allows me to soak up some much-needed Vitamin D, and keeps me fit.

It's also a real treat to go with Liam or Josh to auctions. You can't beat the atmosphere around cowboys. Their raw yet humble energy excites me. Even though my first love is numbers, cowgirling it up, breathing in the fresh country air, runs a close second.

I shake my head and let go of my inner musings to refocus on the columns of numerals before me on the desk for the hundredth time. Much to my best friend's irritation, I arrived yesterday at our cabin in Idaho. Honestly, I needed a few days alone to focus without the distraction of school, the chores at the ranch, or my brothers. But for whatever reason, the numbers swirl and jumble, and nothing makes sense. I've got a pretty good idea why I can't concentrate. I scented Nox on my walk this morning, and the anticipation of seeing him ramps my nerves into overdrive. I itched to get closer for a quick glimpse of the sexy brute, but I didn't dare venture too near. The vampire would perceive my presence from a mile off. According to Liam, Nox is the finest tracker in the Vampire Nation.

"He's like a damn bloodhound," my big brother told me one evening at the ranch. "It's the damnedest thing," he continued with a shake of his head, taking a sip of his whiskey. "I'd venture to say his tracking ability rivals mine when I'm in beast form."

"No way," I breathed, enthralled with any iota of information regarding Nox. Home for the weekend, we lounged on the outdoor patio by a roaring firepit, each nursing a drink after spending all day moving a herd from one pasture to the other.

"No, it's true." He nodded just as Josh sauntered outside shirtless, with gray sweatpants hugging his lean hips, a glass of bourbon dangling from his fingertips.

"No one's a better tracker than you, big bro," Josh commented before taking the wicker loveseat opposite me.

Liam chuckled. "While I appreciate the praise, I freely admit Nox is *slightly* better than me."

"But how do you know for sure?" I inquired, being careful not to show an interest, or my brother would shut down the conversation in a heartbeat. "Have you gone on a hunt with him?"

Liam's eyes narrowed as he studied me, but much to my relief, he answered the question. "Yes. And because of Nox's skill, we discovered a nest of rogue vampires hiding out in the sewer system of New York." He shook his head in wonder. "How he scented them amidst all the rank odors, I'll never know."

Coming back to earth, I toss the paperwork and memories away in disgust and rise from the desk. I'm too antsy to sit inside and work on numbers. I'd love nothing more than to shift and run as a wolf, but I must settle for a hike as an average human until my transition occurs.

The cool evening air hits my face, and I breathe in the fresh scent of pine and earth. As a werewolf, even one who hasn't shifted yet, my body temp runs several degrees higher than a mortal, so I disregard the coat rack by the backdoor.

I'd like to say I don't have a clear destination in mind, but I'd be kidding myself. Christoph Nox calls to me with more power than an Alpha's command, so I turn due east at a brisk pace despite the fact the only light to guide me is the sifting moon through the trees.

Maybe I'll get a glimpse of him shirtless. Gawd. Just the thought puts a spring in my stride and accelerates the thumping of my heart. Perhaps I'll be brave enough to step from the shadows and have an actual conversation with the sexy vampire this time.

I pick up the pace with an eager smile, needing my Nox fix.

Chapter 2

Cellica

A calmness overwhelms my spirit whenever I'm surrounded by nature. Is it merely my consciousness seeking peace, or is it my inner animal making her presence known? Either way, the sounds of the birds, critters scurrying to hide, or the rush of the wind through the trees calls to me, and I seek this solitude as often as I can.

At the homestead, I find solace via horseback. The pressures of school, graduation, and the overwhelming idea of the big imperfect world out there for the taking melts away. Liam wants me to work for the ranch. To reside on the property, either at the homestead or in my place somewhere on the thousands of acres. So the day each of us hit eighteen, my dad drew up plans for houses for his kids, hoping we'd all stay and raise our own families on the ranch.

Liam also wants Josh and I to settle at the Wild Beast, and while I'm pretty confident Josh possesses no desire to leave, I'm not so sure I want to spend the rest of my life in Montana. Besides, most of the time, Nox resides at the Vampire Nation in the remote area of Nunavut, Canada.

Wait. Stop planning your future around Nox, dumbass.

Besides, I've heard him talking to my brother, and it's clear the vampire has no desire for a permanent woman in his life. He enjoys playing the field too much. Anger bubbles to the surface at the thought of him fucking other women. Those large hands fisting their hair in the throes of passion. His fangs sunk deep into their flesh as he brings them to orgasm.

"Fuck, Cel. Get a grip," I mutter as my insides ache for those fantasies. But Nox has never looked at me with anything more than annoyance. Instead, he merely sees me as Liam's little sister and as off-limits.

Could the Guardian be my mate? Who the fuck knows? I could walk right by my fated male every day until my transition and never realize it beyond a strange sense of familiarity. Or so I've been told.

I pause when I hear the deep rumble of King Darath. What the hell is he doing here? I ease forward, apprehension tingling up my spine. The demon king is kinda scary. Not that he's mean, just the opposite. Darath has been jovial with me the few times I've been in his presence. But something about the power radiating off the creature, combined with those eerie red irises, raises the hair on my nape.

"Is yours the only home?" King Darath asks.

"No, but I own twenty acres on either side. Listen," he gestures to the log structure, "why don't you come inside, and we can contact Nicole and find out what the heck happened to you."

Tingles race across my skin at the sound of Nox's voice, but I ignore them and walk into the clearing in front of the vampire's cabin. I stop in my tracks at the sight of the demon king's sculpted ass on full display.

What the hell? It looks like he has a shirt tied around his waist, but for what reason? "Nice ass, King Darath," I giggle and step closer.

"Does Liam know you are consorting with his little sister?" Darath asks, raising an eyebrow at Nox.

"What?" Christoph exclaims, his cheeks darkening. "Yes. I mean, no–nothing is going on between Cellica and me. She and Josh own the cabin on the next property."

"Convenient," Darath sneers, adjusting the shirt covering his manly parts. "What became of Kleora?" he demands. "Did she return?"

What does he mean? I obviously missed something huge since nobody has bothered to keep the little sister informed. On anything.

"No clue," Christoph replies, his frown deepening the more I continue to ogle King Darath's chiseled torso with avid interest. "Neither one of you surfaced."

What the hell does that signify?

"Jag," Nox barks. The irritated expression fixed permanently on his face when I'm around glares at me. "Seriously, dude, conjure pants."

"Never took you for a prude, Vampire," I smirk, jutting my hip, my fingers splayed out over the denim covering my waist. Nox's irritation with me raises my hackles, and of course, I mouth off just to watch his anger escalate. "I'm more than fine if you want to drop the shirt, Demon." I smile enticingly at Darath.

The low growl emanating from Nox stalls the breath in my lungs and an emerging part of me craves to lower my gaze in subjugation like he's my damn Alpha. What the holy hell is wrong with me?

"Go home, little girl," Nox thunders, his beautiful mismatched eyes sparking. "Nobody wants you here."

His remarks pierce my heart, but I refuse to let it show. "One day, you will regret those words, fanger." My tone is livid, squelching the hurt simmering below the surface. Why does he hate me so much? And why can't I control my anger and mouth? Maybe if

I carried on a normal conversation, as a damn adult would, he wouldn't treat me like an unwanted child. And I'm sure I wasted the obscenity *fanger*, which hails from the TV show *True Blood*, on Nox. Besides, he's more like a hyped-up version of Dean Winchester from *Supernatural* than Eric Northman.

Sparks on the edge of the clearing catch my attention, and I gasp at the vision of Priestess Tanagra—the deceased Priestess Tanagra—engulfed in flames, her body shimmering like a specter.

Holy shit! She's a ghost.

"What the fuck?" Nox whispers, his eyes wide with disbelief.

"Kleora," Darath growls low, pulling a smoldering projectile from his shoulder. She shot him. Skewered him with a flaming arrow. Wait. I thought they were a couple. Now she's trying to kill him?

In the next instant, Nox is in front of me, the entire width of his shoulders and back a hair's breadth away when the Priestess lets loose another fiery arrow at Darath. When the big demon sidesteps the flaming bolt at the last second, the projectile sinks into Nox's chest instead.

"Chris!" I scream as his body plows into me, knocking us off our feet. The heat of the fire sears my skin as I rip the arrow from his flesh and frantically slap at the flames rapidly spreading over his torso with my bare hands. "Nox," I shout. "Are you alright?"

His long lashes flutter. The dual-covered glow nearly blinds me when his lids lift. His blazing gaze takes me in before shifting to the Priestess. His fangs drop, and a vicious snarl escapes those fantastic lips. Lust slams through my body at the sight of them.

What the heck is wrong with me? We are in a dire situation, and all I can think about is dropping to my knees before Nox and doing anything he commanded. I'd crawl across the forest naked if he demanded it for a small iota of his affection.

Jesus, Cel. Get a fucking grip.

And then it happens. Nox rolls, pinning me beneath him, and I nearly combust. Large hands cradle my skull as the weight of his body covers me from chest to toes. His breath warms my neck and ear and I clutch his waist, overcome with desire.

Nox's chest expands as he inhales deep, his head jerking up, his gaze trapping mine. The bright irises drop to my parted lips, and I freeze, waiting for the feel of his mouth on mine.

"Baby girl," he whispers, and I groan at his nickname for me. Dampness floods my panties, and I spread my legs to accommodate his hips. But the second his hardness contacts my fiery center, his jaw hardens, and he leaps to his feet, dragging me behind him.

He shouts something to King Darath, but I can't hear anything over the buzzing in my head. Holy shit. Nox's hard body covered mine, and he almost kissed me. I'm sure of it. I may not have much experience in this area, but the heat in his gaze was lust. And it was directed at me.

Does Nox secretly desire me? God, I fucking hope so. I can work with that if it's true.

A sudden fire devours my mind, robbing me of my breath. Horrible images of death and destruction invade my skull, and a vile presence consumes my spirit. My body convulses with no authority to stop it.

"Cel? What's wrong, baby girl?" Nox's voice sounds distant, like cotton fills my ears. I want to respond, scream at the agony coursing through my frame, but when I open my mouth wide, no sound emerges, and I can't seem to control the convulsions rattling my bones.

Am I dying? Did one of Priestess Tanagra's arrows pierce my heart?

I barely feel the powerful arms engulfing me, and I can't make out where they're taking me. Then, within seconds, darkness shrouds my vision as I'm sucked into what feels like the very bowels of Hell.

Chapter 3

Nox

Dread fills my gut as I lay my precious bundle on my bed. Her skin is waxen, and I barely detect the rise and fall of her chest. What the hell happened out there? My senses endured a gambit of emotions in only a few seconds.

When Cellica walked out of the forest, ogling Darath's ass, jealousy and rage hit hard. I wanted to rip the demon to shreds. I peer down at the charred flesh on my chest, wincing as my skin flakes off and crumbles down to the floor. It's healing, but magic laced whatever fire Kleora wielded because, usually, I'd have healed in seconds.

I gently lift Cellica's tiny hand, remembering her frantic efforts to smother the inferno. Sure enough, angry red blisters cover her palms. The little idiot tried to save me.

I peer at her face, brushing a blue strand from her cheek. When her body convulsed, fear raced through my veins. Now she doesn't even stir, and my heart stutters. It's almost like she's a sleeping vampire—still as death.

I can't do anything about her unconsciousness, so I slip into the guest bedroom closet and drag out my mobile medicinal kit. Human, immortal, or animal medicine are all pretty close in the way that they work. Since I'm often called away to handle emergencies, I keep a fully stocked medical bag here at my cabin and in my room at the castle in Canada.

As I wet a clean washrag with cold water, I reflect on my alternate career choice. Surprisingly, I'm not the only veterinarian in the immortal race, but we are a rarity. So I have to be prepared to transport anywhere in the world to treat and care for the immortal's pets. Dogs, cats, and even exotic animals—our kind own a gambit of species.

My queen has no issue with my second job as long as it doesn't interfere with my Guardian duties. And I agree. My allegiance to Queen Giordano, and my responsibilities as second in command, must come first.

I ease onto the bed next to Cellica and place the open bag on the floor. Holding the cool washcloth to the inflamed area for several minutes, I clean her palms with gentle care. Unfortunately, the little werewolf doesn't stir throughout the process, and my anxiety rises with each passing minute she remains unconscious. What caused her body to seize? Is she damaged somehow?

Since I first opened my eyes as a baby, my parents deemed me a defective misfit. The colors of my irises were different. My family shunned me, treating me like the hired help instead of their son. My father tried to beat the disfigurement out of me, and my mother acted like I didn't exist. When I trained for the Guardians, they laughed in my face. "Do you honestly believe the king will accept you? We should have killed you the second we realized you were flawed."

Yeah, that was my upbringing, but I proved them wrong. Logan and Sebastian didn't care that my eyes were different colors. All they cared about was my loyalty and skills. They became my family, and I would gladly lay down my life for either of them in a heartbeat.

Once the burns are cleaned, I retrieve a tube of silver sulfadiazine, a topical burn cream, and apply it to both palms before wrapping them in gauze and cling wrap. My gaze continues to bounce from my task to her face, hoping to see those enticing whiskey irises staring back at me.

I grind my teeth as I remember the intoxicating perfume of her arousal outside. The little wolf desired me, and even amidst the chaos, my cock responded to her scent. But Cellica is forbidden. She's my best friend's little sister and a werewolf who hasn't graduated college yet or transitioned into her immortality phase. Her whole life lies before her, spread out like a fully stocked blood bank.

I rub my nape, bolting to my feet with nervous energy. The kicker? Cellica is my one true mate, but the connection won't solidify for sure until after she transitions. Not that it matters. Liam will have my balls if I even look sideways at his baby sister. And I can't really blame him. She can do so much better than me.

Since the day of my rebirth—how I refer to morphing into immortality—I never wanted a mate. Still don't. Especially not a beautiful, exotic, sheltered werewolf. Although the second I laid eyes on Cellica, electricity nearly short-circuited my brain. The urge to grab her by that crazy blue hair and mark her as mine seized my muscles in readiness.

Fortunately, the mating bond wasn't as strong as I'd heard, and I resisted. Once she transitions, however... how the fuck will I keep my hands and fangs to myself?

Not that it matters, she's the sister to a king. I'm just a lowly Guardian with weird colored eyes, a questionable background, and a notorious reputation as a ladies' man. I have nothing to offer her besides endless hours of solitude. My responsibilities consume my nights, and I sleep when the sun rises through the sky. My werewolf does not.

A low moan snags my attention, and I trace to the bed instantly. Thick, dark lashes flutter as I sit on the mattress next to her.

"Cellica?" Her lids pop open, and those whiskey irises zero in on me with eerie precision and directness that startles me. "How... how are you feeling?"

She doesn't answer right away, merely studies me, as if trying to analyze everything about me in mere minutes. No fear or uncertainty resides in her scrutiny as she silently takes in me and the room.

"Baby girl?" I inquire again with a frown. There's something off with her. Maybe she hit her head when she fell.

"Christoph Nox," she finally replies, as if asking a question.

"Umm, yeah. How do you feel?"

"Free," she breathes with reverence, and I scowl at her response.

Free? What the hell is that supposed to mean? "Do you recall what happened?" I ask.

"Yes. I remember it all." She sits up, coming face to face with me. "But you wish to know what I retain most?"

I swallow my desire as her gaze seems to heat, and her tone lowers to a husky whisper. "No. What?" I foolishly query.

"Your cock pressing against my pussy."

What. The. Fuck.

"Excuse me?" I rasp, shocked by her explicit candor.

"I need to feel your length inside me, Nox. Pounding into my flesh, our bodies slick with sweat until we both explode into nirvana."

My cock hardens in an instant, visualizing her naked body writhing beneath mine. No! What the hell is happening?

I leap to my feet, putting some distance between us, but the sexy werewolf simply rises to stalk me across the room.

"I felt the hard thickness of you against me, Nox. You want me. To take me from behind, to pound into my pussy. Or maybe you're an ass man. Is that what you would like, vampire? To fuck me in the ass?"

I can only stare at her, my jaw practically on the floor. What the hell happened to my insecure little werewolf with eyes that danced with equal amounts of anger and devotion? Standing before me is a totally different female. One I'd bed in a heartbeat if she were anyone else.

"Cellica. Stop this," I bark, the command watered with the gruffness of lust. The dirty talk is getting to me, and I need to shut this down pronto.

"Stop what, Nox? Cease craving your cock in my mouth? Your fangs in my neck as you thrust deep inside me?"

"Fuck." I can't hold the groan in. Before I know it, I've retreated into a corner of my room, the only exit blocked by the wanton hellion prowling toward me. Every molecule of my being craves to grab her by that glorious mane of blue hair, shove her to her knees and fuck her foul mouth. My dick pulsates with profound need. One I haven't experienced in my century and a half of life.

Bandaged hands glide over my naked torso, and my skin twitches under her touch. Blunt nails trace the family crest over my right peck and down my ribcage, and I grit my teeth to maintain my clenched fists at my sides.

"You hail from Eric Bloodaxe's line?" Surprised eyes find mine. "Fuck me like the Viking you are, Nox. Hard. Soft. Slow. Fast. However, I don't care. I just need to fuck."

"Jesus, Cellica," I moan, snatching her roaming hands by the wrists, careful to keep away from her burns. "Knock it off."

"Or what, vampire?" she whispers, leaning into me, the heat from her body clenching my muscles. "Will you punish me? Spank my bare bottom red?"

I nearly lose my grip on reality. "Is that what you'd like, baby girl? A spanking?"

What the fuck am I doing? I should shut down this conversation, not escalate it with fantasy talk. Just visualizing her lying prone over my lap, her perfect ass exposed and ready for discipline, the evidence of her need slick on her thighs has my cock jerking in my pants.

"Oh yes. Spank me, degrade me, whip me. I want it all, as long as your dick is my reward."

Christ. This can't be happening. "Who are you?" I whisper in awe, my arms encircling her waist to bring her flush against me, my reservations like mist in the wind.

"Anything you want me to be," she replies before leaning in and claiming my lips in a searing kiss to seal my doom.

Chapter 4

Nox

The softness of Cellica's lips nearly brings me to my knees. I've fantasized about her mouth. Of running my tongue along the plump seam, listening to her needy moans as I nibble at the lush bottom lip. Or the exotic feel of those smooth pillows wrapped around my cock as she takes me down her throat.

With a deep growl of need, I grip a fistful of her silky hair and jerk her head back, enabling me more control to take her lips in the manner I crave to claim her luscious little body. Cellica grips my waist, her nails digging into my skin as her tongue duels with mine, a give and take dance matching the pounding in my groin.

With how Liam and Josh have protected Cel her whole life, I assumed she was inexperienced with males. Until tonight, her shy, heated glances proved it. So this aggressiveness—attacking my mouth with desperation, like the little minx knows what she wants and how to get it—is entirely surprising.

How many guys has she allowed to fucking touch her?

The mere notion of another man's hands handling what belongs to me ramps my anger to a fever pitch, and I grip her biceps, breaking the kiss to stare into her eyes. Our panting breaths fill the space between us, and my muscles clench at the dark, determined lust consuming her expression. The warm brown of her irises takes on an eerie, red-tinged glow. While my body is more than willing to answer her blatant plea, logic assumes command, knowing I'm treading dangerous waters here. If I don't shut this down in the next few seconds, my craving for her will override my brain.

"Cellica," I warn. "We must stop."

"No," she growls low, and my eyebrow jerks up at the menacing quality of her tone. "I need you, Nox. Now."

With astonishing power, Cel shoves me against the wall with enough force, my shoulders dent the plaster. Before I can process this change, she rips off her bandages and flings them on the floor. Her shirt follows in an instant.

My eyes widen with shock when she reaches behind her to unclasp her pretty lace bra.

"Wait," I bark, holding out my hand to emphasize my point. "You proceed, and I will hogtie you to my bed. I mean it, Cellica. Stop this right now."

"Oh," she smirks. "You wish to tie me up and have your wicked way with me, Nox?" The bra hits the floor, and it takes all my control not to glance down. "I'm so fucking on board with that."

"Goddamnit, Cel."

She steps toward me again, but before those breasts touch my chest and make me lose my shit, I bend down and grip her jean-clad thighs, flipping her over my shoulder. I retrieve her shirt from the floor before striding into the closet with my package in tow.

I'm not strong enough to resist what she is so brazenly offering. So the one way to preserve this situation until someone can intervene is to get her restrained, and my cock as far away from her as possible.

I stride to the back of the wardrobe. Cellica caresses my shoulders, and down my spine, before reaching into the waistband of my jeans to grip my ass.

"Cellica, knock it off for fuck's sake," I growl, my cock hardening to painful proportions.

"But you have an impressive body, Nox. And this ass… yummy."

Christ, I'm in trouble.

When I arrive at the cabinet, I jerk the door open with more force than necessary, breaking the hinge. I ignore the damage and grasp the long braids of rope hanging neatly on the pegs. Since she's pre-transition, the cords should hold her.

Throughout my life, I've enjoyed many diverse aspects of sex. Fantasy play, BDSM, sex in public, group activity, straight vanilla, or whatever strikes me or my partner's fancy at the time. Although one thing has always remained consistent—control belongs to me. I'm an Alpha male. I wouldn't have made it into the Guardian program or through my shitty existence if I wasn't. Now that's not to say I wouldn't allow my partner a little authority once in a while, but I could never submit to a female. So I'll never understand how Liam, the king of werewolves and the ultimate Alpha, does it for his mate Viessa, a known Mistress.

Ropes in hand, sweat beads on my upper lip. I attempt to ignore Cellica's roaming hands and the feel of her hardened nipples rubbing against my skin with each move as I stride to the bed. Instead of dumping my precious bundle on the mattress, I stare at it for several seconds and contemplate how the hell I'm going to get her shirt back on without the visual of those lush breasts bringing me to my knees.

Come on, Christoph. You're a trained soldier, a goddamn veterinarian. Just treat this as a clinical situation. Pretend she's a fucking dog if you have to, but get it done.

"Nox, please touch me. I'm dying here."

Pep talk over, I dump her ass on the edge of the mattress and quickly shove the shirt over her head. But in record time, Cellica has my jeans unzipped and is caressing my throbbing length over my boxer briefs.

"Fuck," I can't help but groan as pure pleasure radiates through my body, and desire clouds my brain. The sensation of her small hands kneading my aching cock is beyond bliss.

"Wow," she breathes, arching her scrumptious neck, her gaze direct. "You're a big boy."

Jesus.

I gnash my teeth, even as heat builds behind my irises, lighting up her face in turquoise and blue. "Put your arms through the goddamn shirt," I rasp, hoping she obeys, my resistance weakening by the second.

"Please, Nox. Let me taste you. Just for a second."

My swallow fills the room. I want her mouth on me with a desperation that scares me. Still, as I open my mouth to say yes, Liam's livid face pops in my mind, cooling my ardor as effectively as a dip in the arctic.

"No." My deep growl startles her, but I ignore her pout. Instead, I shove one arm through an armhole and put as much contempt behind the following words as possible. "I prefer a *woman* on my dick, not a fucking child."

The pretty irises narrow at the barb, but it distracts her momentarily so I can finish shoving her other arm into the shirt. When the back of my hand accidentally brushes the side of her breast, we both moan at the contact. I want nothing more than to feel their weight in my palms, tweak the nipples, and suck them until they are turgid peaks of pleasure.

No. No. No. Focus, Nox.

Much to my irritation, my fingers tremble as I finish my task, despite Cellica continuing to fight me—swatting at my hands as she reaches for my crotch again. Once her shirt is in place, I re-zip my jeans and tie her wrist and ankles to the rings in the headboard and footboard with supernatural speed, installed for this very purpose. Well, not for this purpose. But observing her tied to my bed is fucking with my head.

No sex with the little sister, for fuck's sake.

"My pussy is all woman, vampire. She weeps for your touch," Cellica cries out, lifting her hips off the mattress.

Jesus. I've got to get out of here.

"Knock it off, Cellica. Your behavior is pissing me off," I snort inwardly. My cock is far from pissed. On the contrary, it's eager for everything the petite minx begs from it.

"I know," she pouts prettily. "I'm a bad, bad girl, Daddy. I need a spanking."

"Fuck me," my agonized whisper escapes before I can stop it as my gaze roams the gyrating, deliciously enticing body trussed up and ripe for the taking. The precious little werewolf has morphed into every fantasy I've imagined over the years, all rolled up into one tempting package. If I don't escape the sexual heat coming off her in waves, this night will end with my dick buried deep in her pussy.

An image of an enraged Liam in beast form dominates my mind as I turn my back on what my cock is screaming to claim. Few can defeat Liam when his beast takes over, especially if the creature is beyond pissed. Besides, he'd have every right to take my head if I violated his little sister.

"Sorry, kid, I make it a rule to steer clear of innocents. And were-wolves." A blatant lie. Since meeting my potential mate—*potential? Who are you fucking kidding, Nox?*—I've fucked every willing werewolf I could find to banish those whiskey irises from haunting my dreams. I've been deliberately mean to her, treating her like an annoying teenager instead of a grown-ass woman ready to transition into immortality. But it was the only way to keep my inner vampire at bay and throw suspicion off from my best friend.

Too impatient to walk to the living room, I trace to the front porch and head straight for my pile of logs needing chopping. If I don't work off this lust, it will snuff out my conscience, and

I'll storm back into my cabin and plunge deep into the forbidden fruit, shouting for all she's worth for a thorough fucking.

Christ. What happened to my life? This alternate universe where demons come crawling up from the earth in front of my house, ghosts shoot arrows with hellfire, and my lust rages for my best friend's little sister, fucks with my hard-earned control.

If Liam ever suspects Cellica could be my one true mate, he'll beast out, rip my limbs from my body one by one, and beat me bloody with them. I'm in over my head. Maybe it's time to seek help.

Chapter 5

My eyes snap open. Cold sweat covers my shaking body, and if I were a mere mortal, the pounding of my heart would scare the shit out of me. What the hell is happening to me? Flashes of my interactions with Nox dance in my vision. Why couldn't I control my actions? Why couldn't I have shut my mouth? I witnessed every horrifyingly embarrassing sexual move or word I made toward Nox. It was like I was a bystander with duct tape over my lips, and a puppeteer controlled my limbs.

But holy shit, the blazing lust in Nox's colorful gaze set my body on fire, and I wanted it to be me saying and doing the things that drove him crazy with desire. I've coveted it since the first moment I laid eyes on him. But it wasn't me he was reacting to. And doesn't that take another huge chunk out of my self-confidence? Until tonight, he scorned my lame attempts at flirting with a sneer or snide remark about me being a kid.

A dark presence has taken residence inside me, and even though I was fully aware of what was happening, I couldn't stop it to save my life. Whatever controlled me wanted to fuck my vampire with a desperation bordering on psychotic. I'm somewhat mollified he treated the entity the same way last night before he traced away.

Not that I blame it for having the hots for Nox, but the things I said... it said and did, spread warmth across my cheeks. Holy shit, never in a million years would I dream of being that aggressive. I begged... dammit, *it begged* for Nox to fuck me... shit... *it*, and there wasn't a thing I could do to stop it.

With a deep breath, I take a second to assess my inner situation. The depraved being still exists deep down but seems dormant. The big question is, what is it, and how in the green acres did it get inside me? Has a demon possessed me? I remember a portal opening right before my mind seized with fire. I've never heard of a demon possessing an immortal before. Wait. Is it because I haven't transitioned yet, so I'm fair game?

I attempt to sit up, forgetting Nox hogtied me to his bed. I suck in a breath through my teeth as the ropes dig into my sensitive flesh. How long did the creature inside me struggle? The skin on my wrists is tender and red. Luckily, my socks protected my ankles from the same fate.

I can't believe the vampire fucking tied me up. He loathes me so much; he'd rather bind me and disappear than touch me.

I ease back on the mattress and close my eyes, replaying every detail from the moment I walked from the forest. I recall being outside Nox's cabin, and King Darath was naked. My brows pinch, trying to remember what happened after that. How did this passenger consume me?

Oh shit, an image of Priestess Tanagra appearing out of nowhere and in flames pounds through my brain. I jerk on the ropes, reliving the moment she shot Nox in the chest with a fiery arrow. I freaked the fuck out as his immense body plowed into mine. A strange fire consumed his torso and burned my palms as I stamped it out. But then he rolled on top of me, and in those precious few seconds, he peered at me with hunger. I would've sworn he was about to kiss me. *Me.* Not whatever possesses me now.

Gawd. The feel of him between my thighs, the heat radiating from his muscular physique, will get me off for months to come. Warmth spreads through my lower stomach. Could Nox desire me? His best friend's little sister and a werewolf a quarter of his age? It doesn't matter. Until I can figure out what is riding shotgun within me, I need to steer clear of Nox.

How the fuck are you going to do that, genius, when you're strung up like a thanksgiving turkey on a spit? I clench my fists in anger, but they meet fabric instead of my nails digging into my palms. I glance up at my bandaged hands. Wait. Didn't I fling those off so I... it... could touch Nox? How long have I been out?

'*Three days of blissful silence,*' a voice growls inside my head. *Either shut up, or I will take over again and shove you farther into darkness.*'

What the fuck? The rich, male voice came from deep inside me. "Who are you?" The wobble in my tone pisses me off.

'*Your salvation,*' he chuckles.

"How did you possess me, demon?"

'*Ah, not just a pretty face,*' it sneers.

"A limited number of immortals can occupy another. Since King Darath was present, I can only conclude you are a hell demon. Care to tell me what the fuck you want?"

'*I saw a chance at escape and took it. You happened to be in the right place at the right time.*' His sinister laugh grates along my nerves. *Just need to get the sexy vampire on board and take care of your little barrier. Convince him to let us go, and the fucking world is ours.*'

Oh crap. I'm in it deep now. I saw the struggle on Nox's face when the creature was seducing him. Felt the hardness of his arousal in my hand. If he surrenders to the demon and unwittingly takes my virginity, there's no doubt in my mind the monster will play on Nox's guilt to connive and cheat his way out of here. But, if it came down to a fight, Nox would do everything in his power not to hurt me, giving the asshat the upper hand.

I shudder at what the creature will force me to endure if he's unleashed on the world. I must stop him. If he enacts the dark fantasies in his head, I won't survive. At least I've gained control for now.

'*You're not gaining anything sycophant. I just need rest.*'

"If you're going to violate my mind and body, at least tell me your name."

I recalled a movie or a book a long time ago, or maybe someone told me—if you knew a demon's true name, you had power over them.

'*Uh Uh Uh. Naughty little wolf.*' His amusement confuses me because I sense the dark, hungry power emanating from my hijacker, swirling around my spirit.

"Well, I can't keep saying, 'Hey you,' all the time."

'*You, soon to be immortal, can hail me, Master.*'

"Fuck off," I whisper-growl, jerking on the ropes.

His mischievous laugh grates on my nerves. '*Fair enough. Since we will soon become one, you may call me...*' he pauses as if he needs to think about it. Which means, whatever he's about to utter, will *not* be his real name. Pity. '*Moe,*' he states and spreads my lips wide in a wicked grin.

"Why were you trying to seduce the vampire, *Moe*? Why not just bust out of here and find someone else? Someone willing?" I can't help but ask.

'*You mean your fated mate?*' At my gasp, he chuckles. Fucking chuckles! '*You might as well get used to it, little one. The second I merged with you, I perceived and understood everything about you. Your wants, desires, thoughts. You're a naughty girl, Cellica. Why do you keep your passions buried under all those boring numbers?*'

I struggle against the bonds. "I have no idea what you're talking about, you sick asshole."

The entity sighs dramatically. '*You are nothing more than a scared, insecure virgin who desperately needs to fuck, and I'm just the demon to make that happen. Remember, my dear, I perceive every thought and fantasy flitting through your brain. Be grateful I have the cajones to get us both what we want.'*

"Please let me go," I whisper, disconcerted at realizing the creature isn't wrong.

"If you behave, I will," a familiar voice states from the doorway.

My head whips to the side as Nox enters the room. Unease shines in the beautiful mismatched irises as he regards me. But before I can inform him of my inner passenger, the demon roars in my brain, and sudden blackness surrounds my vision.

"No! Stop," I sob, yanking on the restraints with everything I've got. "Please, don't do this."

"Cellica?" Nox questions, approaching the bed.

Oh God, stay away! I shriek, but no sound emerges. Moe has taken control.

'You will thank me later, little wolf. Now sit back and watch a pro at work.'

Chapter 6

Nox

Little did I realize when I went barreling through the door to seek my queen's assistance with Cellica, I'd interrupt a damn meeting. I really needed to pay closer attention to the emails Sebastian sends me. My only excuse? I've been a little distracted.

As expected, Liam took the watered-down version of the issue with his little sister... badly. He fought his beast to keep from tearing me apart, even though I kept the majority of what transpired to myself. I'd be seeking medical attention if it weren't for Nicole's barked order to stow our shit.

Looking back, I can't believe I decked Darath. I rarely let his goading get to me. In fact, I find him downright hilarious, but when he referred to Cellica as a bitch in heat, red filled my vision, and I lost it, plowing my fist into the King of Hell's jaw.

What still rankles me is Liam's apparent belief I'm not good enough for his sibling, but I can't say I blame him. I've earned my reputation with the ladies. Until I came in contact with Cellica, I relished a different woman on my cock every week. No emotion. No promises of a future. Just pure, unadulterated enjoyment. I never lost control, and I made sure I completely satiated the females before taking my own pleasure. Rough or soft, I enjoyed it all but kept my emotions out of the mix.

Now, my other brain thinks of one thing—sinking deep into a certain werewolf with eyes the hue of nutmeg. Her lush little body haunts my dreams during the day, forcing me to relieve the ache in my cock before I go postal.

I shake my head in wonder as I ease closer to the bed. Darath's revelation regarding Cellica explains so much. He informed me she's controlled by a lust demon. The aggressiveness, lewd comments, and power behind her actions were not my little wolf. A fucking demon manipulated her.

I replay Darath's warning—*"Your mission, if you choose to accept it, is to guard the little possessed werewolf, but to keep your hands to yourself no matter what she says or does."*

I peer down at my assignment and snort. I've survived a shitty childhood, years of Guardian training, skirmishes, and wars, but keeping my distance from my mate when she's coming at me with both barrels will be the biggest challenge of my life. And even though I know a fiend influences her actions, Cellica's distressed sob urges me to calm her fears.

"Hush, baby girl. I'm here," I soothe and ease my hip onto the mattress, ensuring our bodies don't touch.

"Please, Nox. My wrists hurt."

Actual tears gather in her eyes, and my jaw clenches. Is this Cellica or the demon? "Are you going to behave?"

"Yes," she hiccups, nodding in agreement. "I promise."

I reach over and retrieve my medical bag. "I can put an ointment on your wrists and change the bandages on your hands."

"What... what about your blood? Won't it heal me instantly?"

She's lowered her lids submissively, and uncertainty cramps my gut. How do I identify if who I'm dealing with is my wolf or the fucking demon? I square my shoulders. Until I know for sure, I must treat her like a hostile hostage and assume it's the monster in control.

"You will never taste my essence, little girl," I state matter-of-factly as I remove the bandages without untying her wrists. Cellica watches my movements with a frown, and I almost smile. The minx hoped I'd untie her first. Not gonna happen. I barely escaped the last time. I won't repeat my mistake.

"Why do you hate me so much, Chris?"

My gaze shoots to hers. Rarely does she utter the shortened version of my given name, but warmth spreads through my chest when she does. Is this Cellica? The hurt in her expression sears my soul, and I grit my teeth to keep from caressing her cheek and reassuring her I do care. I care too damn much.

"I don't hate you, Cellica, but your doe eyes need to look elsewhere. We have no future. I require a vampire, and you should be with another werewolf." I hope my gentle comment gets my point across.

"I can't be with another wolf," she whispers, lowering her lashes.

"Why not?" I ask with a frown.

"Because... because you are my fated one, Chris. My destiny is with you."

Fuck me.

"No, Cel. You're mistaken. You haven't transitioned, so you do not know who your fated mate is yet."

"I'm close enough. I sense my wolf, and she's claimed you."

I sit back and stare at her in stunned silence. Is this true? Or is this the demon trying to trick me? Not that it matters. Liam will never allow his sister to bond with me.

Shit. Why the hell am I thinking about bonding? I don't want a mate. I have no space for a damn female in my head, knowing my every emotion, speaking to me telepathically at any given moment. My life is my own. I work hard to play harder, and my duties to my queen and profession consume me. It's the way I prefer it. By the time dawn arrives, I'm so exhausted that I barely make it through a shower before collapsing nude on my bed to sleep like the dead for eight hours. I don't have time for a clingy, needy she-wolf. But the idea of plunging my cock inside Cellica's warmth while feeding on her neck, her cries of pleasure in my ear, hardens me in an instant. Fuck. Who am I kidding? My inner vampire would sacrifice anything if she was mine and not complain one bit. In fact, I'd rejoice for every second we could find together.

"Nox? Did you hear me? You're my fated one, and I suspect I'm yours."

The pleading in her brown depths pierces my heart as effectively as a silver blade. I crave to tell her she's spot-on, to untie her and wrap her in my embrace. But Darath's warning and Liam's enraged eyes keep the words at bay.

Enough of this guessing bullshit. Time to call the demon's bluff. "If you think an inexperienced, spoiled little werewolf could be my one true mate, you are way off base, *Demon*." A single eyebrow arches instead of anger or aggression, and I watch in horror as the beautiful whiskey irises transform into a deep ruby red. "There you are," I growl, leaning over her body.

She shrugs. "Busted." Her smile raises the hair on my arms. "What gave me away?"

"Your king." The familiar yet foreign eyes widen for a moment before hardening to stone. Ah, so the demon fears his king. Good to know.

"It doesn't matter," It states with an unnerving calmness. "You can't deny my effect on you, vampire. The hardness of that big, beautiful cock revealed the truth." It sits up, straining against the bonds. "You relished the feel of her breasts on your back, her hands roaming your glorious body, but mostly, you craved to do everything I pleaded for. Admit it. Together, she and I are all you desire."

Jesus. It's right. Goddamn it. I offer a menacing growl and lean down, showcasing my fangs. "Fuck off, and let me speak to Cellica."

"The little wolf can't come out and play just yet," the demon grins.

I wrap my fingers around her neck and squeeze. "Cellica, come to me."

The demon-looking eyes widen in shock, as Cellica's body thrashes against the ropes. "No!" it bellows. "I'm not fucking done yet."

"That's it, baby girl," I encourage, my tone still Alpha strong. "Fight it and come forth. Now."

I watch in amazement as the red bleeds from her irises. The hardened expression melts into the adoring countenance it always holds when she observes me when she thinks I'm not paying attention. Slowly, the tension in her body eases, and she sags against the comforter. I wait patiently for her to recover without a word.

What the fuck just happened? How did my command summon her from wherever the demon shoved her consciousness? Only an Alpha wolf has such domination over another wolf. I'm certainly not her Alpha. That role falls to Liam.

"Chris?" the sob snags my attention, but I remain motionless. Is this Cellica? "I'm so sorry." Tears stream down her temples into her hair. "I can't fight him."

Him? Fuck. The beast who tried to seduce me is an actual dude? When Darath informed me that *he's* set his sights on me, I assumed *he* was metaphorical, not a literal him.

"Is it really you?"

"Yes. Please. Bring King Darath. He'll know what to do to get this asshole out of me."

Relief drops my shoulders. It is her. No way the demon would ask for the one entity with the power to extract him and shove him back in Hell.

"Baby girl," I caress her cheek like I craved to do earlier, and she breaks. Sobs shake her body, and I suddenly don't care about the consequences—I have to hold her.

I untie her wrists with hurried movements, leaving her ankles bound just in case, and gather her in my arms. "Hush, Cellica," I murmur, cradling her against my chest. "You're safe now. I've got you."

Her fists clutch my shirt as she cries out her fear and misery. I'd give anything, sacrifice anything to take this burden from her, to never see another big fat tear fall from those brilliant eyes. But, as her weeping soaks my shirt, it finally hits me like a sledgehammer to the skull, and I can't deny it any longer. This little forbidden fruit *is* my one true mate. I will move heaven and earth to get this fucking demon out of her. Whatever the cost, I will pay it.

Chapter 7

Cellica

God, he smells fantastic. Like cedarwood and spice. Even as upset as I am, the warmth of his embrace and his scent invading my nostrils calms me. Just as his commanding tone dragged me from the dark depths of my consciousness.

Since Nox talked to Moe directly, he understands I'm possessed. I don't want this to end, but I can't cry indefinitely into his shirt. I lean back and wipe the moisture from my face, embarrassed by my outburst. He already thinks I'm nothing more than a kid. Liam's little sister. What must he think of me now? Could I be more fucking pathetic? And to top it off, I've never been a pretty crier. My eyes puff up, my neck turns blotchy, and my nose runs. Yeah, queen of ugly crying right here.

Nox gets up and heads to what I can only assume is a bathroom, coming back with a box of tissues in his hand. I glance at him quizzically as I pluck one from the top.

"Why does a vampire need a box of Kleenex?" I ask before blowing into the tissue. Loudly. Yup, I can't even blow my nose like a lady. I'm all cowgirl through and through.

Nox fights a grin as I snatch another to mop up my face before he sets it on the nightstand. "I often have non-vampire guests," he states before sitting down on the mattress next to me.

My jaw hardens. Ah yes. The perpetual playboy. Even I've heard the rumors. Just the image of some woman in this bed, enjoying orgasmic pleasure from my vampire, heats my blood.

"Right," I state flatly and lower my lids so he doesn't see the hurt and anger simmering below the surface.

"How are you feeling?" he asks, tossing the used tissue in the wastebasket by the bedside table before picking up my hand and removing the rest of my bandages. The skin is not as fiery red, and the blisters have opened, and because I'm not fully immortal, the healing is taking its damn sweet time.

"A little shell-shocked," I admit as he reaches into his black bag on the floor. I wince as he gently applies one salve to my palms before applying another to my chafed wrists.

"That's understandable," he murmurs, re-bandaging my hands with quick efficiency before covering both wrists with a thick gauze. "Are you aware of what's happening when the demon is in control?" He never lifts his concentration from his task, and I understand exactly what he's asking.

"I'm cognizant of everything," I whisper, scrutinizing his reaction even as my face heats with embarrassment. A muscle pulses in his jaw, and a surprising blush darkens his cheeks. I bite my lip to keep the smile at bay. His desire for me embarrassed the sexy playboy.

No. Not me. Moe. *Ugh.*

"If you wish to hit me for kissing you, I'd totally understand." As he tidies an already perfect bandage, his muttered comment sends butterfly wings flapping in my stomach.

"It wasn't your fault, Chris."

"Yes. It was. I should've had more control," he growls, throwing the supplies back in his bag.

"To be fair, he was extremely... persuasive."

"I thought it was you," he blurts out before his eyes widen in shock at the admission.

I gasp, and my heart leaps into my throat. He desired me? Not the demon. Holy shit. "Nox...."

"No. Forget I said that." He rises with fluent grace inherent to his kind and backs away several steps.

"Why is wanting me such a bad thing?"

His lids lower, and his hands clench into fists as he fights his inner demons. The ones telling him how his best friend's little sister and a member of royalty is off-limits. Not to mention, he's a vampire and I'm a werewolf. Not as taboo as it once was, thanks to Queen Giordano, but still. Nox lived through a time when the law forbade mixed-species mating. Years of indoctrination are hard to fight.

"Cellica. No future exists for you and I. Do you understand? I value Liam's friendship. I am a goddamn vampire Guardian. A soldier who enjoys playing the field and who comes from shady beginnings. I'm no good for you."

Was Nox's childhood horrible? The image of him as a small boy, enduring whatever he suffered to mold him into today's male, puts a vice around my heart.

"We don't get to choose our fated one, Nox."

"No. I am not your fated mate. You have no way of knowing until you transition."

"How do you think I fought Moe? The command in your voice gave me the strength to push forward." I reach down and untie my ankles.

"That's not a good idea, Cel," Nox mutters, backing away from me. "And who the hell is Moe?"

"The demon. That's what he said to call him."

"I still can't believe it's a fucking dude." He shakes his head, and I grin at his scandalous expression.

Needing out of this bed, I swing my legs over the edge and stand, but my thigh muscles are still shaky from lack of use, and I stumble. But like a flash, Nox is there to grab my elbows and keep me upright.

"Thanks," I mutter and grip his forearms. Before I think it through, I rest my forehead on his sternum with a sigh. "Despite popular belief, I am not a child, Chris. And my shift is close enough for me to sense my wolf. She hungers for you." I lift my head and peer up into the most beautiful eyes I've ever encountered. The right one is stunning turquoise. Like the crystal-clear waters of the Caribbean. While the left is a vivid blue like the purest sapphire. I could drown in the magnetic intensity of his gaze. "Can I ask you a favor?"

"Anything." His reply is husky, and his hands move from my elbows to my waist, even though I no longer need aid to stand.

"Will you kiss me? Not him, but me?"

"Goddamn it, Cellica. You tempt me beyond reason."

"Please, Chris. Just a kiss, that's all I seek." I crave to experience his lips on mine, more than my next breath, so I clutch his shirt and draw closer to his warmth. I'd suffer Moe for all eternity, to be crushed in Nox's embrace, his desire for me snapping his control.

A low growl is my only warning before his mouth descends.

I've been kissed by a few boys, and while it was pleasant, it wasn't the earth-shattering, soul-fracturing epicness of being devoured by my vampire. Instead, Nox's full lips consume mine like he's been starved for them for far too long, and I moan in surrender.

Muscular arms band my waist, lifting me from the ground, and I grip his strong shoulders before wrapping my legs around his fit waistline. Within seconds, the softness of the mattress meets my back, and Nox's hard length grinds against my aching center.

His hands come up and frame my face, continuing to nibble and suck at my lips. I trace my tongue along his lips, and he responds by sucking it into his mouth. He tastes like cinnamon and whiskey, and I'm drunk on his flavor. I've never had a kiss set my whole body on fire. I'm not sure if it's our connection or Nox's skill, but whatever it is, I never want it to stop.

When his large hand encompasses my breast, kneading the flesh over my shirt, I break away for a deep breath and arch my neck as dark yearnings course through my veins. "Chris," I pant, pushing into his palm.

"Christ, Cellica. I fucking want you."

"Yes. God, yes."

I've dreamed of this moment for what seems like forever, and it's more than I could've imagined. His weight against me, the hardness of his cock pressing against my sex rhythmically, is better than any fantasy I conjured in my head.

"You're wet for me, aren't you?" he groans. "I can smell your desire, and it drives me fucking insane." He thrusts faster, and I hate the barrier of our clothes. "Need to taste your pussy as you come."

Oh, Jesus. No mouth has ever been down there before, and while I've watched my fair share of erotica on the internet, I desire Nox to be the first. I want all my firsts to be with Nox. "Please, Christoph," I plead, my skin on fire.

"You want my tongue on your cunt, baby girl?"

Shit. The dirty talk ramps my lust to a feverish pitch. "Yes," I cry out, gyrating against the hardness behind his zipper.

As he raises up to unbutton my jeans, a shrill ringing floods the room. *No! Please don't answer it.*

Nox stiffens before reaching into his back pocket and extracting his cell. "This better be fucking important," he growls into the phone, his bright gaze devouring my face.

His expression shuts down like a flash of lightning, and he leaps off me as if I'm filled with leprosy.

What the fuck?

"Sorry, bro. I didn't realize it was you," he says, rubbing the nape of his neck in agitation, and my heart plummets. Our brief epic episode is over. Whoever is on the other line snuffed out the lust in Nox's regard and replaced it with shame and guilt. One guess on who it could be—my fucking brother.

"Sure, Liam. She's in control right now if you want to talk with her."

Goddamn it. He's done it again. I'm never gonna get laid.

Chapter 8

What the hell was I thinking? That's the problem. My *other* brain took over, and all I could focus on was diving between her thighs and drowning in her flavor. I disregarded my vow to steer clear of the little wolf. Yeah, a total fucking failure. My fangs dropped low and saliva pooled in my mouth for a taste of her pussy. My inner vampire demanded we claim her as ours, and the fact she's my best friend's little sister and a pre-transition wolf never entered my mind until Liam's growled greeting cooled my lust as effectively as a dip in the arctic and kicked my guilt into high gear.

The werewolf king, not to mention my queen, trust me to keep my hands to myself and babysit the package without pawing her or marking her as mine. Granted, Darath gave us no choice, but still, she's my responsibility, and I need to treat her like an assignment and not my own personal plaything.

"Get your shit together, Nox," I mutter as I unload the groceries I abandoned earlier when I heard Cellica's plea to let her go. I bought way too much shit, but since I didn't know what my little wolf liked or didn't like, I pretty much bought everything. She's probably starving after being unconscious for so long. Speaking of starving....

I push aside the emergency blood bags to make room for her food, grabbing one for later. Part of my problem is I haven't fed in a while.

Yeah, hunger is why you kissed Cellica. Keep telling yourself that, and you might believe it.

I toss the bag in the microwave to warm it up while I gather ingredients to make my prisoner some dinner. Her conversation with Liam is plain as day with my vampire hearing, and it's starting to piss me off. How many times does she have to reassure him she's fine? He treats her like a little kid who doesn't know her own mind. I snort. Isn't that the pot calling the kettle? I do the same, but for very different reasons.

She ends the call and pokes her head around the corner. "Do you mind if I take a shower?" she asks quietly, holding out my cell phone.

I grab a duffle bag off the barstool and exchange it for my phone. "I went to your cabin and grabbed a few things. I hope you don't mind?" The dangerously tempting whiskey irises widen in surprise. "I also brought your guitar." I nod to where it's leaned against the pool table. "By the time you finish up, dinner should be ready."

"Wow. Um, thanks." Her fingers brush mine when she takes the bag, and I grit my teeth against the tingle of electricity racing up my arm at the contact.

"Did Liam teach you to play?"

"No. Our dad taught all of us." The sadness in her smile tightens my chest. "We used to have jam sessions as a family, but when Daddy died, Liam and Josh's responsibilities, plus my studies, kinda brought that to a halt."

"I'm sorry about Jimmy. He was a great man."

"Yes. He was the best." Her gaze drops to the bag clutched in her hands.

"Cellica." When she glances up at me, I step into her personal space, pocketing my phone. "If you sense the demon rising, call out. Do you understand?"

Her lids narrow. "I'm not an idiot, Nox."

"Do you understand?" I repeat, leaning down until we are eye to eye. The last fucking thing I need is the demon forcing Cellica to escape.

Her lashes lower submissively in the face of my aggression. "Yes," she grits out between clenched teeth as if the admission is against her will. "I understand."

"Good girl," I praise, and her shoulders relax somewhat. "Use the guest bathroom to get cleaned up while I make you something to eat. And then maybe later you can play me something."

"Sometimes, I really don't like you," she admits with a dramatic huff, spinning for the bathroom down the hall, her sapphire hair flying out around her shoulders.

If that were true, this situation would be way easier. Instead, as I watch that tempting ass until the door slams shut, I can't help but grin. My mate has a quick temper and a smart mouth. I'm going to enjoy teaching her who's in control.

No. No, you're not. You'll cultivate her anger by doing precisely what she loathes—treating her the same as every other male in her life—like a teenager who needs direction. It's the only way to keep my sanity and my hands to myself. Although, her feistiness makes my cock twitch.

Damn it.

The sound of the shower running fuels my imagination of a wet and naked Cellica. With shaky hands, I mentally will my erection to stand down and snatch the blood bag from the microwave, snap off the end, and down the contents in record time.

God, I hate bagged blood, but I can't very well tie Cel up to appease my hunger somewhere else when she's coherent and in control of the demon.

Even though I shouldn't, I will take this time we have together to get to know my wolf. When we were hiding out at Viessa's lake house, I could only observe her from afar, concerned Liam would catch my lustful stares toward his little sister. Still, Cellica made it difficult to avoid her. She constantly sought my company, and as much as I wanted to take her in my arms and learn everything there was to know about her, I couldn't. So instead, I belittled her and pushed her away so she'd leave me in peace because I had difficulty doing it myself.

The wolf and I are going to have a little chat over dinner. We need to determine what "Moe the demon" actually wants, stall his actions until Darath can get his ass over here, and fling that fucker back where he belongs. As much as I enjoyed the blatant sexuality the demon brought out in Cellica, I crave my little mate's defiant personality and demure countenance more. I'm not above admitting I get off on her naïve adoration, as misplaced as it might be.

I adore her expressive face and how every emotion plays across her beautiful features, no matter how much she endeavors to hide it. The second I laid eyes on her at her ranch, interest and desire etched into every line of her expression. From the unconscious way she bit her bottom lip when aroused, to the embarrassed blush warming her cheeks when I picked her up in my arms to trace her to the castle. Or the fire and hurt in those whiskey irises when I rebuffed her the instant we landed, and every time thereafter. Cellica would never survive poker night.

I'm a vampire, so I have no need to cook, but I have been known to grill like a pro for my non-vampire friends at parties or for a female or two. Since Cel is a werewolf, red meat is undoubtedly a staple for her. I fire up the barbeque on the back deck, season a thick twelve-ounce ribeye before chopping and seasoning some broccoli, tossing it in the steamer pot. I also poke holes in a potato before wrapping it in tinfoil and placing it on the grill.

That done, I set the table for one with all the condiments I purchased earlier, pour a glass of wine for her, and fill another glass with more bagged blood for myself. It's going to be torture watching Cellica place big chunks of meat in her mouth over and over again, but she requires food and my inner vampire craves to nourish her. Plus, it will give us an opportunity to talk. So as my queen is fond of saying, suck it up, buttercup.

When the shower shuts off, I test the potatoes and start the vegetables before slapping the meat on the grill and setting my timer for four minutes. Cellica strolls into the kitchen dressed in jean shorts that showcase her lean muscular legs and a varsity shirt from Montana State University by the time I've flipped the steak. Her long hair is damp, subduing the blue tinge. Her face is free of any makeup, making her appear even younger and highlighting the intense brown of her gorgeous eyes.

Fuck. I want my little wolf with a desperation I'm finding extremely difficult to control. I actually take a step toward her, needing to get my hands on that tanned skin when my timer chimes, saving me from making another huge mistake.

"Can I help?" she asks, following me out on the deck to retrieve the steak. A cool breeze blows through the trees, stirring the fragrance of pine and cedar.

"Nope," I say, placing the steak and potato on her plate and shutting the gas off to the grill. "Your dinner is ready."

"I didn't know vampires cooked," she grins, taking the plate and heading back into the kitchen. She scoops a spoonful of seasoned broccoli on her plate before sitting at the table by the window.

I grab my blood and join her. "Most don't, and I'm only proficient with the grill." I watch in fascination as she prepares her potato with butter, sour cream, and salt and pepper before digging in.

At her first bite of steak, her eyes practically roll back in her head, and she lets out an appreciative groan that tightens my groin with need. Damn, she's sexy as fuck, but totally oblivious to her allure.

"Oh, Chris," she moans, and I grit my teeth, craving to hear her scream my name with my tongue buried in her pussy and her fingers digging into my scalp. "This is either the best steak I've ever tasted, or I'm hungrier than I thought."

The petite wolf savors every morsel, combining each element on her fork with every bite. I've never cared to watch people eat. And while the aroma can be somewhat pleasing, food is not something I have any knowledge of.

"Describe the taste for me," I ask, placing my chin in my hand and watching her with rapt attention. She possesses a healthy appetite for someone so small, and pleasure runs through my veins at feeding my mate.

The fork, laden with steak, broccoli, and potato, pauses halfway to her mouth as her gaze collides with mine. When she lowers the utensil to her plate, a blush steals across her cheeks, and I mentally kick myself for interrupting her enjoyment.

I hold my breath as she takes several moments to gather her thoughts, taking a sip of the red wine. "Well," she finally begins. "I imagine a steak would be similar to blood taken from a person who eats a lot of spices and drinks bourbon."

I snort in amazement. She just provided me with the perfect analogy. Something a vampire would well understand. I've drunk humans and immortals alike, infused with those very elements. When they describe food, most people tend to do so as if I've eaten a steak or know what broccoli tastes like. But Cellica put it in terms a vampire could relate to, and the little wolf wormed her way into my heart a little more. My forehead creases at the thought.

"Does that make sense?" she asks tentatively, taking my frown for not understanding.

"Yes, it does. Please continue." I wave at her food to indicate she should finish. I'm relieved when she resumes eating, devouring the entire meal. "Damn, do all werewolves have such a healthy appetite?" I ask, picking up her empty plate and taking it to the sink.

"Yeah." Another blush stains her cheeks. "Because of our body heat and high metabolism, we require copious amounts of protein."

"It's not a bad thing, Cellica. I enjoyed cooking for you. It pleases me to provide for you."

"Spoken like a true mate."

Something in her tone has me scrutinizing her more closely as I resume my seat and refill both of our glasses. She eyes the blood with curiosity instead of revulsion.

"Let's talk about that for a minute." As much as this topic puckers my sphincter, I need to make it clear to her, bond or not, we have no future. "You graduate soon, don't you?"

Her eyebrow lifts in surprise at the question. "Yes. What does that have to do with anything?"

I take a sip of blood. "My point is, you have your whole life ahead of you. Your daytime life. Werewolves' lives revolve around the sun. My life revolves around the moon.

"What a lame-ass excuse," she sneers, and I'm taken aback. "King Ruse and Lucretia make it work. My brother and Viessa do just fine." She leans back and crosses her arms over her chest. "What else you got, vampire?"

Shit. Why do I love her attitude? "Your brother is my best friend and loathes the idea of me anywhere near you." She can't deny that.

"My brother loathes the idea of *anyone* near me," she grumbles. "Don't take it personally."

"I'm 150 years old, and you haven't even transitioned yet." I realize I'm grasping at straws, forcing her to see reason to keep me from splaying her across this table and feasting on her for dinner.

"Semantics."

"Goddamn it, Cellica," I growl and rise to pace the kitchen. "I'm trying to be gentle and the adult here."

"The adult?" Anger sparks in her gaze as she too rises, striding toward me with purposeful steps. "Fuck you, Nox," she practically shouts. "You didn't think I was such a kid when you wanted down my pants. Did you?" Her eyes widen, the comment surprising us both, but it doesn't stop her. "I don't understand you, Chris. First, you look at me like you want to devour me, and the next minute you act like you can't stand being in the same room with me. Is this talk about trying to dissuade *me* from a relationship or yourself?"

Perceptive little wolf. This conversation about relationships and devouring her makes my skin crawl and my cock stand at attention. I almost crave the appearance of Moe so I can shut this down, tie her back up and get the hell out of here.

"I'm just trying to make you see reason in all of this." I swallow, guilt eating at my gut as I deliver the final blow. "You're like the little sister I never had. That's all I will ever feel for you."

"Oh, really?" she scoffs. "You kiss all your little sisters like that? You tell them you crave to suck their pussy until they come? If so, that's pretty sick, Nox." The little minx has me cornered against the fridge, jabbing her finger into my chest with each word. "You want to know what I think?"

"No."

She ignores me. "I think you want me so badly you make this shit up to keep me at a distance over some misplaced guilt regarding my brother." Her palms skate up my chest, causing the muscles to twitch in their wake. "But let me make one thing clear. I'm an adult with the wants and desires of a woman, and I crave everything about you. I get myself off every damn night thinking of you, Chris. You're like a cancer in my brain that keeps growing, consuming my every thought."

Jesus. God help me. My fists clench with the need to crush her to me and fulfill every one of her fantasies.

"Look me in the eye and tell me you don't want me. If you can do that, I will move on with my life—after I get rid of Moe—and find someone who desires me. For me."

Son of a bitch. Fire burns through my veins at the thought of some asshole touching what belongs to me, or the lips I crave locked on another's. Those long tan legs wrapped around some asshole's waist as he takes what the fates designed for me alone.

Red fills my vision, blocking out any rational thoughts about why I shouldn't care. Instead, I grip her biceps hard and lift her until we are eye to eye. I witness the bright ember of my fury reflecting from her pupils. Instead of extinguishing my rage, it merely adds fuel to the fire.

"If anyone dares touch you, I will rip their spines from their bodies and dance in their blood, then I will fuck you into submission over their corpses. Do you understand me, Cellica? You. Are. Mine," I snarl before capturing her lips in a fierce kiss.

Chapter 9

Cellica

Oh, my fucking God! Nox's words are dark, violent, and downright bewitching. His talented lips and tongue dominate my mouth while my feet dangle around his knees. It's erotic as hell. I can't move, can only experience his domination, the way his kiss touches me everywhere.

When Moe was in control, arousal pierced through the fog, but the connection felt diluted. Like the demon was a cloth filter, blocking the full effects of how my body was responding to Nox. Now? Intense sensations bombard me from every direction, and it's overwhelming. I want to slow down and savor his touch. The glide of his tongue across mine, the slight sting as I scrape against one of his fangs. The utter authority of his kiss as he consumes my lips like a vampire deprived of blood for weeks.

My nipples are hard, aching points I itch to rub against his solid chest, my lust soaks my panties, and my inner walls clench for something it's never experienced. Fuck. The bombardment of sensations is way better than my imagination, and I can't get enough. I need to be closer, to rip the barrier of our clothes away and experience the scorching heat radiating from him in waves against my skin.

In the next breath, Nox pivots, shoving my back against the wall before pressing into me, a muscular thigh thrust between my legs. I groan at the pressure against my clit and shamelessly gyrate against him. One hand clutches my waist in a death grip while the other closes around my throat, his strong fingers holding me in place as he continues to lick, suck and bite at my lips and tongue.

"Chris," I gasp when he nibbles and kisses his way across my cheek to my ear, his thigh pressing harder into my crotch. I can't deny the tempest building in my core, but I require more. Of what, I'm not sure. "Touch me, please," I beg, clutching his shoulders.

"Tell me what you desire, baby girl?" he whispers, and I shiver at the sensation of his breath at my ear.

"More," I croak out, my mind unable to assimilate words.

"Uh uh." He leans back, and I gasp at the beautiful array of brightness shining in his irises, those sexy fangs on full display.

Holy crap. I'm making out with my vampire. And he wants me just as much as I want him. His grasp on my throat tightens, and an answering ache unfolds inside me. Is this turning me on? Fuck yes, it is, and I don't care.

"Be specific, Cellica. What is it you want me to do to you?"

Shit. My mind replays all the dreams and fantasies I've enjoyed of Nox, but I'm scared to articulate my lewd thoughts. What if he rejects me like he has so many times in the past? I can't handle the rejection again, not after he's set me on fire.

'*Allow me to help,*' Moe pipes in, and I freeze. '*I won't take over,*' he quickly assures me. '*Just assist you in overcoming your insecurities and ask for what you most desire. What we both crave from your vampire.*'

"Cellica?" Sensing the change in my body, Nox leans back further to frown down at me. "You okay?"

Should I warn him Moe resurfaced or authorize the demon to aid me in revealing my desires? Shit, this is so wrong. My brain shouts at me to shut this down. But knowing Nox, he will truss me up in his bed once more and disappear if he suspects Moe has joined our foreplay. So, against my better judgment, I allow my hormones screaming for the release only my vampire can give me to dictate my actions.

'*Fine,*' I hiss mentally. '*But only this once, and if I sense you attempting to take control, I will shout it at the rafters. Are we clear?*'

'*Crystal,*' the demon grins, and a smidgen of shame warms my chest. If Nox knew I was communicating with the entity possessing me to help seduce him, livid wouldn't cover the scope of his emotion.

Just as Nox tries to release his hold and step back, my grip on his shoulders tightens, and I allow Moe to voice what I couldn't. "Please, Nox. I need your fingers on my pussy. Make me come, vampire."

Nox stills, eyeing me with uncertainty. "Is this you, Cellica?"

Oh shit, he knows.

'*No, he doesn't. Trust me.*'

"Yes." We breathe the lie so easily. "I only hesitated because I didn't know what to ask for first."

Nox grins. "Tell me your fantasies when you got yourself off at night, and I will make them come true."

"Umm," Moe hesitates demurely, just like I would. Son of a bitch. I hate that this creature knows me so well already.

"Baby girl." Nox gently pinches my chin, lifting my gaze to his. "Never be embarrassed to voice your desires with me."

I bite my lip. Will Moe reveal what's in my head? "I want your hand squeezing my throat while you finger my clit until I shatter."

"Fuck me," Nox groans. "That's the hottest goddamn thing I've ever heard."

Firm hands grip my ass and hoist me up until I wrap my legs around his waist before he pivots and heads to the bedroom, his lips sucking on the skin above my vein.

"No biting," Moe asserts, and I perceive his anxiety. Would Nox sense the demon's presence if he drank from me?

'Yes,' he growls in answer. '*And this would be all over, and he'd tie us to the bedframe once more.*'

Nox halts next to the bed before sitting on the edge, my ass settling in his lap. "I would never bite you without your permission, Cellica."

"Oh. Okay," I... Moe... says lamely.

"Before I begin." he pushes my mostly dry hair from my face, gazing deep into my eyes. "Is there anything else you wish to confess?"

Confess? What a weird way to phrase that? "I think I've revealed enough for now. Don't you?" the demon answers for me.

"You certain?"

'*Moe? Maybe you should...*'

'*It's fine, little wolf. Trust me.*' "I'm positive," he assures Nox. "No more talking, vampire."

Disappointment clouds Nox's expression, and nerves rattle down my spine. Something's not right here. The demon may be confident that Nox is clueless, but I'm not so sure.

"I agree," Nox sighs before swiveling and pinning me beneath him on the mattress.

Oh, maybe Moe was correct, and Nox believes it's me? I ignore the guilt warming my chest and grip the back of his neck to bring him in for another soul-shattering kiss. His lips are firm and insistent. And while it still sends tingles straight to my nipples, it feels different from before. In the kitchen, Nox was ravenous, his restraint gone. This seems practiced. Controlled. Angry.

As warning bells clamor in my skull, stiff rope encircles both wrists, yanking them above my head and securing them to the center of the headboard.

"Did you think I wouldn't be able to tell the difference between you and my innocent little wolf?" Nox growls, straddling my hips and glaring down his nose at me.

Son of a bitch. '*I fucking told you, Moe.*'

The demon laughs. Well, to Nox, it's me laughing, I guess. "You do not understand how innocent."

'*Shut up, Moe,*' I growl, fearing he will announce my secret.

"She gave me permission to join the play since she's too afraid to voice her passions out loud."

'*You fucking bastard!*'

"Is that so?" Nox states with an unnerving calmness. "Cellica." Oh, no. By his tone, he's going to command me forward like before, and I won't be able to deny him. Inevitably, my stupid guilt will force me to confess my sins. "Come to me."

'*Moe, please. I can't. I'll die if I have to reveal I was such a coward that I summoned you to help. He scares me a little when he's pissed, and this will make him beyond angry.*'

'*What are you saying, wolf? Are you giving me control?*'

Shit. As much as I want to hide behind my unwanted passenger, concocting deals with demons is bad juju. *Time to own up to your shortcomings, Cel, and deal with the consequences of your stupidity.*

'*No. Go away. I will handle this,*' I respond with more bravery than I'm feeling.

'*I will acquiesce, for now, but do not say I did not warn you,*' he murmurs before receding into a corner like a petulant little demon.

I blink rapidly for effect, tugging on my bonds. "Nox?" I question as innocently as possible, praying he buys my act.

"Baby girl," He plants both palms on the mattress by my armpits, his expression hard as stone. "Was the demon telling the truth? Did you give him permission to come forward while I had my mouth and hands on you?"

"I... I...." Fuck, his anger is a frightening sight.

"Do not lie to me," he growls fiercely, and alarm slithers up my spine.

I swallow, lowering my focus to his fangs. Oh shit. I so want to lie, but Nox possesses a strange power over me I don't understand. It's like he's my Alpha, and his tone compels me to do as he orders, but Liam is the only Alpha currently in my life.

"Yes," I whisper against my will. "I'm sorry."

"Why?" His stunned expression says more than words could, and I bite my lip as shame heats my face. "Why would you do that, Cellica?"

"Because!" I holler, my embarrassment turning to anger. At myself mostly, for being a complete and utter coward. "He's bold enough to ask for what I cannot. There. Are you satisfied?" I yank frantically on the restraints. "Now fucking untie me."

Nox sits back on his heels, keeping the bulk of his weight off my legs. "That's not going to happen. You've proven I can no longer trust you. The ropes stay."

"You can't keep me tied up forever, Nox."

"Not forever, Cellica. Just until Darath retrieves his demon. Then you may go on your merry way, finish school and resume your life. And I can finally do the same."

Pain pierces my heart at his words. I'm merely a burden to him. The second I'm free of Moe, Nox will discard me like week-old trash, get on with his Guardian duties, his playboy ways, and stay as far away from me as possible. I swallow the sob at the mere notion and shove my misery down deep to keep the demon company.

"You're right," I state coldly. "The sooner I'm free of you both, the better."

Chapter 10

Anger warms my skin. How could she fucking bring that bastard forward? I craved *her* passions to override her insecurities and confess her innermost fantasies to me. I heard the acceleration of her heart rate when I closed my fingers around her neck. The hitch in her breath told me it excited her. My little wolf wishes to be dominated, but to what extent? Does she enjoy pain with her pleasure? Or merely submission? I wish I could determine if what the demon voiced were Cellica's wants or his.

Why does it matter, Nox? When this is all over, she will run back to her life, hopefully demon-less, to graduate, and either scuttle off to the ranch under Liam's protective wing or find her own path. A path that does not include a vampire. But damn, I can't let go of my disappointment and anger at her letting the demon take control during an intimate moment.

"Do you know what happens to bad little girls with smart mouths, Cellica?" I question calmly, leaning forward until our lips are almost touching. As I gaze into those perfect brown irises the color of dark whiskey, a plan forms in my brain on how best to dole out punishment for her actions.

Her body stills, and she swallows, her eyes narrowing in wariness. "Go fuck yourself, vampire," she whispers breathlessly.

"Answer the question," I snarl, and she immediately sinks back into the mattress to get some distance from my fury.

"N... no. I said I was sorry, Nox. It won't happen again. I swear." Her brows knit.

She's trying to reason with me. How cute. But her pleading will not derail what's coming.

"I'll tell you what happens—a thorough spanking," I murmur low before rising from the bed to grip her hips and flip her over onto her stomach. The motion forces her wrists to crisscross above her head.

"Don't you fucking dare!" The pillow muffles her shout as she attempts to get on her knees, but I shove her down, with a palm at the small of her back.

She really does have a delectable derriere, and I'm going to enjoy turning it bright pink.

"Maybe tanning your hide will make you think twice before sicking your passenger on me again."

She struggles in earnest when I reach under her to unzip her shorts. "No. Please, Nox. I am sorry. I won't ever do it again. I promise."

On some bizarre level, her begging sends pleasure straight to my groin, hardening me to stone in a second. It washes over my skin like the warmest blood. Maybe I am more of a Dom like Logan and Sebastian than I thought. "Tell me why you did it, and I might reconsider," I offer, rubbing her muscular ass cheeks through her loosened shorts, not wanting this to end in the slightest.

Her body goes limp, and she burrows her face in the pillow. "Because...."

I wait, but when she doesn't continue, I do what I've been itching to do since the first moment the words formed between us like a dark fantasy of need. The hard smack is not as gratifying as bare skin, but it's a fucking start.

"Ow!" she hollers, clenching her butt against the sting.

"Because why?"

"I don't owe you a damn thing, Nox. If you strike me again, I will never forgive you."

I laugh. "Brave words, little girl." I lean down and brush the long locks from her face, running my tongue over the outer shell of her ear. "But you want to know what I think?"

"No," she growls before biting that enticing lip.

I ignore her response, and my aching cock throbbing behind my zipper. "I think you've fingered your pretty pussy to visions of me brightening your ass red with my palm. I bet the imagined sting sent you over the edge time and time again." I rub her bottom as I whisper my naughty words into her ear. "Admit it, little wolf. You'd love nothing more than to surrender to your vampire."

Her lids lower, and her breath hitches. "N... no. You're wrong. I... I would never..."

Smack. "Uh uh. Bad girl. No lying." Slowly, I slide her shorts down her hips to rest them just below the curve of her butt, leaving her pretty lace panties in place. Fuck me. Her ass is flawless. Heart-shaped with tanned glutes begging for my bite, my tongue. "Did your pussy spasm when I wrapped my fingers around your throat and squeezed? Your answer will determine what happens next." I run my fingertips across the exposed flesh above her underwear, and goosebumps sprout along her skin.

"Yes," she breathes, and now I'm conflicted. On the one hand, I couldn't be more ecstatic that she finally admitted the truth. Still, I was hoping she would continue to defy me since my need to discipline her is a living, breathing entity wrapping around my body like a demented lover.

"Good girl," I rasp in her ear. "I enjoy dominating you, baby. Seeing your eyes dilate with lust, hearing your seductive moans of pleasure." Gently, I run my fang over her lower back, and she arches in response. "Did you ever masturbate to fantasies of me spanking you?" I ask again, desperate for the answer. She goes motionless. The only movement is her chest's rapid rise and fall with each breath, and I hold mine in anticipation.

"Yes."

Fuck. "Are you wet right now, thinking about it?"

"Yes."

"Goddamn, Cellica," I pant, my lust for her out of control. "I fucking need to spank you. Tell me you want me to?"

"Yes," she moans, raising her hips in the air as if in offering. I nearly come undone and I'm forced to call on my inner vampire for strength. I stand, adjusting my cock to a more comfortable position and observe the writhing female tied to my bed, ass raised and ready. Shit, I want this with a desperation that should make me hesitate. Cellica is so young. Her brother is my best friend. She's not even immortal yet. Do I end this before it goes too far?

Fuck no. Nothing will stop this from happening. If my queen knocked on my door, I would ignore it and proceed. That's how frantic I am to lay my hands on Cellica.

I grab an extra pillow off the bed and shove it under her hips. "Do you have a safe word in case it gets too intense?" I think to ask as I gather the edges of her panties and pull them into the crease of her ass, keeping it bunched in one hand, so it stays tight against her pussy.

"A what?" she asks, already pumping against the cloth.

So... no. "If you wish for it to stop, say the word... *fanger*," I smirk.

She huffs out a laugh in reply but nods her agreement, and without preamble, I slap her butt cheek with my free hand. Her gasp floats through my ears like a long-lost lover, hardening me further. If this is her initial spanking, we should take things slowly at first. I massage the handprint marking her flesh, and she bows her back in response. I give a tug on the panties, rubbing it against her pussy and anus.

"Chris," she moans, and I glance over my shoulder at her.

Her fingers white knuckle the rope, blue hair flows down her spine, and her cheek rests on the pillow with eyes closed and mouth open as she pants with desire. Fuck, that's a beautiful sight. A deep ache builds in my chest. The need to hear her cries of ecstasy is all-consuming. I turn back to the delectable picture before me and set in, alternating cheeks and setting up a rhythmic pull with her underwear. Soon her ass is bright red with my handprints, and her juices soak the material of her panties.

"You fucking smell delicious, baby girl." Her arousal fills my senses, and I'm desperate for my tongue buried between her folds, lapping up every last drop. Soon, but right now, we're enjoying this spanking too much, and I want her to shatter against her delicate undies. "Do you like your spanking, little wolf?"

"Yes. God, yes. Please, Daddy. Make me come."

Holy fuck! My cock jerks. "Does my baby girl need to explode against her panties?" I fucking love the dirty talk. The dirtier, the better, but many females don't appreciate it, so most of the time, I keep the dialogue in my head. Deep down, brought out by her raging lust, my remarkable mate gets off on it as well.

"Yes, Daddy. Please. Harder."

"Since you beg like my good little slut," I growl and smack her ass vigorously, watching the muscles ripple with each hit, tugging the underwear faster and with more force. "Come for Daddy, baby girl."

"Oh... Oh god... yes!" Cellica's hips pump frantically as she flies apart. I shove aside the fabric and plunge two fingers into her soaked cunt, glorying in the convulsions of her sex. Next time it will be my cock she clamps down on like a sweet delicious vice.

"Good girl. Ride it out," I instruct, pumping into her gently while I kiss and lick her low back and ass, listening to her little mewling sounds as she slowly comes down. When the convulsions calm, I withdraw, bringing my fingers to my mouth and sucking them clean. Goddamn, she tastes like pure honey.

Once I settle her panties in place and pull her shorts up, I ease the pillow out from under her and grab her hips to flip her over. Her whole body stiffens, fighting me. "No. Please don't turn me over."

What the hell? I lean over to see her face, but she buries it in the pillows. Is she embarrassed about what happened?

"Cellica. You do not need to be ashamed of your needs. I fucking loved it."

"You did?" she asks tentatively.

I roll her over and untie her wrists, bringing her palm to my raging erection. "Do you doubt it now?"

"Damn," she breathes. "You're like steel."

"This is what you do to me. What your desires do to me. Not the fucking demon. You, Cellica."

A flush spreads across her cheeks. "I never imagined I liked that kind of stuff outside of my dreams."

I keep my grin at bay. "What stuff?"

The blush deepens. "You know...." She clears her throat. "Spankings and dirty talk."

"Oh, baby, we've only just begun."

Chapter 11

Cellica

Who the hell am I? What the fuck just happened?

The vampire I've fantasized about for over a year made me come in my panties harder than I ever have while he slapped my ass with such vigor, I never wanted it to stop.

Jesus.

I'm a whore. No, I'm worse than a whore. I'm a goddamn submissive whore. My college professor would pull her hair out if she saw me now. The feminist movement slapped its forehead and shook its head at me in disgust, and I can't seem to give two shits. In fact, I crave to do it all over again. What does that say about me?

What surprises me the most is my urge to obey Nox. Yes, I answer to an Alpha—my brother and king and when Liam interjects that tone, my mind has no choice but to bow to his wishes, which makes me an omega, I guess. But I've never felt the compulsion with anyone but my pack leader. Until now. Is it because Nox is my mate? But that can't be. He's not a shifter, therefore *not* my Alpha and we are not bonded. So why do I feel compelled to submit to Nox's commands?

Because you fucking get off on it, sicko.

Like my current yearning to drop to my knees and take his enormous length down my throat. With the awkward boys I've been with, I never once possessed the inclination to go down on them. My dreams, on the other hand, were saturated with images of me kneeling before my vampire, his fingers fisted in my hair as he pumped his length down my throat. I crave to live out that fantasy right now even though deep down my insides quake with the certainty I could be an utter failure at it.

Just as I'm about to strangle my insecurities and drop to the floor, the ringing of Nox's cellphone interrupts us. *Again.* First chance I get, I'm smashing that "fuckerinteruptus" to smithereens. To hell with Nicole and her stupid assignments.

"I'm on my way," he growls into the phone. "Yes, my queen. I will make sure."

When Nox glances at me with that permanent frown creasing his forehead where I'm concerned—shame and humiliation return full force. I mentally scream at him to leave so I can avoid facing what I've done.

I don't blame him. I... no correction... *Moe* fed off my fantasies and pushed Nox relentlessly. He stroked the embers of the male's desire until it was a raging inferno of lust, and I became the outlet. Deep down, where I refuse to analyze, I understand the outcome of this night would've ended with a thorough fucking if I was anyone but Liam's little sister. Because of Nox's sense of morality and no doubt some stupid bro code, instead, I received a spanking of epic proportions. My mind cringes when I realize I'm a filthy, submissive slut. One who shatters into a million pieces from having her ass beat and her wrists restrained. I find myself in a *what the fuck am I doing?* moment. One of many since meeting my vampire.

When the warrior squats down in front of me, I lower my lids in embarrassment. His heavy sigh constricts my heart, but I refuse to look up and see those beautiful eyes smoldering with regret.

"Let me guess," I sneer to hide my shame. "Your queen *demands* your presence."

"Yes. We are restoring Kleora's soul tonight, and I must attend."

I jerk my gaze to his. "Restoring her soul? What happened to her?"

"It's a long, long story, and I'll tell you all about it another time." His hesitation speaks volumes, and I grit my teeth against what's coming next. "I'm sorry, Cellica. This could take some time. I must restrain you again in case...."

He doesn't need to finish the sentence. Moe is the sole reason Nox and I were shoved together. The vampire wouldn't have given me the time of day without my deviant passenger riding shotgun, proven by our past interactions. But not one part of me regrets a single, solitary moment of my forced imprisonment with my mate. Even if it was the lust demon, and not me specifically, who fired up Nox's passions. I lived out a fantasy with my mate I will cherish for the rest of my days.

Dutifully, I lay down on the mattress without another word, button my shorts, and stretch my arms and legs wide. Nox once again hogties me to his bed to leave me alone with my destructive thoughts. He makes quick work of the ropes before ducking into his closet and emerging seconds later in full combat gear, a sword strapped to his back.

Great balls of fire, he's hot as fuck in that outfit. It's not the first occasion I've seen him dressed for battle, but it affects me every time. Most of the males around me are warriors with extreme fighting skills, yet he is on another level.

I can ride and rope, shoot a rifle or handgun with pinpoint accuracy and calculate complex numbers in my head in seconds, but Josh and Liam never taught me how to fight. I wouldn't understand the logistics of how to defend myself without a gun. Hand to hand and swords are a complete mystery to me.

"I'll return as soon as I can," he says, hesitating by the bed. "Do you need anything before I go?"

Yeah, another shower and a chance to pee. "No," I say instead, looking everywhere but at him. "I'm fine."

"Cellica...."

"I'm fine, Nox," I interrupt, knowing he's about to inform me how sorry he is and what happened was a mistake. Shit, my head hurts.

"Behave," he demands before vanishing from the room.

Hours pass and my bladder is a living monster demanding release. I shift to ease my torment, but it's useless with my arms and legs spread eagle. If Nox doesn't arrive in the next few minutes, I'm gonna wet the bed. Just the image of the sexy brute returning to find me soaked in my own urine is enough to tighten my muscles, keeping the dam from bursting.

A sudden tapping on the front door stops my heart. Who the hell is visiting at this hour? One of Nox's lady friends? A fuck buddy, perhaps looking to score? I glance at the bedside clock. It's two in the morning. Nox has been gone for five fucking hours. More knocking. Do I yell out? My bladder screams, yes.

"Cellica? Are you in there?"

What the hell? Jessica? How in the world am I going to explain why I'm tied to Nox's bed?

"Cellica. I've been trying to reach you all night. If you're in there, please open the door."

"Jessica!" I shout. "I'm here."

"Oh, thank God. I've been looking for you everywhere. Can I come in?"

"If it's unlocked, come in." Please let it be unlocked.

I hear the nob jiggle. "It's locked."

"Then bust a damn window."

"What the hell? Are you alright?"

"No." I bite my lip to keep the tears at bay. "I can't get to the door. Please, Jessica, break a window or something."

"Oh, my God. Okay. Hang on." I hear the frantic fear in her voice a few seconds before the sound of glass breaking, followed by the squeak of a window lifting. "I'm in. Where are you?"

"In the back room."

"You're freaking me out!" she shouts as I listen to her opening doors in an attempt to find me.

When the bedroom door finally swings open, I almost laugh at her horrified expression, but I don't dare at the risk of losing control over my bladder. "Untie me before I pee my pants."

"What the fuck?" Her big blue eyes, wide with fear, dart around the room as if she expects Freddy Krueger to leap out the walls and slash her with his finger blades.

"Jessica," I whine. "No one is here, and if you don't undo these ropes in two seconds, I am gonna soak this mattress with pee."

"Right. Okay." She sprints over to the bed and attempts to release the knots, but her fingers shake so badly it takes forever.

"Hey," I say to snag her attention. "It's okay. No one else is here, so calm down. The worst thing that is going to happen here is me wetting myself."

Jessica draws a deep breath, her blonde hair fluttering around her shoulders before she refocuses on the ropes. "*Why* are you tied up?" she asks, moving to my other wrist.

Well, crap. What do I say? *Oh, I have a demon inside me, and my vampire fantasy tied me up to protect himself from my sexual assault and spanked me until I came.* Ha! She'd run for the hills to get away from her mentally insane friend. "I'll tell you all about it after

I pee." Which should give me time to come up with a plausible story. Hopefully.

Once both wrists are free, I sit up to help her untie my ankles and then beeline it to the restroom, doing the pee-pee dance as I struggle with my shorts and underwear. I spin in a circle in utter dismay when I realize there's no toilet. What the ever-living-fuck!

I dash out of the bathroom, run by a dazed Jessica with my fingers pressed into my crotch as I beeline it to the other bathroom I utilized when I showered. Who doesn't have a goddamn toilet in their master bathroom? A fucking vampire, that's who. When you don't eat or drink anything besides blood, you do not need to have bodily functions like the rest of us lowly immortals and humans.

I sigh with relief when I reach the guest bathroom and quickly take care of business, groaning as the pressure vanishes. God, it's never felt so good to piss.

Jessica peeks her head around the corner when she hears the flush. "You want to tell me what the hell is going on here?" she demands, leaning against the doorjamb with arms crossed over her chest.

"Let's get out of here first, and I'll explain everything." Or at least a watered-down, non-supernatural version. When Nox discovers I disobeyed his order to behave and took off, the vampire will be beyond livid. I shudder at the notion of an enraged Nox but shove it aside.

"Were you kidnapped by your neighbor?" Jessica asks as I grab my bag and head for the front door.

"Sort of," I answer vaguely, flinging open the door and heading for my cabin. Jessica hurries to keep up with me.

"Shouldn't we call the police?"

"Absolutely not."

'*Where are we going, wolf?*' Moe emerges with renewed interest.

"Shut up," I blurt out.

"Excuse me?" she scowls next to me.

"Not you," I stupidly say.

"Then who are you talking to?" She searches the timbers for a threat lurking in the shadows.

I ignore her question and sprint through the forest, Jessica hot on my heels demanding answers, but I have none to give a human that won't send me straight to the loony bin.

Once I reach my cabin, I race inside my bedroom and begin shoving more clothes and toiletries into my bag. I have no clue where I'm headed, but the sooner I get the hell away from Nox and my family, the better.

'*A road trip, Goodie,*' Moe pipes in, but I shut him out and concentrate on my task.

"Where are you going?" my friend asks, following me from room to room. "Finals are this week, you know. You can't just disappear."

Shit. Why does that seem so inconsequential now? "I have to get out of here for a while. Please don't ask me to explain."

She eyes me for several seconds, and when she grabs me by the shoulders, I'm startled by her fierce expression and firm grip.

"Sorcerer of darkness, demon of fright, I call you now into my sight."

Pain explodes in my chest, and I sense Moe surging forward, shoving me into obscurity. *No!* I mentally shout, grinding my teeth with the effort to hold on, but Jessica repeats her strange chant, and my consciousness plunges deep, and this time, I'm unsure if I'll ever emerge again.

Chapter 12

"Hello, Witch. Who's the vessel?"

"A simpering college student, but a friend of the wolf's," she responds with a sneer. I perceive the witch's true visage floating just below the surface, and I grimace at the charred condition of her skin. "I could ask you the same damn question, demon." Her glower makes me smile. "The plan was to occupy the vampire guardian. Not this wolf child with no connection to the queen."

"I couldn't break through his barriers in the seconds I had available. So Cellica was my only option," I growl. Abigail Brevil is a total bitch, and ordinarily, I wouldn't give her the time of day, but she possesses something I want. "But fear not. The guardian has a thing for the little wolf. She's his one true mate."

"No shit? Well, no matter. Since I'm not functioning on all cylinders, I'll make this quick." She glances down at the bag in my hand. "Wait. Where the fuck are you going? Leaving is not part of the strategy, Asmodeus. You need to stick with Nox, remember?"

"I'm well aware of the plan, Abigail, but after several days in Nox's presence, I'm still not able to break through his barriers and possess him. Therefore, I require the aid of some old acquaintances."

"Who?" she asks, following me out to the driveway after I snag Cellica's purse and laptop off the kitchen counter.

"None of your concern, Abi,"

"You're not going soft on me, are you, Asmodeus?"

I halt in the drive, spin toward her, allowing the red glow from my eyes to shine through. My fire wings appear over my shoulders. The witch rightfully takes a step back. "I have a vested interest in assisting you with your foolish vengeance, otherwise I would rip you to shreds and be on my merry way. Do not think you control me, Abigail. I am a fucking Prince of Hell."

"My apologies, my lord, but time is not on our side. If we don't organize this right, then everything we have set in motion will be for naught."

"I am well aware of my part in your little scheme, witch, but if I have any hope of possessing the vampire, then I require aid. And in your weakened state, you are of no use to me." I glance over at the two vehicles in the circular drive. "Which car did you arrive in?"

"The twat drives the fucking Prius," she growls, and I can't help but laugh at her disgust.

"Thank Lucifer," I chuckle and head for the massive black vehicle. The little wolf owns a god's honest ranch truck. So many delicious layers to my vessel.

"The vampire will hunt you down," Miss Obvious states.

"I'm counting on it, witch. Now leave me alone. Go finish healing and give that big hunk of a male a sloppy kiss from me."

"We both know I can't do that. Troy can never discover what we are planning until it's over."

"Afraid he'll kick you to the curb?" I smirk.

"He'll fry both our asses."

"It wouldn't be the first time," I grumble before fishing the key fob from the purse and hopping into the truck with an enormous grin. It's been eons since I drove. This should be fun.

"Hey sweetheart," the good-looking wolf next to me rumbles. "Can me and my buddies buy you a drink?"

My insides clench with need as I peer over my shoulder at the two friends waiting in the wings. I've been on the road for a week seeking information on my fellow brothers, dodging Nox at every turn, and so far, I've come up with squat. Finally, I landed in Grand Forks, North Dakota—the last known whereabouts of my brother, Mammon—but the sheriff, along with every other goddamn human in this town, had no memory of the female he possessed. Tomorrow, I head to Devil's Lake to question the mortal directly. If Lucifer exercised Mammon, my final hope is back in Hell and of no use to me.

Irritation at my failure rides my shoulders, but one glance at the werewolves and, for the first time in a week, sexual energy scuttles to my groin. As the demon of lust, I require massive amounts of sex to stay in control. Since I'm not ready for the vampire to catch me yet and provide that diversion, these boys might be a pleasurable distraction. Here's hoping they are as energetic in the sack as they look and can recharge my depleted batteries.

I have endless reserves in Hell, feeding off the debauchery all around me and only requiring a bout of rough sex once a week or so. Here on earth, the heaviness of gravity and lack of visual stimuli saps my energy, necessitating some sort of release daily. Masturbating is not cutting it. Every time I frantically rub her clit, forcing an orgasm from her reluctant body, I sense the little wolf fighting for dominion. I'm not quite ready for her to emerge yet, but if I don't fuck within the next few hours, she might gain the upper hand.

My only regret is offering these youngsters the gift of Cellica's virginity. I may be a Prince of Hell and a deviant prick, but I'm not so heartless I don't feel a slight twinge of remorse at denying her wish for her first time to be with Nox. But desperate times and all that.

"You sure can, big boy," I smile, flipping Cellica's blue hair over her shoulder as I swivel to eye the beefy wolf up and down. I almost laugh as his face lights up and he signals to his comrades. Cellica stirs in outrage as I trap the one bold enough to approach me between my thighs. The others form a semi-circle around me.

"What are you drinking, beautiful?" the blond to my left asks.

"Elijah Craig bourbon," I whisper, grazing Cellica's fingers down his massive chest.

His big brown eyes widen. "Expensive taste."

"Am I not worth it?" I ask seductively, with a raised eyebrow.

"That's yet to be determined," the redhead on my right murmurs, boldly rubbing the wolf's petite waist.

"Oh honey, you buy me another and I'll make damn sure you understand how worthy I am."

The one caught between my thighs snuggles deeper, gripping my legs in his big beefy hands, his green eyes intent. "Order her whatever she wants, Dave," he commands the redhead. "This little wolf is in for the ride of her life."

About fucking time.

'Don't do this, Moe. Please.'

'You'll thank me later, wolf. We are going to give you a crash course in the ways of sex that your vampire will appreciate, so sit back and enjoy.'

'You son of a bitch.' Her growl is quite impressive, low, and menacing. *'I hope you choke on their dicks.'*

I bark out an internal laugh. *'I choke, you choke, so be careful what you wish for.'*

When my bourbon arrives, I savor a small sip and strategize how best to accomplish this without hurting Cellica unnecessarily. These brutish wolves could do severe damage, and I've grown fond of my vessel.

"Can I let you boys in on a little secret?" I ask before downing the rest of my drink as if I need the fortification for what I'm about to confess.

"You can tell us anything, darlin'," Dave the redhead murmurs, grazing his lips over Cellica's neck, causing goosebumps to pop up over her arms.

'You enjoying this, wolf?' I grin at her.

'No. Please walk away. I don't want this.'

'I think deep down you're curious, but too ashamed to admit it. Even to yourself.'

'No, you're wrong. Nox is the only one I choose.'

'Too bad he doesn't feel the same.'

Her silence speaks volumes, so I proceed with the hunky werewolves. "You promise you won't disappear on me?" I ask them, portraying an air of nervous anticipation, hoping their protective instincts will reign supreme.

The heavily muscled blond proves me correct. "You have nothing to fear from us besides sexual pleasure, sweetness."

"Mike's right," the big boy between my legs pipes in. "I'm Luke. This is Mike." He points to the blond. "And the redhead is Dave. We'll take good care of you. We vow it."

"I'm Cellica," I announce demurely. "And as much as I fancy what you're offering, I have to be honest and let you know... I'm still a virgin." Their eyes widen, and Dave takes a step back. "But I crave to experience everything. Will you three gorgeous wolves be my teachers?" Fuck, I should win an Oscar for this performance.

Luke seems unphased by my revelation. In fact, the giant wolf cups Cellica's cheek and leans down to press his lips to hers. "You honor us, Cellica."

Well, aren't they just delicious beasts with huge, chivalrous hearts? '*See, little wolf. These three are perfect for your first time.*' She doesn't respond, but I sense her seething in a corner. Her fear and anguish that I'm robbing her of this with Nox kicks me in the chest, but I ignore my stupid conscience attempting to rear its head. I'm a Prince. We do not do guilt.

"I have a hotel room across the street," I offer helpfully.

"Perfect," Luke says with a wide grin and throws a hundred-dollar bill on the bar. He's obviously the leader of this trio. "Show us the way, beautiful."

Just the mere notion I'm going to be plowed in every orifice has renewed energy sparking through my veins. I eagerly hop off the stool and lead my new entourage out the door, swaying Cellica's hips enticingly in her denim skirt. I'm like the fucking pied piper leading the children with his flute. Although what I have planned for these gruff wolves will be an adult-only pornographic extravaganza.

Just as I step off the curb, Luke grabs Cellica's right hand, and Mike clutches the other, entwining our fingers as if the wolf is a toddler and requires the buddy system to cross the road. I mentally roll my eyes as Dave brings up the rear.

"You guys share a lot?" I ask curiously. Werewolves are adventurous, sexual creatures who only become possessive and controlling when they find their mates.

"We love women," Luke shrugs, matching his strides to Cellica's smaller steps. "And we found three dicks are better than one for pleasuring females. There will come a day that will change, but for now, we are having fun."

"Do you boys ever cross swords, so to speak?"

Mike chuckles. "It's been known to happen in the heat of the moment, but if you're asking if we fuck each other, the answer is no."

"Pity," I pout. "I'd love to observe that."

"Darlin'," Luke leans down and purrs in my ear. "You'll be so busy coming, you won't know which end is up, let alone have time to watch anything."

Where have these wolves been all my life? I chortle to myself. They'd run for the hills if they knew a male demon was orchestrating this whole situation. And while it will be Cellica's body they are relishing, I too will experience the euphoric high her orgasms bring, sharing everything right along with her.

'*You're a sick, disgusting pig,*' Cellica snarls, and I chuckle inwardly.

'*No, love, I'm the originator of lust. I invented sex. The more outlandish and deviant, the more I thrive. But don't worry. I guarantee these males will make sure your initial time is beyond pleasurable, and if it becomes too much, I'll just slit their throats.*'

Her shock at my words swells my chest. Everyone always assumes that because I'm the demon of lust, I'm the docile one, out only for love and sex. But, first and foremost, I'm a Prince of Hell.

As we stroll across the lobby toward the elevators, patrons turn and stare wide-eyed at our foursome. The women openly ogle the males, their expressions dark with envy, craving to be Cellica. The men glare at the prominent predators in their midst, but their eyes dart to my wolf with lust. I nearly clap Cellica's hands in excitement. This evening is going to be one for the record books. I feel it in my bones.

Tonight, I recharge. Tomorrow, I find out what happened to Mammon and either discover a way to possess Nox or abandon hundreds of years of meticulous planning to reunite with what belongs to me.

Never. I will *never* give up until I reclaim what that bitch Abigail stole from me.

Chapter 13

Cellica

This can't be happening. How am I equally furious at Moe manipulating the loss of my virginity and turned on by the prospect of being taken by three wolves?

I wanted my first sexual experience to be with someone I cared about and who cared for me. Namely Nox. If I'm honest, haven't I been attempting at every turn to lose my last barrier to womanhood for the past four years? Now's my chance, and all I can think about is the fact I'm somehow betraying my vampire.

He's made it plain and clear from the moment we met—he prefers female vampires closer to his own age. Not a werewolf who hasn't transitioned into immortality yet. I personally feel he's worried about damaging his friendship with my brother and possibly hurting me if he loses control. Or at least that's what I keep telling my stubborn ass, who refuses to believe it's because he's not into me.

Although when my mind flashes back to the cabin, his actions and the hardness of his enormous cock portray a different story. Oh yeah. Based on that alone, he was definitely into it.

'What blood-redded immortal wouldn't in such a situation, Cellica?' the asshole taunts as our foursome enters the empty elevator.

'Fuck you, Moe,' I grumble.

'Oh, baby, it's you who's about to get fucked beyond anything your naïve little mind could conjure.'

'I don't want to be present for this. Please knock me out again as you did before.'

'No can do. I want you front and center.'

'I really hate you.'

'Aw, that almost hurts my feelings.'

As soon as the elevator doors swish shut, Luke pivots to pin my back against the back wall with his big body and takes my mouth in a blistering kiss. Holy shit. He's skilled, I'll give him that, and as much as I want to shove him away and scream at them to let me go, fucking Moe moans, clutches the brute's waist with one of my legs, and buries my fingers into his dark locks. With my skirt high on my hips, the hardness behind his jeans presses into my panties, causing a delicious friction.

Oh, God. This is happening, and there's not a damn thing I can do about it. I'm helpless—Moe's puppet to use and abuse to assuage his insatiable lust. I attempt to block out the assault on my senses. Even though I'm mentally screaming at them to stop, my body betrays me, responding to the stimuli.

'Quit fighting it, Cellica, and enjoy the moment.'

The redhead, Dave, steps to my side and lifts my hand from Luke's hair, placing it over his raging erection behind his cargo pants. He bends, running his lips along my shoulder. Mike mirrors him on my left.

While Luke ravishes my mouth, his cock rubbing against my clit over my panties, the other two have effectively pinned my hands against their dicks. Moe rubs my palms up and down their lengths and pumps my hips against Luke. It's too much. Too many sensations bombarding me all at once.

'This is fucking bliss, little wolf. These males will cherish your body. You have nothing to fear from them. I vow it.'

Right before the door dings, Dave and Mike step back. Then, without breaking the kiss, Luke lowers my leg and straightens my skirt. It's like being surrounded by a wall of testosterone and sexual tension. The lust permeating from this trio is immense, and I whimper in agitation, scared to death of what comes next.

An elderly couple goes to enter the lift, but when they take in the three lethal-looking men sandwiching li'l ol' me in the middle, they halt in their tracks, eyes wide, and immediately step back, claiming they forgot something in their room.

Luke chuckles as the doors slide shut. "Humans. So easily spooked."

"Are you ready for the best night of your life, Cellica?" Mike asks, rubbing the small of my back in a strangely soothing gesture.

No. Absolutely not.

"Yes," Moe answers instead. "I'm nervous but excited."

"We will take good care of you, little wolf," Luke adds over his shoulder. "You have nothing to be nervous about."

Ha! Says every serial killer ever! I shout as the doors open to the correct floor. As the four of us move in unison, I dig deep for my inner wolf. Even though she hasn't presented herself yet, I know she's there, simmering under my skin, waiting for the perfect opportunity to be free. *Well, now would be an ideal time*, I whisper. *I need you to stop this.*

Nothing, not even a tingle of a response. Damn it.

I watch with growing trepidation as I slide the keycard into the slot, and Luke swings the door open. I go to follow, but Dave and Mike grab my elbows, keeping me in the hallway while Luke investigates the room. Is he worried I laid a trap for them or something? Moe is suddenly quiet, and I'd relish the chance to punch the demon bastard in the throat.

Over the last week and a half on the road, I've sensed Nox's presence several times. No doubt Liam and the vampire queen have the entire task force and every werewolf territory on the lookout for me, but so far, the demon has stayed one step ahead of them. I can't deny it. I'm impressed with Moe's ability to remain hidden and fly below the radar, especially with a world renowned tracker on his tail.

Please hurry and find me Nox before it's too late.

The reality is if he hasn't caught up with us yet, the odds of him doing so before my virginity is just a memory is slim to zero.

Once Luke secures the suite, Dave and Mike usher me inside. The door slams shut, causing Moe and me to jump at the sound.

'*Fucking calm down, female. You're making me jittery as hell.*'

'*Good,*' I growl back.

As I gaze around the room we've spent the last couple of nights in, I notice Luke was busy in the few minutes he took to scout the area. He turned on the bedside lamp and threw one of my shirts over it, giving off an erotic red glow. The curtains are wide open, showcasing the twinkling lights of the town below, and a pleasant breeze flutters through the room. The setup is sensual and warm, and instead of calming my nerves, it ramps my anxiety up several notches.

The sight of Luke prowling toward me, the heat of the other two banking me in on both sides, causes my insides to flutter—and not in the way that I'd hope. This is it. I'm about to have sex with three strange men in some random hotel in the middle of who the fuck knows where.

If I didn't possess a fucking puppet master pulling the strings, I'd never put myself in this position. Not even if my fated one wasn't in the picture. These powerful males could gang rape me, rip me to pieces, and discard my body with no one the wiser.

Luke brushes my hair behind my ear, and some of my anxiety must shine through cause his next words are soothing and seem sincere. "Darlin', the boys and I will make tonight something you'll remember for the rest of your life. No matter who you mate or settle down with, you will look back on this night, and your heart rate will pitter patter faster, your sweet-smelling cunt will weep with need, and you won't be able to catch your breath. Whoever you're with will reap the benefits.

Well, damn.

Moe grins. "Based on your kissing skills, I have no doubt, Luke."

"Let's get you out of these clothes, shall we?" Mike murmurs against my ear as he moves in behind me and unbuttons my shirt.

The fucking demon boldly reaches out and cups Luke's sack, and I want to scream. The male's eyes darken with lust as he slips me free of my skirt in a blink. Warm air caresses my skin, and I'm covering my bra and panties with my hands imprisoned in my own body. Outwardly, Moe straightens my shoulders and lifts my chin with a tenacity I envy.

'Be proud of your body, Cellica. Confidence is sexy as fuck.'

"You're beautiful, little wolf," Luke murmurs, cupping my breasts and rubbing his big thumbs over my nipples through the thin fabric.

Against my will, the traitors tighten with need, and my insides clench. Moe leans my head against Mike's shoulder as Luke pops a breast free to suck a nipple between his lips. At the same time, Mike's beefy hand slides down my belly and slips into my panties and my slick seam.

"Fuck, she's so wet for us."

Luke groans and moves to the other breast to gift it with the same attention. Dave steps forward, gently tweaking the nipple Luke just abandoned. Moe grabs the red head's buckle, opens his trousers, and dives in to grip his raging erection.

"Goddamn. Are you sure you're a virgin?" Dave pants, pinching my nipple a little harder.

My body jerks at the pleasure spiraling from my breasts, straight to my clit which Mike is rubbing with delicious circles. Shit. If this keeps up, I won't be able to hold back the pending eruption.

'*Fucking don't hold back, Cellica. We need this.*'

'No,' I lie. '*You need this,*'

When Luke drops to one knee and slips my panties down my hips and thighs, flinging them across the room, the realization of what he's about to do has me thrashing in earnest. No! I want Nox's mouth on me. Nox's fingers bringing me to orgasm. My vampire's cock claiming my virginity. Not these strange men, no matter how vigorously my traitorous body is responding.

A second before Luke's lips contact my sex, a tremendous roar shakes the walls right before the door bursts open, impaling the drywall. Luke leaps to his feet and shoves my naked ass behind him. The other two take up flank positions.

What the ever-living fuck was that?

Moe tries to peer around their massive shoulders, but the boys are like an impenetrable wall. '*Find our damn clothes, Moe,*' I holler at him, jumpstarting his brain into gear. We bend and snatch my shirt and skirt off the floor when whoever was at the door finally speaks. We freeze in disbelief.

'*No fucking way,*' he growls in frustration.

'*Oh, thank the gods,*' I sigh at the same time.

"Cellica, come to me." Nox's deep timber sends chills down my spine, but the demon refuses to budge. "Cellica. Now goddamnit."

The Alpha command shoots through me like a shot of adrenaline. I wrestle for control, growling in anger.

'*You win, for tonight, little one,*' he whispers before sinking back and giving me power over my body.

If I don't diffuse this situation, in his rage, Nox will slaughter these men. This rendezvous wasn't their fault. I tap Luke on the shoulder, and he peers over at me. "You want us to wipe the floor with this vampire, sweetheart? Just say the word."

"No. He's... a friend. But if you keep me from him, he will kill all of you."

"We are not afraid of a lone vampire, darlin'," he growls, his eyes glowing the bright green of his wolf.

"He's a Guardian, and if you don't allow me to pass, you will be," I plead, clutching my clothes to hide my nakedness.

My words seem to surprise the werewolf. "You belong to him?"

"Yes," Nox states coldly with an eerie calm tracing fear down my spine. "She is mine. You've breathed your last breath, dog." Nox strides further into the room, and I get a peek of a muscular arm flexing as he draws his sword from inside his leather duster with an ominous ring.

Luke steps to the side slightly, and I gape as I behold my mate. His nostrils flare as he scents the room, the vast expanse of his chest rises and falls at a normal rate, like he's at a cocktail party and not about to annihilate three wolves. But the brightness of his eyes proves he's about to detonate.

My heart kick starts at the sight of him, beating as fast as the little drummer boy at Christmas. My entire body shakes. Not with fear, more like... a coming home.

When Nox's eyes land on my shivering form, clutching my clothes to cover my shame, the mismatched irises light up the room, and he lets out another ear-piercing roar. His lethal fangs drop low, ready to rip open flesh. My brain screams at me to stay behind the protective barrier of the wolves, but I ignore the stupid organ misfiring in my skull and shove against bulky arms to run to my vampire.

He snatches me with one arm and shoves me behind him. "Get dressed," he growls, never lifting his focus from the males in front of him. "You reek of wolf."

"I am a wolf, you jackass," I dare to throw back as I scramble into my clothes. "Please don't hurt them, Nox. It wasn't their fault. Moe took over and enticed them."

"Did they touch you?" he counters calmly, his concentration never deviating from the trio in the room.

"I...."

"Aye, we did," Mike taunts, and my eyes widen in dismay. What the fuck is he doing. "And if you step back out, vampire, we can finish what we started."

"She's a fucking delicious morsel," Dave pipes in with a cold, menacing smile.

"We were about to give her the ride of her life when you interrupted, *Guardian*," Luke sneers the title, his irises glowing with retribution, and my heart leaps in my throat. These idiots have no idea who they are challenging.

Nox slams his palm into my chest, knocking me into the hallway. I scramble to my feet as my mate wrenches the door from the plaster, but before he slams it shut, locking himself inside with the massive wall of testosterone, he shoots me a glare and my heart stutters to a halt. It promises retribution and I gulp in equal parts fear and anticipation of how Nox will punish me.

The door slams with a resounding boom. "No!" I shout and launch myself at the metal barrier. But without the keycard, all I can do is listen in growing horror to the massacre taking place on the other side.

Chapter 14

Nox

A red haze clouds my vision, and a loud buzzing fills my ears. They touched what belongs to me. My wolf. Their paws were all over her naked body. My body. My fucking mate.

As I throw punches that crunch bone, refusing to utilize my sword, craving to prolong their pain as long as possible, something in the back of my brain warns me not to kill them. The consequences of a Guardian slaying three werewolves in a fit of jealous rage will bring down a harsh sentence. But my inner vampire, the creature who claims Cellica as its own, shoves rational thought aside to seek justice for violating our female.

The wolves possess fighting skills. I'll give them that, and they work well as a team, indicating this isn't their first brawl together. But they are no match for a Guardian blinded by rage and fueled with the need to protect its mate.

When the tall asshole who was about to place his mouth on Cellica's pussy pulls out a knife, I smile but still refrain from raising my sword. Not yet. The redhead charges from my left. Without breaking my stare off with the big wolf, I side-kick him in the gut, sending him flying through the sliders and over the balcony railing to the street seven stories below.

One down. Two to go.

"You're gonna pay for that, vampire," blondie shouts, charging me with a large hunting knife lying along his forearm.

I spin low, knocking his legs out from under him, and slam my fist into his throat. The wolf rolls to his side, gasping for air. I swivel and rise to my feet as the big one plunges his blade into my gut. It burns like a motherfucker. So the werewolves are using silver blades. Interesting. He jerks it free and tries again, aiming for my heart.

I block the move with my forearm and hiss against the pain as it sinks into muscle. We grapple for the knife, throwing punches and kicks until the one I throat punched earlier slams into us. The potency of his blow sends us careening over the balcony railing. The wolves strike the asphalt with bone-crushing force, but I trace mid-fall to land softly beside the trio writhing on the dirty ground of the alley.

The demon—who Darath informed me when I barged in on him and Kleora in a panic after an entire week of tracking Cellica with no luck, is none other than Asmodeus, a powerful Prince of Hell—didn't choose the best location to stay in. The danger he placed Cellica in pisses me off even more. I bend down and pick up the enormous wolf, tossing his ass through the window of the abandoned warehouse next to the hotel. The others moan and groan, attempting to stand. Their irises light up as they fight the shift.

I ignore them and trace inside the building. If the dogs want a piece of me, they can follow me in, or I will take care of their asses later.

The second I detect my mate getting closer, I draw my sword. She must have raced through the lobby and out the front to follow the battle like an idiot. Enough of this bullshit, I need to get her out of here and back where she is safe. And once I calm the fuck down, I'm going to find out precisely what that goddamn demon wants and get rid of him.

As I approach the wolf, he bends and pulls another blade from his boot. Well-armed, I see. "Cellica wanted us to be her first, vampire. So I guess you haven't had the balls to make her yours yet."

His comment stops me cold. Cellica is a virgin? Anger and pride tangle in my gut. Why didn't she tell me? Not that I didn't suspect she was pure from the moment I laid eyes on her, despite her bold comments and quick temper, but this moron confirmed it. I'll make damn sure I'm her first everything.

"Those really going to be your last words, dog?" I taunt, easing closer.

"Nope. Her tits tasted mighty fine and her cunt smelled delicious."

My fury echoes through the abandoned structure as I charge the idiot, decapitating him in seconds. The brawl was merely foreplay, building the anticipation of their deaths, but his remarks sealed his doom.

The other two come charging inside but skid to a halt when they see their decapitated leader on the floor. My heart stops. Clasped in the redhead's meaty hands is Cellica, a knife to her throat. The defiance in her gaze guts me. The little idiot will fight with everything she has and get herself hurt or killed. Why didn't she fucking stay in the hotel?

I have to protect her, to impede whatever is about to happen. This fiasco is all my fault. I should've watched over her better, made sure her bindings were secure, and sought my queen's help the second I realized Cellica was gone. Instead, my arrogance in my tracker abilities clouded my judgment. Now, my defiant mate is about to pay the ultimate price.

My head swims with fear, scrambling my brain as every instinct pushes me to charge the fucker holding Cellica. I take a huge breath and dig deep for the cold warrior.

"You fucking killed him!" the blond shouts in disbelief.

"He touched what belongs to me," I counter calmly, even though my insides are in turmoil. I fucked this up once. I refuse to do it again. "Hand her over and I might consider letting you go."

The redhead snorts, pulling Cellica harder against his chest. "We both know that's a fucking lie."

"Look, man," Blondie boldly steps forward. "We didn't realize she belonged to anyone. We were just looking for a little fun and she seemed willing."

"They didn't know, Nox," Cellica beseeches. "It's not their fault. Please," she jerks against Carrot Top. "Let me go to him and no one else needs to get hurt."

"You think we can allow the murder of our pack Alpha to go unpunished?" Blondie growls low, and my gut clenches. "He took from us. Now we are going to take from him."

"Come and get it," I growl, brandishing my sword coated with their buddy's blood.

"Not from you, vamp."

"You harm her, and it will be the last thing you do."

"Please, Dave," Cellica pleads. "Don't do this."

"Sorry, love," he murmurs in her ear, and my insides go cold.

Without thinking things through, I trace to the redhead with more speed than I've ever accomplished and swing my sword, but I'm not fast enough. The wolf slides the edge of the knife across Cellica's throat.

His body crumbles behind her, his head rolling into a corner. For several seconds, it's like we stand frozen in time, staring at each other in horror and disbelief. Cellica clutches her neck in a futile effort to stem the blood flow as she gazes at me with an expression that will haunt me for the rest of my long existence.

I reach for her, pierce my wrist with my fangs, and bring the open wound to her mouth. "Drink, baby girl," I urge in a hoarse whisper, lowering us both to the floor, cocooning her in my arms.

Right now, I couldn't care less that the last wolf stands in wide eyed disbelief from several feet away.

I'd gladly give my life to save hers. Cellica, I've come to realize too late, is my everything. Before those whiskey irises landed on me, my course was just an endless list of jobs, assignments, duties, and meaningless sex. She changed all that, and I'll be damned if I lose her now.

After the first swallow, the precious essence seeping from the wound slows. Then, with several more gulps, the muscles, arteries, and skin slowly stitch back together. Even when the area is merely a pink line smeared with dried blood, I continue to provide my mate with what she needs. Fuck, I would gladly give it all to save her.

Her lashes flutter open, and those precious eyes meet mine. I almost shout with elation until a pair of powerful hands grip my shoulders and haul me away from Cellica, tossing me across the floor.

Apparently, the wolf's shock wore off.

I skid to a stop, thanks to a concrete pillar, but gain my feet in a heartbeat. Dizziness swamps my vision. Shit. I might have given her a little too much of my blood.

I spot my sword a few feet from Cellica struggling to her hands and knees before refocusing on the wolf charging toward me. Of the three, the blond is the most skilled fighter, and it takes everything I have to block and counter his attacks. Of course, I'm weak from not feeding for over a week and now blood loss, but I'll be damned if I leave my mate unprotected.

I require nourishment, so in a last-ditch effort, I tackle the wolf and sink my fangs deep into his neck, cleaving through muscles and tendons and taking down as much red octane as I can in a few seconds. The male roars in fury, jerking me from his flesh before flinging me across the room toward Cellica and within reach of my weapon.

The slight kick of energy from the wolf's blood allows me to trace to my sword and swing just as the wolf reaches me. His head bounces next to his Alpha's, and I sag in relief, dropping to one knee. Not sure how much longer I could've withstood his attack.

"Chris?" Her soft, tentative voice washes over me, bringing back all the rage and fear of the last hour. I almost lost her. The horror of watching that wolf slit her throat, her life essence cascading down her chest, nearly destroyed me. Was that the plan all along? Were the wolves going to fuck her, then kill her and drop her body in the alley like trash?

Goddamn. Possessed or not, the little minx is mine. My world means nothing without her in it.

Rational thought flees my brain as I recall the scene in the hotel room. The blond held my female from behind, and his fingers touched her pussy. She clutched the redhead's dick in her petite hand while he pinched a nipple, and the leader kneeled before her, ready to lick the sweetness that belongs to me.

Before realizing what I'm doing, I grip Cellica by the throat, shove her against the concrete wall, and sink my fangs deep into her neck, marking my claim. Effectively, I'm pissing on my territory, calming my inner vampire and reasserting she belongs to me. In an instant, my cock is hard as stone, rubbing my erection against her pelvic bone to relieve the ache.

"Christoph," she breathes, clutching my head to her neck, and I shudder at the sound of my full name on her lips.

She is mine, and no one will ever touch her again.

Chapter 15

Cellica wraps both legs around my waist, hiking her skirt above her hips and I realize she is panty-less. Fuck. The aroma of her arousal misfires something in my brain and I reach between us and finger her clit. Goddamn, she's wet for me, and I want nothing more than to impale her on my cock while drinking her blood to mark her as mine forever.

She's a virgin, chants through my head and somehow, I find the sense to refrain and ease my fangs from her flesh. Even though I could gorge myself on her succulent offering to restore my strength, I crave another treat right now.

"Is your pussy wet for me, baby girl?"

"Yes, Chris. Only you."

"Good girl. I'm going to remove any lingering images of those filthy wolves touching you while their sightless eyes watch us." Her eyes widen at my grotesque comment, but I'm beyond caring. I need to eradicate every molecule of their encounter. "Grab the steel bar above you and don't let go. Do you understand?"

"Yes," she groans and grips the round metal a foot above her head.

I rip open her blouse, sending buttons flying into the congealed blood and gore around us, and lean in to sever her bra with my teeth. Fuck me, her tits are spectacular. Full and succulent, with rosy areolas puckered tight.

"I'm going to suck and bite your nipples until my lips and fangs are all you remember." I cup her wet sex, diving a finger inside. She arches, clutching the rebar harder. "Then I will do the same to your sweet pussy until you cum all over my face."

"Yes, God yes." She writhes against my digit, but I withdraw.

"Uh ah. You are not in control here, Cellica. Daddy is. No coming until I say so." Before she can respond, I kneel before her and take a turgid nipple in my mouth, sucking it deep. The spent life essence of the fallen surrounds us, but I don't care. It merely adds fuel to the fire of my lust, reveling in their deaths. My inner vampire preens with satisfaction. We destroyed the fuckers who touched what is ours. Cellica cries out when I pierce her puckered flesh with a fang, and rapture flows over me as I suckle like a starved man.

"Chris," she pants, gazing down at me. "I love when you bite and drink from me. I can't get enough. It feels so good."

I grin and pinch the other nipple, rolling it between my thumb and fingers, and her head drops back. Her moan of pleasure shoots straight to my dick, hardening me to painful proportions.

Before we leave this blood-soaked warehouse, Cellica won't remember the goddamn werewolves. Unable to deny myself a second longer, I hike one of her legs over my shoulder and take my first taste of my mate, sweeping my tongue from her wet opening to the clit.

"Oh, shit," she gasps, gazing down at me with wonder.

"Has no one tasted this pussy before, baby girl?" If they have, I will find out who they are and make sure they never remember a damn thing again.

"N... no."

A feral grin spreads my lips. "And no one but me ever will, Cellica. You. Are. Mine."

With that threat hanging in the air, I lean in and feed on the sweet, succulent flesh that now belongs to me. I love I'm the first to give my wolf pleasure with my tongue, and a low possessive growl rumbles from my chest.

Fuck, she tastes as good as she smells and every muscle vibrates with the need to devour her whole. I contain my inner vampire and relish her, swirling her clit before sucking it gently into my mouth. I monitor the subtle changes in her breathing. Each moan that escapes, or the way her body shudders in desire helps me determine her exact pleasure points to transport her closer to climax. I want this initial time to be epic for my little wolf

"You taste so damn good," I rumble and slowly insert a finger into her soaked opening. Christ, she's tight. I'll need to make sure I well prepare my little virgin in order to handle my size.

"Christoph, oh God. Yes, right there." I follow her directions, giving her exactly what she craves as she gyrates her hips, grinding her sex on my face.

I fucking love the way she lets her inhibitions float away with the wind and lays bare her soul for me in the throes of lust. "Who owns this pussy, baby girl?" I growl in between laps and gently insert another digit.

"You do, Daddy," she moans, gripping the steel tighter.

"And what will happen if you ever run from me again?" I ask, pumping my fingers faster, curving them to graze that sweet spot on the inside.

"I... You..." her head drops back, unable to answer the question.

"I'll tell you what will happen, baby girl. I'll whip your ass with a belt and then fuck you for hours, denying you release. Do you understand me, Cellica?" My manner is all command and my trembling wolf responds by gazing down at me, taking in the brightness of my irises and my fangs riding low, ready to plunge into her in a second.

"Yes, Christoph. I understand." Her serious expression and solemn tone calm my vampire.

"Good girl. Now shatter for me, baby." I set back in, flicking her clit and plunging my fingers deeper, skimming that soft spot every time. Cellica digs her heel into my spine, her muscles quivering with need, her insides fluttering. Even though I know she's close, she doesn't plunge over the cliff. Not that I care. I could stay right here for hours, savoring my mate's sweet sex, but she obviously needs something more.

If I'm learning one thing about my wolf, it's that she relishes a little pain with her pleasure, so I reach over her leg with my other hand and rub her needy clit, while continuing to plunge inside her with the other. I scrap my fangs down her inner thigh before plunging them into her femoral artery without warning.

Cellica jerks at the discomfort, but within seconds her insides convulse and her scream of ecstasy has my cock twitching for release. Easy boy, I reprimand him as I gulp her restorative blood, not relenting on her pussy in the slightest. In record time, another orgasm rocks through her and her fingers delve into my hair, holding my head against her vein as her sex spasms. Goddamn. Cellica is a fucking goddess and I can't get enough of her body.

When the tremors ease, I withdraw from her thigh, licking the wounds closed before nuzzling her sex and lapping up every drop. I'm addicted to my little wolf's taste. Her blood. Her pussy. I crave to mark the entire surface of her body to demonstrate she belongs to me, but the sobering reality is she doesn't belong to me. Even though I suspect I'm her fated mate, until her transition, we won't know for sure.

A twinge of pain suffuses my chest at the idea of her walking away from me and mating with another. I don't think I could ever look at Liam again and not experience the crushing agony of knowing his sister is my one true mate but belongs to someone else.

A furious rumble threatens to let loose, but I tamp it down and lower Cellica's leg to the floor, straightening her skirt before rising to cup her cheek. "You released the bar, baby girl," I admonish with a teasing grin.

She fiddles with her shirt, tying the ends in a knot to bring the sides together as best she can. The hint of her cleavage enthralls me for several minutes. "Yeah. Sorry about that," she mutters, refusing to lift her gaze.

Something is off. "Cellica, look at me." When she doesn't comply, I grip her chin and force her face up. Tears fill her eyes and my chest tightens at the sight. Fuck, did I harm her? I'll never forgive myself if I'm the cause of her anguish. "What's wrong, baby? Did I hurt you?"

"N... no," she stutters and to my utter dismay, the floodgates open and sobs shake her slim form.

At a loss, I enclose her in my embrace and press her head to my chest, whispering soothing words. Within minutes, her tears soak my shirt and her little fists grip my waist. "Tell me what's wrong, Cellica. Whatever it is, I'll fix it."

"He... he made me... with the wolves... I had no control. Moe was going to let them... all three of them...."

Son of a bitch. That's the last visual I need in my head, but I shove aside my wrath at the demon and try to soothe my wolf. "It wasn't your fault, Cellica."

"Yes, it was," she murmurs and moves away several steps, wiping the tears from her face. "I was the one who left your cabin after Jessica broke in to rescue me. I planned on taking off to the ranch."

My body stills, anger warms my chest, but I continue to watch her intently, my features hopefully blank. "Why?" I ask quietly. "You were safe with me."

She shakes her head, her gaze frantic. "No. I wasn't. And neither were you."

What the fuck does that mean? "Explain."

"Moe has...." she halts and her entire demeanor changes. The shoulders slumped in grief mere seconds ago, straighten and her chin lifts with a confidence I would now recognize anywhere.

"Cellica has nothing more to say. Except that I enjoyed the cunnilingus immensely. You have a very talented tongue, vampire. Thank you for the orgasm."

Fucking demon.

My skin crawls at the thought of him being cognizant of our intimate moment. I reach into my pocket for my cellphone. "Your king is very interested in knowing where his wayward prince went," I say, typing out a rapid text to Darath. "He sent the hellhounds on your trail. Lucky for you, I found you first."

Cellica snatches the cell from my fingers and hurls it across the deserted warehouse where it smashes against the same pillar my spine did before falling to the ground in several pieces. "Not quite quick enough, *Asmodeus*," I sneer and reach into my back pocket for the silver handcuffs I didn't want to have to use. "Come peacefully, demon."

"Ah, so Lucifer tattled on me, huh? It matters not." He shrugs. "I will tear her apart before I allow you to take me back to Hell," he growls in a demonic voice that sends tingles down my spine. "Besides," he sidesteps to the gaping opening to the alley. "We both know you won't hurt the little wolf to get to me."

I trace in front of the doorway, blocking his escape. "I can't let you leave, demon."

"Pity," he says with actual remorse, and my eyebrow lifts in response. "I was starting to like you, vampire, especially after you fucked me with your mouth so thoroughly."

Before my mind can process that comment, Cellica... Er... Moe launches himself at me, fists flying. I block and evade, but the demon is stronger than I expected and I'm doing my damnedest to not hurt my mate. When her fist connects with my jaw, blood spurts and the force knocks me back several steps. Rage fills my vision at the horrifying sound of the bones breaking in Cellica's hand. I charge, attempting to wrap her up in a hold, but the demon writhes like a slippery snake before plowing her knee into my groin.

Pain buckles my knees, but I lock my legs and push past the agony. "Cellica, stop him before I hurt you," I shout, hoping she hears me.

The wolf's body spasms and her eyes widen. "No!" the demon shouts, clutching her head.

"That's it, baby girl. Come to me."

But instead of Cellica advancing to overtake him, a sudden explosion rips through the warehouse, sending me careening into the opposite wall. Pain stabs through my spine and torso, and I can't catch my breath. The impact fractured my left arm; the humerus broken and protruding through the skin, and my right ankle sits at an odd angle. Neither of those injuries is keeping me from rising. Something else is pinning me to the surface. I peer down at my chest. Thick rebar, about two inches in diameter, protrudes from my sternum, impaling me against the brick in a seated position, my legs straight out along the floor.

Well, shit.

Chapter 16

"Cellica, I might need a little help here," I mutter through clenched teeth as I watch my life blood stream down my torso, soaking my hips before pooling on the surrounding ground. If I don't deal with the flow soon, we could have a problem.

I raise my head to peer around the building. "Cellica?" Did she gain control of the demon, or did he force her to slip out the doorway and disappear into the night again? And what the hell was that explosion?

"Cellica!" My shout is pathetic, the metal rod through my chest restricting my breathing. Panic nibbles at my brain with the focus of a beaver, but I shove it aside for the moment. Was she also injured in the blast, knocked unconscious behind a pillar?

"Goddamnit, answer me."

A soft whine to my right snags my attention, and I whip my head in its direction. Crouched in the darkness, undetectable by the human eye, a large black wolf lays in wait. Its fur so dark, it's almost bluish. Slanted cerulean irises study me with unnerving directness. Shit, did one of the wolves have time to call for backup before I killed them? I glance across the dirty ground at my sword glinting in the muted moonlight by the doorway.

Fuck.

I'm in no condition to ward off an attack from a werewolf. Right now, I'm earnestly wishing the communication with my queen went both directions. I can only hope my text to Darath sent before the fucker smashed my phone to smithereens.

Sweat dots my forehead as I grit my teeth and attempt to slide forward off the rebar with my good arm. Agony skyrockets through my chest and down my spine, and I groan against the immense pain. Typically, having ingested Cellica's blood, my bones, tendons, and muscles would've mended by now, but with the amount of blood saturating the surrounding concrete, healing is merely a distant dream.

Another whine comes from the darkness. *Just fucking stay there, dog, until I get myself out of this predicament, would ya?* My breathing shallows, and my vision tunnels. Shit. I must find Cellica. She could be lying injured somewhere, or the fucking demon is attempting to find another hookup before they disappear.

Rage is the catalyst to propel me forward again, but in my weakened state, I merely slide a couple of inches before the excruciating agony becomes too much, and I almost pass out. That's all I need—blacking out with a hundred and fifty-pound wolf salivating in the corner, waiting to rip me to shreds.

A shuffling sound spikes my heart rate, and I peer over at the wolf. It's up on all fours with its head hung low as it prowls toward me. Well, fuck.

"Easy boy," I coo and grip the steel in my chest with my good arm. Maybe I can snap the end and slip off.

No, that's stupid, Nox. You barely moved two inches.

What if I yanked it out of the wall? Then I could grab it and slide it from my body. I snort. Just moving has taxed my strength. Having the power to pull the bar from solid brick is a joke, but I can't give up. The second I do, the hunter in the shadows will pounce and eat me alive.

As a vampire, I'm an apex predator—the one pursuing others. It's humbling to be the prey, and while I've always known I'd die on the job—dreamed of it often—unease tingles across my scalp at the notion of dying without my sword in my hand.

The black beauty stalks closer, emerging from the shadows into a beam of light from a gaping hole in the roof. The low whine is eerie, but the intense irises are somehow soothing, and I can't take my eyes from the beast.

"Aren't you beautiful?" I whisper, clearly delirious at this point, thinking the object of my demise to be strangely captivating.

A sudden brilliant flash, pursued by a booming clap of thunder, surprises me, and I jerk, hissing against the pain. I peer up at the Swiss cheese of a roof to see thick dark clouds above. Great. That's all I need, a good soaking on top of everything else.

A mere three feet from my fractured arm, the wolf's whine turns into a menacing growl, and I brace for the attack, for the agonizing sensation of its canines sinking into my body. But instead of leaping on me, ripping my throat open, and devouring my flesh, the wolf crouches low on the concrete and shuffles closer in a submissive gesture. I tilt my head in confusion. Why isn't it attacking me?

The powerful jaws come within inches of my useless arm. I tense. My sword hand clenched in a fist, ready to pound its skull. I won't go down without a fight. A visual of the wolf chomping down, tearing my limb from my body, and slinking back off in the darkness to relish its meal, plays like a morbid slideshow through my brain. But instead, the wolf's long tongue flicks out, licking the gaping wound, its wary gaze darting to my face as if to gauge my reaction.

I take a moment to examine the creature as dizziness swamps my vision. Why am I not more afraid? Have I lost so much blood my mind and body are numb to the possibility this wolf could precipitate an agonizing end to my hundred and fifty years? Or is it something more? Maybe this is a stray who means me no harm, who just happened by and saw the carnage.

Fuck, you are delirious, Nox.

When I make no move to reach for it, the animal slinks closer, and the warmth emanating from it leaches into my side. Then, with slow grace, the beast rises to its feet, easing its large muzzle toward me, and that's when I realize the wolf is female. Hot breath fans my forehead as she sniffs my face, and a warm tongue licks my cheek.

You stupid son of a bitch, Nox.

"Cellica?"

The beauty whines in response, licking my neck.

"Holy shit. The blast was you?" Another whine as she lowers her head as if in remorse. My baby girl just experienced her first shift. Undoubtedly, the trauma of the last few hours catapulted her into finally transitioning. Liam confessed during a poker night not too long ago, that he was concerned by the fact Cellica hadn't shifted yet, and if she didn't transition by the end of the year, he, as her Alpha, would have to take matters into his hands and attempt to force the event. Which apparently involved some serious messed up shit because the look on Liam's face clenched my gut in the moment.

She sniffs the steel protruding from my chest before lowering her front legs onto my lap, her long body flush against my thigh. She chuffs, peering at me with those bright sky-blue eyes before dropping her muzzle to lick up at the blood pooling on my hips. Blackness dances around my vision, but I shake my head to clear it and sink my fingers into the thick coat at her neck.

Darath's words come back to haunt me. He said if Cellica shifted while the asshole still possessed her, the Prince would bind to her soul forever. Please, God, I silently pray. Don't let that be the case. Cellica is pureness and light. Asmodeus is deviant and dark. His presence defiles her spirit.

"If I don't make it, I want you to know how proud I am of you. You've had some serious shit thrown at you the last couple of weeks, and have handled it like a warrior."

Cellica whines low.

"Hush, baby girl. Do you think you can shift again and get help?"

She huffs and closes her eyes as if in concentration. When nothing happens after several minutes, I realize she has no clue how to transition back, and my heart sinks.

"It's okay, baby. I'm sure King Darath is on his way." But, even to my ears, the words sound hollow, and Cellica arches her neck and lets out a soulful howl into the rafters just as the first drops of rain stain the concrete.

I try to reassure her, rubbing my fingers through her coat and murmuring soothing assurances to calm her fears, but it's getting harder to speak. Blood loss saps my energy until my hand falls to my side and my vision blurs. It won't be long before my body shuts down entirely to preserve strength. The warning tingle of dawn tightens the skin on my nape.

"Cellica," I whisper, and she lifts her head from my lap to gaze up at me, her ears perked forward. "Your wolf is stunning, and no matter the outcome, I'm glad I was here for your first transition."

Her low whimper breaks my heart because I know the darkness is about to consume me, leaving her defenseless and far from home.

Chapter 17

Rage and terror pour through my heart, and my wolf, my glorious wolf that I'd love to take the time to relish, howls in agony and helplessness.

Nox's chin rests on his chest, his beautiful mismatched eyes closed. How he's still alive boggles my mind as I examine the situation. Of course, in animal form, I can't help him. I need to fucking shift back. But no matter how hard I concentrate or how much I pace and growl and plead for my inner beast to let go, nothing works. Nox is gonna die because of me, because I'm too weak and stupid to control my wolf.

He saved me. My beautiful, complicated, lethal warrior slaughtered those wolves like they were pesky flies. I trot over to Luke's headless body, pawing at his clothes with my claws, praying one of these assholes has a phone on them. Not that I could use it, but maybe I could rouse Nox enough he could call for help. I glance at the spot where my vampire shoved me against the wall and sank his fangs into my neck, then where he'd kneeled in the fallen's congealed blood and worshiped my sex with his talented mouth. It was deviant and sick, but goddamn, if his dominance and aggression didn't ramp my lust to such a degree, I would've performed anything he demanded.

What does that reveal about me? It exposes one thing for sure. I'm a submissive. With Nox anyway. He commands, and I obey. The notion doesn't sit well with me. Yes, I'm an Omega who answers to an Alpha, but I would've never guessed I was a true submissive. I make my own decisions. Rule my own life. Like Julia Roberts muttered in Pretty Woman—"I say who, I say when; I... I say who..."

Not finding a phone on Luke, I move to Steve, ripping at his clothes. I bark in triumph when a cell phone drops out of his pocket. As gently as possible, I pick up the device between my teeth and trot over to my vampire. Fear spears through me at the paleness of his skin.

Please don't die on me, Chris. I beg silently as I drop the mobile in his lap. He doesn't even stir, so I bark a couple of high-pitched yips and his body jerks. Dull eyes zero in on me and I paw at his hip, mentally screaming at him to look down.

"What is it, baby girl?"

His voice is so faint. If I wasn't a wolf, I probably would've missed it. I nudge his lap again, lowering my head and bumping the phone with my nose. Nox glances down, and his eyebrows raise at the object resting on his groin.

"What the hell..." he frowns, lifting his undamaged arm to bring the screen to life. "Did you get this off one of the wolves?"

I chuff in response and position myself along his side to offer warmth, facing the entrance. It terrifies me how cold his body feels.

"Good girl," he whispers. When his lids flutter and lower, I rise and lick his face and neck, needing him to stay conscious long enough to call for help. His head jerks up, he shakes it several times before refocusing on his task.

I watch him closely as his fingers move sluggishly across the screen. "Thank God the dumb bastard didn't password-protect his phone," he mumbles. After a second, the ringing sound echoes through the building, mixing with the spatter of rain soaking the floor.

"Please tell me you found her, Nox?"

I haven't spent much time in the vampire queen's presence, but I'd recognize Nicole's husky tone anywhere.

"Yes," he whispers before rattling off street names. How he even knows our location boggles my mind. "We are in the abandoned warehouse next to the hotel," he rasps out, and I can tell he's struggling to stay conscious. "Bring blood. Hurt bad." My low whine at his words lifts to the rafters.

"Team is on the way, but was that a dog?" Nicole asks.

Nox lays his hand on my neck, and pleasure at his touch spreads through me. "Need Liam. Cellica shifted."

"Fuck. Shit. Okay, hang in there, Nox. I forbid you to die on me. You hear me?"

"Yes, my...."

My gaze swivels to Nox's face. His chin rests on his chest once more, and his fingers slip from my fur to land with a splat in the surrounding blood.

"Nox?" Nicole's tone is frantic. "Nox!"

I howl my anguish. This is all my fault. I'm weak and pathetic. I couldn't handle the demon. I couldn't control my shift. And it appears I'm stuck in wolf form, unable to aid my mate, who's dying.

Weak. Weak. Weak.

With an agonized whine, I rest my head on Nox's lap.

"Stay with him, Cellica. Help is on the way," Nicole reassures before the line goes dead.

I shuffle closer and pray the team gets here pronto. I'm not sure how much longer Nox can hold on.

I no more get the thought out of my brain when six figures materialize in the middle of the warehouse. The gentle rain falls like sparklers around them, casting a sinister vision, and a sudden fierce protectiveness surges through my chest. It consumes and blinds me to everything. A mantra pounds in my skull like a bass drum in a marching band—protect my mate. Protect my mate.

When the shadows move toward us, I rise to all fours, placing myself over Nox's legs. The hair down my neck and back spikes with aggression, and I snarl a warning, baring my teeth.

Protect Nox. Protect our mate. Kill any who try to harm him.

"Easy, Cellica," a familiar werewolf soothes, stepping forward, his palm outstretched. "We are here to help."

My lips quiver with each step until my low, feral growls surround us.

"What the hell happened here?" the big shifter whispers as he gazes at the headless bodies by the entrance.

"Cellica. Stand down." The Alpha command causes my muscles to spasm with the need to obey the familiar tone. Yet, somehow, I ignore the directive and leap forward, snapping at his hand.

"What the fuck?"

My wolf whimpers at the male's stunned expression.

"Why can't you control her, Liam?" the shifter asks with a frown.

"I'm not sure." The Alpha werewolf replies. "I think her instincts have taken over and her demand to protect Nox is overriding everything else."

"From us?" a tall female vampire standing next to the shifter asks. She's covered in black leather, similar to my mate, a long, dark braid hanging over one shoulder.

"From anything she perceives as a threat."

"We must get to Nox," a male vampire with striking blue eyes demands, and I snarl at him. "If he doesn't take blood in the next few minutes, it will be too late."

No! My mind screams. *We must save him.*

"Cellica. As your Alpha, I command you to move aside."

My body shudders at the absolute power in the wolf's tone, and I whine in response but ignore the directive. Instead, I ease down over Nox's lap, refusing to budge.

"Baby girl."

My mate's soft entreaty perks my ears. I huff in submission and pleasure when his fingers grip my scruff.

"They are here to help. Back down," he commands.

I immediately obey, shifting to the side to allow the group closer, watching every move they make. With Nox's words, the protective haze subsides, and my brain clears enough that I recognize the werewolf is my brother.

Liam watches me with a strange expression as he leans down to examine the rebar impaling Nox. Sebastian and Lu dump blood down Nox's throat from numerous bags while the petite redhead, Alex, approaches me with cautious steps.

"You are a beautiful wolf, Cellica," she whispers, her big blue eyes round with amazement. "It's an incredible feeling to be one with your animal."

"Red," Sebastian barks. "Do not get too close."

She rolls her eyes with a grin, and I yip in response, rising on all fours. She's so petite that my head reaches her chest, but she doesn't seem intimidated. In fact, she takes several steps closer, her arm outstretched with her palm turned up, her lips curved in a slight smile.

"Goddamn it, Alex," the vampire commander growls, tracing to her and shoving her behind him.

Internally, I grin at his protective gesture. So like Nox. Like every male immortal, really. I again retreat to my mate, respecting the vampire's right to guard his female, and refocus on the team working to extract Nox.

"Just grab my shoulders and drag me off the fucking bar," Nox snaps, and I'm relieved to see he's gained some of his strength back, thanks to the two dozen bags of blood scattered across the floor.

"Lucretia, protect his broken arm as we pull," Kurtis orders, and she moves to his damaged arm, healing at a snail's pace.

"Alex, keep his ankle from twisting more while we move him," Sebastian directs, watching me. "Liam, you grip under his right arm, I will grab his left and Kurtis, you hold him around his torso."

The pain in Nox's expression agitates my wolf, and I pace back and forth off to the side, low warning growls vibrating my chest, rain soaking my coat.

"Nox," Sebastian warns. "On the count of three we move, but whatever you do, do not cry out or I am afraid Cellica will attack us."

"I'm not a pussy, commander," Nox snarls between gritted teeth. "Just fucking do it."

"One," the vampire I always liken to Henry Cavill, counts down. "Two. Three."

The large males slide Nox off the rebar with quick efficiency while Lu cradles his broken arm and Alex secures his busted ankle. My warrior never makes a sound. Instead, those penetrating irises stay glued to mine as if to offer *me* comfort when he's the one in excruciating pain.

The second his body is clear of the steel, Sebastian props him against the wall and tosses several more blood bags onto his lap. I watch in fascination as Nox sinks his fangs into the bag, downing the contents in seconds, and I ease forward, needing to be closer. The others move back, making room for me.

"Cellica," my brother halts my path. "You need to turn so we can teleport out of here."

I whimper in response, deflated by my failure to transition. Again.

First, I couldn't shift into wolf form. Now I can't turn back. If Nox hadn't commanded me to stand down, my inability to control my wolf's instincts could've killed my mate. His death would be on my head. This whole situation is my fault. The deaths in this abandoned building are because I had no hold over the demon. My shame sits heavy on my soul, and I ease away from the group, my stare never leaving Nox's, watching him down more blood as his body mends and heals.

"Cellica. I command you to shift," my brother orders again in that Alpha tone. While my muscles ripple in response to the power in his voice, and a part of me itches to obey, I refuse with a low snarl.

Kurtis helps Nox to his feet, his ankle and arm mended. The bright, multicolored stare spears through me with regret, and I soon realize why when he reaches into his back pocket and pulls out a pair of silver handcuffs. Dread weighs down my shoulders.

"What the fuck are those for?" Liam demands, stepping between Nox and me.

"Are we forgetting why we are all here?" he urges quietly. "If Cellica shifts, Asmodeus will take over again."

A sudden dark, tempting manifestation permeates the atmosphere seconds before King Darath appears, Kleora, his mate, at his side. "What did we miss?" he asks with a wicked grin.

Something moves in my solar plexus, and my wolf growls in agitation. Fucking Asmodeus is responding to his king's presence. It's getting awfully crowded in here. If I'm not careful, circumstances will force my brother to institutionalize me until they rid me of my pesky passenger.

Darath's crimson gaze scrutinizes me as he slowly approaches, and the regret in his expression spreads dread through my gut. "Asmodeus has no control while your little sister is in wolf form," he informs Liam and the group. "Unfortunately, neither do I until she shifts." His comment soothes the demon, and he settles.

"Dawn looms," Sebastian announces. "We need to make a decision."

"What about a silver cell in the castle?" Lucretia asks.

"No fucking way," Liam growls.

"A silver prison won't hold a Prince of Hell for long," Darath informs them.

Nox rakes his fingers through his disheveled locks, darkened by the rain. "I'll take her back to my cabin."

"Yeah, because that worked so well last time," Liam snarls, waving his arm to indicate our current location and the carnage. "What happened here, Nox? Why are three of my wolves missing their heads?"

"We do not have time for this line of questioning," Sebastian implores, and I sidestep my brother to ease closer to my vampire's side. His anger and agitation cause my nerves to draw tight.

"You all leave. I will shift and stay with Cellica during the day. Teach her to control her wolf."

"No. I'm not leaving her in some random town she's not familiar with. She's scared and restless." Whether or not he realizes it, Nox's fingers sunk into my fur as he spoke, massaging my tense muscles.

I glance up at the hole in the roof above us, and fear claws through me. Clouds tinged with soft pink showcase the approaching dawn. If the vampires don't leave now, the sun's rays will fry their skin from their bodies in minutes in this unprotected building. Even with the cloud cover.

"Nox," Sebastian barks, gathering Alex into his embrace. "Head to the castle. Now."

Lu mimics the commander's actions with Kurtis, readying to trace away. Needing my mate protected, I step around to face him and lick his hand before nudging him toward Sebastian and Alex.

Understanding softens his expression, and he nods. "Stay with your brother, little wolf. Be safe. I'll see you tonight." He tosses the handcuffs at Liam who hisses at the contact before shoving them into his back pocket. "Just in case."

As he disappears, something in my soul splinters. Nox is such a worthy male. Second in command of the Vampire Guardians. A skilled veterinarian with a warrior's spirit. His sense of right and wrong guide his decisions. It kills him that I'm his best friend's little sister, and our bond severely strains their friendship.

He's stated in the past that he thought I was immature and too young to know what I wanted. In the last few days, I've proven that's true. I'm incapable of controlling the demon inside me, even willingly letting him direct our actions with Nox, because I'm too much of a coward to take the initiative. With the three wolves, I objected to being controlled, objected to not having a say in what was happening. Still, a part of me I can't acknowledge burned with lust at the notion of being fucked by three males at once. It scared me shitless, but excited me nonetheless. And even though I've finally connected with my wolf, I lack the strength to command her or shift back. I may be from royal blood, but my spirit and character are less than.

I am less than.

Chapter 18

Cellica

The second the others disappeared, Liam guided me out the rear of the building through a run-down subdivision and an abandoned construction site until we finally slipped into a wooded area.

"I think we should run together until you tire, then I'll shift again and talk you through controlling your change. Sound good?"

I yipped my response.

"Turn around while I undress," Liam ordered, and I gladly gave him my back, not wanting to see my brother's nude ass. Not that it would be the first time.

Living in the same house, I've strolled in on him and Viessa on several occasions. Of course, if they kept their damn sexcapades to their bedroom, I wouldn't have to worry about it. But noooo. Kitchen, laundry, living room. I even walked in on my brother kneeling before the Oracle one time—with his mouth latched onto her pussy—in the fucking wine cellar.

I can never unsee that.

My mind flashes back to the warehouse and Nox devouring me against the wall, and I shift restlessly. I love our dirty talk, and calling him Daddy tightens my pelvis. I'd do anything he commanded. The vampire could tie me up—which he's done but unfortunately not for sexual reasons... no wait. That's not entirely true. He spanked me as I came against my panties while restraints pulled at my wrists. That definitely counts.

The moment I laid eyes on Nox, my dreams morphed into a porno slide show, and even though they were loaded with sexual tension and angst that had me sliding my fingers beneath my panties they remained blurry and vague because I honestly didn't comprehend what my body wanted. Until Asmodeus. Boy did that fucker open my mind. Like wide open. Every lewd, graphic image he threw at me played an active role in my dreams, morphing them into High Definition.

I would allow my mate to collar me, demand I crawl across the room to him, whip me, or spank me. Everything he desired, I would submit to and obey as long as my reward was his praise, mouth, touch, and cock.

Why do I subjugate myself to Nox? It's not because I'm weak or have no choice. I do it because it makes me feel good. Happy. In control. It's a powerful feeling, owning the passion of a vampire like Christoph. I'm his equal, but he's dominant, the Daddy directing his baby girl to be his willing whore, and I'm addicted to it.

But I have to question if that's genuinely me craving those things, or is it my unwanted passenger—the fucking demon of lust? How do I trust that what I'm aching for is me and not Asmodeus? The only way to find out is to get the fucker out of me and see what happens. Will I revert to the shy, awkward idiot, unable to articulate my wants and desires when in Nox's presence? Or will I retain some of the demon's sexual confidence?

A quick flash has me turning back to my brother.

Now is not the time to dwell on the what-ifs. Today, I need to conquer my wolf and learn to control her impulses and the change. Then I'll worry about Asmodeus and Nox.

Baby steps.

Liam's wolf is enormous, with piercing blue eyes and snow-white fur. He trots over, standing a good foot taller than me at the shoulders. My wolf's instincts take over when he headbutts me, nipping at my neck with a low growl. She forces us to the ground submissively, rolling to her back and presenting her Alpha with her most vulnerable areas.

The woman in me grinds her teeth at submitting to my brother even though I've done it my whole life. Nox dominates the woman in me, but Liam is king, pack Alpha, and controls every wolf throughout the vast Providence.

So who do I listen to? The woman? The wolf? Or the demon? My situation is absolute chaos and I'm being ripped in two. Or three in this case.

Liam sniffs me, snarling when he encounters Nox's scent deep in my coat. His blood still crusts the underside of my neck, where my wolf laid her head in his lap.

My brother bites at my jugular. I whimper but make no aggressive moves even though mentally I'm still gnashing my teeth. Then, after a few seconds, Liam barks and takes off running, so I leap to my feet and give chase. My wolf preens, glorying in the freedom of stretching our legs for the first time as my Alpha and king sets an unrelenting pace, leaping over streams and logs, his long stride swallowing up the forest floor as I push harder to keep up.

Mile after mile, we run, play, and hunt. Liam teaches me how to stalk prey and corral them as a team like we do when herding cattle. I thought I'd balk at killing and eating Bambi's mother, but my wolf relishes the meal, tearing into the muscles like it's the best banquet I've ever feasted at.

With our tummies full, we trot back the way we came, stopping to clean our muzzles in a stream, washing down our supper with refreshing spring water. When we reach Liam's pile of clothes, which he hid under a bush. I settle down among the pine needles with my back to him, my tongue hanging out the side of my muzzle as I pant with exhaustion.

The forest area sits up on a hill overlooking the strange city below. I realize I have no freaking idea where we are since Asmodeus directed our path. I willingly went along for the ride, not even trying to fight him.

In all honesty, I think I'm going to miss the demon when he's gone. He's the yin to my yang. Confident where I'm hesitant. Strong when I'm weak. We are so interconnected now that I'm unsure who I am without him. He pisses me off, but on the flip side, I love his sense of humor and adventure. He's deviant, naughty, and cares about one thing—himself, his sexual gratification. But he also boosts my courage, forcing me to look deep inside myself. He knows my darkest fantasies and is willing to help me achieve them.

Liam sits down next to me, fully dressed, his arms draped over his bent knees. Now comes the hard part—shifting back and hoping Asmodeus doesn't take over.

"I'm proud of you, little sis," Liam says, gazing out over the valley. "Your wolf is spectacular." He picks up a pine needle and fiddles with it like he's unsure what to say next.

I study him intently. My brother always seems so confident, sure of himself and his decisions. So this hesitancy surprises me.

"I need you to know that I love you no matter what. Whether you move away to discover a different path and pursue a career elsewhere, or you stay and work the ranch." He turns and looks me directly in the eyes. "But I'm not okay with you and Nox. I realize it's your life, and you're going to do whatever you prefer regardless of how I feel about it, but Nox..." he hesitates. A low rumble builds in my chest, knowing he's about to make me furious. "He is a player, Cellica. I've never seen him with the same female twice. He drinks from them, beds them, and then discards them. I don't want you to get hurt, and as much as I love him like a brother, he's not good enough for my baby sister."

His words have the opposite effect than what I expected. They hurt. Like a mother fucker. Am I just another conquest to the vampire? No. I don't believe that. I won't. He's possessive, jealous, and claims I'm his. Those aren't the traits of a love 'em and leave 'em kind of guy.

A part of me—the hesitant, afraid of her own shadow part, wonders if Liam's right. Am I merely a duty to Nox? King Darath tasked him with babysitting me, and things got out of hand. He's a vampire with a mighty sexual appetite. Was I just convenient? The willing woman tied to his bed with the demon of lust after his cock in a relentless pursuit he had no hope of escaping?

Please don't let that be true.

"We need to get you shifted. Deal with three dead werewolves, and then I require answers." Liam stands, and I rise as well. "Wait here while I try to find you some clothes. Do not move from this spot." His command races down my spine, and I sit on my haunches to show I understand. "Good, I'll be right back."

I watch as my brother jogs down the hill and maneuvers through the construction site before disappearing into the bowels of the city. I glance up at the sky. The clouds disappeared as the day wore on, but I'm surprised to discover the sun rests low on the horizon once more. It's almost dusk, and a tingle of excitement mixed with apprehension skates along my nerves.

In a couple of hours, Darath is set to remove Moe, and I'll see Nox again. I'm not sure how I feel about that. Will he want me when his responsibilities to his queen and best friend are over, and I no longer carry the demon of lust? Or will he turn away from me and revert to his player ways to save his friendship with Liam?

I wish I felt more assured of Nox's feelings for me. Yes, a biological link binds us, now more than ever since I've transitioned, but does the vampire care for me beyond the connection? Is he willing to put me first? Above his duty and friendship? If I were a betting girl, I'm not sure I'd take such a bet.

'Asmodeus? Wake up, you bastard. I might need you.'

I sense the lustful entity submerged deep in my subconscious, but he doesn't stir. I remember King Darath said the demon has no control when my wolf rules, so maybe he's merely biding his time until I'm in human form so he can gain power once more.

Chapter 19

Until Cellica, I rarely dreamed, but today my inner vampire seems agitated and pissed off. We left our mate when she was most vulnerable. For the first time in my existence, I loathed being a vampire controlled by the sun.

A part of my brain understood Liam would defend his little sister with his life. Few would dare go up against the werewolf king, but she is my mate, mine to protect and care for, so handing such a precious package off to my friend killed me. But what good was I to Cellica if the daylight fried me to a crisp?

From the second my head hit the pillow as the shutters slammed over my windows, I tossed and turned, my mind in utter turmoil. I'm not powerful enough to fight the sleep as Logan or Sebastian can at only a century and a half. I'm toast if I don't trace to a secure location before the sun rises. Literally. My brain and body shut down for at least seven hours. An enemy could walk right up to me and stab me through the heart. I would be none the wiser until my soul, if I even possess one, went wherever it's destined to go in the afterlife.

But today, it took over an hour before I fell into a restless slumber. Nightmares of Cellica running from me, being torn apart by those wolves, the ice-blue eyes of her wolf condemning me, plagued my sleep. I shouted to her in my dreams and ran at full speed through the darkness to reach her. Unfortunately, I never acquired her in time. I was forced to watch in horror as the wolves ripped her apart, her form morphing from wolf to human and back again. Her agonized screams shattered my heart and marked me as a failure.

Then the dream changed. Asmodeus rose from the carnage. Red irises zeroed in on me with eerie precision. His body was in full demonic mode—pale skin, horns pointed straight up from his head, and enormous wings of fire. I skidded to a halt, knowing I was no match for a Prince of Hell.

"Christoph. Come to us." His voice boomed inside my brain, and my eyes widened in disgust at my desire to obey. "We have need of release, boy," he crooned low, grabbing his huge phallus and stroking it, his irises bright with lust.

I scrambled backward, falling on my ass in my haste. The demon laughed, stomping toward me, his bare feet slapping against the ground. "No!" I shouted, struggling to stand, but chains pinned my arms and legs to the darkness beneath me.

When Asmodeus halted between my spread limbs, still gripping his dick, I jerked against the bonds in full-on panic mode.

"Time to suck us off again," he murmured, his face and body fluctuating, becoming Cellica for brief seconds before reverting back. "You pleasure us so well."

The dream morphed again, and a completely nude Cellica, her pussy glistening with desire, kneeled over my face. My cock hardened in a second, and saliva pooled in my mouth, desiring a taste of her sweet cunt.

"Nox," she groaned, cupping her succulent breasts as she lowered further, bringing what I craved closer. "Make me come."

"Gladly, baby girl," I moaned and lifted my head to latch onto her pussy. The chains at my wrists rattled with my effort to pleasure my mate. From the first swipe of my tongue, my lids closed in bliss, but a second later, a foreign object slammed down my throat. I gagged, my eyes popping open.

Asmodeus kneeled over me. A giant hand gripped the back of my skull as he forced my mouth over his engorged dick. I jerked against the restraints in horror and revulsion, but they held firm. I felt helpless. Frozen. Unable to fight or move as the demon fed me his cock.

"Ahhh, so fucking good, Nox. I am going to enjoy you for centuries now that the wolf and I are one."

"NO!" My shout reverberated through my room as I bolted upright, my body drenched in sweat, my dick pulsing with need. Bile burned the back of my throat, and I leaped from the bed to hightail it to the bathroom and dry heave in the sink.

What the ever-living fuck!

After brushing my teeth and gums raw, I take the longest shower of my life, hoping to wash away the images of my nightmare. The throbbing in my dick disgusts me, so I slap it several times with a command to calm the fuck down. But the pain escalates the lust running rampant through my veins. How will I ever look at Cellica again without shame and horror crushing my chest?

She shifted while still being possessed by that fucker. So, according to Darath, the demon and Cellica are now bound forever. This means that every time I kiss or touch my baby girl, Asmodeus is a voyeur and maybe an active participant in our intimacy. A shudder racks through my body at the notion.

Dressing quickly in my combat leathers, I hightail it down to the dining area for first meal and a situation report on vampire business. It seems weird that the world continues to rotate on its axis after the events of last night. This circumstance is so fucked up and changes everything. For her and me.

A fissure cracks in my heart, recalling the beauty of Cellica in wolf form—the midnight fur glistened with raindrops. The cerulean blue of her irises pierced my soul. As did her utter devotion to me. Cellica defied her Alpha. She fought Liam's control to protect me from what she perceived as a threat. When she submitted to my command, against her inherent instinct, it solidified my suspicion that I am her fated male.

I halt at the dining hall entrance and scan the group of Guardians seated at the enormous table. They either suck on bagged blood, drink it from wine glasses, or partake in the human volunteers. They stay at the castle to offer us nourishment. Not because we give them false promises of turning them for their servitude, as King Dimitri did, but because they crave to be bedded by a vampire. Many of the unmated soldiers are more than happy to fulfill their fantasies in exchange for their life essence and vow of silence. For years, I was one of them, not caring that we shared the women among the males. It was easier than seeking my own source, especially when I didn't have the time or energy. And the natural course of feeding for a vampire is fucking.

Cellica altered my wants and needs. The second I realized she was my one true mate, drinking from another or having sex with anyone else soured my stomach. Not that I didn't give it the old college try, burning my way through the humans and seeking willing werewolves to ease my lust for Liam's little sister.

Even though I loathe the taste of the bagged shit, it offers the meager nourishment needed to keep my system running. Like it did in the warehouse last night. I would've healed ten times faster if it had been Cellica's blood I was gulping down, but with Liam standing guard and my mate unable to shift back into human form, it was my only option.

Now that I've tasted Cellica, nothing compares to the burst of her sweet, spicy flavor on my tongue, down my throat. After the battle with the wolves, it revitalized me in a way human or bagged blood never has.

"Nox," Sebastian calls out. "Feed. We have much to discuss."

Before the echo of his words fade from the room, a volunteer, Trixie or Tina, I can't recall, blocks my path to the standing refrigerator housing our nourishment. "My lord," she bows, and I grit my teeth. "Might I be of service?"

The lust in her gaze disgusts me, but I work to keep my emotions from showing. "No thank you, human. Not tonight." She pouts, but I move past her to grab two packs and head to my seat next to Bastian. Quickly downing the contents, the remnants of my nightmare shudder through me, and my traitorous cock stiffens.

You'd better be thinking about Cellica's pussy, you fucker. I mentally growl and toss the pouches in the trash just as Nicole waddles into the room, Logan close on her heels. I'm surprised when Darath and Kurtis enter a second later with their mates glued to their sides. We usually reserve these meetings for vampire business only.

"Before we get to our regular agenda, King Ruse has a few questions," Nicole announces before settling awkwardly into her chair at the head of the table.

The queen's due date has come and gone by a week, and we are all worried about her birth. Unfortunately, vampire pregnancies are rare to begin with nowadays, and when the females do go to full term, the delivery is often fatal to the baby or mother. Sometimes both. I peer at Logan hovering by her chair, his anxious gaze never surrendering his mate. The former commander almost lost Nicole once, and it nearly killed him. If he were to lose her permanently, I suspect he'd take his own life to follow her into the afterlife, leaving the Vampire Nation without a ruler.

But this unborn miracle is the prophesied king. According to the ancient prophecy, he's the first child born of a vampire and a Halfling—half-vampire, half-human. He will walk in the sun, and while he'll require blood, he can also eat regular food. He will gift every offspring with the same abilities until, one day, the daylight will no longer rule vampires.

What I wouldn't give to run and hunt with Cellica during the day. To swim and hike and travel without the restrictions and limitations of my species. Just mentally visualizing my little wolf sunbathing nude has my cock twitching behind my zipper.

Now that's a damn fine reason to stand at attention.

When the hell did I start talking to my dick?

"Nox," Kurtis begins, jerking me out of my internal musings. "Liam asked me to represent him tonight since he's still busy with Cellica. Do you mind explaining why you butchered three werewolves and wound up impaled to the wall?"

Chapter 20

I take a moment to gather my thoughts before I answer Kurtis. What did he mean Liam was still busy with Cellica? Was she unable to control her wolf and shift back, or did the demon take over?

Fuck. I need to get to her.

"I tracked Cellica to the hotel adjacent to the warehouse to discover…" I clench my fist against the rage, recalling the wolves surrounding and touching my naked mate. "To discover Cellica stripped of clothes and surrounded by the three wolves, their filthy paws all over her."

"They were attempting to rape her?" Nicole questions with fire in her gray eyes.

"Well… no. Not exactly." Shit. How do I explain she was willing but not? "Asmodeus was in control, egging the wolves on."

"How do you know my demon was at the forefront?" Darath asks with a curious tilt of his head. "Normally, only another demon can detect one of their own."

"I… I just know when he is present. It's the way she holds herself. The things she says. They aren't her."

"We will get back to that," Sebastian interjects, turning to the soldiers around the table he says, "You all have your assignments.

Head out but keep in touch with any problems." When the hundred plus soldiers file out of the room like ants on a mission, my commander turns to Kurtis. "What is it Liam wants to know, Kurtis? Whether Nox killed those wolves in self-defense or cold blood?"

"Exactly." Kurtis shifts his focus to me, his blue gaze direct. "Were you defending Cellica against an attack?"

Fuck. Fuck. Fuck.

"Yes and no." I'm in deep shit here.

"Explain, Nox," Nicole orders, and I frown at the paleness of her skin.

"If it was actually Cellica who had wanted to be... taken by those wolves, if it had been *her* encouraging them, I would have grabbed her from the room and traced her back to my cabin until Liam could retrieve her." I wait for Nicole to call me out on the lie. It wouldn't have mattered who was in control. They touched what belonged to me, so they had to die.

When my queen continues to stare at me with a lifted eyebrow, my concern for her ramps up another notch. The halfling is the equivalent of a human lie detector, but she gives no outward indication she's aware I lied through my teeth.

I frown but continue. "Cellica had no control. What was happening was against her will and all the fucking demon's fault." I plunge my fingers through my hair. "I admit, I lost it. But so would've any of you in the same situation."

"I'm going to ask you this because Liam's not here to lose his shit," Nicole's voice snags my attention. "Is Cellica your one true mate?"

Silence shrouds the room, the eyes of my closest friends rest on me, waiting for my reply. If I admit it, every immortal in this room with a mate will understand why I lost it, but the revelation does nothing to help my cause.

I blow out a breath and lower my head. "Yes," I whisper in the oppressive silence.

"Damn it," Nicole swears softly.

"The Werewolf Province will demand retribution for their fallen, Nox," Kurtis says, his gaze filled with worry. "King Scott will decide what that retribution will be. The fact she's your mate will be a strike against you, proving you lost it because you couldn't control your inner vampire. I hate to ask this, but I know Liam will. Did you have sex with Cellica while she was in your care?"

"No," I grind out between clenched teeth. "Not that it's any of your goddamn business."

"Normally, I would agree with you, Nox," Sebastian interjects from across the table. "But you murdered three wolves because of your connection with Cellica, so we need to be wholly transparent about every aspect. Now," he lays his cellphone on the wooden surface and taps the screen, no doubt recording my confession for Liam to rip apart later. "Start from the beginning and don't leave anything out. We will question Cellica when she returns."

The thought of them interrogating my mate sends rage slithering through my veins, but I clench my hands under the table and give them a detailed play-by-play of last night. I omit the part where I shoved her against the wall, drank her blood, and sucked on her sweet cunt until she exploded. That would not go in the "pro" column of my defense.

"Like I said, the blast from Cellica's shift injured me," I state again for the fifth time. We've been at this for over two hours, and I'm about to lose my shit. Not in fear over the consequences of my actions, because I would do it again knowing what I know now, but on whether Cellica is alright.

"Depending on the reaction from the families of the fallen to your confession, and what pressure they put on their king for retribution, your actions last night could jeopardize relations between the Vampire Nation and the Werewolf Province," Nicole states. "Relations Liam and I have worked diligently to procure. You are a Guardian, first and foremost, Nox, and you represent our Nation as such. Your lack of control reflects badly on all of us."

Well, fuck. Shame and sorrow weigh down my shoulders. The last thing I ever wanted to do was disappoint my queen. And I see it reflected not only in her weary gaze but also in Logan's and Sebastian's.

"You're right, my queen. I've shamed us by my reckless behavior and willingly submit to whatever punishment you deem appropriate."

"It's not up to me, I'm afraid. If it was, I would slap your wrist, put you on probation for a week, and call it good. In my eyes, you didn't do anything that Logan, Bastian, or any other mated vampire wouldn't have done. No matter the circumstances, the bottom line for me is you eliminated the threat to your mate, whether or not she was aware of it, and for that, I can't fault you. But King Scott and the families of the fallen will have a different opinion, and unfortunately, they are the ones to decide your fate."

"My fate?" I question with raised eyebrows. Jesus. Are we talking about punishment here or something worse?

"The families may demand your head," Kurtis interjects quietly, and my heart stops.

"I will *never* allow that to happen," Nicole growls at Kurtis, rising to her feet. "Don't think for a fucking minute I will permit them to take Nox's life. He did what he did to safeguard his mate. I will declare war before I ever let that occur."

My chest warms as Nicole bastions my case. She's a hardass for sure, quick to temper with a mouth like a sailor, but she would defend those she cares about with her life. That's what makes her an outstanding leader. But in good conscience, I can't be responsible for a war between the werewolves and vampires. She and Logan have worked too hard to procure peace, and I will not be the downfall of the prophecy.

"Nicole," Logan coos next to her. "Calm down, baby. It's not good for you or the baby."

Kurtis raises his hands. "I'm just the messenger, Nicole. However, I understand Liam's precarious position. If he doesn't satisfy the families, he could have a real problem on his hands."

"I need to talk to Liam. Alone." I rise from my chair and skirt the table to kneel before my queen. "Maybe he and I can come to some kind of understanding. Allow me to fix this, my lady. It's my mistake to rectify."

"Your problems are my problems, Christoph. We will deal with this together," she commands, her tone final.

"Yes, my queen."

"Now get me some fucking pancakes and coffee before I take someone's head," she says with a wicked grin, easing back down into her chair.

"Maybe you should go lie down for a bit, love," Logan suggests calmly, shoving a pillow behind her back.

"Stop fussing, Logan. I'm fine. Just hangry."

Chuckles circle the table as I gain my feet and signal for the maid to fulfill her request.

A muscle pulses in Logan's jaw, and I see it's taking all his restraint not to pick her up and carry her back to their room. Our friends watch her with wary concern.

Suppose something happens to her or this baby... In that case, everything she accomplished in the immortal world as the prophesied bringer of peace will unravel. She is the beacon of light that brought us out of war and chaos. Even our most recent enemy, the dark fae, now ruled by Syn Grayflame's son Rordrick, has come on board, signed a peace treaty, and now has a seat on the Council of Unity.

I tap my foot under the table with impatience, thoughts of Cellica consuming my mind as I observe Nicole devour her blueberry pancakes with gusto. I'm pleased to see her appetite hasn't diminished even though her strength has, and the pallor of her skin frightens me.

While Nicole sips her decaf coffee, Sebastian turns to me and dread drops like a stone in my gut. Based on his expression, I'm pretty damn sure what he's about to say.

"Nox, in light of recent circumstances, I think it would be best if you stayed off patrol for a while. Just until the issue with the werewolves resolves. In the meantime, I am placing you on guard duty for your queen."

Fuck, I knew it. "The highest of honors," I murmur, and Nicole snorts.

I snag Kurtis' attention when the meeting breaks up. "Have you heard from Liam?"

"Yes. It took some doing, but Cellica finally shifted. Liam is questioning her about last night and then together they will present the bodies of the fallen to their families."

"What? Why is he putting Cellica through that? It wasn't her fault." I can imagine my kind-hearted wolf being ripped to shreds over guilt as the families cry and wail over their kin. What the fuck was he thinking? It should be me. Not her.

"I believe he described it as a 'teaching moment,'" Kurtis shrugs. "It's not our place to question his methods."

"Nox," Darath joins our little trio. "We should discuss the ramifications of Asmodeus now residing permanently inside Cellica and examine how best to help her control him.

Nicole waddles up, Logan right behind her. "How so?"

"As you recall, we discussed using the Princes in locating the breeder females."

"Yes. That's hard to forget when my *mother* is a breeder. And I still hate that name, by the way."

"Agreed. But now with Cellica and Asmodeus joined at the hip, and she learns to commune with the Prince, through my help, she might convince him to aid in the search for these women without us having to strike an outrageous bargain. Which would ease both our minds."

"Might?" I ask, sensing Lucifer is holding something back.

"Princes are tricksters, fine manipulators. They can strike a deal in their favor and make it seem like your idea." Darath's crimson gaze focuses on me, and I swallow. "Asmodeus has an ulterior motive. I sense he desires something. What that something is, I won't know until I can probe his mind, but it might be just the leverage we need. The less contact we have with my fellow fallen, the better."

"Did you know from the very beginning the demon would fuse with Cellica if she shifted?" I grind out, anger roughening my tone.

"Vampire, I was unaware a demon could even possess an immortal. That's not how I designed them. God's chosen were their mission. If I'd paid better attention to the goings on in Hell over the last century, I would have picked up on Asmodeus's schemes long before they happened. As it was, it took a little recon of my own to discover the logistics of what happens when a possessed immortal shifts." He shakes his head but offers no apology. Typical.

"Like I said, something motivated the Prince to not only escape Hell but occupy an immortal. I do not believe his original target was Cellica, she just happened to be in the wrong place at the wrong time. However, his priorities changed and his reason for punching through the portal transformed to something or someone else."

My nightmare flashes through my mind. "And if that something is me?" I ask, my face heating with embarrassment as everyone stares open-mouthed at me.

"Well," Darath breathes, fighting a fucking grin, and I want to punch him in the face. "If it's you he's after, pucker up, boy. You're in for a wild ride."

Chapter 21

Cellica

"Last one, Cel. You doing okay?" Liam asks as he carries Luke's body up a long drive in his arms.

No, I'm not okay. This is ripping me to shreds. The guilt and sorrow suffocate, making it difficult to breathe. "I'm fine," I mutter obediently, following my brother. The two previous houses were brutal. The mothers sobbed, and the fathers demanded answers. Liam handled it with diplomacy and grace, and I couldn't be prouder of him, but this is all my fucking fault.

I shiver as I recall the drastic maneuvers my brother used to get my wolf to retreat. After several hours of explaining what to do over and over again, and me concentrating until my eyeballs bled with no change, Liam finally grabbed me by the scruff like a damn puppy and pinned me to the ground. His growl shook my frame, and my wolf whimpered in submission. I, on the other hand, was livid. And even though it was fucking humiliating, it worked.

As my wolf retreated, I memorized the sensations skittering across my spine. The surge of power poking my skin like a thousand mosquitos in order to replicate it again. And thank God I did, because my big brother forced me to shift five more times before he felt satisfied with my ability.

My insides hum with the regenerating power of my wolf, and I'd love time to relish her presence, but she completely ignores me and seems to be in love with Moe. If she whimpers at him one more time, I'll lose it. And he's no better, cooing to her like she's a baby or a goddamn puppy. They need to get over it already. My fucking brain is full enough.

I let go of my issues and knock on the front door of a quaint cottage on the outskirts of Lansing. It still blows my mind that I drove from our cabin in Idaho to middle-mitt Michigan with no clue how I got there. For an entire week, until we landed at that hotel, Moe kept me suppressed. Did he attempt to have sex with anyone else along the way without my knowledge? God, I hope not.

A large burly man with short blond hair and a beard opens the door. His eyes blaze a bright green as he takes in his son's headless body wrapped in blankets in his king's arms. Then, without a word, he steps forward and snatches the precious bundle from Liam before peering down at the basket in my hands.

"Follow me," he mutters, ducking back through the doorway and into the darkened house.

We trail the wolf through a cozy living room with a lit potbelly stove, down a long hallway to what appears to be a spare bedroom. The father lays Luke's body in the center of the bed. I watch in horror as he unwraps the cloth. Fuck, I can't do this.

I take a tentative step back when those emerald irises, filled with rage and grief, pin mine. "Don't move an inch, pup," he barks, and I jerk in response. "Luke is... was my only son and since his mother passed two years ago, I require your assistance to prepare him for mourning."

I glance at Liam, and he nods. "Yes, sir," I respond. "I'm so sorry for your loss."

"Don't give me your platitudes, just bring me my son's head."

I tread warily over to the other side of the bed. At the same time, he continues to remove the coverings, exposing Luke's massive chest covered in blood. Bile burns the back of my throat, but I swallow it down and set the basket on the mattress. This robust werewolf is dead because of me. Nox may have struck the killing blow, but Luke and the others would've never been in that hotel room if it weren't for me and my inability to control the demon inside me.

My heart breaks as I watch this brawny wolf clench his jaw to hold back the tears that are surely burning his eyes. If he demands I wash and prepare the body, I'll do it. It's the least I can do.

"Go fetch towels in the bathroom," the father directs. "And dampen several washcloths."

I immediately spin and beeline it to the powder room we passed down the hall, allowing the men time to remove the soiled clothing.

Tears cascade down my cheeks as I hold the cloth under the sink, dropping my head and giving free rein to the emotions I've bottled up for the past several hours. Luke, Mike, and Dave were all good guys, looking for a bit of fun. And even though Dave slit my throat in retaliation, they didn't deserve this end. For their lives to be snuffed out in such a gruesome way.

I'm not angry at Nox. He did what he felt was right to protect me—his mate. Any immortal walking in on three males touching their naked female would've lost it. Besides, the wolves could've walked away and diffused the situation. But they chose to fight, even though I begged them not to engage with my vampire. We made sure they knew we were connected, yet their macho pride couldn't let it stand.

Men. So primitive and barbaric. But then I grimace as I recall what Nox and I did in the aftermath while their sightless eyes looked on. The heat spiraling through my pelvis shames me as I remember the exquisite sensation of Nox's mouth on my sex. How one heated glance, one naughty word from him, made everything else drift away, and my sole focus became him.

Wiping my tears on the dry towel, I squeeze the water out of the washcloths and return to the bedroom, stopping short at the sight of Luke's head sitting on a pillow, lined up with his shoulders like he's resting. Liam and the father stripped the garments from his body, using part of the shroud to cover his groin.

"Don't just stand there. Bring those here so we can wash his remains," the big wolf barks.

For the next thirty minutes, we bathe this man's son, preparing him for the parade of friends and family soon coming to pay their respects.

Once we complete the task to his satisfaction, he ushers us into the living room. "Now, King Scott," he begins, waving at us to sit on the couch as he takes the recliner by the stove. "You mind telling me what the fuck happened to my son?"

As my brother relays the story I confessed earlier for the third time, I keep my head bowed, and my hands clasped in my lap, not wanting to draw attention. The other parents never spoke to me, addressing their anger and grief at their king.

"You confirm this, girl," the father, I now realize is Jeremiah, asks me directly, and my gaze darts to his in surprise. Does he dare question Liam's story?

"Yes, sir. I'm so sorry. Luke's death is on my shoulders."

"Not the way I heard it," he says gently before turning his attention to Liam. "I want that vampire's head."

My gasp fills the room, my wide-eyed regard bouncing between this mountain of a wolf and my brother as panic sets in.

"Jeremiah...."

"That Guardian stole my only son from me. The one thing left in this world that mattered to me. As my king, I expect you to offer me justice."

"Anything but his death," Liam states calmly. "I'm not willing to start a war with the Vampire Nation over a male protecting his one true mate. If I did that, I would execute more than half of our species." Liam shakes his head, his whiskey irises filled with remorse. "What else can I offer you, Jeremiah?"

The wolf leans back in his chair, contemplating the two of us with a shrewd expression, and my heart skips several beats. "Before I answer that, I expect it best if I confer with Mike and Dave's parents. They have just as much say in this as I do."

"That's a wise decision. Discuss it together, but keep in mind what I said. Nox believed Cellica was there against her will. Would you have reacted any different if you'd found Dorothy in a similar position?"

"I'd never leave my wife's side if a demon possessed her, King Scott, so we would never have been in that situation, to begin with. I demand justice for my boy and one way or another, I will take it out of the vampire's hide."

"And if the vampire queen objects? What then, Jeremiah? Are you willing to resume the war with the vampires and spit in the face of the prophecy to avenge your son? Because I am not." Liam stands, and I rise with him, my palms sweaty. "You present your terms, but as your king, my priority is to all my people, not just the grieving parents of three dead wolves. Nox will suffer the consequences of his actions, but execution is off the table. Are we clear?"

Jeremiah's muscles twitch at the power in his Alpha king's command. "Do right by us, King Scott, and we won't have a problem." The wolf stands, his body tight with grief and anger as he escorts us to the front door.

The second we are out of earshot and back in my pickup, I turn in my seat to face Liam. "This wasn't Nox's fault. I should be the one taking the punishment, not him."

He shoots me a sideways glance but says nothing as he fires up the engine and heads to Interstate 96 toward Detroit. "We're leaving your truck at the airport. I'll have one of my guys pick it up and drive it back to the ranch later."

"Liam, don't shut me out. I have every right to know their decision."

"No. You don't, Cellica. I will handle this. You're going back home where I can keep an eye on you until Darath helps you with this menace inside you. After which your ass will head back to school, finish your degree, and forget any of this ever happened."

I stare at him, my mouth hanging wide open. He can't be fucking serious? "Nox is...."

"Nox is none of your goddamn concern," he growls at me, and my jaw snaps shut. "He was reckless and irresponsible and because he couldn't control himself, three of my wolves are dead. He's a Guardian, Cel. He should've known better."

"I throw the same question you asked of Jeremiah. Are you telling me you would've reacted differently if it had been Viessa in my situation?" A muscle pulses in Liam's jaw, and his fingers grip the steering wheel so tight, I'm afraid it will snap in two. "You can't, and you know it."

"Regardless, Nox must answer for what he's done. If I ignore it, Jeremiah will form a rebellion and take matters into his own hands. It wouldn't be the first time."

"What does that mean? How will he have to answer? And shouldn't I suffer the same punishment?"

"You had no authority over your actions, Cellica," he sighs with exasperation. "Asmodeus controlled you. What happened wasn't your fault."

"So because I'm a weak pathetic wolf, Nox must deal with the consequences?"

"You are not weak and pathetic. Don't ever fucking say that about yourself. And Nox is the one who beheaded those wolves, not you."

"Are you forgetting that one of them slit my throat? I would have died if Nox hadn't given me his blood."

"Yes. I am grateful to him for saving your life, but it never should have escalated to such a degree in the first place. Nox handled the situation badly."

I open my mouth to go at him again, but Liam jerks the wheel, skidding to a stop on the side of the road. When he turns to me fully, his eyes are the bright blue of his wolf.

"This discussion is over. We are flying back to Montana, getting this... *thing* inside you under control, and then you will finish your degree and graduate. Are we clear?"

I grind my teeth as the power of his command pricks my skin. "Don't speak to me as if I'm one of your subjects or a child, Liam. I'm a grown-ass woman who can make her own decisions. Whether you like it or not, Nox is my fated mate, and if he still wants me, I will be by his side in a heartbeat."

Liam snarls, and I instinctively draw back until a familiar dark presence warms my chest, demanding the right to surface.

'*Allow me to aid you, little wolf,*' Asmodeus pleads. '*Per our agreement, I won't take over. Just give you the strength to face off with your king.*'

I sniff. '*Fine. But no funny stuff. He's my fucking brother.*'

'*Agreed.*'

"Liam put your canines away. You're scaring me," Moe informs my brother, who rears back in surprise.

"I'm sorry. I don't mean to scare you, Cel. I'm petrified you are going to throw your dreams aside and never achieve the life you deserve."

"You're mated to a vampire, Liam. Is it so bad?"

"No, of course not. I often wish we had more time together. Her duties as Oracle keep her away from me far too much. Lately, her visions seem to be non-stop, and I see her struggle to interpret them. I sense it along the bond, but she refuses to share with me."

"Why?"

"She claims they are too disorganized and unclear, that she can't make sense of them yet, but the mental chaos isn't lessening, and I'm worried." He rakes his fingers through his hair in agitation. "But putting aside her calling, if I'm honest, there are times I lament the fact we can never have children or ride and work the ranch together, but I would do it all again to be with her. Viessa is my life."

"Even with her sexual proclivities?"

'Demon,' I warn. *'Knock it off.'*

"It must be hard for an Alpha to submit to his female. How do you do it?"

"I'm not discussing this with you," he growls and puts the truck in drive, peeling out onto the interstate.

'Enough,' I admonish again, and Moe, surprisingly, retreats.

Huh. Maybe this inner threesome thing—me, my wolf, and the demon—might work. When I presented my plan for us to coexist peacefully together, it shocked me at how readily he agreed. Or that I even suggested it. I figured he'd fight me for dominance or find another host if he couldn't get his way.

I'm not stupid. I realize the demon possesses a secret agenda of his own, but I've come to rely on Asmodeus's strength, confidence, and boldness. Does that make me pathetic? Yeah, kind of. But Moe pushes me to be a better person. With him inside me, I feel like I can accomplish anything I desire.

A girl, a wolf, and a demon walk into a bar....

Chapter 22

Defying my queen makes my skin crawl, but I need to see Cellica and to determine for myself that she's all right. And it's not as if she confined me to the castle. She merely forbade me from going out on patrol.

Heavy, dark clouds obscure the moon as I materialize outside the Wild Beast Ranch homestead, lurking around like some creepy stalker for a glimpse of my mate. Of course, if Liam found me out here, he'd lose it, but I'm beyond caring.

Movement catches my eye, and I trace closer, keeping to the shadows. Thanks to all the windows, I can track that bright blue hair shining under the recessed lighting as she walks down a hallway.

My insides unclench for the first time in days. She looks as beautiful as ever. Dark jeans hug her lean hips, and a leather halter exposes her back and arms. My eyebrows raise when I notice a tattoo across the top of her back. I'd been so focused on keeping her dressed that I never noticed she had ink during her captivity.

The swirling design spreads from one shoulder blade to the other in the form of a howling wolf. It's intricate and beautiful. My precious Cellica has finally bonded with her inner animal and is fully immortal. Pride fills my chest. I crave to take her in my arms and show her how much I worship every inch of her.

She stomps into what I can only assume is her bedroom and disappears into a closet for a couple of seconds before emerging with a suitcase. She flings it on the bed, then strides to a dresser under the window nearer to my location, and I get my first full view of her face.

A black leather choker encircles her neck with a metal ring in the center. My cock twitches at its sight, imagining the collar proclaims she belongs to me. That my baby girl belongs to Daddy. Now and forever.

Mine.

Upon closer examination, I observe the puffy, red eyes, and the pinched expression, as if she's in pain. What the fuck? Cellica dumps an armful of clothes from her drawer into the open suitcase. Where is she heading? She needs to be supervised until Darath can help her control the dickwad inside her.

I'm about to trace into the room and demand answers when Liam plows through the doorway, temper brightening his gaze.

"Where the fuck do you think you're going?" he demands.

"I'm getting the hell out of dodge, away from you and Josh. I need some space," she replies with a calmness that contradicts the anger pinking her cheeks.

"I forbid you to leave until Darath gets here," Liam commands, and for once, I'm in total agreement with my friend. Her shift made the demon a permanent passenger, and she needs to learn how to manage him.

"I'd gladly stay if you let me talk to Nox," she counters.

Why is she trying to get in contact with me? Even though I know it's a bad idea, I ease closer to the window. If Liam scents me, I'll trace away before he can confront me.

"I will deal with Nox," he growls. "Right now, your primary concern is dealing with Asmodeus."

Exactly.

"I need my mate, Liam, so unless you chain me with silver, I'm leaving to find him."

Whoa. Wait a minute. She's admitted to her brother I'm her fated one? I snort inwardly. I bet that conversation didn't go over well.

"Cellica, don't fucking tempt me."

She ignores him and continues to dump garments in the suitcase, enraging Liam further until he walks over to the bed, grabs the case, and flings it across the room. Clothes fly everywhere, and the baggage busts in half against the log wall.

Rage fills my vision, and before I can think it through, I've traced inside to face off with my friend, Cellica tucked protectively at my back.

"Nox," my wolf breathes behind me, but I focus on her brother.

Liam sneers. "I wondered when you were going to stop creeping around my house and show yourself."

Damn werewolf senses.

"I would like to talk with Cellica for a minute, Liam, then I'll go."

"You've got five minutes, then meet me in the living room. The team is assembling and you and I need to talk."

I nod, and he pivots, slamming the door behind him.

I turn to my mate, and the adoration in her gaze tightens my chest to painful proportions. "Why are you defying your brother?"

"Why were you lurking outside my house?" she counters, taking a tentative step toward me. "Are you stalking me again, vampire?"

There's something different about Cellica, and I can't quite put my finger on what. Is the demon directing her, or is this my female hitting her stride as an immortal with full control over her wolf? Either way, it's sexy as fuck, and I want to shove her against the wall and demonstrate how much I crave her... but Liam waits in the living room, and I'm pretty confident I know what he wants to talk about. The consequences of murdering three of his wolves and my contact with his sister. Namely, me staying away from her.

"I wanted to make sure you were okay after the warehouse," I say, brushing a lock of her silky blue hair behind her ear.

"I'm better now that you're here." She reaches out and grips my waist with both hands, and my muscles clench at the heat penetrating my t-shirt.

"Listen to me, Cellica. You must obey Liam. He will protect and watch out for you."

"I don't need his protection anymore. I need you."

Fuck. My vampire is screaming for her with a desperation bordering on psychotic. I grit my teeth and ignore him. "Now that Asmodeus is a permanent fixture in your life, you're going to require Darath's help to handle him."

She stumbles back a step, her mouth gaping at my words. "How did you find out about our deal?"

My body stills and I frown down at her. "What deal, baby girl?"

"I... wait. What are *you* talking about?"

"What deal, Cellica?"

"Nothing. It's nothing," she mumbles, busying herself with picking up the clothes scattered about the room. "I will listen to King Darath's advice regarding Moe and how he wants to extract him."

"Moe? You're back to calling him Moe?" What the fuck? She acts like she and the demon are besties.

"Why not?" she shrugs, still avoiding looking at me.

"Wait. Cellica. Did Liam not clarify the situation with Asmodeus? Did the fucking demon not explain?"

She stops, clutching garments to her chest as she turns her confused gaze to mine. "What situation?"

Christ. He didn't tell her.

With purposeful strides, I reach her and sink my fingers into her hair, gripping her head. "The second you transitioned, the Prince of Hell bonded to your soul. There is no getting rid of him."

"What? No, we had an arrangement." She steps back and flings her clothes to the floor, her body taut with anger. "That wily son of a bitch. He played me."

"What are you talking about?" Did she make a pact with the demon? "What goddamn deal, Cellica?" I grab her by the elbow and spin her to face me. "What did you do?"

"I... I invited him to stay."

"You..." I stare at her in utter shock for several seconds, unable to process her comment. "Why the fuck would you do that?"

How could she bargain with that bastard? My nightmare flashes to the forefront, and I drop her arm as if scalded. He's there. Inside her. Hovering below the surface, biding his time until he can get his clutches into me.

I pace the room, running my fingers through my hair in agitation. This can't be happening. I understood from Darath that Cellica and Asmodeus fused as one the second she shifted. Still, I figured the demon king would teach Cellica how to keep the demon repressed so he couldn't pop in anytime he wanted. I told myself I could handle that.

But now, my mate is informing me she made a pact with the beast, meaning she has no desire to place him in lock down. The idea of him controlling her, our intimate moments, repulses me.

Yeah, Nox? Then why is your dick hard as a rock at the prospect of taking them both? Metaphorically, of course.

"Chris. Please hear me out," she pleads, her anxious expression unsettling my vampire.

"Hear you out? Damn it, Cellica. You just admitted you're giving the demon free rein over you. Over us. How in fuck's sake do you expect me to respond?"

"It's not like that. We agreed—"

"I don't give a shit what you agreed to. I want nothing to do with him, Cellica. You will work with Darath to shove the fucker into the background. Permanently. Do you understand me? Her eyes suddenly flash red, and I rear back.

"Methinks thou doth protest too much, vampire?"

"Asmodeus," I growl, my fangs dropping low.

"Please, call me Moe since we are going to be so intimate and all." Cellica prowls toward me, and I retreat for every one of her strides forward. "Tell me, Nox." Cellica shoves me against the wall, pressing her tempting body against mine. "Have you dreamed about me?"

My eyes widen in surprise. How could he possibly know that?

"Did you imagine sucking my cock while devouring the wolf's succulent pussy? Or maybe you visualized bending me over and fucking me while you fucked her tight cunt? Did you cum fantasizing about having us both, Nox?" Cellica's hand rubs down my engorged length behind my jeans. I'm turned on and disgusted at the same time.

I shove my possessed mate across the room without thinking, repulsed by my reaction to the demon's words. Her back slams into the foot of her bed, and her slight moan rips my heart in two.

"Your deal doomed us, Cellica. I will never accept the demon having any amount of control."

She rubs her head and rises to her feet. "We are a team, Chris. I help Moe get what he wants, and he helps me be a better version of myself."

"Yeah? And what is it he wants?" I stupidly ask.

"You. We both want you."

"No fucking way. *You* can have me, baby girl. I'm all yours, but I will never accept him as an active participant in our relationship."

"You relish and benefit from how bold he makes me. The confidence he helps me project. It's still me, only better."

"You are perfect just the way you are, Cellica. You don't need him."

Why the fuck can't she see how beautiful and resilient she is all on her own? Under that rebellious attitude my wolf is shy and insecure. But that's part of her charm. What makes her unique. The boldness and confidence will come with time, age, and experience.

"According to you, whether we like it or not, he's here to stay."

"Yes, I know that, but you can learn to keep him repressed and out of our lives."

"And if I don't want to?"

I close my eyes and grit my teeth for patience. "I could command you to obey me," I hiss.

Her eyes widen briefly with hurt before they harden to stone. "You could," she murmurs with a nod, her irises flashing the blue of her wolf for a mere second. "But, thanks to Moe's help, I have the strength to disobey both you and my brother."

"I see." A bleak future spans out before me, and I want to bash my head against the wall and roar with anger. "So, you're choosing him over me?"

"No, Nox. You are."

Chapter 23

After Nox slammed out of my room, I collapsed among my clothes and sobbed my heart out while Moe murmured soothing words in my brain, telling me our vampire would come around, to just give him time.

"I can't lose him, Moe," I wailed aloud. "And all you do is provoke him."

'You won't. The vampire wants us both. So I push him in hopes he can learn how to get past his own stubborn head.'

"Maybe I'm asking too much of him. The whole concept of you and I as one seems to be a breaking point for him."

'A hard limit?' Moe smirks, but I find no humor in this situation. He quickly sobers. *'Your only other course of action is to follow the commands of my King and shove me into a dark corner of your subconscious. Is that what you want? To back out on our agreement?'*

"You tricked me, Moe. When you bargained for our deal, you already knew you were bound to me."

'I've grown to care for you, little wolf, but I am still a Prince of Hell and I must look out for my interests. Do you think I'd relish being locked away in your soul with no way to sense what's going on around me or speak to you when I'm lonely? Without sexual stimulation, I will wither. Put yourself in my shoes, Cellica,' he pouts, and I roll my eyes

at the drama. '*I had specific plans of my own that your transition brought to a halt. Strategies centuries in the making. They were the whole reason I escaped Hell, to begin with.*'

It never dawned on me that Moe had other interests besides possessing me and sex. "What plans?"

'*It's of no importance now. I've adapted to my circumstances, my new home.*'

I resume picking up my discarded clothing as we talk, taking comfort in his presence, not wanting to think about the conversation going on in the living room. I glance at the clock. No doubt the task force has assembled by now, deciding Nox's fate and mine. I should be in there, but my brother adamantly refused. It's not like I could lurk around the corner and eavesdrop. Every immortal in there would sniff me out the second I stepped foot outside my door.

A soft knock startles me. "Come in," I call out.

When the regal Oracle, dressed in her customary leather pants and backless halter top, strolls into my room, I sense Moe vibrate with wariness. Hmmm. The Prince is afraid of Viessa? Interesting....

"Hello, Cellica. Might I have a word with you?"

"Of course." I still struggle with the concept that my sister-in-law is an Oracle. A Dominant no less. I can't even comprehend how they make that work. My brother is the Alpha of all Alphas. How he denies his true nature for his mate is beyond me.

The door closes, blocking the sounds of an argument between Liam and Nox with a soft click, and I feel as if the sound triggered my downfall. Now who's being dramatic?

"Actually, I wish to speak to Asmodeus, if I may?"

"He's always with me, so he can hear you."

"I need your plan to move forward, Prince," she states in a quiet ethereal voice, and tingles skate across my skin. Viessa knows his plans, but I don't? Why does that bother me so much?

"I'm bound to the wolf, Oracle. What you ask is no longer possible," he responds.

"I see all, demon, and I understand the depth of your desires. Your original plan is what you crave. Cellica is not for you."

"I'm well aware, Tribrid," Asmodeus snarls, and my apprehension grows. "What is it you are offering me?"

"A compromise," she steps closer, and her power skates across my nerves. "You scratch my back and I will set yours free."

"Free," Moe scoffs. "You mean imprisoned in Hell? As much as I enjoy Lucifer's special brand of torture, I think I'll pass."

"Not in Hell," she states, and my demon perks up. "The Council of Unity requires aid. The kind only a Prince can provide. In exchange, I will liberate you from Cellica and insert you in the place you most desire."

Asmodeus practically quivers with anticipation, and jealousy claws at my gut. He prefers someone else. Based on his reactions, Moe would discard me for this other vessel in a second. A fucking demon wants someone over me. Why the hell does that upset me so much? I should be glad to be rid of him. Nox would welcome me back if I was no longer possessed.

'*You fickle bastard. So much for you caring for me, huh?*'

Moe ignores me, and the hurt spreads.

"What is it the council requires specifically?" he asks.

"Do you care?" she counters.

"Not really," he shrugs. "But I don't like going into a contract without all the details. So until you reveal them, no deal."

"Very well, Asmodeus. When you're ready to sign on the dotted line, you let me know." She turns to leave.

"Wait. Have you talked to him? Did he agree to your little plan?"

The Oracle hesitates. "Not yet, but is there a reason he'd object?"

"Yeah. I'll give you one fucking reason. Abigail Brevil."

"And if the witch was no longer in the picture?"

Wow. Viessa is a ruthless negotiator. Who knew? Not that I understand this conversation in the slightest.

"That's a big if, Soothsayer. Abi is almost impossible to kill."

"So I've discovered. Answer the question," she demands with a quiet potency, and I see why Liam is so drawn to her. She's a combination of vulnerability and stealthy power.

"If you can guarantee you will eliminate the witch and join me with my beloved, then you have a deal, Oracle."

"I'll keep in touch," she says with a nod. She turns to leave without a glance in my direction, strolling out the door, as if I wasn't even in the room.

"What's going on, Moe?" I demand the second I no longer hear her retreating footsteps down the hall.

'Not to worry, little wolf. The bitch's plan will never work. Oracle or not, she will never take down Abigail. Her father proved it's impossible.'

"But who is your beloved? I thought you bonded to me?" Shit. I sound like a petulant child who just had her favorite toy taken away.

'I am connected to you, but long, long ago, I linked to another for centuries. We fucked and played without a care in the world, and he was my universe. Until he met Abigail. His physical body bonded to hers, and for a while, we were a threesome. I tolerated it. I even enjoyed relentlessly abusing her sweet cunt the way she craved, but Abigail became obsessive, demanding Troy keep me suppressed for long periods.'

"Troy? You mean Troy Tenebris, the male witch?"

'Ah, you've heard of him.' The pride in his voice has the green-eyed monster raising its head.

"He's assisted the team a time or two," I grumble.

'Really? That is surprising. Anyway, Abi demanded that Troy get rid of me or she would leave him. At first he refused, and when she left, I was ecstatic. It was just the two of us again. But the bonded immortal was miserable without her, and I couldn't stay and watch him slowly

deteriorate from sorrow. I convinced him to let me go and be with his mate. It wasn't long before Lucifer found me and cast me back into Hell.'

"Wow. I'm sorry, Moe. I didn't realize you had such a strong connection to someone else."

'It was not your fault, little one. I am the one who possessed you. And while I have quite enjoyed our time together, you no longer need me. You have your wolf now. She makes you strong and brave.'

"No, Moe. *You* do. Your presence gives me the courage to say and do things I'd never be bold enough to do on my own. My wolf makes me physically strong, sharpening my senses, but you've seen into my mind. Understand my secret fantasies and desires, the ones I've got myself off to, but couldn't voice."

'Even so, your vampire doesn't wish me here. If whatever Viessa has planned is successful, I can't let go unless you release me, Cellica. As much as I adore you and crave Nox, he's laid down the gauntlet. Him or me. Which is it going to be?'

Good fucking question. Why can't I have both? I crave both... even if I shouldn't.

It's strange. When I transitioned and my inner wolf awakened, I thought she would loathe the demon, and her possessiveness of our mate would cause her to fight Moe's presence. But he seems to have the opposite effect on her. It's like she sees both Moe and Nox as ours. Equally.

The demon encourages every deviant imagining in my head. My wolf escalates my emotions. He intensifies my lust to such an extent, I sleep, eat, and breath Nox twenty-four-seven. My wolf champions his cause.

Deep down, my mate relishes my newfound sexual fearlessness. He enjoyed fulfilling my passions, dominating his baby girl, and granting every lascivious thought in both our heads.

But maybe Asmodeus is right. Could I find my inner strength in my wolf alone? Pain sparks in my chest, and the agony nearly brings me to my knees at the prospect of never seeing my vampire again. Never experiencing his caresses, his wicked words, his dominance mixed with softness. Nox is the perfect combination of both. Fire and Ice. Possessive but loving. Dominant but caring. My life isn't complete without him in it.

'*I think you've made your choice, little wolf.*' The sadness in his tone breaks my heart.

"I understand you a little better now, Moe. As much as I treasure having you with me, I would never deny you a chance to be with the one you love."

'*You might not get rid of me that easily, Cel. I have serious doubts on whether the Oracle possesses the ability to deliver on her promise. And if destiny forges us together, I will do everything in my power to bring Nox on board. Ease his reservations and concerns. We can make this work however he's comfortable. Without suppressing me. As much as I adore you, I refuse to live as the unwanted partner in a threesome again. I'd rather go back to Hell.*'

"Time will tell, my friend."

Chapter 24

Nox

"The families of the fallen demand retribution, Nicole," Liam informs my queen and Logan, looking on from the big screen TV.

With Nicki's delivery date so overdue, Logan has confined her to the castle suite in order to minimize her stress. I guess I've thrown a wrench into his plans with the murder of three wolves.

"I get that, Liam, but what are they demanding?" she asks, and I'm relieved to see her color has returned to normal.

"Thirty lashes with a cat-o-nine in a very public setting," he replies quietly, and Alex gasps in surprise. My stomach clenches at the perceived pain I'm soon to endure.

"Thirty?" Sebastian growls. "Too extreme."

"I agree," Logan pipes in. "Why not ten?"

"It's thirty or they will form a coalition to dethrone me for not properly protecting my people," Liam sighs. "Now, normally I don't respond to threats, but these wolves were good, upstanding members of my pack that didn't deserve to die. If I refuse to make an example of Nox, you can kiss our treaty goodbye."

"It's fine," I say, stepping forward. "The last thing I want is to instigate a war, and even though I'd do it again to protect Cellica, I respect the families' need for justice."

"Who is doling out the lashes?" Kurtis asks.

"I granted the three fathers ten lashes each."

"Fuck," Nicole pales. "They will tear him up. I cannot allow it."

"My queen, I'm a vampire. I heal."

"Thank you, Mr. Obvious," she grates out with a frown, and Logan lays a hand on her shoulder. "I want to be present."

"No." Logan and Sebastian bark at the same time.

"It's not up for debate, boys." She turns to Liam. "We'll travel the traditional way, in my truck." A small smile graces her full lips.

Alex snorts with humor. "Careful you don't give birth in the backseat of Riddick."

"Wouldn't that be epic?" Nicole grins back.

"I hate to burst your bubble," I interrupt. "But have you forgotten? There are no roads to the castle. How do you propose you get to your truck?"

"Damn it."

"The rest of the team will be at your side with bagged blood at the ready," Sebastian states.

"Umm," Darath raises his hand, and I glare at him. "Now that Nox has found and tasted his one true mate, bagged blood will not possess the same healing powers as Cellica's."

"Maybe not, but it will have to do. I don't want her anywhere near me if I'm crazed for blood."

No fucking way do I wish her to witness the horror of my disciplinary action, either. Knowing her, she will take full blame for what happened, and seeing me being tortured for it will cause guilt and anguish to consume her. I won't allow it.

"I'm going." Cellica strides around the corner casually, and my heart leaps in my chest. "You'll need me."

"No," Liam and I state simultaneously, and he glares at me.

Cellica gazes at the assembly in the room, but she shuffles back a step when her eyes land on Darath.

Jagorach smiles, his irises flashing a bright red for several seconds. "Hello, Asmodeus," the Devil purrs seductively. His mate Kleora bites her lip at his deep, alluring tone. "You've been a very naughty boy."

Cellica recovers, her whiskey irises brightening to crimson as she takes a stride forward with a tsk. "You are a little late, my king." I shudder at the authentic voice of the demon speaking through Cellica. "The wolf and I have already bonded." She saunters closer. "It is a shame, really. I so enjoy your special brand of discipline." She turns to Kleora with a wink. "Am I right or what?"

Darath growls, but the Priestess merely giggles. "We should swap notes, Asmodeus," she says, and my eyebrows raise in astonishment.

Darath shoots a wide-eyed stare at his mate before roaring with laughter. "Ah, peach. You never cease to surprise me."

"Could we get back to the business at hand, please?" Asmodeus states. "We are going to this farce of a trial. Cellica's life essence is more potent now because we are three. Our blood will heal him in a matter of seconds."

"Three?" Nicole asks with a frown, and Cellica turns to face the monitor.

"Yes, Queen Giordano. Cellica, her wolf, and me."

"That must be awfully crowded," Alex murmurs with a grin. "How is Cellica coping with so much noise in her head?"

"Apparently just fine," I mutter and rake my fingers through my hair.

"Asmodeus," Darath commandeers the demon's attention. "Is the bond reciprocal?"

"What the fuck does that mean?" Liam snarls.

"Yes," Moe... er... Asmodeus answers, and my heart plummets.

"Cellica, come forth," the demon king orders. The ruby irises flash for a split second before they settle back to their warm, inviting whiskey color.

"Hi, King Darath," she says with a shy smile, and I want to freeze-frame that look for all eternity because my gut clenches with need at my mate's naïve, innocent beauty. The female I'm obsessed with. The one I slaughtered three wolves for because they dared to touch her.

"Hello, little wolf," Darath smiles gently. "I've suppressed the prince so he can no longer hear us. I want you to speak freely. Okay?"

"Okay."

"Do you sense an ulterior motive below the demon's charm?"

She frowns. "I'm not sure what you mean?"

"If given the opportunity, would Asmodeus leave you?"

Sadness pinches her eyes. "Yes," she whispers.

Fuck, yes! I nearly shout.

"Would you like him to go?" he asks quietly. I hold my breath as Cellica's gaze zeros in on mine.

"No. But I won't force him to stay."

I grit my teeth at her fierce expression and the collective gasp around the room. "Goddamnit," I whisper and squeeze my lids shut against the fury rising to the surface.

"You *want* the demon to possess you?" Liam's pale face would be comical if the situation wasn't so fucked up.

She bites her lip and turns to her brother. "He strengthens me. He understands me."

Liam stares at her wide-eyed, at a loss for words, and I totally relate.

"Cellica," Darath interrupts the stare-off between the siblings. "As much as the thought horrifies everyone, you can coincide with Asmodeus in such a way it benefits you both, but I need to train you to control him. No matter what he has told you, if you allow him free rein, he will take ultimate authority over you and your wolf, rendering you helpless."

"No," she shakes her head. "He said we would all learn from each other and coexist peacefully."

"And you fucking believed him?" I grate out, desperate to spank some sense into her. Darath holds up a palm to quiet me, and I growl low but bite my tongue. I know my friend has Cellica's best interests at heart.

"Tell me exactly what he suggested."

Cellica glances around nervously. "Can I talk with you in private?"

"Of course, child, but I think Nox should be involved as this pertains to him as well."

"No," she says, her tone ice cold. "He's made his point clear."

"Cellica, I...."

You what, Nox? What will you say or do to fix the hurt and anger in your mate's gaze? Nothing. As long as Moe lives in my wolf, you will do absolutely nothing.

Fucking coward. And when the hell did I start referring to the demon as Moe?

Son of a bitch.

Darath cuts me a glare as he escorts Cel to her room for privacy. My skin crawls with the demand to go after them. To yank her away from the Devil, whisk her back to my cabin, beat her ass bright red, and make her understand reason. She doesn't require the fucking demon. She's perfection, just the way she is. Why can't she see that?

"Liam," Nicki grabs the wolf's worried gaze from his retreating sister. "When and where is Nox's disciplinary action taking place?"

"Two weeks from now in the Great Hall at Province Headquarters," he sighs, rubbing the back of his neck. Viessa strolls over to him, hooking her arm through his as a show of support. Some of the tension eases in his face as he smiles down at her before lifting his gaze to me. "The families have invited the entire territory to witness the event."

Nicole's fierce gray eyes land on me. "Nox, if I squirt this kid out before then, I will be there in a heartbeat," she says. I nod before she and Logan sign off, and the screen goes black.

Liam swivels to face me. "We need to fucking talk. Trace us to your cabin." He brushes his lips over Viessa's. "Please be here when I get back. I need you."

Her eyes brighten. "Of course, my king."

Liam latches onto my shoulder without a word, and I scatter our molecules to recollect in the middle of my living room. Cellica's scent hits my nostrils, and it nearly buckles my knees. Fuck.

Right before we left, the werewolf king confessed his necessity for Viessa. I can only relate. My vampire weeps for our mate. Her blood, her succulent juices running down our chin, and the sound of her sweet cries as she comes apart under us as we plunge deep inside her core. But it's not merely sexual. I seek her smile. Her adorable giggle. The enticing way she eats. Or her quick temper and bashful blushes. I desire to know everything about her. All her dreams and aspirations. Her favorite movies, songs, and color.

"Nox." Liam snags my attention as he heads to my bar and helps himself to a healthy pour of whiskey. "What are your intentions with my sister?" He downs half of it before refilling and striding over to the sole couch in the room, leaning back with one ankle resting on his other knee. "Is she your one true mate, and if so, what do you plan to do about it?"

Good fucking question. "Yes, and no clue," I answer sincerely. "As long as she embraces Moe, I cannot claim her."

"Moe?" Liam asks in confusion.

I sigh and collapse into one of the beanbag chairs. "The Prince. Asmodeus. Cellica calls him Moe, and honestly, it just seems easier to say."

"Fuck me," he whispers.

"Tell me about it."

Liam regards me for several moments, and I let him, needing the time to collect my thoughts. I must come to terms with the fact the demon isn't going anywhere. He's now a permanent fixture.

A bonded vampire never shares. Would even kill if anyone looked at their mate suggestively. Hence the reason I'm about to suffer unimaginable pain. But for some strange reason, my vampire seems calm with the concept of metaphorically sharing Cellica. Why is that?

"Darath hinted that Moe might have an ulterior motive for escaping. Do you think that's true?" I ask Liam, pushing aside my distracting thoughts.

Liam snorts. "According to Viessa, yes. His reason for escaping through the portal was the witch Troy. Viessa believes she and Troy can transfer the demon from Celica to him."

"No offense, but if Plan A doesn't work, then we require a Plan B—submerging that son of a bitch so far inside her, he never rises."

After several minutes, the wolf leans forward, elbows on his thighs as he examines the alcohol in his glass. "Nox, did you have sex with my little sister?"

Well, shit. "No," I answer honestly.

"But you drank from her?"

The quietness of the question unnerves me. "Yes," I state as matter-of-factly as possible. "It was in the battle's aftermath at the warehouse."

"Do you wish to claim her?" He raises his head and pins me with a direct stare.

Fuck yes, my soul cries. "Not while Moe rides shotgun," I say instead, even though I'm no longer sure that's true.

"Good answer. I want that motherfucker out of my sister, and you, me, and Viessa are going to make it happen. No matter what Cellica wants."

Finally, a goddamn plan I can sink my fangs into. "Count me in."

He downs the rest of the whiskey, pinning me with his irises the exact color of my precious mate's. "When this is over, I want you out of my sister's life." He holds up a hand when I growl an objection. "Not forever, Nox. Just until she matures into her wolf and gets her life in order. If at that point, you still desire to claim her, and she you, you'll have my blessing."

"No offense, Liam, but I don't need your approval to claim my mate. If Cellica still wants me after the demon is gone, no force on this earth will keep us apart. I value your friendship, but you know better than to stand between bonded immortals."

Liam sighs heavily. "I love you, Nox, but you're not good enough for my baby sister."

I scoff. "I'm well aware."

Chapter 25

Cellica

It was challenging to confess my ill-conceived pact with Moe to King Darath, but if he's right and the demon *is* out to take complete control over me, I have to stop him.

"I'm surprised Asmodeus told you about his love affair with Troy, but let me make something clear," Darath hesitates. I fidget, plucking at a loose string on my comforter as I sit on the edge of the bed facing the Devil, who perches precariously on my small desk chair.

The king is intimidating, but his towering height is even more so. However, the tension in my shoulders eased somewhat when he lowered into the chair instead of leering down at me. Otherwise, I might have embarrassed myself and pissed my pants in fear.

"Asmodeus did not bond with Troy, no matter how much he wanted it to be true. The Prince of Lust has a hard time determining between sexual gratification and genuine affection or love. Right now, I sense a conflict within him. For centuries, he believed Troy was his mate, but when the witch chose Abigail over him, it devastated him." Darath smiles affectionately. "He wreaked some serious damage and mayhem before I caught up with him and locked him back where he belonged."

I swallow. I do not fancy knowing exactly what mayhem he's referring to.

"He seems to have developed an attachment to you, but I sense his driving motivation, for whatever reason, is now Nox."

"What?" I frown at the Devil in confusion. "I thought his underlying objective was Troy?"

"If given the opportunity, Asmodeus will choose Nox and you over Troy and that is damn surprising, since he's been seeking a way to get back to the witch for eons."

"So, is Moe gay? Or is that even a thing for demons?" I ask, a hot blush spreading over my cheeks.

Darath laughs. "Demons form attachments to either sex. With a possession, like in your case with a straight relationship, he gets the enjoyment of both."

"What do you mean?" And why am I getting turned on by this conversation?

"When Nox is… intimate with you, Asmodeus experiences what you do, as if Nox touches him. At the same time, he can make you discern his body. His hands, mouth, and that beautiful cock designed for pleasure. Asmodeus can heighten your desire, giving the feeling of being enjoyed by two men. One internally. One externally. Do you understand what I'm saying?"

Holy shit!

"I… I think so," I stammer, my nipples pebbling. I quickly cross my arms over my chest to cover the evidence of my arousal at his words. "I've experienced the first part of that already, which is what freaked Nox out. Not that I blame him," I'm quick to reassure. "It's a lot for a bonded immortal to handle. If the roles were reversed and a sex-starved woman, wanting to hone in on our intimacy, possessed Nox, I'd be—"

"What, little wolf? How would it make you feel?"

"Angry, jealous, and aroused all at the same time."

It finally clicks in my brain what Nox is going through. My mate is overly possessive. He's resentful of Moe's time with me and pissed off he's invading our intimate moments. But maybe deep down, the vampire is also turned on by the concept, which, I'm coming to realize, terrifies him.

"Nox is a straight Alpha," Darath says as if reading my thoughts. "This will not be easy for him to accept. But if you take the reins, are the driving force able to lead Asmodeus, you can allow him to participate as often or as little as both you and Nox desire."

"And you can teach me to control him like that?"

His grin is wicked. "Devil, remember? There is not much I cannot do."

I snort out a laugh. "Yeah, I seem to recall your pride was your downfall."

"Ouch," he exclaims with mock hurt. "The wolf has sharp claws. Rawwwwrrr."

I chuckle, loving his sense of humor, but quickly sober "When can we get started?" The sooner I learn to take command of my passenger, the better.

"No time like the present," he says and rises to come and kneel in front of me, taking my frozen fingers in his large warm hands. "You already possess his greatest weakness. His name. I want you to call him forward."

I nod and close my eyes. "Asmodeus. I need you," I say aloud, so at least King Darath hears my side of the conversation. Nothing. Although I get a sensation of hurt and anger brewing below the surface as he fights me.

I lift my lids. "I think he's still pissed you shoved him in a corner."

"No doubt. Try harder, only this time, infuse your wolf's power behind the command."

Geez. Bossy. But I do as I'm told and dig deep for the added strength from my wolf. I sense Moe's presence, like a warm blanket seeping into my bones. My trembling eases, and my shoulders relax as he comes forth. Damn it. Am I becoming codependent on my demon?

'I heard you the first time, wolf. I just chose to ignore you. What are you and my king playing at?'

"Moe, you swore you would do everything in your power to bring Nox on board, to make this work, however he's comfortable. Are you still willing to do that?"

'I vowed, didn't I?'

"Stop acting like a petulant child," I scold, and Darath smirks.

"What do you...."

"No," I interrupt his question to his master. "You don't get to speak unless I give you permission, Asmodeus," I growl, and King Darath nods his approval. Maybe I can do this after all.

'Ah, so you've teamed up with the Devil to control me, is that it?'

"This is our only option, Moe. Nox won't accept both of us any other way." Just saying the words out loud sends misery spiraling through my chest, and I rub my sternum as if to alleviate the hurt. I meant what I said. I understand Nox's reservations, but that doesn't lessen the pain of his rejection.

"Good job, Cellica. Now push him back down," Darath demands.

"Asmodeus, please retreat." I don't know why I add the please, but I need his cooperation. The last thing I care to deal with on a daily basis is a pissed-off demon.

'And if I refuse?' Moe inquires, his manner much more subdued as if he's merely protesting for pride's sake.

"Take the demon by the horns, Cellica. He's bonded to your wolf. Use her to command Asmodeus." Darath's barked order straightens my spine.

I nod. "Then you are a liar, and you give me no choice but to force you so far down you will never rise again. Is that what you want? Because I, truthfully, don't." Silence greets me and I hold my breath, gazing into Darath's curious stare. "Asmodeus. I didn't ask for this. You forced this situation on both of us. Comply."

'*Very well, love. As you wish.*'

'*Did you just quote Westly from The Princess Bride to me?*' I question internally, with a teasing smirk, hoping to soften my harsh comments.

'*I do not know what or who that is, but I am glad I made you smile. Inform my king I am cooperating so he will leave me the fuck alone.*'

"He's on board," I say once I'm certain Moe has re-submerged.

"I'm impressed with how well you controlled him, Cellica."

"Your direction to use my wolf helped. I couldn't have done it alone. And like I said, Moe seems willing to make it work."

"Hmmm. Time will tell," he mumbles before rising to his feet. "Keep practicing bringing him forward and pushing him back. Always use his name and your wolf's power if he tries to get out of hand. It's like training a dog. The more you do it, the quicker he will fall in line."

I frown at the analogy. Moe means more to me than a mere pet, but I nod my agreement. "Thank you, King Darath."

"You are more than welcome, little one. Just remain vigilant, and if you have any further issues with my lustful Prince, reach out to me."

Since Nox's punishment for protecting me is two weeks away, after King Darath's brief session, I decided to pack up and head to school. I'll be damned if I'll go crawling back to Nox and beg for his acceptance. If I'm his one true mate, it shouldn't matter if I'm his best friend's little sister or if I have a pesky demon riding shotgun inside me. He should be by my side, helping me cope.

Instead, he turned away from me, cursed me with his eyes, and broke my heart.

I gaze out at the rolling hills streaming by the truck as I drive down the highway, recalling that Josh was not too happy I was leaving before talking to Liam, but I told him our big brother insisted I get my ass to school. Since Nox's persecution is two days away from a full moon, it will be a fucking miracle if I don't shift while watching them lance his back open.

One minute I'm alone in my truck, contemplating life and the rising sun, and the next, a petite, beautiful blond pops into my passenger seat. Startled, I swerve with a surprised squeak, and it takes me a couple of seconds to gain control. When I do, I jerk the wheel to veer to the side of the road and slam on my brakes.

With no seatbelt securing her, the woman's forehead, with the biggest iron crown I've ever seen, slams into the dash.

"You little bitch," she growls, ripping the headdress off and slamming her palm over the gushing cut at her hairline. A violet glow lights up beneath her fingers, and within seconds, the wound heals. Even the blood disappears.

"Who the fuck are you?" I ask, flinging my seatbelt off, readying to jump from the truck.

"Who I am isn't important," she snarls, turning to face me. The malevolence in her sapphire irises turns my blood into ice in my veins. "It's your passenger I want to talk to. Asmodeus, come forth," she orders.

I lock him down tight, just like the Devil taught me. Every meager instinct I possess screams not to let this powerful female anywhere near my demon.

"You're too late," I lie with a sneer, even though I'm shaking in my boots. "King Darath already exercised the Prince."

Pain shoots through my cheekbone when the blond backhands me with such force my temple hits the steering wheel, and I see stars.

"Do not fucking lie to me, dog. I sense the nitwit within you."

I shake my head to clear my vision while reaching for my phone in my back pocket as stealthily as possible. This bitch is clearly unhinged. Magic infused power explodes from her like tiny fire-crackers and her image seems to fluctuate, like what she's presenting to me is a mirage she can't control.

She grips a fistful of hair at the nape of my neck and yanks my head back to peer into my soul. "Asmodeus, come out and play you fucking coward, or I will destroy your vessel."

I sense Moe fighting me, desperate to advance, but I shove him deeper. '*Let me handle this, Moe. Stay put.*'

'*No, Cellica. Abigail will get off on torturing you just to get to me. Let me rise.*'

Oh fuck. So this is the infamous Abigail Brevil. I'm in deep shit.

'*No. Having this bitch control you is way worse than anything she could do to me,*' I say, not entirely convinced that's true. I'm not a warrior. I have no clue if I'm strong enough to endure what the witch might have planned for me, but I must try. "*Stay down, Asmodeus.*"

The demon growls but immediately stops fighting me.

"Sorry, Moe can't come out and play right now," I taunt while fiddling with my phone, hoping I'm actually calling someone. Anyone.

"Ehhhh, wrong answer, dog," she bullies before slamming my face into the wheel.

White-hot pain lances through my nose as it breaks, and blood gushes from my nostrils to splatter across the Ford emblem in the center. Oh fuck, that hurt. I blink back the tears and punch her in the throat with the edge of my phone.

The second she lets go, gasping for air, I fling open the door, tumbling to my hands and knees on the side of the road, blood pouring from my nose. The intense pain blurs my vision as I bring my phone up to my face. My heart skydives. The fall shattered the screen.

"Damn it."

The boom of the passenger door slamming has me vaulting to my feet and taking off across the road. Unfortunately, before I can shift or even manage two steps, a violet glow encases my body, submerging me in a lake of excruciating torment. I scream against the agony, clutching my useless phone to my chest.

"You will pay dearly for that hit," Abigail says, her tone muffled through the bubble of purple pain surrounding me.

"Cellica!" my brother's shout is distant, and for a nanosecond, relief floods through me, thinking he's found me. "Cellica? Where are you? What's going on?"

My heart drops when I realize his voice is coming from my phone. Fuck. "Aaabigaail," I whisper through the agony, hoping and praying he hears me.

"Darath is with me. Tell me your location and we are there."

"Oh no, you don't."

Abigail reaches through the colored sphere and plucks my phone from my stiff fingers with ease. "Who's this?" she demands. I no longer hear my brother as the fierce fire of pain drills into my bones, and darkness finally engulfs me.

Chapter 26

Nox

Before nightfall, a horrific dream played on repeat through my brain. It was murky and distorted, but I sensed Cellica was in trouble. No, more than that—she was in pain. I searched for her, swallowing my panic and utilizing every tracker skill I possessed to zero in on her location, but it was useless. In each agonizing version, I was too late. Her sightless eyes bored a hole through my heart, and her dismembered body brought me to my knees. Then it would start all over again until I finally bolted upright, roaring her name.

What the fuck? Sweat drenches my skin along with the sheets. I lean over, snatch my phone off the charger on the nightstand and shoot off a text, needing to reassure myself she is alright.

Me: Are you okay?

That's when I notice a dozen messages and missed calls from Liam. One text, in particular, stands out and stops my heart.

Liam: Abigail took Cellica! Get ur ass over here asap!!!

No. This can't be happening. The fucking witch is supposed to be dead. There's no way.

I leap out of bed, shower and get dressed with vampire speed, and head to Nicole and Logan's suite. As I raise my hand to pound on the door, Logan swings it open. He's shirtless, his two broadswords strapped to his back, ready for battle.

"Abigail—"

"I know."

"Cellica—"

"I know."

I can't seem to form complete sentences as a fresh wave of panic swallows my voice.

I sense Sebastian and Alex materialize on my right. She gives my bicep a squeeze before slipping into my queen's chambers.

"Guard her with your life," Logan growls at the petite but deadly valkyrie.

"We will, I swear," Lucretia asserts as she appears in the Hallway with Kurtis, dressed for battle. The big shifter captures Lu's nape before she walks into the suite behind Alex, spins her to him, and devours her lips in a quick but thorough kiss. Lu smiles up at him when he lets her go. "I love you," she whispers, walking backward into the room.

"And I you, vampire," he grins, watching her with a heated gaze.

"Stay safe." She peers over at me. "Get her back, Nox, or I will kick your ass."

I nod, still unable to speak. If anything happens to Cellica... I will fucking lose it.

For the first time, I'm relieved Moe dwells inside her. If anyone can protect my mate, it's a Prince of Hell.

Nicole waddles over to our team in her long nightshirt and shorts, her hand on her enormous belly. Lu and Alex flank her on either side. "Find her and bring her back, but don't get dead. You hear me?"

"Yes, my lady," the warriors flanking me murmur, but I can't form words. Fear for my mate has taken up permanent residence in my brain. Besides Troy Tenebris, Abigail is the most powerful witch I know. She's the daughter of an Oracle with the ability to siphon an immortal's powers, meaning no tracing, mind control, telekinesis, or any other power a vampire can possess. We are reduced to mere soldiers, but I'd put my money on this team any night of the week, supernatural strength or not.

"Are Darath and Viessa coming?" I ask, my voice rough with the emotions clogging my throat. If we have any chance of surviving a war with Abigail, we'll need Lucifer and the Oracle.

"They are at Liam's already," Logan answers.

Nicole slaps a palm in the center of my chest, and her energy warms my torso. "Let your fear for Cellica go, Guardian. She needs the tracker and trained killer in you, now more than ever."

She allows her force to fortify my own. I bow my head, shove my terror into a dark corner, and bring forth the primal instincts of my vampire. "I will burn the fucking world down to find her. I vow it."

"Good," she says and steps back between Alex and Lu. "Now, go get our girl."

Logan bends and presses his lips to hers. "Do not go into labor without me," he commands.

She snorts. "I'll do my best, Sir."

We stop briefly at Liam's, obtaining the coordinates of Cellica's last known location, thanks to the GPS tracker Liam had put on her truck, before converging on the scene. The sight of Cellica's blood hits me like an iron mace to the chest and nearly buckles my knees. Shoving the torment deep, I pull up the mask of an ice-cold hunter, settling into my role with familiar ease. This version of me is more comfortable than the raging out-of-control vampire hell-bent on destroying the world to get to its mate.

I take in the scene. The driver-side door hangs open, blood coats the steering wheel and the asphalt, and smack dab in the middle of the street, the screen cracked to shit, is Cellica's phone. The team remains back, guarding my six, allowing me room to work. Liam paces by the side of the road under Viessa's watchful eye.

A faint odor of dark magic taints the air, but inside the spacious cab of the Super Duty, my mate's scent surrounds me, washing over my senses like spring rain. I grit my teeth when I notice the suitcase in the backseat. She was leaving me, going back to her life on campus.

Yeah, what did you expect after you basically told her she was on her own?

This is my fault.

I shouldn't have walked away from my mate.

Pain sprinkles across my chest, but I snuff it out. If I allow myself to feel right now, I'll fucking implode.

My home life trained me to control my emotions long before joining the Guardians. Their rigorous training only amplified my natural skill to sense people down to the molecule level and track their scent anywhere. Fate gifts most vampires with a unique talent, and the longer you live, the more honed that aptitude becomes. At a century and a half, my tracking ability is that of an elder vampire in their first millennia.

I crawl across the seat to the passenger side, inhaling the rank odor of Abigail's magic, and notice a splotch of blood on the dash. Ah, my little wolf got a hit in. Good girl. It will make trailing the witch easier.

I ease back out and stroll over to the phone. The inky residue of sorcery is more potent here as if held in one spot for an extended period. Did Cellica run until Abigail stopped her with magic? I try not to let the fury boil to the surface, but I can't stop the brightening of my irises.

"Does Abigail have the ability to trace?" I ask Sebastian.

"No. But most witches utilize portals for transport."

That's the odoriferous stench. A portal. "Darath, can you open gateways?"

"Of course," he responds, for once the dark humor absent from his expression. "You smell a portal?" At my nod, he arches an eyebrow. "Impressive."

"I need you to launch one right now."

"To where?"

"I don't care. I just need a gateway for tracking purposes."

He nods, holding his hands out, and within seconds, a swirling black mass appears in the middle of the road. I'm about to stride into the mass when Viessa's command halts me in my tracks.

"Nox, stop!" We all shift to her expectantly. "If we enter the portal, pain and despair wait on the other side."

What the fuck?

"Whose pain and despair? Mine or Cellica's?"

"Both." She shakes her head as if to clear it. "And more."

I hesitate for a mere second. "I don't care, I'm going," I bark and turn toward the swirling bulk once more, only to find the Oracle standing next to me, her amber eyes crazed.

"Then let go of your misgivings and trust the one you least expect."

What the hell does that mean?

"I'm going with you," Liam states, coming to stand with me.

"No, Liam," Viessa urges. "This is Nox's journey, not ours. We must allow him space to track Cellica through the gateways. He will contact us the second he finds her."

"I am not sitting around, twiddling my thumbs while that bitch has my sister," he growls at her, the beast heavy in his tone.

My patience is about to snap. We are fucking wasting time.

Darath steps forward. "Viessa is right, Liam. You would just be a scent obstacle for the tracker. Allow him space to work."

A war wages within the werewolf king, and I grit my teeth. "I will contact you the second I pick up her trail. I promise."

"Fine. But I better be your first damn call, vampire."

"Nox," Darath stops me. "I did not open the other side of the portal. When you catch her scent and wish to exit, utter these words. *Aperi ianuam per tempus et spatium.* Got it?"

"Yes."

"This is a bad fucking idea," Liam grumbles again.

Before they can argue further, I step into the hurricane. The need to get to my mate shoots an added layer of ice into my bloodstream with each toss and turn of the moving wind tunnel. I tune out everything but the aroma I've become addicted to—her blood. Her unique scent of roses and woman combined with the earthy fragrance of her wolf and the dark spice of Asmodeus. They are all intertwined and distinct to Cellica now, and my nose follows, not caring where it takes me or eventually dumps me out. As long as my female is on the other side.

Chapter 27

Pinpricks of discomfort rouse my brain, but the more the darkness fades, the more excruciating the agony. I want to crawl into the cocoon of my mind and never emerge.

'Wake up, Cellica!' Moe's shout reverberates inside my already pounding skull. I bite back a moan as awareness slowly returns. Numbness pervades my fingers, and pain slices through my hands when I try to wiggle them.

I take a second, or ten, to assess my situation while trying to appear unconscious. I'm upright, but my feet are not touching solid ground. Abigail must have trussed me up by my wrists from a ceiling or something, hence why my fingers are numb. Despite the pain stabbing my temple, I attempt to pry one eye open.

Two inches from my bare feet is gray concrete, and my toes curl against the cold radiating from the surface. Shit. No wonder my body feels frozen. The bitch stripped me of my clothes, and I'm hanging like a slab of beef in a meat locker, completely naked.

I lower my lids and concentrate on any sound or movement. Nothing. The silence is suffocating like I'm trapped in a void with no life.

'Moe, where are we?'

My demon's presence comforts me. At least I won't die alone.

'*We are not dying,*' he growls. '*And I do not know where we are. When you are out, I am out. But if you had fucking let me take control, we would not be in this situation.*'

'*Really? You're gonna be one of those, "I told you so" assholes?*'

'*Now and forever, sweetheart, so get used to it,*' he sneers, but I sense his underlying alarm, which freaks me out. If my demon is concerned, I should be petrified. Which I am. Totally freaking the fuck out.

'*Let me have authority,*' he demands, and I'm surprised that he hasn't taken control already in my weakened state.

'*Not until I know what the hell she wants. If she's still after Nicole, there's no way I'm going to allow her to manipulate you... me into hurting her, or worse, killing her and the prophesied baby.*'

I sense the hesitancy in Moe. Like the demon is hiding something vital from me, and he's not sure what to do about it.

"Oh goodie, you're awake," Abigail cheers as she saunters into the barren concrete prison as if she's the Queen of Sheba. Her butt ugly crown missing over her ridiculous abundance of pale blond hair. She carries a wooden bowl in her arms, a towel wrapped over the top, which she places on a long table against the wall I didn't notice.

The room is maybe fifty by fifty feet of nothing but bare concrete, with no other furniture in the space but the table and a folding chair propped up in the corner. There are no windows to indicate whether it's day or night.

My blood runs cold when I spy the shiny, stainless-steel tools lined up on the surface of the narrow table. Fuck. Whatever she requires, she's willing to torture me for it.

'*She wants me,*' Moe curses. '*Let me rise before she hurts you further.*'

"No," I whisper, trying to shove my terror away and put on a brave face.

"What's that dear?" Abigail asks absently with her back to me as she prepares whatever the hell she's preparing. Something to inflict severe pain, I'm sure. "Patience, dog. The fun will begin in a minute."

"Where's Troy?" I ask, my voice a mere croak.

The male witch has helped Liam's team in the past. Maybe I could convince him to let me go and kill this bitch before it's too late and the wrath of hell rains down on this place.

I must keep the hope alive that Nox, the best damn tracker in the world, will find me with the full force of our allies. I just need to stall for time.

With no clue where we are, the icy chill in the air causing shivers to cascade throughout my body, we could be in the fucking Arctic. If I were a mere human, I would have gone into hypothermia by now. I grit my teeth to stop the chattering and tilt my head to examine the iron shackles restraining my wrists. I'm surprised she didn't go with silver to sizzle my skin for dramatic effect.

"Troy is no concern of yours," she mutters while adding ingredients to the wooden bowl.

I've never been around a witch before, but having watched enough *Supernatural* on TV, I realize she's concocting a spell. Although, come to think of it, my vampire looks a lot like Dean Winchester with one turquoise eye and one blue eye, but the same sexy features, thick short hair with those luscious lips that should be illegal.

"What... do you... want, Abigail?" My teeth chattering makes speaking challenging, and I've lost all feeling in both my arms. It must be below freezing in here.

'*Moe, I am so damn cold,*' I cry, trying hard not to show any outward fear to the witch, but my demon has big shoulders, and I trust him.

'*Give me control, princess, and I can warm you up.*'

"I want a great many things," Abigail says, oblivious to our internal conversation, as she finally turns to face me. I shiver for an entirely different reason at the malevolence pouring from her expression. "But what I need from you right now is Asmodeus."

"Why?"

Her eyes narrow as if she's irritated that I'm asking questions. Well, too damn bad. Before I unleash the Prince, I want to know what she plans to do with him.

She saunters over to me, her cerulean gaze skimming my shivering flesh from head to toe. When her warm fingers skim my midriff, a part of me wants to lean into the warmth, but instead, I jerk back. With no leverage, my body swings from the chains, my legs flail to find the purchase just out of reach, and my shoulders scream in protest.

Sharp nails dig into my waist, stopping my shivering gyrations. I wince at the power oozing from her fingertips. It takes every last ounce of willpower to gaze into her crazed stare.

Show no fear. Show no fear.

"I see why Asmodeus and the vampire are so infatuated with you," she says, removing a large knife from a sheath at her waist, running the blade's razor edge down my chest. Her grip on my waist prevents me from moving away from the slight sting. "You have a lush little body. If our circumstances were different, I would enjoy teaching you how to please and be pleasured by a woman." She runs the flat, icy section of the blade across my nipples, stiff from the cold. "Men have their place and offer so much sexually, but there's nothing like the enjoyment of a woman's tongue on your pussy."

"Isn't Troy your mate?" I ask to distract her from any sexual thoughts. I'm a dick girl through and through. One dick in particular.

Please hurry, Nox. I pray silently.

"He is, but witches are freer sexually than most mated immortals. We are bound to one individual for all eternity, but our link allows *experimentation*, if you will." When she leans forward and latches onto my puckered areola, my body stiffens in shock. I assumed her words were meant to frighten me, nothing more. I didn't think she'd actually touch me intimately.

She pops my nipple from her mouth and studies me with a dark expression that freaks me the fuck out. "Mmm, you taste scrumptious, wolf." She licks her ruby lips, and I'm repulsed. "Maybe a little sample before we begin is in order."

"No!" I panic. "Please stop."

'*Oh, come on, love. Let her pleasure us. It will make the pain more bearable later,*' Moe purrs, clearly turned on. Fuck, who am I kidding? A fly landing on my damn nipple would turn the fucker on.

'*Shut up, demon. You are not doing this to me again.*'

"Tell... tell me why you want Moe?" I ask, hoping to derail the deviant plans I see shining in her calculating gaze.

"Moe?" Her heated expression morphs into humor. "Is that what you're calling the Prince of Hell?" Her laugh rings out, and the demon is the one shivering now, but not from the cold. Geez, his sex drive is ridiculous.

'*Come on, love,*' he groans in my head. His lust is getting to me. *Let's play.*'

When I feel hands caressing my breasts, I gasp and glance down at Abigail. But she's not touching me, merely observing me with curiosity.

'*What the fuck are you doing, Moe?*' I demand, gasping when he tweaks both nipples. '*Stop it. Right now.*'

The witch laughs again and drops to her knees. "I see *Moe* is on board with a little foreplay, so sit back and enjoy, wolf, because I suddenly crave to devour this pussy whether you like it or not."

"No!" I shout and try to kick her in the face, but she merely digs her nails deep into my thighs, drawing blood. "Please, I beg you.

Don't do this." Tears threaten my vision, which shames me. I'm clearly not a strong, valiant warrior like Lucretia or Nicole. They would never beg. But if pleading for mercy keeps her mouth off of me, why the hell not?

"You'll be begging for an entirely different reason in a few minutes. Now shut up or I will gag you so you don't ruin my enjoyment."

"You fucking bitch. I will kill you for this."

She laughs again. "I doubt it."

'Moe, goddamn it. Do something.'

'Give me control,' he demands, pinching my nipples, and delicious pleasure shoots through my body; more tears gather, blurring my vision. *'And I will end this.'*

'I can't,' I wail. *'She will use us to kill Nicole and the baby. I know it. She wants you to come forward for a reason.'*

'I am a powerful Prince of Hell, wolf. She has no power over me,' he pants.

I sense the uncertainty behind his words, but lust clouds the demon's brain. All he can think about is the euphoric release of an orgasm. Not how the witch is using his own weakness against him.

The problem is, I'm the one who is actually suffering. Well, not *suffering* per se, like actual torture, but still. This is against my will. I don't want that traitor's mouth on my sex, and I despise how my body is betraying me.

I jerk against the first swipe of her warm tongue up my slit.

'Yes,' Moe moans, pinching my nipples harder, and I whimper as the slight pain shoots straight to my pussy.

"Goddess, you are delicious," Abigail whispers. "I taste Asmodeus's spicy flavor too. Can you feel me, demon? My tongue tasting your hardness? Like old times?" She's fucking playing him like a master puppeteer, and my traitorous body responds to the relentless assault from them both.

"Do you crave to fuck her sweet cunt while I suck on her clit, Asmodeus?"

'*Fuck, yes!*' he shouts, wholly lost to his desire, the demands of his cock.

Moe is a lust demon. No, more than that. He was once a powerful archangel, but his consuming necessity for sex, the more deviant the better, and his devotion to Lucifer, got him thrown out of heaven alongside his king.

Being attached to me has seriously limited his sexual freedom. Because of my restrictions on him, he's now incoherent with lust. Not caring, I don't want this. That it's a violation of my body and mind.

Tears stream down my cheeks at their unwanted assault, but I can't help being affected by their desire, passion, and skill. Wetness coats my inside, and I find I'm pressing into Abigail's face, gyrating against her talented tongue and forcing her to consume every drop. Her nails no longer hold me down. Instead, she lifts my legs over her shoulders, spreads my lips, and spears me with her tongue before coming up and flicking my clit. She fucks me with abandon, sucking, biting, moaning, and eating me like a starved woman. All the while, Moe tweaks my aching nipples, bucking my hips, and when I feel a fullness pushing against my core from the inside, I lose it, the climax hitting fast and hard.

'*Fuck!*' Moe shouts. My orgasm rips through him, gifting him what he needs. What he craves above all else—release.

When the tremors finally ease, my head hangs limp, my hair flowing down my back as Abigail continues to lick and suckle at my sex in a leisurely pace.

"Such a pretty cunt," she murmurs. "Tell me, wolf. Are you a virgin?"

I lift my head to gaze down at her as humiliation and rage burn my throat. The enemy brought me to orgasm. I'm as much a fool as Asmodeus. More so because I'm not a mindless demon ruled by his dick. Bile rises, and I swallow, gritting my teeth to keep it down, blinking against the tears threatening.

'*I will never forgive you for this, Moe,*' I whimper as the flood I tried to hold back cascades down my cheeks to darken the concrete of my new prison.

'Trust me, love,' he urges. '*We both need me strong to conquer this bitch. She's not using me. I'm using her. The more she brings us to climax, the stronger I become.*'

Yeah, but will I survive it?

Chapter 28

At every twist and turn of the portal, I hesitate, inhale deeply, weed out all the other scents, and search for the sweetest aroma that lights up my insides like a live wire. Over and over. Left and right. Forward and back, until finally, her distinct essence fires through my nostrils, and my heart stops.

"Aperi ianuam per tempus et spatium," I whisper, and the black void lightens. The swirling wind, which tried to hinder my abilities at every bend, intensifies, concentrating on a single spot in front of me. At first, it's the size of my fist, but soon the round sphere expands. Wider and higher until it becomes large enough for me to step through.

As I peer out through the portal, I'm shocked by the barren, icy landscape. It may be summer in Montana, but wherever this is, it feels as if winter has dug in its claws, determined to stay despite the season. Off in the distance, barely a dark spot on the horizon, a concrete building looks strangely out of place in the harsh environment. My instincts ignite, and I am confident this is where the witch is holding my wolf.

I quickly assess my weapons throughout my leather duster and draw my sword before stepping out of the portal. I'm shocked by the icy blast of the wind as it smacks me in the face, but I ignore the discomfort and forge ahead. My destination? The concrete bunker.

I should call the team, but I decide to do a little recon first before everyone converges. If Abigail is here, it changes everything. Our odds of winning diminish under her powers. But I have to remain hopeful. With King Darath and Viessa on our side, we are sure to defeat the foul witch and rescue my girl, no matter how powerful she is. To think anything else will distract me, and I need to stay focused. For Cellica.

A hundred yards in, a soul-sucking click freezes me in place. Fuck. Land mine.

I glance down at my right boot with dread. I'm uncertain I could trace fast enough to avoid any damage.

A sharp screeching noise jerks my head to the left, and my heart rate kick starts into high gear. A flock of wyvern dots the darkened night, the flapping of their mighty wings reaching my ears. The creatures are similar to dragons but only possess two legs with a barbed tail. They are also highly venomous and survive on pure instinct.

Their appearance confirms my location. I'm on Baffin Island in Nunavut, Canada. My home fucking territory. The witch parked her ass practically in our backyard.

A quick calculation of their speed means the wyvern will be on me in minutes. *Think, Nox.* I remove my phone and shoot my coordinates and a warning to Sebastian before pocketing it to analyze my situation.

What are my options here? I peer over at the bunker with desperation.

Option one: if I time it perfectly, I might be able to take out several of the wyverns the second I disengage from the land mine, and probably salvage my legs, before I jump back into the portal and hope they don't follow me in, but the team could arrive right when I detonate.

Option two: I fight while attempting to keep my foot in place until help arrives. I snort. The odds of my weight shifting enough to detonate the bomb are pretty high, and then I'm truly dead. There's no coming back from being blasted to bits, even for a vampire.

Option three is looking like the more likely choice: I teleport to the bunker and hope my legs don't get blown off in the process or kill my friends, and the wyverns devour me, anyway.

Fuck it. Bunker, it is.

I twirl my sword, readying to trace the second they are in range. Their screeching intensifies as they dive in unison, like a flock of enormous, scaley birds with poisonous teeth.

An icy calm settles over me as I await what could amount to excruciating pain at the very least. If Cellica's life didn't rest on my shoulders, I'd glory in the battle to come.

My Viking heritage roars to leap into the fray and slash and kill, to die as a soldier should, with his sword in his hand, fighting until the very end. But my mate is in trouble, relying on me to rescue her, so I will do everything in my power to survive and get to her, or at least live long enough for the team to arrive.

The seconds slow, and my focus sharpens. Dozens of predatory eyes zero in on me. I smile, my fangs on full display and my irises lighting up the dark night. An enormous wyvern in the front puffs his chest, preparing to flay the skin from my body with his fire. I pluck a large dagger from my jacket, ready to fling it at his heart, when an arrow whistles by my ear, straight into the creature's chest.

It screeches in agony, dropping to the ground with a loud thud, but the dozen in its wake keep coming. They scent prey, and nothing will sway their absolute focus.

I glance behind me as Kleora, shimmering with translucence, emerges from the portal, several more arrows nocked in her bow.

"Land mines!" I shout.

Another creature dives for me, ignoring the wraith completely. I hold my position, my sword raised and ready, until hot putrid breath hits my face. Then, I swing for its neck, keeping most of my weight on my right leg. I see three more fall from the sky out of my periphery, with arrows protruding from their chests. One drops on a mine and explodes, sending chunks of bloody meat in every direction.

The giant head I just severed, lands with a sickening splat two feet from my foot, and the body ignites on another mine. The blast rocks through me, and I dig my sword into the ground to keep my weight on the detonator.

When Darath, in full Satan mode, blasts through the portal with his gigantic black wings stirring the air with the force of a helicopter, I can only stare, open-mouthed. Of course, I've seen this form before when he crawled from the earth in front of my cabin. Still, to witness him battling the wyverns mid-air, hacking their heads from their bodies with his claws, or gripping their gaping jaws and ripping their faces in half while his mate protects his six with a barrage of deadly accurate arrows, is a sight to see.

I peer back at the portal, and Sebastian flies through the tunnel to battle alongside Darath. I wish I'd been gifted with the ability to fly, but then I never would've found Cellica without my tracker ability. The other shadowy outlines of our team hover at the entrance. Unfortunately, with the land mines dotting the landscape, it's too dangerous for them to engage.

The remaining creatures, realizing they are fighting a losing battle, bug off, and Kleora floats over to me.

"Right foot," I say, and she nods.

"How fast can you teleport?" she asks.

"I guess we are about to find out."

Darath hovers above us, the beat of his wings kicking up snow. "Peach, get to the building," he orders, and she immediately obeys. His rubies penetrate my skull. "Faster than you ever have in your life, vampire," he growls. "You die and I will torture you myself in Hell."

I nod, and he soars into the sky, veering off to join Kleora. I notice the rest of the team line the bunker wall, their worried gazes watching me.

My muscles quiver in anticipation, my mind fixated on placing the full power of my strength into tracing. A fresh round of creatures crests the hill twenty yards to my left, dropping low to the ground like a flock of pelicans over the water. I inhale deep, waiting as long as possible. Then, when the front row is within mere feet, I expand my molecules, snapping them toward my destination with more force than I've ever used.

Pain.

Screeching.

Burned flesh.

I shoot forward so fast that my spine slams into the side of the concrete bunker when I reemerge, dropping me to the frozen ground with a loud thump. Groaning with pain, I roll over and prop my back against the building to assess the damage. My left boot is completely gone, the skin on my foot flayed off down to the bone, but at least it's still attached. Thank fuck for the small things.

"That was fucking impressive, Nox," Logan says, kneeling to evaluate the destruction. "I am not sure if even I could trace that fast."

Agony sears through my foot as the wound begins its healing process. Fuck, it's almost worse than it being blown to shit, but I grit my teeth against the ache. The remaining wyvern circle in confusion over the fallen in the distance, attempting to pick up my scent.

"Gonna need new boots," I mutter.

Sebastian disappears.

By the time I lay my head back against the cold wall and close my eyes against the discomfort of my regeneration, Sebastian's tossing me a blood bag. I quickly down the contents as he drops a pair of shitkickers and socks on the ground next to me.

"No doubt the witch heard the explosions," Kurtis states, having discarded his usual AR-15 for a sword, with knives strapped to his massive thighs. During the battle at the Dark Fae castle, Abigail proved guns were useless against her shields.

"Is Cellica in there?" Liam jerks his head toward the building at my back, clutching a sword.

I toss the bag and reach for the socks. My foot completely healed. "Yes," I say, shoving my feet into the boots Sebastian brought. I rise, bending to pick up my sword, undamaged from the blast.

Damascus steel. The best in the world. Its ability to flex and hold an edge is unparalleled. The secret of the material is the high carbon content, up to twenty times as much carbon as standard "mild" steel, but none of the chromium which would make it "stainless."

The vampire ruler gifts every Guardian with a Damascus sword if they survive the rigorous years of training and engrave their family crest or emblem on the handle. This blade will survive long after I am nothing but ash.

"What do we know?" Sebastian inquires, his two broadswords, like his brother's, strapped to his back. In battles, the legendary warriors always sport bare torsos. Their matching tattoos on opposite sides are on full display over their massive chests and shoulders, no matter the temperature.

"Nothing, besides the fact I sense Cellica." I brush snow off my leather pants, burned and tattered at the hem, grateful for their warmth. "And Abigail," I add with dread.

"Fuck," Logan mutters.

I glance around and note that Darath and Kleora are absent. "Where did Jag go?" I ask with a frown.

"He said he'd be right back but to wait for him," Viessa answers. She's wearing her usual halter and leather pants, but a long white coat protects her skin against the numbing cold.

"Any foresight to help us, Oracle?" I request hopefully.

"No," she shoots an agitated glance at Kurtis. "But I suggest some of us remain here and guard the door against further attack."

Liam rubs her arm. "We require all hands on deck for this one, sweetness. Just stay behind us until we call for your powers. I don't want you getting hurt."

"Yes, my king," she responds demurely, and I peer at her in confusion. She's a powerful Oracle, able to defend herself with relative ease. However, I also sense she sees something but is keeping her lips sealed.

The Tribrid possesses as many characteristics as she does species in her blood. How Liam keeps up with it all, I'll never know. It would drive me insane.

I snort. *Says the vampire whose female plays mental house with a wolf and demon.*

While we wait for Darath, Sebastian brings up satellite images of the surrounding area on his phone and an infrared live stream video of the structure.

"How the hell did you do that?" I ask.

"Hacked into the military satellites and drones in the territory," he answers with a shrug.

"Oh, is that all?" I grin, but the smile vanishes when I see numerous red blips on the screen.

"This bunker is mostly underground," Sebastian informs us. "Three to four guards stationed at every level, and it looks like Cellica is on the bottom floor."

"How can you tell?" Liam asks.

"It's the only blip not moving, and it appears they chained her arms to the ceiling."

Fuck. Fuck. Fuck.

"Where the hell is Darath?" I growl. "If he's not here in the next few seconds, we are going in."

"Abigail probably already knows we are here," Kurtis reiterates. "So we no longer have the element of surprise."

"I don't care," I snarl at him. "I'm getting to her with or without you."

"With, buddy. Always with. I merely want us to be prepared."

I sigh and rub the back of my neck. "I know. I'm just... my skin is crawling with the need to get to my mate."

"We all are, Nox," Logan says. "But we wait for Darath. Besides Viessa, he's the most potent among us and hopefully immune to her magic."

"You flatter me, Logan," Darath purrs as he materializes next to me with Kleora by his side. He shed the demonic visage in favor of his full battle gear. "A mere witch, no matter how powerful, cannot control the Devil, so I might need to shift again. I'll require a safe spot to alter my form so I could vanish for a minute." He rubs his hands together in eagerness.

"Let's do this. It's fucking freezing out here and the Devil hates the cold."

I lead the group around the corner to the steel door with a shake of my head. No matter what lies behind it, we will fight to the death to retrieve one of our own. My mate. My life.

Hang in there, baby girl, we're coming.

Chapter 29

Cellica

I no longer feel my body. I think it's completely frozen. If I hadn't transitioned into immortality, I'd have died of hypothermia hours ago.

But it's my inner turmoil keeping me conscious.

They forced me to betray Nox. Not once, but twice. And I can't say it was just Abigail who coerced me into an orgasm. Oh no, it was a combined effort.

The witch assaulted me from the outside while Moe attacked my body from the inside. And my fucking flesh betrayed me, feeling pleasure when it should have felt revulsion. So I hung there, my thighs clutched around Abigail's head. My hips gyrated against her mouth to get her lips attached to that perfect spot to send me spiraling over the edge when I should have snapped her damn neck.

You're weak. Pathetic. Ruled by the untrained demands of your body, your fantasized lust. You're no better than the goddamn Prince. You might as well let him have control.

"How are we feeling?" Abigail asks as she enters my prison once more.

After her little cunt munching session, she backed up to the table, lifted her thick wool skirt, and fingered herself while staring at me. It fucking creeped me out, and I closed my lids to block the visual. Still, I couldn't evade her escalating moans from searing my eardrums as she brought herself to climax.

When silence prevailed once more, I opened my eyes and watched as she licked her fingers clean, dropped her skirt back in place, and then strolled out of the room with a huge grin.

I felt sick. Humiliated. Violated. My body may have gotten off on what they did to me, but my mind screamed for them to stop.

Even if Nox rescues me now, I'm not sure I can face him after what happened. He'd look at me with disgust and horror, and I wouldn't blame him. I allowed our sworn enemy to strum my clit with her tongue until I shattered with pleasure.

But I determined one thing—Nox is way more talented down there than Abigail. No matter how much she boasts, a woman does it better, I hold the notion close, letting it keep my heart warm against the chill.

Nox knew exactly how to bring me to climax in the warehouse, and oh fuck did I enjoy it. My finale with him was ten times stronger than the meager one Abigail and Moe forced out of me.

"Are you ready to let Asmodeus out of his cage?" she asks, holding a wicked-looking knife. "You enjoyed my mouth more than I imagined, so maybe a little pain will work better."

"Fuck you." I'm so mentally and physically depleted that my curse is a mere whisper.

Abigail smiles, nodding to the table. "We might get to that later. I'd love to be the one to take your sweet virginity. Or ruin your ass with iron." She clicks her tongue. "It won't have the same effect as it does on a fae, but..." her blue eyes light up. "Oh, but we could use silver."

The witch is fucking psychotic.

When she runs the edge of the blade across my stomach, and my skin sizzles from the silver. I whimper against the pain, jerking against my bonds. I eye her warily when she walks over to the counter and replaces the knife with a phallus-looking device. My insides congeal with fear.

'*Give me control, Cellica,*' Moe rages, but I ignore him.

My greatest nightmare is not the torture devices the witch laid out on the table to taunt me. No. I would readily take whatever pain she wished to dole out to avoid a repeat performance that terrifies me down to my bones. Is she trying to enslave me with lust so I'll willingly do her bidding? Is that Moe's plan as well?

His betrayal hurts the greatest. He said he did it to gain strength, but it's like a thousand tiny cuts on my soul. I trusted him. Foolishly believed he cared for me. For Nox. But all the fucker really cares about is his next orgasm, being fucked, and getting his cock stroked by whoever is around.

'*Cellica, I'm sorry,*' Moe whispers in my mind, and even though I sense his remorse, I harden my heart to it.

'*Don't fucking talk to me. I hate you right now.*'

'*I admit, I lost control. It just felt so good and as I said, I needed the recharge.*'

'*I don't fucking care,*' I growl as more tears slip down my cheeks. *You raped me. Almost took what doesn't belong to you.*'

Silence.

'*Yes, but I didn't,*' he has the gall to say. '*And you have to agree, it's been one of your recurring fantasies since I took up residence—being taken by two people.*'

'*Yes, Moe. By Nox and you. Not my goddamn enemy, you son of a bitch!*' I scream at him, my rage so big it's hard to keep inside. I sense the darkness threatening to balloon out of control, and I almost welcome it. My wolf whimpers, her fierceness overshadowed by Moe and my anguish.

Silence again, as if he's choosing his words carefully.

Abigail runs the silver dildo across my sex. I cry out against the pain as my flesh sizzles.

'*You are right. But if you had given me control, I could have stopped it. I can end it now.*'

'*Bullshit. You couldn't stop it even if you wanted to, which you didn't, so don't lie to me. I perceive what you feel, remember?*'

'*Let me make it up to you,*' he coos, his hands caressing me from the inside, up over my waist to my breasts.

'*Don't you fucking dare,*' I growl and jerk against my bonds, my body swinging from the chains.

'*Then give me control.*'

'*I said no, Moe.*'

'*Your lips say no, but your body screams yes.*' He pinches my nipples, and I cry out. They are so painful from the cold and his roughness from before; it feels like he just shoved ice picks through the tips.

The sensation of warm fingers caressing my sex causes wetness to dampen my opening. Finally, I lose it, screaming at the top of my lungs, fearful I'll never quit.

'*Cellica!*' Moe snaps. '*Stop it.*'

But I ignore him, wailing and screeching my helplessness. My pain. My hurt. Nox walked away from me because of Moe and his friendship with my brother. In essence, he chose them over me.

Moe, the demon I foolishly believed I could trust, who cared for me, bonded to my wolf, violated me against my will. Effectively he craved his own gratification over me, no matter his reasons.

I can't... I can't take any more rejection, pain, or betrayal. From them or from my own damn body. I struggle relentlessly against the bonds as my agonized screams fill the room and my legs kick out at Abigail. The shackles dig deeper, and warm blood trickles down my arms, but I no longer feel the ache in my flesh, only the misery in my mind and heart.

Abigail clamps down on my thighs, the silver burning my inner thigh. "Settle down, dog," she demands. "We are just beginning."

My screams turn into hoarse moans of agony as she sears my clit again, and I drop my chin to my chest in defeat. They won. I can't deal with this anymore. The rendering of my soul is too much to bear. If I don't retreat, insanity will cloud my thoughts, and I will lose all that I am.

'*I grant you control, Asmodeus,*' I whisper brokenly before retreating deep into my subconscious, where I'm unable to discern anything. Where the dark pillows of nothingness cradle my soul and shield my mind against the horrors sure to come.

Chapter 30

Asmodeus

I think I broke my new toy.

Cellica's pain and misery prick at my conscience. I am not used to feeling this emotion, so I push it aside to glare at the bitch I want dead more than my desire to ease the wolf's fears.

I was truthful when I admitted I'd lost control. The second Abigail's lips touched Cellica's pussy it was like she'd taken my cock into her hot little mouth and sucked the life out of me. My eyes rolled back in my head, and my one prevailing thought was getting off.

If I'd been in my proper form, I would have taken both of them in a frenzy of hunger, not caring if I ripped Cellica's virginity from her against her will. And knowing Abi as I do, she would have relished the fucking, giving as fiercely as she took, from both of us.

But even with the distraction of my driving lust, my primary focus never faltered—gaining power and getting my vessel to safety. Cellica's adorable wolf scented the vampire the second he entered the concrete structure, and my dick hardened to stone in an instant. We crave the same thing, my little wolf and I, but with one distinction. Even though I desire her mate, I also wish to pleasure Cellica *together* more. To feel his cock sliding into her sex while I take her from behind, our movements in sync, stroking her, stroking us. For him to lick and suck her pussy, effectively stimulating my cock. And when Cellica wraps her lips around his engorged length, mine will be right there with her, licking and swallowing his delicious firmness or fingering her clit to orgasm at the same time.

Dear Lucifer, I crave that more than my next breath.

The sensation of Nox's presence washed over me and I lost focus, rubbing my hardness to fantasies I would do anything to bring to fruition. Which means I'm teasing Cellica's pussy while Abigail tortures her with silver, causing the lick of sweet pain to add fuel to my fire. Fortunately, my fragile little wolf has retreated so deep that she didn't even respond to the stimuli. Worry for her mental state deflates my raging erection in a second, and I concentrate on the bitch watching me with curiosity.

Does she realize a contingent of immortals has breached her compound, making their way through the numerous levels to get to her? I doubt it. She's too calm. Either that or confident enough in her abilities they are no threat. If that's the case, I need to draw on every iota of strength I possess to pull my power through Cellica and kill Troy's bitch. Another added benefit to our recent orgasms. Climax through a vessel doesn't juice me up as it does when I'm in my own body, but it will have to do.

If Cellica, or the strait-laced Nox, ever beheld my true form, the vampire would drop to his knees and beg for any ounce of my affection. The same with Cellica. Her desire for me would overshadow every other rational thought. Her lust would rule her, making her salivate for a taste of my body.

My beauty is legendary. My appeal is irresistible. Some claim it's a curse. I call it a gift. Do I require sex? Yes. And often or my strength wanes. But because of my magnificence and sexual allure, I never lack a partner willing to satiate my deviant needs in Hell. There isn't anything I haven't doled out, performed, or granted in the sex arena. Male or female, it matters not, although I love a sweet juicy pussy on my face as much as the next demon, but a cock will do in a pinch. Especially if it's the vampire's thick hardness ramming down my throat. I'd kill for a taste of his salty goodness. Unfortunately, I've never been allowed to maintain my true form on earth. Hence the reason I must possess someone to stay here.

"Well, he finally makes an appearance," Abigail purrs. "Did we traumatize the little virgin into retreating?"

"We both know that was your plan all along, witch."

"I couldn't have done it without your help, Asmodeus. Or should I call you 'Moe'?" she snickers.

"*My Prince* will do just fine."

"We don't have much time, demon. When the vampire Nox barrels into this room, I will perform a binding spell to attach you to him. I already unbound you from the pseudo werewolf earlier when I brought her to orgasm."

Son of a bitch. How did I not perceive the link breaking? And it seems Abi is well aware of the raid, which is surprising.

Wait. Pseudo werewolf? What is she playing at? I sense the bond with Cellica. It is as strong as the second she shifted. I want to laugh out loud. She does not know the wolf is fully immortal now or that our connection is unbreakable because of it. The witch is slipping.

Absolutely delicious.

"Remember the plan. Once you are in the Guardian, stay hidden until you are close to the vampire queen. Then and only then do you take over and slip the poison into her food."

"Why do you hate Nicole so much, Abi? As far as I know, she did nothing to you."

"My father chose her over me. The halfling's destiny became his obsession, to the point he allowed me to be taken by witches and never bothered to look for me, so focused on setting events in motion to ensure *her* birth. I should have been the next Oracle, not the filthy hybrid Viessa. He had a daughter, but he refused to acknowledge me in order to sire another. One linked to Nicole."

"If I remember rightly, you went dark, my kind of sinister, and he disowned you."

"I went dark *because* he disowned me!" she shouts, and I grin internally. Apparently, I hit a nerve. So fucking easy.

"And if I refuse to give up my current vessel?" I ask, working to keep a straight face because even if I could leave Cellica, it wouldn't be to possess Nox—although being inside the delicious vampire, teasing and touching him while we fucked Cellica would almost be worth the fallout—it would be as my true self, and the stupid little witch would drop to all fours and beg me to fuck her. Her centuries-old grudge or her daddy issues would shatter. Like every immortal about to barge into this room, she would fall under my spell.

Oh, what a visual. An orgy of epic proportions. Too bad I couldn't maintain my form long enough to enjoy it.

"You have no choice, demon. Not if you want Troy. You know, your supposed mate?"

"Yeah, I might have been a little hasty on that one. Sex can cloud one's reasoning."

Grunts and screams finally penetrate the thick door, and my insides tighten. They are close. Abigail realizes the same thing and scrambles for the table. Before I understand her intent, she shoves a large dagger deep into Cellica's gut. Pain slices through me as they kick the door inward with such force, it's blown across the room. The wolf doesn't even stir at the misery, and concern prickles my nape.

Our eyes lock. The dual-colored irises light up with fury at the sight of his mate hanging naked from chains. A blade hilt protrudes from her gut as blood pours around the projectile to stain the concrete a dark maroon.

His snarl electrifies my spirit, but Abi merely smiles. "Come any closer and I will spill her intestines all over the floor. *Ligare vires.*" She quickly whispers the spell to bind their powers. I watch the light drain from the vampire's eyes, his supernatural abilities gone. Along with the other immortals who pour into the room, forming a line against the exit. The legendary Moretti brothers, Kurtis Ruse, the shapeshifter king, and Liam Scott, Cellica's big brother and king of the werewolves.

"What is it you want, Abigail?" Logan asks, his bloody broadswords still clutched in both hands.

"Why, revenge, of course, you stupid vampire."

"You got your revenge," Sebastian states, and I realize two significant individuals are missing from their group. The Oracle and Satan. Hmmm, interesting. "Icarus is dead."

"You just don't get it, do you? But it will soon be clear." A violet glow rises from Cellica's feet to enshroud her body and encase the witch.

A shield? Really?

"Powers of the witches rise. Course unseen across the skies. Hear me beckon, hear my plea. Spirit Asmodeus, I summon thee!"

Oh fuck. The intensity of her spell wraps around my throat, squeezing with such force I suck in a desperate gasp of oxygen.

"By the power of the elements, I bind thee here and now to the vessel of my choosing be!"

No! Blackness swarms. The tie with Cellica's wolf bows taunt, refusing to release, ripping me in two. "Stop, Abigail!" I bellow, but she ignores my command.

"Guardians of the ancient towers, grant me now thy sacred powers! Let this spirit never be set free, for such is my will, and so mote it be!"

When the group charges in an effort to halt the spell, Abigail throws a ball of magic. It shoots through the barrier with ease and smacks Kurtis square in the chest. The force slams him into the opposite wall, his body lit up like a giant Christmas tree, knocking him unconscious.

Viessa slips into the room and kneels next to the big shifter, her amber glow working to dispel the violet fire before it consumes his life.

"Now, Darath!" Nox shouts, never taking his eyes from me.

When my king ducks through the doorway in full Satan form, Abigail reels back in terror, the knife slicing across Cellica's abdomen. Agony pierces through us, and my little wolf stirs for the first time.

'*No*,' I command. '*Stay down.*' She doesn't need to endure this after everything I've already put her through. The least I can do is take the suffering for her.

Lucifer quietly chants, his large palm held out toward Abigail, his red irises almost blinding. My king commands my attention so arduously, I don't notice Abigail frantically intonating a spell, her free hand outstretched and glowing.

"No!" Abi shouts. "I will kill her." But even as she screams her warning, the violet shield surrounding us melts, oozing onto the floor around the witch's feet.

As red-hot pain penetrates me from every angle, my spirit digs deep to hang on to Cellica. The fire in my belly consumes me, and I couldn't be more grateful my delicate little vessel stays buried, oblivious to the torment and agony I'm enduring.

When I think I can't take anymore, a vast portal opens, and a dark, familiar presence joins the room, one I would recognize anywhere. A creature I once assumed I was destined to spend eternity with. Now, I merely feel disgusted and furious that he's come to rescue his piece of shit witch. Again.

Relief floods Abigail's expression when she sees him. "My love," she whispers, and I grind Celica's teeth together.

Troy glances around the room, he nods to Lucifer before swinging back to me. "Asmodeus?" he says in a shocked gasp.

So he wasn't aware of his female's plans. Interesting.

His furious dark stare drops to his mate. "Abigail. What have you done?"

Her beaming smile falters in the face of his anger. "What needs doing," she responds.

If my agony wasn't so intense, I'd laugh at her show of insanity.

"Darath only restored your body because I vowed you would never come after them. And now I find you torturing one of their own possessed by Asmodeus?" His fists clench, and I see the misery and regret in his expression. "I can no longer save you, Abi."

"What? We are mated. *Bound.* You can't just stand there and allow them to kill me." Her fearful gaze darts to Lucifer.

"I have a special place waiting for you in Hell, Abigail," the Devil taunts with a wicked grin. "Let go of the blade or you will spend an eternity regretting it."

Big blue eyes widen before they bounce to Troy and then me. "I cannot do this without you, my love. Our combined power will destroy them all."

"Abi, please. Come to me. Let your revenge go. We have a chance at happiness."

"But she still lives," Abigail wails, manic darkness consuming her expression. "I will never be happy until the Halfling is dead."

Logan's growl is almost demonic in its intensity. "You will never come near my mate or son, witch. Your head will roll this night."

"Why are *you* here, Asmodeus?" Troy asks quietly, snagging my attention and that of everyone in the room.

Oh, fucking hell. My deal with the witch cannot come to light.

"I escaped to locate you." It's not a lie. It's just not my priority any longer. Do I still crave a connection with Troy? A part of me does, but my attachment to the wolf and her vampire overshadows what I experienced with him. "Cellica was the first vessel I came in contact with and then she transitioned before I could find another."

Again. Not a complete lie. Nox was my intended target per my agreement with the stupid witch. I was to possess Nox, stay dormant until I was close enough to the queen to drug her and transport her here for Abi to play with and then murder. In return, she'd bind me to Troy, and the three of us would live happily ever after. That is until I convinced Troy to kill the bitch.

"Ah," Abigail says. "That explains how you can resist my spell, but how easily you omit the major facets of our arrangement."

"Shut up, bitch," I growl, and she digs the knife deeper, forcing a guttural moan of pain from my lips.

"The truth is way more exciting."

"What arrangement?" Nox asks quietly, and I lift my regard to him. He's holding up a palm to stop Darath from whatever he was about to do and studies me intently. "What agreement, Moe?"

I swallow. "We don't have time for this. Cellica needs your blood. Kill this bitch."

Nox studies the witch, then the blade before dropping his hand.

"I cannot without harming Cellica," he mutters.

Abigail smiles, and what I see in the blue depths scares me more keenly than the wrath of my king.

"Abigail, no!" Troy shouts as she slides the knife horizontally across Cellica's abdomen. Nox charges with a roar, but he'll never reach her in time without his ability to trace. My little wolf's guts will cascade from her body and end her life.

It suddenly hits me. My spirit didn't just bind with Cellica's. I absolutely *adore* my innocent, brave werewolf. The thought of her light slowly ebbing from this world has me throwing my head back and wailing with demonic power, joining in Nox's misery.

Chapter 31

No. No. No.

Time slows, each step sluggish as I race across the room. Fear I won't make it clogs my heart, propelling me forward faster, needing to get to my wolf, feed her my blood, and pray it's enough.

Moe's roar emanates from Cellica when her stomach splits open just as I slam my hands against the damage, not caring my back is to the witch. I trust my friends will guard us.

"She felt nothing," the demon whispers in my ear as I work to keep the two sides of the wound closed, but my fingers are slick with her blood. "I made sure of it."

"And for that, I might let you live," I snarl. "Liam!" I shout, only to see him next to me, working on the irons to free her.

"We need your blood, Nox," Moe states, his voice growing fainter by the second.

"I know," I growl, mentally urging Liam to hurry the fuck up. I have no idea what is happening behind me with Abigail, Troy, or our team. Right now, my sole focus is keeping my mate alive.

When the shackles finally release, Kleora lays Viessa's long coat on the ground, and Liam eases her down on top of it. At the same time, I work to keep the deep, jagged wound from opening and spilling her intestines.

"Liam, take over. I need to get my blood into her."

His hands quickly replace mine, and I see tears streaming down his face, but he doesn't utter a sound, lost in his own grief. I have no words to offer him. If Cellica dies, my life is over. I wouldn't know how to move on from her light being snuffed from my heart. My existence.

Shoving my fears aside, I slit my wrist with my fang and place it over her mouth. Moe's eyes flash red in her whiskey depths before he latches on, sucking for all he's worth to get as much of my healing blood into her system. I hope it's enough. If she were a mere human, this injury would be fatal.

"Moe, is it working?" I ask, not caring I'm talking to the entity who brought this storm to my female. I'll deal with my rage at him later.

"She's buried deep, Christoph," he mumbles around my wrist. The sound of my name, in his dark gravelly tone, skates goose-bumps down my arms. "But your blood is healing her internal injuries. Soon the skin should close."

My shoulders drop in relief at his words. As long as she lives, we will deal with everything else together.

The demon continues to suck at my vein, his red irises brightening with each second, and my brows furrow when my cock twitches in response. I'm just responding to the visual of my mate drinking from me. Nothing more.

"The wound is closing," Liam exclaims, and I glance down her torso to witness the two sides of the opening stitching together.

The raw, damaged skin around her wrists where the shackles dug into her flesh is so covered in dried blood I can't tell if they healed or not. I do a quick assessment of her body but see no other injuries. Thank fuck, we must have arrived before the witch could utilize any of the torture devices on the table by the wall. When I spied the shiny silver tools, my blood ran cold.

"Retreat, Asmodeus. Bring Cellica forward," I order, tucking the Oracle's coat around my mate's nakedness.

"I'll try," he responds, closing his eyes to concentrate.

I glance over my shoulder to see Darath raise Abigail off the ground by her neck. His black skin radiates power, his sockets consumed by red, and his massive wings twitching to unfurl.

"Please, Lord Satan," the witch croaks out, her feet kicking at the air, her nails digging into his wrist. "Spare me, and I can be a powerful tool for your bidding."

A soft chanting snags my attention on the other side of the chamber. Viessa crouches over Kurtis's enormous frame, lying at an awkward angle on the concrete. The engravings on her back pulse with her power. Logan and Sebastian stand vigil next to them. Their anxious expressions cause my heart to drop into my gut.

A frantic Lucretia materializes in the room. The second her amber eyes land on her fallen mate, a cry escapes, and she slides to her knees next to her sister. "Kurtis. Oh, God."

"Give him your blood, Lu," Viessa urges, and the shifter queen rips open her wrist without a wince and places it over his lips, opening his mouth and massaging his throat to get him to swallow.

Come on, Kurtis, I mentally shout at him. *Fucking drink.*

I peer down at Cellica. Her lids remain closed as Moe attempts to make her rise from her subconscious before glancing at Liam. I don't have to say a word. He understands exactly what my heated regard is begging for.

"I've got her," he murmurs. "Go. Go do what your vampire—what *we* all demand."

Fire ignites in my eyes, lighting up his face. My fangs drop low in a snarl as I soar to my feet, draw my sword, and head toward the witch. The need for retribution, to slash and kill, burns a hole in my gut.

Troy steps in my path, his eyes a demonic black. "Nox, please reconsider. I know she has taken much, but allow me to deal with her. I can make sure we disappear, never to return. I vow it."

I growl. "Your vows mean nothing, *Witch*. Get the fuck out of my way or your head will roll with hers."

Troy slaps his palm in the center of my chest, whispering nonsensical words. Fire ignites in my torso, spreading with a swiftness throughout my body. Jesus, his power is immense.

Cellica's sudden, agonized shout stabs through my heart. I peer over my shoulder to witness her spine arch, agony contorting her beautiful face, and her mouth opening wide in a silent scream.

"I regret what my female has done, old friend, but I cannot allow you to hurt her."

I swing my focus to Troy, blocking my path. How dare he say that to me? After everything, we've been through? After the immense turmoil his bitch has caused?

Absolute rage clouds my vision, and before I realize what I'm doing, I rear back and sink my sword deep into Troy's gut until it protrudes from his spine. His eyes widen in shock, and a part of me feels regret at ending his long life. But the visual of Cellica's insides threatening to ooze from her body snuff every emotion but vengeance.

"NO!" Abigail screams, going limp in Darath's hold.

An unrelenting fury rides my actions as I rip the blade from the male's flesh, spin with the sword raised over my head, to bring it down across Troy's neck. I observe with a detached sort of sadness as his head hits the hard concrete with a sickening splat before wobbling into a corner.

Well goddamn. That hurt more than I thought it would.

"Troy!" the witch screams, her hands igniting in purple fire. She torches Lucifer, who roars and flings her across the room. Her back slams into the brick wall and Kleora's arrows pin her arms before she can recover.

"I will fucking kill you all, and your bitch queen!" she shrieks, struggling against the projectiles shot with such force they embedded deep in the bricks.

I approach the witch with slow, sure strides, her arms splayed wide. Three feet from her, I fix her with my bright gaze. The agony and horror in Abigail's expression pleases me, and as much as I'd like to draw this out, savor this kill, Cellica needs me. I twirl the sword with a malevolent grin and back up a step to give myself room.

"You...you killed my mate," she rages, a purple light flickering in one of her palms.

"You tortured and tried to slay mine," I respond quietly. Ice pulsates in my veins even as a strange, inky darkness spreads throughout my soul, seeming to take over.

Her laugh is manic, grating along my nerves, forcing the malevolence to ignite in a burst of power. "I didn't torture your mate, vampire. I..." Before she finishes the sentence, I leap at her and slam my fist into her jaw, snapping her skull to the side. The only thing keeping her upright is Kleora's well-placed arrows.

She spits blood before raising her gaze at me with smug defiance. "I pleasured your succulent female with my mouth and she came all over my face," she cackles, and I lose my last hold on sanity.

No one stops me. They stand strong to bear witness to my vengeance as I swing my arm with a victorious snarl. Before the Damascus steel slices through skin, muscle, and bone like it was paper, the wall shimmers behind her, sucking her and the concrete blocks into the void. I roar with anger at being denied the chance to end her once and for all. With a heaving chest, I glare through the gaping hole into the next room.

Fuck. No telling where and when that bitch will show up again. One thing is for certain—she's not done yet.

I stare at Troy's dark, sightless eyes, and something catches in my chest, but I squelch it. He made his choice. He picked a side. It just happened to be the wrong one. The incorrect decision cost him his life. *She* cost him his head.

I watch as Lucifer steps over Troy's body like he's inconsequential before stopping a foot from me. I crane my neck to look up into the cruel beauty of the Devil as his enormous hand comes down on my shoulder. Something inside me shudders.

"You are a true mate, Asmodeus. You attempted to avenge your wolf, but now you must release Nox."

Wait. What?

"What the hell are you talking about, Darath?" Dread drops like a led weight in my gut, and my eyes widen. "That fucker possessed me?" I respond with a growl.

"Not by choice, I'm afraid. Troy siphoned him from Cellica and placed him in you before you took his head. He wrongly assumed their previous bond would hold sway and he could convince him to spare her life."

"But how could he do that so quickly when Abigail tried for hours to get to me… him?" My confusion over my identity is proof I'm not alone in here. It's the weirdest sensation.

When I stalked Abigail, I felt this strange darkness rise up inside me but never actually experienced Moe's presence. I still don't.

"Troy was ten times more powerful than Abigail. He just never cared to reveal all his might to the world the way she did. His downfall was his love for her. It blinded him to the real threat—Asmodeus and you."

"What do you mean?"

"Your rage over Cellica powered Asmodeus. You alone would've never destroyed Troy. He was innocent of Abigail's crimes. But the Prince felt betrayed by Troy for choosing the witch over him time and time again. Combined, the volatile emotions consumed you both. He took his revenge as you tried to take yours."

"Where he succeeded, I failed."

"For now, young vampire."

"Liam." Viessa's frantic call has us all glancing over with worry.

"Do something, Oracle," Logan bellows, and the werewolf rushes to his mate's side in an instant.

I bend down, gather the bloodied coat around Cellica's body, and pick her up in my arms before striding over to see what's going on with Kurtis.

The stillness of my friend terrifies me, as well as the tears streaming down Lu's cheeks.

"What happened?" Liam asks. "Is he okay?"

"I... I don't know what else to do? Abigail's magic damaged his heart, and mine is not healing it."

"And Cellica won't wake up," Liam utters, worry etched in every line of his face, matching my own as I glance down at the bundle in my arms.

"Nox, we must take care of Asmodeus," Lucifer insists.

"Wait a goddamn minute, Jag," I shout back, uncaring, I just growled at the Devil. "Fix Cellica first."

"I cannot until the Prince is where he belongs." His irritation is pissing me off.

I spin with my treasured load and face off with Satan. Probably not a brilliant move. "We can't waste precious time while you cart your demon to Hell."

"What I mean is, the only one who can revive your mate *is* Asmodeus. Therefore, I must rejoin him with Cellica's wolf, or they will both perish."

"What the fuck are you talking about?"

"Asmodeus bonded with Cellica and her wolf when she transitioned, fusing them all together. Just as Cellica can't survive away from her wolf, neither will she survive without the demon. Nor will he."

Fuck. I could still lose her?

"He suffers inside you, infused with pain at being ripped from his other half," Lucifer explains. His deep, grating voice washes over me. "As does Cellica."

"Do we have time to trace her out of here and do whatever the fuck you're gonna do somewhere warm? She's frozen."

"Of course," he says.

"Converge at the castle," Sebastian commands, shoving his swords into the sheath at his back and bending to pick up Kurtis. Lu clutches his hand in desperation. "Dawn will arrive soon."

Cradling my precious wolf tight against my chest, I scatter our molecules and head straight for my room. I must save her. No matter what it takes.

Suppose Moe is bound to Cellica, and they can't survive without each other as Darath proclaimed. In that case, I have some serious decisions to make. Because even though the thought of sharing her with the demon enrages me, I won't endure a life deprived of my mate by my side.

Chapter 32

Nox

Without easing my hold on Cellica, I hunch down and get a fire going in the fireplace against the wall facing the end of my bed. Worry over Kurtis's condition plagues my mind, but if anybody can pull through, it's the big shifter. My first priority is to see to my mate's needs, then I'll check in on my friend.

Once the fire is blazing, I grab a pair of my sweats and a t-shirt along with a pair of thick winter socks from my dresser and toss them on the bed before strolling into the bathroom and flipping the hot water on high in the shower.

Sitting on the edge of the tub, I unwrap the blood-soaked coat from her body to examine the wound. I am relieved to see it's just a raised pink line now. With more of my blood, it should be gone by tomorrow.

Through it all, Cellica doesn't even stir and my heart constricts. "Please don't leave me, baby girl," I whisper and brush a blue lock behind her ear. "I need you."

'*As do I*,' the now familiar voice whispers in my mind and I jerk at the sensation. I'm used to having Nicole intrude in my skull, barking orders, or teasing me with her sarcasm, but to have a male voice in my head, seeming to come from everywhere, is downright bizarre. Between her own thoughts, her wolf's primal instincts, and Moe, how does Cellica separate them out and keep from going insane?

I rise, and awkwardly undress while keeping a tight hold on my female. The others will be here any minute, but I need to get the blood rinsed off my wolf. It's a constant reminder of what I almost lost.

"Asmodeus, while I take care of my mate, we need to have a little chat," I say, adjusting the temperature before dropping the coat on the floor and stepping under the warm spray, Cellica cradled against my chest.

'Not functioning on all cylinders, vampire, but I will try.'

My brow furrows at how weak he sounds. "Suck it up, demon," I growl at him. "You need to be strong for her."

'I know,' he sighs. *'State your demands,'*

Before I answer, I lower Cellica's feet to the tile floor, holding her tight against my chest as I tilt her head back under the spray, careful to keep the water out of her face. There's no way I can shampoo her hair and hold on to her at the same time, she will have to do that later when she wakes up. And she *will* wake up.

I grab the bar of soap, and with my foot on the low bench, I sit her on my leg like a puppet. Her head rests on my shoulder as I rub the soap over her belly where the wound that nearly took her from me still mars her perfect skin, and down her legs to wash away the blood. Remembering the witch's words, I run the soap over her sex to wash away her vile touch.

I work to keep a clinical filter over my brain as I wash her luscious body.

Is my dick rock hard? Yes. But since I prefer my partner conscious and an active participant, I merely admire the beauty of her body as I clean the sweat and blood from her skin.

"Was Abigail lying when she said she went down on Cellica?" Why I'm asking that question, I don't know, but it burned into my brain the second she uttered it. The demon seems to hesitate. "Moe?"

"*No.*"

"Why do I feel like there's more to the story you're not telling me?"

'*I may have revved things up a bit,*' he mutters, and I sense his guilt.

I grit my teeth against my immediate anger. "What did you do?"

"*Cel didn't want what happened, but I'm the demon of lust and I need to get off on a regular basis. It's like with a succubus. Sex is their fuel source. Without it, they die. If it had just been Abi seducing her, our wolf would've fought tooth and nail, but I ramped up her endorphins, seducing her from the inside until her body betrayed her even though her mind raged at me to stop.*"

He pauses and I grit my teeth, wanting to rip the fucker to shreds for violating her.

'*I told myself I did it to gain the strength I would need to fight Abi, but afterward, I felt something I've never felt before—shame. Remorse. Guilt. I was so damn sorry for what I did. I apologized to her and now I'm asking for your forgiveness as well, Nox. Cellica loves you and I want to make this work. I want her to be happy.*'

I'm so livid I can't speak. Instead, I finish rinsing us both, pick her back up and step out of the shower, wrapping her up in a fluffy towel. As I dry her, Moe's words penetrate the rage. Cellica loves me? Does she understand the difference between the mate bond and genuine emotions? God, I hope so, because I crave more.

With sure strides, I head back into my room and gently lay her on the bed. I toss the towel in the corner and dress her in my clothes as quickly as possible.

'*Nox, did you hear me? I'm sorry.*'

"You've done nothing but manipulate the both of us from the second you hijacked her body. I can't bear the sound of your voice right now. Shut up and go sit in a corner until I call you forth," I growl, pissed beyond words.

'*Are you going to discipline me, Sir?*' he murmurs and my head nearly explodes.

I yank on a pair of gray sweats, not bothering with a shirt since the fire has warmed up my room nicely.

'*Shit. I'm sorry. I can't help it.*'

"Shut the fuck up, Moe," I demand in a fierce whisper, scenting the approach of the others. I tuck my mate beneath the covers just as a knock taps on the door.

Before I can say come in, Liam barges through the entrance, his gaze zeroing in on his sister in my bed. "You bathed her?" he asks between clenched teeth.

"Of course. Blood covered her skin," I frown. I don't need Liam's fucking attitude. I'm already ruffled by Asmodeus' comments.

He and that bitch violated my little mate, forced her to orgasm. Knowing her, the guilt she endured was far worse than the act itself. I don't blame Cellica. I place guilt where it rightfully belongs—at Abigail and Moe's feet.

Back in his normal form, Darath ducks through the entryway decked out in a black three-piece suit, white shirt, and red tie the color of his eyes. One by one, the individuals as close as any family file into the room, making way for a very pregnant Nicole cradled in Logan's arms and dressed in a long nightshirt, that I suspect is Logan's, and black leggings. He sets her in the chair by the fire with such ease it's almost painful to watch. Nicole peers over at me and rolls her eyes. I smile for the first time in what feels like weeks.

"We are here for support," she states, rubbing her belly. "Have you spoken to the demon inside you, Nox?"

"Briefly," I admit.

"Is he going to cooperate?" Sebastian asks with a raised eyebrow.

"He needs her as much as she needs him, so yeah, he'll do what must be done."

Viessa steps forward, her features drawn tight with worry. "Nox, may I speak with Asmodeus?"

I eye her warily. "How is Kurtis?" I ask first.

Tears gather in her eyes and she shakes her head. "Not good. Lu took him to her room. Only she can help him now."

Fuck.

A heaviness slams into my chest. I've lost fellow soldiers in battle. It hurts, but I understood it was expected. If Kurtis dies... I can't even finish the thought. Instead, I focus on the Oracle and her inquiry.

"He's very weak, Viessa, so he can't take control, but I can relay his answers."

"Fucking eh, this is so weird," Alex whispers, stepping closer to Sebastian, who wraps his arm around her shoulders.

"Asmodeus, you broke your word and killed the one vessel with the ability to detach you from Cellica." Her harsh tone surprises me. Viessa is always so soft-spoken and humble in the presence of others. And what does she mean *to detach* him from Cellica? I thought that wasn't possible now.

"You're making deals with my demons, Oracle?" Darath asks with a frown.

"Asmodeus agreed to aid the council in locating the breeder females. In exchange, he'd be bound to Troy permanently."

"Wait," Nicole pipes in. "I thought it bonded with Cellica and if they separated, they would both die?"

"Very true, my lady," Viessa answers. "But Troy has successfully unbound a demon in the past. So I hoped he'd do it again."

"Detaching a demon from a human is easy peasy," Darath says. "But severing a link between a Prince of Hell and an immortal has never been done before."

"It has, King Darath. *Once* before. Although never with a newly shifted immortal." She turns back to me, her amber eyes hard, unrelenting. "Troy destroyed the link to you, Asmodeus. Otherwise, you could have never left him permanently. He craved Abigail. His true mate."

An eerie stillness settles in my center. Moe's emotions run the gambit. Disbelief. Anger. Denial. Sadness. And finally, acceptance. I want to tell him I'm sorry, but I've yet to learn how to communicate with him mentally, so I say nothing. Besides, I'm still pissed at the motherfucker.

A hushed, expectant silence blankets the group as we all wait for Moe's response to Viessa's revelation. We killed the one entity with the ability to sever his connection to my mate.

Son of a fucking bitch.

"I'm sorry to deliver such devastating news to you, Asmodeus," Viessa states coldly, clearly not sorry at all.

The Oracle is not a big supporter of demons in general. She and Darath butted heads a few times in the past and rightly so, since he snatched his mate's soul from entering Heaven and Viessa is the mouthpiece of the gods.

"But I need to know if you still plan on helping the council in their search. Only a Prince can detect their underlying power."

"So you're saying there is no way to set Moe free now?" I ask.

'*Still eager to get rid of me, vampire?*' the demon murmurs, sorrow in every syllable.

Am I livid at him for his shenanigans? Fuck, yes. Would I prefer him out of our lives? Again, fuck yes. I peer over at my unconscious mate, recalling what she said the last time I laid down an ultimatum.

Whether I like it or not, Cellica has formed an emotional attachment to the demon. She believes he bolsters her courage, makes her fearless and able to voice and act out her inner desires.

I can't lie. I relished and benefited from her newfound sexual confidence. Would her inner desires have come out on their own? Probably, with some gentle coaxing from me, but there's no denying Cellica thinks she wants… no, she needs him and it would hurt her physically and mentally to lose him.

I will always choose her happiness over my own. Moe seems amenable to my dictates, my commands. If I lay down the ground rules, we might be able to make this work. After having him inside me, my tolerance for him has raised an inch. Will he push my buttons and fuck with me? Yes and often. But with Cellica's help, we can make an unpleasant situation endurable.

"Moe?" Alex giggles. "I like it."

Sebastian smirks down at her, tweaking her pointed ear.

"Troy was the only individual with the knowledge and power," Viessa confirms. "But I promise to scour every source available to me to discover a way to reverse their bond if that is what you desire."

"Moe agrees to help in the search if Cellica is willing," I say, not caring if he does or not. The females we seek are important to not only our race, but many other races as well. With the number of miscarriages, stillborns, and mother's deaths during delivery on the rise, we need these humans with the ability to breed with our kind now more than ever. Our numbers are dwindling fast.

'*Yeah, what he said,*' Moe agrees with a weak moan.

"So how do we transfer Moe back into Cellica?"

"There is only one spell I know of with the power to link souls," Darath states. "But the longer we sit here chitchatting, the more they weaken and the odds of success disintegrate."

"What do I need to do?" I ask.

Darath glances at Liam with a devilish smirk before addressing me. "Strip boy, you're about to have sex with your mate."

"What?" I exclaim.

"Not funny, Jag," Liam growls.

"Oh shit," Nicole exclaims with a laugh. "He's fucking serious."

Darath sits on the edge of the bed, patting the mattress with his big palm, his eyebrows wiggling up and down. "Time to claim your mate, Nox. It's the only way to transfer him from you to her. Your threesome is about to begin."

Chapter 33

"**I**'m not fucking having sex with my mate while she's unconscious," I growl at him. "Or with a goddamn audience."

"Unfortunately, I need to be here to perform the spell and guide Asmodeus since he is so weak, but the others will leave."

"Lame," Alex mutters.

"I can rouse her spirit enough so she is lucid before I go," Viessa states as she strolls to the other side of the bed.

"Damn straight. Because I am not doing this without her consent," I respond, rubbing the back of my neck. This situation is totally fucked up. Cellica lost authority over what happened to her at the hotel with the werewolves and at the bunker, so I refuse to mate with her unless it's what she truly desires.

"Agreed," Liam says, and for once, we are in total accord regarding Cellica.

Viessa places her palm over my mate's forehead. Then, with her eyes closed, she softly chants. The amber glows from beneath her hand, brightens Cellica's face. From the other side of the bed, Darath watches the Oracle with curiosity.

My breath hitches when my wolf's lids flutter and a soft moan escapes her lips.

'Ah. There's our girl,' Moe sighs in relief.

"My girl, you bastard," I mutter under my breath, and Liam frowns at me, but I shake my head, and we both refocus on Cellica.

I didn't get the opportunity to lay the ground rules with the demon before everyone converged in my room, and apprehension claws at my insides. As much as I loathe him being involved in our lives, Cellica now requires him. But she has an issue with putting her foot down where he's concerned, and his growing attachment to me is disconcerting. I don't bat for that team, and his sexual innuendos and involvement in our intimate encounters drive me insane. If Cellica and I hope to have a chance at a relationship, something needs to change.

"Jag, can I speak with you privately?" I ask.

His ruby eyes pin mine. "Of course," he says, rising to his feet to follow me into the bathroom. I don't want to leave my wolf's side, but I need a working understanding of how I can control Moe once he's back in Cellica because she gives the demon too much of a leash.

"I must warn you, Nox," Darath says loudly as I close the door. "Kleora is extremely jealous, so whatever you have planned for us in here, best to keep your moans to a minimum."

I snort at his wicked grin.

"I have enough issues with Asmodeus. I don't need to add you to the mix, Jag."

"Pity," he pouts before sobering. "How can I be of assistance?"

"Cellica has proven she can't command Moe, despite your tutelage. Is there a way I can direct him when he's inside her?"

Darath sighs. "I wish I could tell you, yes, but only the vessel has ultimate control over the demon, especially a bonded Prince of Hell. But I might persuade him to heed your commands."

"Do it," I growl, running my fingers through my hair in frustration.

'I will behave, Christoph. I swear,' Moe whispers.

"Yeah, I don't believe you for a damn second," I answer, and Darath tilts his head, studying me like a bug under a microscope.

"May I?" he asks, holding out his hands to my neck. I nod, and he grips both sides hard enough to make me wince.

His cardinal irises brighten, and I find I can't look away. In fact, I grip Darath's waist in eager anticipation. Of what I have no clue, but if someone were to walk in here, it would appear as if the king of Hell and I were having an intimate moment.

"Asmodeus." Darath's tone is all demonic. A shiver runs down my spine, and I'm appalled to discover my dick is rock hard. "Hear and obey your king."

"Yes, my lord," the demon utters through my lips. Okay. I'm not the one reacting to Darath with submissive eagerness. It's Moe. Thank fuck.

"Heed the commands of Cellica's Alpha. When she submits, you submit. Cellica is your Mistress, but Nox is your Master in all things." My dick twitches when Darath steps closer, his eyes blinding. "Do you understand?"

"Yes, my lord," Moe utters.

The thoughts running through the demon's head have me gripping Darath's waist tighter. Moe wants nothing more than to drop to his knees and worship his king with his mouth. I nearly gag at the thought of Lucifer's cock down my throat even as my dick pulses with the need to be free.

"Can I encourage or make suggestions to enhance a situation?" Asmodeus asks quietly.

"Absolutely. Pleasure is the goal, but only with consent. Understand?"

"Yes, Lord Lucifer. I hear and obey."

When Darath releases me and steps back, I stagger with him, my grip on his waist refusing to let go. The Devil smirks. "Sorry, friend. I just don't love you that much," he teases before gently removing my hands from his sides. I lurch backward, appalled by my… no, by the demon's actions.

Good lord. Has Darath fucked Asmodeus in the past?

'*Oh yes*,' Moe breathes. '*He subjugated all the Princes of Hell. Sometimes for pure pleasure, other times to discipline us for wrongdoings. Either was fucking incredible.*'

"Too much information, Moe," I groan and will my erection away before opening the bathroom door. Darath's deep chuckle follows me out.

My gaze zeros on Cellica sitting up against the headboard, and my chest swells with relief.

"Hey," she says with an awkward wave, her lids lowering.

"Hey, back." The dark circles under her eyes and the paleness of her skin worry me. But I keep my concerns hidden and sit on the edge of the mattress while Darath strolls to the other side to mirror me.

"Nox," Cellica whispers, tears threatening to overflow. "I can't feel Moe anymore. I'm just… empty." She rubs at her chest as if it aches, and my jaw clenches at the realization of how deep Cellica's emotional attachment is to the demon. Jealousy burns my throat, but I shove it aside.

"I know, baby girl. Currently, he's with me." Her eyes widen, roaming my face as if she could see him. "But we are going to put him back with you, okay? If we don't you both will… die." Just saying the words sends pain spiraling through my veins.

"H-how did that happen?" she asks.

"Cellica," Darath snags her attention. "We do not have time to explain. We have to perform the ritual to rejoin you two."

"Great. What do I need to do?"

"You must…."

I hold up my hand to stop him. "Anyone who doesn't need to be in here, can you please clear the room?"

"We will just be upstairs in Nicole and Logan's suite, okay, Cel?" Liam declares, squeezing her foot reassuringly.

When she nods, big brother leads everyone from the room.

"Damn it," Nicole mutters as Logan lifts her in his arms. "I wanted to grab some popcorn and watch a live porno."

"Not in your delicate condition," the warrior states, striding for the exit.

"The minute this kid is out of me, you better...." The door shuts, cutting off the rest, leaving the three of us... technically four of us, alone.

"What did she mean?" Cellica asks, her gaze bouncing between me and Darath, a frown marring her forehead.

"Cel," I begin. "In order to put Moe back in you, we need to complete the mating ritual."

She blinks several times. "You're referring to the... the sex, biting, and blood thing?" A deep blush stains her cheeks as Darath chuckles. "If that's the case, why are you still in here, King Darath?"

"I must control Asmodeus. He is too weak at the moment and might not have the strength to perform the... jump, for lack of a better word. Don't worry, I will keep my eyes closed the whole time," he grins.

"I fucking doubt it," I respond before scooting up the bed closer to Cellica. "The point is, I wanted to make absolutely sure you were on board with this. Once mated, there is no undoing it. You will be fully mine until my dying breath. We will perceive each other's emotions as our own, be able to communicate telepathically, and... I'll need to drink from you regularly."

She eyes me for several seconds, her expression closed off, and I find it difficult to discern what she is feeling. "Are *you* okay with this?" she asks quietly.

"The alternative is unacceptable."

"That's not what I asked, Chris," she whispers.

"Cellica," I take her hand in mine. "I would do anything to protect you."

She closes her eyes briefly as if in pain, and Darath puffs out a frustrated sigh but says nothing.

'What are you doing, Nox?' Moe groans. *'Fucking express how you feel. I'm in your head, remember? Reveal to her she is your universe and that without her, your life is nothing but darkness. Fucking tell her how much you love her, dumbass.'*

"When Abigail chained me to the ceiling," she announces, her gaze lowered to our hands intertwined. "Not grasping whether I was going to live or die." Cellica's whiskey irises lift to spear through me. "My one comforting thought was knowing you were looking for me. I never doubted, for a second, you wouldn't find me. I'm your one true mate. Your inner vampire would never rest until I was safe." She swallows, her strength visibly dwindling. "But I hoped it was for a different reason. That you actually cared for me and not out of obligation or a damn biological link. I'm sure it doesn't come as a big shock, but I love you, Christoph Nox. Even so, I refuse to bind you to me just for the sake of saving my life. We will discover another way."

"Cellica," I groan, my heart bursting at her confession. "I am such a fool." I grip her hand tighter. "I put my friendship with Liam ahead of my wants and needs. Of yours. I deluded myself into thinking I was doing the honorable thing by keeping my distance because you were too young. Fuck Cel, you hadn't even transitioned until recently."

I brush a lock of hair, still damp from our shower, behind her ear before gripping her chin. "Despite all my good intentions, I couldn't stay away from you, no matter how hard I tried. Every time I was at the ranch, I prayed for a glimpse of you. Your timid blushes, sweet smiles, and even your outrage when I called you kid."

"But you were always so mean to me," she whispers as a tear rolls down her cheek, crushing me.

"It was the only way I could keep Liam from suspecting my feelings for you. No matter how much your presence fired my lust, I had to carry the anger like a wall between us or I would've fallen to my knees and begged for any small scrap of your affection." I sigh and rub my nape. "And then Moe fell into the picture, adding an additional layer of brick to that wall. I worship you, baby girl, but the mere notion of another involved messed with my brain. I didn't understand your desire or your need for him. And to be honest, I still don't. You are perfect all on your own. I fell in love with you long before Asmodeus joined us. Your inner fire. Your resilience and drive. Your innocence and naivety. Those are the traits I adore."

Tears stream down her cheeks, and she inhales a deep breath. "But I would never have been able to say or do the things I did without Moe. I need him. I love him. Not as deeply as I do you, but we bonded nonetheless. Can you accept he's a part of me, a part of us?"

I shrug. "I'm not going to lie and claim it will be easy, but I'm willing to work through it to be with you. I choose you. Nothing else matters."

She smiles, and a weight lifts from my shoulders. I would sacrifice, kill, or maim anyone to witness that smile every day for the rest of my existence. To be the reason it brightens her face. I don't deserve the look of adoration in her eyes, but I'll take it just the same.

"One more thing," she whispers, another blush darkening her cheeks as she shoots a shy glance at Darath before picking at the comforter. "Since we are about to mate, I thought it might be prudent to inform you... to tell you that I'm a... a virgin."

Thank all the gods. Moe said as much, but hearing the words from her lips and knowing I'm blessed to be her first and last suffuses my soul with warmth and I can't contain my grin.

"Congratulations, Nox," Darath murmurs, and for once, he seems sincere. Although I really wish he wasn't in the room right now.

"Baby girl? Look at me." When she immediately obeys, my cock hardens. "Your confession pleases me. I'm honored to be your first and only. Thank you for bestowing upon me the wondrous gift of your innocence. And despite the circumstances," I dart a glare at Darath. "I will make your initial time as pleasurable as possible."

'*We will,*' Moe interjects.

"We will," I amend aloud, pointing at my chest so she understands I don't mean the Devil about to bear witness to her deflowering.

"Now that we have the emotional shit out of the way," Darath says, rising next to the bed. "Let us get down to the nitty-gritty of fucking, shall we?"

Chapter 34

Cellica

Oh. My. God. I'm about to have sex with the male I've lusted after since the moment I laid eyes on him, and we have a damn voyeur in the room. The king of Hell has a front-row seat to the spectacle of me losing my virginity.

UGH.

"Do you have to stand so fucking close, Darath?" Nox growls in annoyance as if sensing my unease.

The demon king sighs dramatically. "Since you are both such prudes about this, I will wait in the hall with Kleora. When you have your dick buried, Nox, and you are ready to claim her with your bite, holler, and I will quietly slip in and help Asmodeus."

My shoulders relax somewhat. Thank the fucking stars.

The second the door shuts, I turn back to Chris, my nerves ramping up. What if I suck at this? I want to please him, but I'm not sure how.

Nox rises, and I hold my breath, thinking he's about to drop the sweats, but he merely grabs his phone and fiddles with it for several agonizing seconds before setting it in a docking unit on the nightstand. When the sexy notes of Ride by SoMo fill the room, the knot between my shoulders loosens even more, and I laugh.

He turns it up with a smile before dropping his knee to the mattress. "No one can hear your moans of pleasure now but me," he whispers against my ear, and a shiver dances down my spine. His lips press against my pulse point, and I tilt my neck to give him better access.

The nervous flutters in my gut morph into spasms of anticipation. I've dreamed of this moment, and I won't allow anything or anyone to spoil it. Not even me.

Nox lifts his knee, flips the blankets to the end of the mattress, grabs me by my knees, and drags me down the headboard until I'm lying prone. I'm practically hyperventilating as he comes over me with such control and grace. It's almost as if he's floating. The mismatched irises burn with desire, and his fangs peek through his slightly parted lips.

"You are so fucking beautiful, Cellica," he moans, easing down until his lower body is flush with mine.

I spread my thighs, and he nestles his hips between them. When his solid length pushes against my sex, my eyes widen. Shit. I forgot how big he is. Will it even fit?

He rests his upper body on his elbows, and I can't deny my desire to explore his bare skin a second longer. Hard muscles twitch when my fingers travel over his ribs, tracing the beautiful tattoo.

"Fuck yes. Touch me, baby girl."

His groan liberates me, and I boldly run my hands up and down his back, loving the feel of the thick muscles flexing with each pass. Finally, his face lowers, and I hold my breath, gazing into the turquoise and blue glow.

His kiss is gentle, a simple brushing of his lips against mine. Even though my body trembles with the unknown, I groan, needing more. The kiss intensifies, and my mouth opens to his. His tongue sweeps in to dance with mine, and another needy moan escapes. The ache between my legs is almost unbearable, it demands relief, so I unashamedly gyrate my hips, seeking that impressive hardness. When it runs over my clit, the friction of the cotton scraping in such an exquisite way, I break the kiss and tilt my head back with a sob, clutching his ass to pull him tighter against me.

"That's it, Cel. Take what you need."

A large palm slides under the borrowed shirt, finding my breast as his hips set up a delicious rhythm while his lips suck and nip down my neck. "Chris," I gasp when his fingers tweak my nipple, shooting intense pleasure straight to my clit.

Nox sits up, straddling my hips. My gaze devours his sculpted chest and abdomen before widening at the enormous tent in his sweatpants.

Jesus.

He whips the burrowed shirt up over my head in record time, and when those striking irises zero in on my bare breasts, they brighten with need. "God, you've got the greatest tits, Cellica," he says, bending to latch onto a nipple, sucking it deep into his hot mouth. I cry out, arching my back and gripping his biceps at the exquisite sensation. "I could lick, suck, and bite them all night."

When he pinches the other at the same time, I nearly come out of my skin at the fire he ignites in my body, and my sex floods with desire. It throbs, shouting at me to relieve the building inferno spreading through my veins.

I allow my lust to take over, shutting off the part of my brain that says I'm not good enough to hold a male like Nox's attention for long and tentatively trace his erection through the sweatpants with my fingers. I crave to give him as much pleasure as he's giving me right now.

He groans, thrusting against my hand. "Open my pants and take me in your hand, baby. I need to feel your fingers gripping my skin."

I swallow and do as he commands. The second my fingers contact his cock, his moan deepens, causing shivers to dance along my skin.

"Fuck, Cellica. Look what you do to me," he whispers before sitting back, still straddling my legs, giving me more room to play. And I do. *Look*, I mean. My eyes nearly pop out of my head at the sheer size. I can barely reach all the way around his girth. But I am enamored by the silky skin stretched over the cast iron, and I lick my lips at the drop of pre-cum emerging from the tip, daring me to taste.

"You look like you crave my cock in your mouth, baby girl."

"Yes, Daddy," I reply automatically, and my sex clenches at his answering growl of approval.

"Have you ever given head before?" he asks, and heat spreads over my cheeks.

"No. Teach me?"

"Just a taste, because I have other plans for you."

When he clasps the headboard with one hand, leaning up over me and gripping his hardness in his other to guide it to my salivating mouth, my pussy flutters at the sight of him. Ripped muscles quiver. The intricate tattoo up his ribcage, chest, and arm adds to his sex appeal, but it's his cock that grabs my attention. When he taps the head against my lips, I run my tongue over them and groan at the salty goodness left behind.

"Look at me," he commands, and I obey, peering up his torso to the hypnotic glow shining down upon me. "Open your mouth. Take us between those soft lips.

My eyes widen at the term, *us*, meaning he's allowing Moe to play an active role. A thrill jolts through me. What I do with Nox, my demon will experience as well. I get to pleasure the two most important beings in my life simultaneously, and a rush of wetness dampens my sex.

While holding Nox's gaze, I open my mouth as ordered and stick my tongue out slightly. "Good girl," he murmurs, tapping the bulbous head on my outstretched tongue several times before dipping the tip inside and then retreating.

My vampire repeats this over and over again. Tap. Plunge. Tap. Plunge until I'm gripping his thighs to keep from reaching for his cock and devouring him. I crave the dominant, whom I know and love, to come out and play and for my males to grant me the pleasure of them fucking my mouth.

As if reading my thoughts, Nox's words almost have me diving my fingers between my slick folds to alleviate the pulsing ache. "We are going to fuck your mouth like a good little whore."

I whimper, scissoring my legs.

"Is that what you are, baby girl? Our perfect little whore?"

"Yes, Daddy," I moan, opening my jaws wider in invitation. I worship at the altar of Nox's dirty talk. The naughtier, the better.

I'm one sick, messed up puppy, but I don't give a fuck right now. All I care about is pleasuring my vampire and demon with my mouth.

Without another word, Nox slips his cock, coated in my saliva deep, hitting the back of my throat. My eyes water, and I gag slightly, but I relax and close my lips around his goodness.

"That's it, baby, choke on my cock, take us down." He commands before cradling my head and setting up a steady thrusting between my eager lips. "Relax your throat."

I'm so turned on, I can't help but reach down and cup my sex over the cotton pants. A sharp slap to the side of my breast has my eyes popping open.

"No. We own your pleasure, Cellica. You belong to us."

"Mmmm," I moan, placing my trembling hands back on his thighs.

"Your mouth feels so good," he groans, thrusting faster and deeper, and I thrill at the rough taking. I want everything this

male can dish out. I desire to be cherished, degraded, loved, dominated, flogged, spanked, tied up, or made beautiful love to, whatever, wherever it doesn't matter. I embrace and trust him in all
things.

"We can't wait to sink into your sweet cunt, taste the gift of
your innocence on our tongue," he groans, clearly lost in the lust
swirling inside him, amplified by Moe, no doubt. The demon
sends his cravings and needs to a higher level, just like he did with
me. You forget everything but your passion, the feelings of sexual
euphoria sweeping through your brain.

His thrusts quicken and I know he's close, so I relax my throat
even more and watch my mate lose himself in abandon. It is erotic
and beautiful, and I dip my fingers inside his waistband to fondle
his tight sack.

The grip on the back of my head tightens and Nox drives deep
one last time. "Fuck, Cellica. Swallow my cum like a good girl."
With my lips pressed against his groin, I've gobbled his entire
length. My eyes water as thick liquid shoots down my throat, but I
consume it all, humming with pleasure. "Yes, baby. Just like that."

Nox's irises flicker from his unique dual color to red and back
again, and I realize Moe released alongside my mate and pride fills
my chest. I did that. I pleasured Nox and Moe to completion with
my mouth.

I'm a freaking rockstar!

Chapter 35

Nox eases away, and I trail after him, cleaning him with my tongue, swirling it around the enormous head, and running it over the slit, making sure no drop escapes. I want to chase after his yumminess, but I don't have the strength, so when he steps from the bed I collapse among the pillows. Nox discards his sweatpants before leaning over and removing mine, leaving the warm socks in place.

"You sucked our cock perfectly, baby girl, but now we crave a taste of you." His fingers graze my pussy, and I shiver with need. "Look at your sweet cunt. It weeps for my touch." Nox kneels at the end of the bed and drags me so my ass is on the edge, my legs draped over his wide shoulders. "Fuck, you smell amazing."

"Chris," I whimper, shamelessly lifting my hips in invitation.

"You have a pretty pussy, Cellica. All pink and glistening." He blows on my sex, cooling the wetness.

"Please, Daddy," I beg. "Make the ache go away."

"I fucking love you," he groans before he leans down and swipes his tongue up my slit from my opening to my clit. I nearly levitate off the bed, but Nox clamps his arm across my hips to keep me in place, his fingers spreading my lips. When he takes my swollen nub into his mouth, sucking and swirling, I grip fistfuls of the blanket under my ass, my heels digging into his shoulders.

"Chris!" I scream as the orgasm grabs me by surprise. My vampire growls low, keeping a steady rhythm to prolong my climax. My body quivers and my eyes roll back in my head at the sensations bombarding me.

"That's it, baby girl. Come all over my face. Again."

He inserts a finger while flicking my sensitive clit with his tongue and I moan, another orgasm building fast. When he thrusts a second digit inside, curling them slightly to tap that perfect spot, I cry out. The wet sounds of his fingers plunging into me should appall me, but I'm beyond caring. My only thought is climbing up the next cliff so I can nose dive off the edge into utter bliss.

When a third one joins the others, the stretching overwhelms me, but I love it. Is this what his cock will feel like? If so, what the hell are we waiting for? I need to experience his girth.

"Chris, please." What am I begging for, I've no clue until Nox bites down on my swollen clit, thrusting harder. I shatter, screaming his name as tiny explosions fire through my body like the Fourth of July, the music swallowing my shout.

Holy fuck. Oh, God. Shit.

I've lost the ability to form a complete sentence as intense pleasure continues to travel from my sex, that Nox still laps at, to my heavy, aching nipples I didn't realize I pinched so hard they throb. Geez. I think I enjoy it rough.

Nox eases his fingers from my tender sex, and I prop myself up on my elbows to watch in fascination as he licks them clean, his glowing stare never leaving mine.

"You taste fucking incredible. I can't get enough of your sweet cunt."

I bite my lip. Every time he uses the C-word, my insides clench in response and a tightness simmers in my belly. I always hated that term, but when Nox says it, it lights me up. Same when he refers to himself as Daddy. Or how he's gonna treat me like his little whore or slut. His words should make me outraged and offended, or something, but instead, my pussy floods with wetness, and I envision a collar around my neck as I crawl across the floor to him, ready to perform any deviant sexual act he desires.

These cravings are all me. Moe isn't inside me yet and I'm fantasizing about every lewd and filthy thing I've always wanted from my mate. Which means these passions were always present. Moe just brought them out and gave me the courage to pursue them.

I want more. I need to be controlled sexually by Nox in a manner that should repulse me, but doesn't.

Nox kisses his way up my abdomen, and I collapse back as he runs his tongue across the fading scar marring my skin before giving each sore nipple a gentle suck. He settles between my hips as he nuzzles my neck. I wrap my arms around his shoulders, needing him as close as possible.

"Nox," I whisper, shivering as his fangs scrape my neck. A profound lethargy attempts to steal my strength, but I dig deep, searching for my wolf. Her answer is weak, but enough to fortify me for the moment.

"Yes, love?"

I take a sharp breath and tumble forward. "The things you make me crave sexually scare me."

His body stills before he lifts his head to peer down at me with a bewildered frown. "Why do they scare you?"

"Because," I say, avoiding direct contact with his stare and swallow. "I'd like to think I'm a tough, independent girl. So yearning to submit or perform the darkness in my mind seems wrong."

Instead of laughing, as I expected him to, Nox clasps my chin to lift my regard. "Cellica, whatever we play at in the bedroom, does not reflect who you are in your day-to-day life. You *are* a strong, resilient, courageous, woman and I couldn't be prouder of you."

Tears shimmer in my vision. "But you don't understand half of what I fantasize about," I admit breathlessly.

"And where do these fantasies come from, love?"

"Porn in the past," I shrug and lower my gaze in embarrassment. "Now from Moe, mostly."

"Yes. Moe is willingly sharing some of it with me right now." His fangs drop low with a groan and his irises brighten. I squirm under his weight. "Goddamn, Cellica. I crave to act out every fantasy in your mind, but more importantly, I need you to feel safe enough with me to voice them yourself. Do you trust me?"

"Yes, of course."

"No. there is no, *of course*. Disregard what the mate bond is telling you. If we weren't linked, would you trust me enough to confess your sexual needs?"

"I..." I hesitate, taking the time to contemplate what he's asking. Would I? Up until Moe, I would've *never* called a guy Daddy or allowed him to spank me or submit to his will. But with Nox, my feelings for him brought out all these debased desires. Even before the demon possessed me, my vibrator worked overtime to keep up with the wicked thoughts of my vampire. Afterward, I felt sick and ashamed that I got off to such imaginings.

Now, Nox encourages it. Moe relishes in them. And I realize that if I wasn't linked to Nox, it wouldn't change my desires or lessen the absolute trust I have in him, to not only fulfill those fantasies but nurture new ones I haven't even considered yet.

I grip his face between my palms and gaze deep into his eyes. "Yes. With or without the link, I'd still entrust you with every kinky request plaguing my brain."

His smile is wicked. "I'm gonna hold you to that, but right now, I want to fuck you senseless and claim you as mine forever."

"Okay," I say softly with a grin before he leans down and devours my mouth with his. When the head of his cock bumps against my entrance, I tense, waiting for the pain, but Nox seems in no hurry.

He reaches between us, the pads of his fingers circling my swollen nub, and I whimper with renewed need. His kiss is possessive, demanding. His fingers relentless against my sensitive flesh and before long, another crescendo builds.

"Chris," I cry out, gyrating my hips to position his cock at my opening, needing to feel his size stretching me, to have him claim the gift fate saved for him and him alone.

"You need my cock, baby?"

"Yes," I breathe and he pushes deeper another inch.

"Damn, you're so tight," he groans.

The stretch borders on pain, but I fixate on relaxing as much as possible as he eases forward inch by glorious inch until he bumps against the last barrier of my womanhood.

"You okay?" he asks, sweat dotting his forehead.

"Yes."

"As soon as I'm buried in this sweet cunt, I'll call in Darath. You concentrate on me and only on me, even after he's in here. You understand?"

"Uh-huh," I mumble and squeeze my lids shut.

"Cellica, look at me."

At the command in his tone, I lift my gaze to his just as his hips thrust forward, breaching my hymen and seating himself to the hilt. I cry out at the pain but somehow manage to keep my focus on his bright gaze. Nox holds perfectly still. The only movement is his chest rising and falling rapidly and the clenching of his jaw.

"Demon, fucking knock it off," Nox growls and for a moment, the ache fades, wondering what Moe is doing to my vampire.

I remember what it felt like to have Moe stimulate me from the inside. How his hands were all over me, pinching, caressing, and arousing. When his dick nudged my opening, it drove my body over the edge. Is that what Moe is doing to Nox right now?

"Let him pleasure you, love," I whisper in his ear. "Just this once." The mere idea of my wicked demon taking Nox while he fucks me is the hottest thing I've ever imagined.

"No," Nox snarls.

"Please, Chris. For me." Why am I pushing him? Better yet, why does it spike my lust into another level? If Asmodeus were a sentient person, I would *not* be on board for a threesome. I'm too possessive and jealous to share. But Moe resides in Nox's spirit and mind. It's just the fantasied visual that dampens my insides as Nox pulls out to slide back in with ease.

"Goddamn it," Nox groans. "Fuck."

"Do you feel him, Chris?"

"Yes," he moans, thrusting again, delivering sparks of pleasure-pain at the friction and immense stretching.

"Darath!" Nox shouts, but I don't turn away from my mate, too enthralled with the look of pure carnality on his face.

I lower him to my neck in preparation for the claiming, but before Moe switches places, I need Nox to tell me what he's experiencing. "Chris," I whisper in his ear. "Describe it to me."

"Fuck," he growls again, thrusting harder and the pain fades, replaced by exquisite sensation. "His lips and tongue are...."

"Are what, love?"

"Swirling my anus and balls. Fucking hell. Stop Moe or I won't last."

I vaguely hear Darath's rich timber in the background as spasms spiral through my core at the visual of Moe pleasuring my vampire.

Before I take my next breath, Nox's fangs sink deep into my neck. I gasp at the sudden attack, but the intruding pain is brief, replaced by sweet euphoria. This is what I've waited my whole life for, what fate designed for me—my mate's cock pounding into my pussy and his fangs buried in my flesh, taking nourishment from my body. Every pull on my vein triggers an answering clench in my sex.

"Oh God," I gasp as the build-up bursts through my system with such force, I can only clutch Nox's head as he pounds into me with relentless abandon. Darkness dances at the edge of my vision and I fear I'm about to pass out—which would be totally humiliating—when a familiar presence nudges my soul.

My wolf whimpers with delight, calling to the demon. Nox licks the puncture marks before tilting his head to the side to expose his neckline.

"Make me yours, as you are now mine."

At his words, all four canines descend. I don't think or fret about the logistics of the act, I just strike, penetrating the muscle between Nox's shoulder and neck. His gasp electrifies me. I'm the first woman to mark him.

A burst of spicy liquid gushes into my mouth and as Nox continues to fuck me with abandon, I swallow down his spicy goodness as stars dance in my vision and my sex convulses, squeezing and milking his cock for what all three of us crave—his warm come saturating my insides, making us whole. Complete. One.

A sizzling sensation dances through my veins as I release his neck. The flesh mends in seconds, but my claim remains for all immortals to witness. Pride warms my chest. With his cock still buried deep, Nox leans up to caresses my cheek. I melt into the gentle touch, trapped by the dual-colored gaze.

"You belong to me," he whispers, and my breath hitches at the significance of his words. At the acceptance. "From this moment forward, we are one. One mind. One heart. One soul. Forever.

Warm tears leak from the corners of my eyes as Moe's strength becomes my own, and my wolf stretches in pleasure and contentment. Nox's spirit swirls with my own and my soul could burst with joy. "I am yours, as you are mine. From this moment forward, we are one. One mind. One heart. One soul. Forever."

"I think I might actually cry, this is so beautiful," Darath murmurs and my gaze swivels to his, totally forgetting he was in the room and a witness to our mating. His wink and devilish smile make me snort with laughter, despite the fact I'm naked and Nox has his cock still buried deep within me.

"Get the fuck out, Jag," Nox growls.

"You are welcome, by the way," he says right before he slips out the door.

"Oh goodness. We just had sex in front of Lucifer," I mutter, slightly appalled.

Chapter 36

"Get dressed, baby girl. We need to go check on Kurtis. He was hurt pretty bad at the bunker."

"Because of me," she whispers, keeping her head down as she slips back into my borrowed clothes.

"No." I kneel in front of her as she sits on the bed, cup her chin, and force her to look at me. "Because of Abigail. Not you, little wolf."

"Troy is dead, and she's still in the wind, plotting God knows what."

"A worry for another day." I rise and brush my lips across hers, tempted to forget everything else and dive back into this bed with her. I'm addicted to her body, and thanks to Moe, I now understand my mate's sexual needs. My dick hardens with eager anticipation to fulfill each and every one of them.

"I love you, Chris," she murmurs.

I'll never tire of hearing that. "Cellica. You are my life. My every-thing. My love."

"And you're sure you are okay with having Moe an active par-ticipant in our relationship?" she asks with a worried frown.

"We reached an understanding with Darath's help. He knows his place and his role." I pull her to her feet, spin her toward the door, and smack her ass. "Now come on. Kurtis and Lu need us."

***

When we enter Lu's old room, fear squeezes my heart when I see Kurtis' dad, Cipher, hovering next to the bed with his mate, Alex's mother, weeping against his rib cage. Cellica clenches my hand tight.

The huge shifter lies in the center of the mattress, motionless, fully dressed, his black shitkickers practically hanging off the end. His usually tan skin is pale, and his breaths barely lift his massive chest.

Lu stretches out next to him, sobbing quietly, her head on his chest, her arm and leg draped over his body as if she can't bear a single inch separating them.

Viessa stands on one side of the bed while Nicole sits on the corner of the mattress, her back leaning against the post, her hand on her belly. When I see the tears flowing freely down her face, my heart stops.

I glance at my commander off to the right, comforting a distraught Alex, and his piercing blue eyes meet mine. The grief and misery in his gaze nearly buckle my knees.

No. This can't be happening. Kurtis is a fucking brute of a male. Nothing can harm him.

"Please, Viessa," Nicole begs. "Save him." Logan stands next to the queen, his hand on her shoulder, his jaw clenched with sorrow and worry over his mate's stress level.

"Isn't there something you can do, Vi?" Liam asks his mate, clutching her hand, his anguished gaze zeroed in on his best friend.

Viessa's breath hiccups, her irises bright as she shakes her head. "I'm so sorry. The magic damaged his heart beyond repair."

"No," Nicole weeps. "I had a dagger through my heart and your father brought me back to life."

"A physical wound," she replies quietly. "Not a magical one."

"Please, Oracle," I whisper, stepping to the end of the bed, a weeping Cellica at my side. "Whatever the cost, I'll pay it."

The weight and reality of this occasion seem surreal. Like at any moment, I'll wake up and realize this was all a bad dream.

"Yes," Sebastian asserts. "Tell us what to do and we will do it."

"Anything," Liam agrees.

"His only chance was his mate's blood, and it didn't work. I'm so sorry, I don't know what else can be done."

I turn to Darath. "Lucifer. You are the king of Hell. Is there nothing to be done?"

"I wish there was, but his soul is not mine to command. I'm sorry."

"But you snatched Kleora from going to heaven," Nicole utters, swiping the tears from her cheeks to focus on Darath.

"Because she was my mate," he replies softly, sorrow brightening his gaze. "If there were a way to save King Ruse, I would take it. I vow it."

Lu bolts upright. "No, no, n-no. You don't get to leave me." She scoots to the headboard and cradles Kurtis's head and shoulders in her lap. Her long dark hair drops like a curtain as she rains kisses over his face. "Please, baby. We haven't had enough time. I need more time. I can't survive without you. Come back to me. Please." Her sobs break my heart.

The big shifter doesn't twitch. We stand helplessly by and watch in horror as our friend's life drains from his body. I grit my teeth against the pain and tears threatening and gather my weeping mate to my chest.

We've lost one of our own—a strong, fair king who loved his people. A strategic warrior ready to jump into battle for the ones he loves. A loyal friend to us all, with a unique bond with Nicole.

His life changed the day he met Lucretia. At the time, the law forbid their love. Still, it didn't stop him from pursuing her relentlessly until she finally accepted him as her own.

How could the gods or God take such a valiant warrior and phenomenal individual from our midst? His absence leaves an immense hole in all our lives.

The only sound in the room is the weeping of those left behind. The males comfort their females while silent tears slip down their cheeks. I've lost fellow Guardians in one battle or another over my century and a half, but never a close friend. Kurtis was a rock to us all, and it's hard to imagine our lives without him.

Lu suddenly throws back her head and screams her anguish to the heavens, just as the shutters slam shut to the coming dawn.

"Lu!" Nicole barks, leaning forward as far as her belly will allow, cutting off the vampire's shout of despair.

Bright, shimmering amber fills the room as Lucretia snarls at her former queen. "Get out!"

"We must prepare him for the burial ritual," Nicole insists, not backing down at Lucretia's tormented rage.

"Get the fuck out of here! All of you!" Her fury stutters and more tears flow from her luminous eyes. "Please, leave us."

Nicole slowly stands to her feet with the aid of Logan. "Sleep the day with him by your side. Say your goodbyes." she informs Lu with a gentleness I've never witnessed in her. But it's soon replaced with tender determination. "But tonight, you and Cipher will take him back to his people to perform the burial ritual and allow them to grieve their king. Do you understand me? You will not sequester yourself in here with him for nights on end."

Lu's lips tremble as more tears escape, but she gives a brief nod of acknowledgment. "How am I supposed to move on without him?" she questions and the desperation in her expression hollows my chest.

Nicole hesitates and tears gather in the turbulent gray depths. "I wish I had the answer for you, Lu. Some magical word or potion to ease your despair. But I don't. All I can offer is my assurance that Kurtis would want you to."

She nods again, brushing his hair from his forehead. "Now, please leave us," she whispers brokenly.

As each couple passes the bed, the men place a fist over their hearts in tribute to their fallen comrade. The women silently touch his boot or ankle in goodbye.

Liam and Kurtis were the closest among our close-knit boy's club, so instead of just placing his fist over his chest and offering a nod, the werewolf drops to one knee. A king bowing to another fallen king.

"I will miss you, buddy," he murmurs, his fist clenched so tight the knuckles whiten.

Viessa places her palm on her mate's bowed head and leans over to squeeze Kurtis' ankle before they both exit the room.

I won't leave until my queen does. Currently, I'm her personal guard, so I watch her as she waddles to the front of the bed and grips Lucretia's chin. "You will survive this or I will personally kick your ass. The shifters require their queen." Not waiting for a response, Nicole bends and brushes her lips across Kurtis' forehead and a big fat teardrop plops on his cheek. "You were always there for me when I needed a friend." Her breath hiccups as she fights for control. "Thank you. Every minute with you was a blessing, and I... I miss you already."

Logan offers his soldier salute before guiding his mate to the door.

Cellica and I quickly pay our respects and follow my queen from the room. How will Lu recover? I'm not sure I'd survive if something happened to my wolf. She's my entire world, my reason for living, and we've only just started our lives together.

I glance back at Lu cradling her mate in her arms, her long hair hiding her grief, and I mourn for her, for the loss of a magnificent male and friend.

Abigail will pay for the death and destruction she's caused if I have to hunt her down to the ends of the earth. One way or another, her head will roll.

Chapter 37

'**M**oe? It's good to have you back,' I whisper, striding next to Nox down a dark hallway as we follow Logan, carrying the queen, to their chambers.

'*While I relished fucking you with our vampire, I'm thrilled to be back where I belong.*'

'*I appreciate you not pushing him beyond his comfort level. What you did was perfect.*'

'*I aim to please, my lady,*' he smirks. '*I enjoyed titillating him, and wow, you took us like a pro, little wolf. I'm impressed.*'

A blush steals over my cheeks, and I duck my head so Nox doesn't notice. '*I'm sorry about Troy,*' I whisper. Although, I don't know why I'm whispering. No one can hear the conversation in my skull. Well, except Nicole.

'*He made his choice, and it wasn't me,*' he growls bitterly. '*My condolences on the big shifter's death. You all seemed to care for him deeply.*'

'*Yes. He was a regular at our ranch as he and my brother were close.*'

I make a mental note to have a private moment with Liam and give him a huge hug and an ear if he needs it.

'*So, you're mated. How do you feel about that?*'

'*Absolutely thrilled. And you?*'

'I've come to care for you passionately and now that I have an insight into Nox's emotions, my obsession with him is unbreakable,' he chuckles. *'Once your tongue is in someone's—'*

'Okay, I get it. You're a funny demon,' I interrupt, refusing to let him finish the lewd comment about my mate's ass.

'Just saying. You need to try it. He enjoyed it.'

The mere notion of tasting Nox down there sends heat swirling through my groin. Of course, since he's a vampire, it's not as taboo. Hmmm, I'd love to swirl my tongue anywhere on his body to watch him come undone.

Nox's nostrils flare, his gaze swiveling to mine. *'Thinking about me, baby girl?'* he smirks inside my head. I jump, totally forgetting the second we mated we'd be able to speak the way Moe and I do.

Geez, my brain is getting congested.

'Always,' I answer tenderly. *'Are you okay?'*

'No. I can't believe Kurtis is gone, and I'm worried about Lucretia. But as long as you are by my side, I can deal with anything.'

We enter the queen's lush chambers, where our friends mingle, whispering softly to each other as they honor Kurtis with their memories. The mighty warrior places Nicole in the wing-backed chair by the roaring fire with such care I nearly swoon. She winces, rubbing the small of her back. Logan disappears, reemerging a second later with a heating pad to place behind her before plugging it into the outlet by the fireplace. She smiles up at him, but it doesn't chase away the sadness in her eyes—in all of ours.

"How are you feeling, baby?" Logan asks, kneeling in front of her to tuck a blanket around her legs and waist. The worry in his expression is plain as day. "I can kick these degenerates out and we can take a nap."

Aww. That's the sweetest thing ever.

She snorts. "Tempting, but no. We need each other for a little while longer. Then we sleep."

"We are here for you, my lady," Nox states, positioning us behind her chair, and it's like his words are a signal for the others to gather around Nicole.

Logan sits at her feet. Sebastian eases into the opposite chair in front of us, with Alex in his lap. Viessa hovers by the fire, her vacant gaze consumed by the blaze while Liam's arms circle her waist from behind, his face buried in her neck.

We all feel Kurtis and Lu's absence from our group as we sit quietly, absorbed in our own thoughts and grief. I can't imagine what she is going through right now. She's lost her one true mate. Her other half. The only one she will get in her long life.

I'm not sure I would be strong enough to recover from something like that. If Nox died, my life would no longer hold meaning.

When Darath and Kleora enter, he grabs another chair from the corner and settles into the cushions with Kleora facing the fire. I wonder if Cipher and Arra will join us or if the previous king's despair over the loss of his son is too much to share.

After several minutes of silence, each lost in their grief, Darath speaks up. "I've released the hounds in search of Abigail. I should have fucking snapped her neck when I had the chance." The torment in his tone rips at my heart.

"It wasn't your kill, Jag," Nicole whispers. "But, if by some miracle, Lu survives this, she will stop at nothing until the witch is dead. And if I know my previous Guardian at all, it will be a slow, painful death that awaits Abigail."

"I'd certainly like another shot at the bitch," Nox growls.

"As would I," Liam says.

"We must remain vigilant," Bastian interjects, stroking Alex's flaming hair. "She is desperate and grieving, but she will come for Nicole and the baby."

"I would like to ask you all to stay here at the castle," Logan states. "We can't safeguard her during the day, so if you—"

"Say no more," Liam interrupts. "We defend each other's six. We are family."

Everyone nods in total agreement. A bloodline may not connect these incredible immortals, but they love and protect each other with a fierceness more profound. "I can bring in my most trusted wolves to patrol the perimeter during the day."

"Thank you," Logan says. "That would ease my mind. Also, I had the staff make-up rooms for each of you, just in case."

"None of us are safe while she still lives," I whisper, remembering the crazed look in the witch's eyes. Nox squeezes me closer.

"Congratulations on your mating, by the way," Alex murmurs with a kind smile. "When this is over, we will celebrate."

"When that bitch is dead, we will honor Kurtis and your union with a decadent party," Nicole mutters, her head resting against the back of the chair.

The vampire queen appears gaunt, her skin pale. No doubt Kurtis' death, Lu's sanity, and her precarious delivery refusing to start, have her at her wit's end.

Viessa suddenly straightens, and her eyes flash brightly. "Oh my," she whispers. "She's close."

Logan jumps to his feet, drawing his sword. Sebastian, Nox, and King Darath do the same. "How the fuck did she get into the castle?" Logan growls.

Like a well-orchestrated play, the males form a protective circle around their females, their backs to us, ready to face any threat. Although I notice Alex has a dagger in each hand, her eyes twin beacons of silver, and Kleora hovers above the fireplace, an arrow nocked and ready in her bow.

I am the only one without combat experience in the room. The first chance I get, Nox is gonna remedy that. I refuse to be a defenseless female, even if I have a strong mate.

'You are not helpless, Cel. You have a powerful Prince of Hell inside you. Next time give me fucking control and I will protect you.'

"Oh gosh," Viessa exclaims. "I'm sorry. I meant Nicole's in labor."

"W-what?" the queen stutters, turning her stunned gaze on the Oracle.

Weapons lower, and I notice Logan is staring at Nicole with equal parts fear and awe.

"The pain in your back is the start, my lady."

"What... what do I do?" the young queen asks, eyeing her stomach like it might burst.

"Might be best if we get her to the bed," she instructs Logan. "This could happen quickly, or it could be hours. Alexandria, grab the protective blankets in the corner and place them over the comforter so they are under Nicole."

Alex nods and rushes to the covers. I rush over and help her spread them over the existing comforter. Logan lowers his mate into the center, sitting behind her with his back to the headboard for support. He wraps his arms around her, stroking her stomach.

"Is this like... happening *right* now?" Nicole asks. "Cause if so, I fucking don't require a damn audience."

"Everyone clear out, except Viessa," Logan barks.

"And Alex," she adds and reaches out to her best friend, clasping her hand. The red-headed valkyrie offers a shimmering smile before sitting on the edge of the bed, ready to offer whatever support is needed.

"I will be right outside the door, Red," Sebastian murmurs, bending to kiss the top of her head.

"It's dawn, Bastian," she replies, grabbing his hand before he walked away. "Get some rest. I'll retrieve you if anything changes." The commander frowns with worry but nods, swooping in for a kiss before heading to the exit.

"My lady," Nox bows. "May the gods show favor upon you and this birth. Do not worry about anything but bringing that baby into this world. We will guard you both with our lives."

She nods. "Thank you, Nox."

We file out, offering words of encouragement as we go. Those not ruled by the solar cycle set up camp in the sitting room adjacent to the bedroom to defend the queen. My heart goes out to Logan. He has a long day of fighting the sleep and supporting his mate through delivery.

Nox grabs my hand and traces us back to his suite. I see the fatigue setting in, but he directs us to the bathroom.

"I need a shower before the slumber claims me." He starts the water, adjusting the temp before turning to me. "You okay with staying with me while I sleep? I have books, or you can watch TV. It won't bother me."

'Aww, how sweet. He's worried about you being bored. Lick his ass. I guarantee that will wake him up,' Moe whispers.

'Shut up, Moe,' I fire back, trying not to laugh. "I'm exhausted too," I tell my mate, lifting my shirt over my head and stepping out of the sweat pants two sizes too big.

"Jesus," Nox mutters, his gaze devouring my nakedness. "It will be a miracle if I actually rest with your lush body next to me."

"I could go and sleep in a spare room," I say with a straight face.

"Never. You belong tucked next to me." He smacks my bare ass, and I yelp. "Now, get in the shower, woman."

The shower was quicker than I'd initially wanted, but it felt amazing to wash the last twenty-four hours from my hair. By the time Nox soaped up, shampooed, and rinsed off, his eyelids were practically closed. Still, it didn't stop his erection from jutting out in readiness. I rubbed against it as often as I could, his growls causing tingles to race along my skin.

"Come nightfall, before I start my shift, your sweet ass will feel the sting of my palm, you little minx."

I giggle. "Whatever do you mean?" I say, batting my eyelashes at him as we dry off and climb into his comfy bed. Before I even get the comforter tucked around us, he's out. I observe him for several minutes.

Never having slept with a vampire before, his stillness is unnerving. I lay my ear on his chest to make sure his heart still beats.

'*Now's your time to explore,*' Moe whispers, and I bite my lip.

'*I shouldn't....*' Even inside my brain, it sounded lame and half-hearted. Because everything within me is screaming to touch, lick, and explore every inch of his sculpted body.

'*You so should,*' Moe encourages like a devil on my shoulder. Literally. '*He'll never know.*'

'*Okay, maybe just a little.*'

I push the covers down to his waist and ogle the fantastic tattoos. Black swirls form a cross over his ribs on the right side, his shoulder, and down his bulging bicep to his wrist. But the one that captures my attention is his family crest covering his amazing pec.

My brother once told me that Nox's lineage was Viking. Hence the shield with an iron helmet in the center. A sword stabs through it from top to bottom, and two axes crisscross behind the helmet. Celtic glyphs depicting his bloodline cover the entire design.

I lean over and run my tongue over the shield, dipping to his nipple to nip at it gently. Nox doesn't even stir. No, that's not true. Something stirs.

I glance down as the covers jerk. I bite my lip, lifting the blanket to discover Nox's rock-hard cock staring back at me. Saliva pools as I remember how he aggressively fucked my mouth, and wetness gathers between my legs. After a quick peek at his face, I bend down and lick the pre-cum, ready to drip onto his stomach.

Damn, he tastes good. Salt and spice.

'*And everything nice,*' Moe interjects, and I smile before replacing the covers and snuggling in next to my mate. My sex throbs with need, but I ignore it. I didn't lie earlier. I'm exhausted. It's been a long grueling night, but I'm safe now, mated to the man of my dreams, my demon back where he belongs, and nestled against Nox's warmth.

If Kurtis' death, Nicole's perilous delivery, and Abigail possibly hunting for a way to get to us didn't hang over our heads, life would be good.

Chapter 38

Cellica

Cold. I'm so cold. My wrists burn, and my shoulders stretch to the point of pain.

"What a sweet cunt you have," a familiar voice murmurs in the dark. I can't see her, but her warm breath fans my sex.

I jerk against my bonds as her wet tongue delves between my folds to tease my clit.

"No! Please stop," I cry, even as I lift my hips for more.

"We will pleasure you beyond your wildest dreams," Moe declares from right behind me.

Wait… His voice wasn't in my head or coming from my lips. Instead, scalding heat warms the skin on my back, and large hands cup my breasts. Oh shit. Moe is sentient?

"I'm going to take your sweet ass while our boy here pounds into your pussy," he groans in my ear.

I open my eyes to see my vampire in front of me, his irises bright as he lifts my legs to wrap them around his waist. "Nox," I breathe. "Release my shackles."

Where the hell did the witch go?

"No, Cellica," he says and pushes his cock against my opening while Moe probes my anus.

"Wait. I can't do it. It's too intense."

"Yes, you can," Moe whispers.

"All good little sluts can take two dicks. You are our perfect little whore. Aren't you, baby girl?" Nox growls, his fangs descending.

His words inflame my mind, but the burn and stretch are too much as they penetrate simultaneously. I struggle, but they only move in tighter, sandwiching me between their massive bodies.

"No, Nox. Please stop. I can't do it."

"Yes, you can," they command in unison before plunging deep.

I scream, flailing from the chains, the shock of pain overwhelming. They draw back and thrust again, and a new sensation dulls the hurt. Pleasure. My inner walls spasm from the exquisite friction, the push and pull along my sensitive walls. The immense heat from their solid bodies buffeting my front and back, causes stars to dance in my vision.

"Cellica."

"Oh, God. Please. I can't... I can't take it." I fight the decadent pain their cocks inflict, gripping the chains tighter, but they ignore my pleas, setting up a rhythm despite my struggling. Within minutes, the discomfort fades, replaced by a euphoric sense of peace. I drop my head on Moe's shoulder and hold on as I relish the intense sensations of being fucked by my boys.

"Cellica!"

Rough hands grip my biceps to pull me away, and I flail, desperate to stay, to find the elusive release.

"Damn it, Cellica. Wake up."

My eyes pop open, and Nox's worried face hovers above me. Two things become crystal clear to my dream-induced brain. One, Nox is fully clothed, sitting on the edge of the mattress, and two, I'm naked beneath the sheets. Of his bed. *Not* in the bunker being sexually taken by my males.

My heart nearly pounds out of my chest, and my sex throbs. Not in pain but in arousal. Jesus. I was getting off on the rough treatment they inflicted. What the fuck is wrong with me?

"Hey, are you okay?"

"Yeah, um, yeah. It was just a dream."

"You want to talk about it?"

"No!" I almost shout, and my cheeks heat with embarrassment. "No," I respond more rationally. "I'm fine. What time is it?"

"The shutters should go up in about half an hour," he says, brushing my sweat-dampened hair from my face. "I got up early to do my rounds and check on everyone. You were sleeping so soundly I didn't want to wake you just yet."

"How's Nicole? Did she have the baby?"

"No. She's still in labor." I see the strain around his eyes and mouth. He's worried about his queen.

"How can Logan stay awake during the day?" I ask.

"He's over six hundred years old, so he's obtained the strength to withstand the pull of the sleep, but not for long. If she doesn't have this baby by dawn tomorrow, he will have no choice but to crash."

I nod. "I should get dressed."

"Tell me about your dream," he demands, plucking me from under the warm covers to drape me over his lap. The coals in the fireplace are mere embers now and I shiver at the coolness of the room. He snatches the blanket at the end of the bed and walks to the chair by the fireplace. Settling in, he tucks the soft fleece around my body.

"I know I was in it because you moaned my name," he says with a smirk, reaching over and throwing several logs from a basket onto the glowing embers before turning a key on the side of the fireplace. Flames burst forth and ignite the wood with a whoosh.

"I don't want to talk about it," I mutter, tucking my hair behind my ear and dropping my head to his shoulder to hide my still flaming cheeks.

Between the warmth of Nox's body, the blanket, and the flickering fire, the shivers cease even as the dream plays through my brain like an erotic slideshow.

"Baby girl? I smell your desire. Tell me your dream or I will spank you."

My eyes widen, and my stomach clenches in a good way. "I can't. It's too embarrassing."

He lifts my reluctant gaze to him with a finger under my chin. "Never be embarrassed with me. Did you enjoy what was happening?" he asks, caressing my cheek with the back of his knuckles.

I squeeze my legs together. "I... parts of it," I admit.

"Tell me then. Every detail."

His hand disappears beneath the blanket to fondle my breasts, and my breath hitches. "I was at the bunker."

His fingers pause on my nipple, a frown between his brows, but he says nothing, waiting for me to continue.

I decide to skip the portion with Abigail since that was the nightmare section of the dream. "I was chained to the ceiling again. Cold. So cold. In pain. But then Moe was there. Not a voice inside my head, but actually there, behind me, and you were in front of me." I take a deep breath and let it out slowly. "You were both naked and...."

Fuck, I can't say it out loud.

Nox tweaks a nipple before dipping his head to my ear. "And then what, Cellica?" he whispers, and shivers run down my spine. "Tell me what happened."

"Moe said the both of you were going to pleasure me. That he was going to take me... from behind while... while you fucked me."

"Mmm," Nox rumbles, his hand sliding down my stomach to cup my wet, aching center. "You wanted it. Didn't you? Your cunt wept in the dream to be taken by both of us. As it does now."

"Yes," I breathe, as Nox parts my slick sex to circle my clit. "It hurt at first," I admit.

"But you enjoyed it, didn't you, baby girl? Moe's cock stretching your anus to the point of pain? While my hardness plundered your sopping cunt?"

'*Fuck. This vampire has perfected dirty talk,*' Moe groans in my mind.

"Yes." I keen low when his fingers delve inside, the heel of his palm rubbing my achy nub with each thrust.

"Jesus, you are so wet for us," he groans. "Moe. Slip a finger in her anus," he commands.

Oh, God. Nox is ordering the demon to participate, to pleasure me right alongside him. I spread my thighs farther apart to give them more room.

I'm draped over Nox's lap, my hip pressing into his raging erection beneath his leather pants and my legs hanging off one side and my head off the other. Somewhere amidst my scandalous confession, Nox discarded the blanket. Between the heat radiating from my mate and the warmth of the fire tickling along my skin, I'm the opposite of cold.

My breath hitches when something presses against my back door, churning and tapping, while Nox continues to fuck me with his fingers.

"Do you feel him?" Nox pants.

"Yes. He's swirling it." I can't believe I possess the ability to respond verbally. Dots dance behind my lid, and I gyrate my hips, rubbing against Nox, mindless with lust as my males worship my body.

"Look at me, Cellica."

Somehow, I lift my head to stare into my mate's bright regard. "Come for Daddy, baby girl." The Alpha command zings through my soul.

'*Goddamn,*' Moe whispers. '*His commands and filthy mouth do it for me.*'

I couldn't agree more. A fiery blaze builds, clenching my insides around their fingers. When Moe spreads me further with a second digit, I skyrocket, forcing my lids to remain open as ordered. Nox observes me explode apart, his heated stare taking in every shift and change in my face.

"You are so fucking beautiful," he murmurs. "I love watching you come. It's the sexiest goddamn thing I've ever witnessed."

"Nox," I moan, collapsing against the arm of the chair again.

"Oh no, we're not done with you yet." He pushes my feet to the floor, positioning me between his spread thighs, my ass in his lap, with my back to him. "Bend over and grab your ankles," he commands, and I do as ordered, even as a blush heats my cheeks at this vulnerable position.

He lifts me slightly to unbuckle his pants. I peek over my shoulder, having no clue what he's about to do until he pulls out his raging erection and positions it at my entrance. Even though I'm soaked with my own juices, Nox's size takes my breath away, and the stretching breaches the pain threshold, but I don't care. I want him to fuck me fast and hard. I'm so desperate for it, I drop my hips, seating him all the way in one swift move.

I cry out at the intense burn, holding perfectly still to allow my quivering inside a chance to adjust.

"Damn it, Cellica," he growls and smacks my butt cheek with such force I gasp at the sting and attempt to rise. "No. Hold on to your ankles and don't let go," he orders, pushing me back down with a palm between my shoulder blades. "I want to watch this juicy ass bounce as I fuck you."

He rubs the hurt away and I moan softly, dropping my head between my knees at the sweet burn. My inner walls clench around him like a vice.

"Did you enjoy that?" Without waiting for my reply, he whacks the other side, and I grind my hips, pushing him deeper. "I love seeing my handprint on your ass, baby girl. I think you need a quick punishment for licking my cock while I slept."

Oh shit, he was aware of what I was doing?

Before I can contemplate the new information, Nox spanks me in earnest, sometimes alternating sides, other times hitting the same spot. The sting of his hits is almost unbearable, and I wiggle to get away from the scalding heat of his strikes. But then, his cock shifts inside me, and the pain morphs into a desperate yearning for more.

Just when I think I can't take anymore, Nox grips my hips and lifts me up his shaft before driving me back down. "Chris!"

"You need a good fucking, don't you, Cellica?"

"Yes, Daddy. Fuck me hard." Did those words just come out of my mouth? Jesus. The things this man brings out in me.

Blood rushes to my head as Nox pounds into me, and I shift my grip from my ankles to his for added leverage. The pad of his finger swirls around my opening beside his cock before rising to probe my anus. I groan and push back, desiring him to fulfill even a fraction of my dream. Nox answers my silent plea, slipping the well-lubed digit inside.

"Oh, God," I whisper, clutching his ankles harder. "More."

He responds by adding a second finger as he pounds into my pussy, his other hand guiding my hips. I squeeze my eyes at the intense burn of his stretching a place that's never been touched before.

The sensation is not unpleasant, and the more ramped up and closer to orgasm I climb, the more I crave. Even though Nox is doing most of the work, my legs shake with effort as he pistons into me.

As Nox fucks my anus with his fingers and pounds into my pussy with his glorious cock, Moe pinches my nipples. I'm surrounded. Overwhelmed. Unsure which sexual act I love more, but never want them to stop. Finally, I plummet over the edge, repeatedly crying out Nox's name as my body convulses around his.

"Fuck, Cellica!" Nox shouts, plunging deep and holding me tight against his pelvis as his hot seed pumps into me. I convulse and squeeze every drop.

'Jesus. I've never felt so satiated and energized at the same time,' Moe exclaims. *'I fucking love you two.'*

"Mmm." It's all the strength I have for a response. Nox squeezes and rubs his free hand all over my ass, his fingers and pulsating cock still buried deep. I've lost all feeling in my legs, but I couldn't care less.

"You fucking amaze me, Cellica. I can't get enough of you, and this ass. I have great plans for this ass."

Still caressing it, he eases from my anus before bringing me upright to recline against his chest. My vision dances as the blood drains from my brain back where it belongs.

"That was... amazing," I sigh as my heartbeat slowly returns to normal, and I catch my breath.

Without a word, he lifts me off his cock and onto my feet, tucks himself away, much to my disappointment, before rising to stand behind me. His muscular arms wrap around me, pinning my arms to my side. "As much as I'd love to spend all night teasing and tormenting your body, I must see to my queen."

"I need to go home, Nox."

He stiffens behind me. "No. It's not safe."

"But I require clothes and toiletry stuff." I pivot into his hold, wrapping my arms around his neck. "My final exams are in two weeks and I haven't even begun studying for them."

"I don't want you leaving the castle. Give me a list and I will send a Guardian to fetch what you desire."

"Nox, be reasonable. Some of it is at the ranch while the rest is at the cabin. It would be quicker if I went. I know where everything is. I'll be in and out in no time and back in your arms. I promise. Liam can go with me."

Worry darkens his eyes. "Not without me."

"Then when can you get away?"

He huffs out a sigh. "Not until the baby is born."

"Nox. Send me with one of the other Guardians, then. Please."

A muscle pulses in his jaw as he regards me, and my insides churn. I can't keep parading around in Nox's clothes that are two sizes too big for me. Plus, I need my books. I've worked too hard to drop the ball now and flush it all down the drain.

"You will do exactly as the Guardian tells you. Without question," he says with a growl, and I know I've won.

"Yes, Sir," I smirk.

"I prefer, 'Yes Daddy, I will be a good girl.'"

My grin widens. "Yes, Daddy. I promise I will be the bestest girl."

'We are sooo not going to keep that pledge, little wolf,' Moe snickers. *We like his punishments too much.'*

Chapter 39

My gut churns at the thought of Cellica being beyond my reach, especially with Abigail in the wind, but I recognize the need for it. I don't like it, but I understand.

When we walked into the sitting room, with Cellica back in my sweats, I halted in the doorway, shocked to see Lu, in full combat gear, standing stoically in the corner.

Shadows marred her eyes, and she clenched her jaw tight against the tears and grief. How she could function at all was beyond me.

What stunned me further was when I informed Liam of what Cellica required, Lu spoke up and said she'd escort her wherever she needed to go. My first reaction was to disagree. Even though Lu is one of the most lethal Guardians among us, she was suffering, and I am worried about her mental state. In her misery, would she miss something and get them both killed?

"I will guard her with my life, Nox," she said, and the desperate plea in her gaze wrenched my gut, so I relented. Lucretia needed a distraction to keep her from spiraling into the dark abyss of grief and despair.

Although Liam sat five feet from us, I pulled Cellica against my chest, dove my fingers into her silky hair, and ravished her mouth for a brief kiss. She gripped my waist, offering a breathy moan that hardened my cock in a second.

Liam had disappeared by the time I let her go, and Lu waited patiently, her eyes devoid of emotion.

Now, I'm sitting in the high-back chair by the fire, attempting to read a book to pass the time. Logan and Nicole lounge on the bed. According to Alex, her contractions slowly increased from every thirty minutes to ten. She walked the halls to speed up the process, showered, and changed into a clean nightgown with Logan's help but refused to eat or drink anything.

I've never seen Logan look so haggard, and it's not merely from lack of sleep. He's plainly worried about his mate since fate stacked the odds against her. Not only is she the only human-vampire hybrid that we know of, but labor and birth for vampires is a crapshoot. The likelihood of the baby being stillborn is exceptionally high, but the chances of her even surviving the delivery are minimal.

Please, God or Gods, I pray silently. *If you can hear me or care, allow them to survive this.*

Viessa and Alex come and go, bringing fresh towels and linens, and keeping a pot of water bubbling over the fire. One of them rests while the other checks on her progress every hour.

Even though she must be exhausted, Alex keeps up a bubbly dialogue that makes Nicole laugh or smile despite the hours of pain.

God certainly knew what he was doing when he decided the woman would carry a baby in their body for nine miserable months and then expel the behemoth out of their *"hoo-hah"*, as Alex is fond of saying.

I shudder.

"Nox," Nicole calls, and I drop the book I wasn't really reading anyway on the table and stride over to the bed.

"Yes, my lady?"

"How is Lu?"

"She actually volunteered to take Cellica to the ranch to grab some of her things."

"You're shitting me?"

"I know. I was as shocked as you."

"And Kurtis?"

"Her and Sebastian took Kurtis and his parents to Shifter Territory to begin the preparations for his burial ritual at sunset."

"Wow. Okay. She's doing better than I would be in her shoes."

"You would do the same thing, love. Anything to keep your mind occupied and off your grief," Logan murmurs without opening his eyes. He rests against the headboard with Nicole snuggled between his spread thighs.

"No," she groans, gripping her stomach as it moves and shifts with another contraction. "I would've met you in the afterlife."

"It is not just about us anymore, baby. We have a son to think about."

"I don't care." She tries to sit up, but he grips her and keeps her in place. "If you leave me, I will find you and haunt your ass for all eternity."

He chuckles, rubbing her tightened belly through the contraction.

Even after all these years, I'm still in awe of Logan and Nicole's unwavering love and devotion to each other. She was the beginning of everything. An ancient prophecy foretold her birth and destiny.

The second the Guardian commander discovered her existence, he plotted, sacrificed, slaughtered, lied, and risked his own neck to keep her hidden and safe until the appointed time.

She defied the odds and executed the powerful King Dimitri, her father, by plunging a knife through her own heart. A plan the previous Oracle, Icarus, helped her execute without Logan's knowledge, discerning it was his destiny to bring her back.

"Logan. Is there anything I can get you? Do you need nourishment?"

As Nicole's due date approached, the warrior refused to take sustenance from her any longer, fearing it would harm her or the baby.

Unlike Nicole, who cannot partake from any source besides her mate without becoming violently ill, Logan has survived on bagged blood for the past two months. The Queen had put her foot down, refusing to let him drink from anyone else. Vampires are incredibly possessive about being their mate's only source of nourishment.

"He does look a little pekid," Nicole mutters with a frown, craning her neck to peer up at him. "Bring him a couple of bags, Nox."

Logan huffs out a sigh. "What I need is sleep, woman. Close your eyes and be quiet so I can get a little ten-minute power nap in."

I grin at Nicole's pseudo display of outrage. "Did you just tell me to shut the fuck up, Logan?"

"Never, my love."

Leaving them to their gentle bickering, I stroll over to my chair when Nicole lets out a sudden scream, jerking upright and clutching her abdomen. Alex and Viessa come rushing into the room while Logan rubs her back, a helpless expression engulfing his face. The legendary soldier has no clue what to do, and it's driving him insane that his woman is in pain.

"Get this fucking kid out of me!" Nicole bellows. "He's ripping me in two."

My heart drops, and fear grips my throat. According to Liam, that's exactly what his mother said right before she died giving birth to Cellica.

Two hours later, Nicole's continued screams of agony have us all on pins and needles. Cellica texted and said she and Lu were having some girl time at the cabin while she packed, but they'd be back soon.

Good. Maybe Cellica can help Lu through the early stages of her grief. Even though the vampire will never have another mate, she can fall in love and have a meaningful relationship with someone else without the bond. Though unlikely, it's been known to happen. She's still young, with centuries ahead of her.

At one point, Logan came barreling out of his chamber and punched a hole in the sitting room wall. His rage and anguish were so extensive that he felt the need to pound something or he'd explode.

"Give me a fucking enemy I can defeat, for Christ's sake. I cannot deal with this. Her misery," he points to his bedroom. "It is tearing me apart and I almost hate this child for causing my female so much pain."

"We are here for you, brother," Sebastian says, clasping his hand on Logan's shoulder. "If you need to hit something, hit Nox."

"Hey," I gape at my commander. Logan has punched me before in training and nearly broke my jaw.

But when the big vampire's shoulders relax, and he shakes his head with a slight grin, it suddenly doesn't seem that important I'm the butt of the joke.

"Thanks, brother. I needed that."

"Just remember, it is not the baby's fault, and Nicole knows how to deal with pain. She will get through this, and so will the baby."

Logan stares at his brother for a long moment. "While I appreciate the pep talk, we both know the likelihood of this ending on a cheerful note is slim to none."

"She's not the average vampire, sir," I reassure. "She is the bringer of peace. The only one of her kind. Not to mention, the prophecy foretold of this child."

Logan nods. "You are right, Nox. I am just exhausted and mentally drained." Another scream rips through the air, and without a word, Logan pivots and stomps back into their room.

Needing air, I turn to Sebastian. "I'm gonna do a sweep of the grounds."

"Coward," he snorts but doesn't stop me.

I trace outside, and the crisp night air clears my head. A half-moon blankets the forest with a dim glow. Not that I'd need it to patrol. I see perfectly in the dark, as do all vampires.

My chest expands with a deep inhale as I stroll the perimeter of the magical barrier that protects the Vampire Nation Stronghold from invasion and curious human eyes.

As I scan the area, my boots soundless on the moist ground, my mind wanders to Cellica. Obviously, Liam still has a problem with his sister being involved with me. He couldn't bear to watch me kiss her. And even though a part of me understands his issue, another part can't help but be hurt by his lack of faith in me.

Granted, Liam watched me flit from one female to the next for years, getting what I wanted from them—blood and sex—before moving on without a backward glance or care about their feelings. I made it perfectly clear upfront what I required and what I offered. A one-night stand with mind-blowing sex and nothing more. They all walked into it with eyes wide open, so if they expected more, that's on them. Not me.

I've proven with Cellica that it's different. I fucking love her. Need her. Can't breathe without her next to me. I rub my nape. But have I? Have I had the "talk" with my mate's big brother?

No.

Liam understands I'm Cellica's mate, and she's mine. He knows it's an unbreakable bond that will never fade or expire but through death. However, I think he still believes our connection is just a biological link and not something more profound. He's worried I'll break his baby sister's heart, hence his demand that I leave her alone until he feels her life is on the right track. Like Logan did for years. He stayed away from Nicole to keep her protected, only visiting her in her dreams until he couldn't even do that. For two fucking years, he never saw her or spoke to her, forced to only hear about her life through the reports from her protection detail.

Fuck. I'm not sure I'd be as strong if I were in his shoes. Even now, being apart from my wolf for mere hours, my skin crawls with the need to trace to her cabin just to get a whiff of her rose-scented hair or watch her move about doing mundane things.

It's not that I don't trust Lu to keep her safe. On the contrary, the warrior would willingly sacrifice her life for my mate, especially now, I suspect. Still, it's not the same as me actually having my eyes on her.

I rub at the ache in my chest and reach out mentally with our new link. *'Baby girl, I miss you.'*

Nothing. What the fuck?

'Cellica. Answer me.'

A dark void expands in my spirit where our connection resides, and my fear takes on a life of its own.

Chapter 40

Cellica

"**C**ellica. Wake up. It's time to start back."

My brain feels fuzzy, and my lids refuse to open. "What?" I croak out, shaking my head to clear the fog.

"You were obviously exhausted," Lucretia says. "The second your butt hit the couch, you passed out cold."

"I did? How strange." I slept like a baby nestled against Nox all damn day. Why am I so tired?

'*Moe? You okay?*' I inquire mentally. No response. Maybe he's still sleeping. I frown and try again. '*Moe. Wake up.*'

"Cellica," Lu sighs, irritation drawing her brows down. "We must go back. Now."

But before I can respond, Nox appears in the center of my living room, his expression frantic. The mismatched irises spark when they zero in on me sitting on the couch, scanning my body as if for injuries.

"Nox? What's wrong?" I ask, rising to my feet in an instant. Dizziness blurs my vision, and I sway. Lu reaches out to steady me, but I'm wrapped in Nox's embrace before her fingers reach my arm.

"Baby? You alright? I tried reaching out mentally, but I couldn't feel you and you didn't respond."

I shake my head. "I zonked on the couch. I guess I was more tired than I thought."

He peers over me at Lu. "Any issues?"

"No," she assures him. "She packed a bag and then we sat down to talk and, like she said, she went out like a light. I didn't have the heart to wake her."

"I can't reach Moe," I whisper, blinking back tears.

"What?" he asks with a frown. "What do you mean?"

"He's not responding."

"Try again," he orders.

'*Moe!*' I shout, hoping he's just out of it. '*Please answer me.*'

Panic bubbles in my chest as I lift a frantic gaze to Nox with a shake of my head.

"Asmodeus," Nox barks, and I jump. "Come forth."

"Could he be sleeping?" Lu questions. "Might be why you were so out of it."

"You should have fucking called me," he growls at Lu.

"And tell you what? Come quick, Nox, Cellica is sleepy?"

"It's not her fault, Chris," I mumble against his chest. "Maybe the transition from me to you and back again was too much for him and he's just gone dormant to recharge."

"Let's get you to the castle and we will talk to Darath." He turns to Lu and slings my bag over his shoulder. "I'm sorry. I didn't mean to bark at you."

She shrugs her shoulders. "It's fine."

"You okay?" he asks, eyeing her curiously.

"Never been better," she replies coldly, turning from him. "Can we just get back to the stronghold, please?"

I rub my aching temples. "You're right, babe, we need to talk with Darath? But my head is pounding. I would like to lay down for a bit first or at least pop some ibuprofen."

"Of course." He gathers me closer and nods to Lu. "See you in a few."

"Wait," she holds out her hand to stop us. "I'm sort of depleted. I haven't fed properly in weeks and now..." she trails off as tears gather in her eyes. The proud, stoic warrior is keeping it together by a thread. "Could I hitch a ride with you?"

"Of course," I agree when Nox doesn't answer, holding out my arm for her to join our circle.

"You positive that you're okay?" Nox questions again when Lu grabs his shoulder.

"What do you think?" she whispers as a tear cascades down her cheek. "I just want to get home and make sure Nicole and the baby are fine."

We materialize in the sitting room a minute later, and nausea rolls in my stomach. Something isn't right. I remember stopping at the Ranch, shoving clothes and bathroom shit into my bag... Then when we arrived at the cabin for more essentials, I recall feeling extremely hungry as I shuffled around, grabbing what I needed.

I asked Lu if we had time to eat, and she was hesitant at first, but agreed. As I made a sandwich while the vampire scouted the perimeter, fatigue hit me like a raging bull between the eyes. My lids felt as if they had lead weights attached to them, and I wanted nothing more than a nap. I left my PB&J on the counter and shuffled to the couch. The last thing I remember was Lu coming in and asking me what I was doing?

Did I even respond?

The second Lu lets go and disappears, Nox traces us to his room. "I have baby aspirin in my medical bag, but I doubt we will find anything stronger here."

"That's fine," I mumble, collapsing on the bed and massaging my temples.

Nox returns from the bathroom with a glass of water and two pink pills resting in his palm. "Don't you think it's strange you have a headache?"

"I used to get them all the time during finals week." I ease up on one elbow, pop the pills and down the water.

"That was before you turned fully immortal."

"I'm fine, babe. I just need a minute."

"You're not fine, Cellica. Are you not concerned why Moe went radio silent?"

"Of course, I am," I mumble. "I just need to stop the pounding in my skull first." I sling my arm over my eyes. "Then we will talk to King Darath."

"You have ten minutes."

"Great. Fine. That's all I need."

I ignore Nox as he paces at the end of the bed and concentrate on slowing my breathing, relaxing my muscles, and clearing my mind.

I must have zonked, because the next thing I know, Nox is rousing me. "How do you feel? Any better?"

I take a second to assess. "Yes. Much better. The headache is gone."

"Do you sense Moe at all?" He asks, helping me to my feet.

"No. Nothing."

"Let's go talk to Jag then. Maybe he can figure out what's going on."

"Darath," Nox beelines for the demon king, lounging in a chair, his mate cuddled in his embrace as I greet my brother with a warm hug. "We think Moe's gone dormant."

"Unlikely," he murmurs, tickling Kleora's ear and ignoring Nox.

When I move to Nox's side, the red irises glance at me without interest, but then he does a double-take, focusing on me with a frown.

"It's true," I say. "He's not responding to me or Nox."

The Devil stands, gently placing Kleora on her feet. "Why did you not come to me right away?"

"I needed to lie down for a bit. It felt like someone was taking a sledgehammer to my skull."

"Walk me through exactly what happened, little wolf. Did you piss the demon off?"

"What? No. I was just packing and then I got hungry. Like really hungry, but by the time I made a sandwich, I could barely keep my eyes open. The next thing I know, my butt's laying on the couch, and I'm zonked."

"How do you feel now?"

"Better after my power nap and some aspirin."

Darath goes to lay his huge palm on my neck when Nox snatches his wrist.

"Watch yourself," my vampire growls, the glow in his eyes at a low simmer.

"What the fuck do you think I am going to do to her, Nox?"

"Why don't you tell me before you do it," he demands.

"I need to touch her in order to sense Asmodeus. Anything beyond that, and my mate would take my balls. Trust me." He grins down at Kleora, and she smirks.

"Damn straight."

Nox releases his hold with a sigh, and I glare at him. God save us all from overly protective males. "Please ignore the caveman, King Darath. You may proceed."

Out of my periphery I see my mate shoot me a look, but I refuse to glance up at him as Darath's warm fingers wrap around the back of my neck under my hair. He closes his eyes in concentration, and a hush settles over the room.

A tingle skates down my spine, followed by another and another until I'm practically vibrating. I shuffle from one foot to the other with nervous energy and think about anything but how my body is responding to the Devil.

Nicole and Logan are the only ones absent from this group. Has she had the baby yet? I should probably ask once we get this Moe situation resolved.

Finally, after what seems like forever, Darath drops his hand and steps back. "Asmodeus is still with you. He is just... dormant. Like you said."

"But why?" Nox demands.

"Tell me, Cellica. Who was with you when you passed out?" Darath questions.

"I didn't pass out," I argue. "I merely fell asleep, and Lu was watching over me."

Darath's eyes sharpen. "Where is Lucretia now?"

"I..." I look around the sitting area. "I'm not sure. Maybe she went up to her room. She seemed distraught?"

"What's wrong, Jag?" Nox asks.

"I am uncertain. Your mating should have charged Asmodeus up like a nuclear plant, so I am confused why he would need to go quiet." He barges past, and my anxiety ramps up another notch. "I must talk with Lucretia."

"I will check her chamber," Sebastian says before disappearing, only to reappear seconds later. "She is not there."

"What is the urgency, Darath?" Liam demands, a frown pulling his brows together.

"I want everyone to listen to me carefully." We all gather closer, my heart in my throat. "Asmodeus would not go dormant for no reason. Someone wanted him out of the way. If the female Guardian was in the room with you, she may be compromised."

"What the fuck do you mean, *compromised*?" Liam asks in an urgent whisper.

Instead of answering, Darath turns to my mate. "Nox, let us ignite your tracker skills. Do you still possess Abigail's scent?"

"Yes."

"Do you detect her essence in Cellica?"

My eyes widen. "You think she's the reason Moe is dormant?"

"Possibly. I will need to talk to Lucretia. Probe her mind."

Nox spins me into his arms and buries his nose in my neck. His attention would thrill me any other time, but the thought of that bitch near me again without my knowledge has me clenching my fists in fury. The rest of the team circles us, their expressions taut with worry.

Nox runs his nose into my hair. Even with the fear circling our group, my stomach clenches at the overwhelming sensation of my vampire all over me.

His big body tenses when his bloodhound senses reach my torso, and he rears back. "Abigail laid her hand on Cellica's chest within the last hour."

"What?" I whisper, blinking against the brightness of Nox's livid gaze. My heart in my throat.

"I just asked Logan if he has seen Lu," Sebastian informs us. Thank God the brothers have the ability to speak telepathically "She is in there with them. "What exactly do you think is going on here?" Sebastian questions in a harsh whisper.

"As I said, I won't know until I probe Lucretia's mind, but if Abigail was in the same room with them, she was attempting to control someone or gather information. I believe she suppressed Asmodeus. What she did to the Guardian is yet to be determined."

"She harms Nicole or that baby—whether it is Lu's fault or not—Logan will take her head."

"I am well aware, commander. Let me enter first, assess the situation before you forewarn Logan. Each of you, file in quietly, but do not alert Lucretia in any way." He turns to Sebastian. "Send one of your Guardians to scout out Cellica's cabin. Abigail may still be there."

"I'll go," Nox says, and my heart dips.

"Not alone," Bastian responds. "Take Morgan and Niall with you, but make it quick."

Nox nods to his commander before bending to brush his lips across mine. "Stay with the team and keep trying to rouse Moe," he commands before disappearing.

"Darath." I halt his entry into the bedroom with a hand on his elbow. "If Abigail is controlling Lu, what are we going to do?"

"I am not sure, little wolf, but we must prepare for anything," he replies before squaring his shoulders and entering Nicole and Logan's suite with Kleora at his side.

Great. Here's hoping no one gets killed this time. Liam takes my hand as we wait to enter the room, and I sense his anxiety, his need to get in there and defend Nicole.

"You okay, Liam?" I whisper, staring at the bedroom door and clutching my brother's fingers.

"That bitch had you in her clutches again. She could have slaughtered you and I wasn't there to protect you."

"Liam, it's not your job to protect me anymore. No one could have foreseen what happened. Even if you'd been there instead of Lu, Abigail would control you now."

"When this is over, you, me, and Nox need to talk. We lost dad. Josh and I won't lose you too." He bends and presses his lips against my forehead.

I sigh. "You're not losing me. You're gaining an awesome brother-in-law and another vampire into the family." I grin up at him.

"That's what I'm worried about."

Chapter 41

I loathed leaving Cellica, but at least this time, she's surrounded by a group of immortals willing to lay down their lives to protect her. I trust them with my precious mate, but it still eats at me to abandon her side when so much uncertainty hangs in the balance.

I can't believe Abigail got to my wolf. Again. I've failed Cellica numerous times over the last few weeks, and shame sits heavy on my shoulders.

It's my duty to guard and protect my female, but my misguided bro code prevented me from securing the most precious thing in my life. Because of my failures, a demon possessed my little wolf and forced her on the run. Three wolves almost sexually assaulted her, and the witch kidnapped, tortured, and nearly killed her.

Jesus. Maybe my father was right. Growing up he always told me my deformity would scare all the females off, and no woman of worth would want me. Certainly not one with a pure heart whose innocence shines bright in her whiskey irises but whose deviant soul matches mine.

When Moe whispered Cellica's dark desires in my ear, it stirred my blood. More than anything, I crave to grant every single one of them and more.

I shake my head. Now is not the time for such thoughts. Abigail is the priority. If that witch and I ever come face to face, I will rip her insides out like she tried to do to my Cellica and let Lu take her head. The final blow rightfully belongs to her.

It bothers me that Moe was so easily shoved deep when Cel needed him the most. It proves how potent Abigail truly is.

The Vampire Nation and our friends need Nicole at full strength. My queen nearly took the witch down once. Granted, she required the combined power of Icarus and Viessa. But maybe between the Oracle, Lucifer, and the formidable Halfling, they can subdue Abigail's magic long enough for us to dispose of her once and for all.

The second we materialize outside Cellica's cabin, the odor of spilled blood hits my senses like a sledgehammer. I freeze. Denial suffuses my brain as I recognize the familiar aroma.

No. Please let me be wrong. Fate can't be that cruel.

With slow steps, I stride around the back of the building. Morgan and Niall don't say a word as they follow behind the vampire bloodhound, well accustomed to my tracking skills.

But the closer I advance to the source, the harder my muscles bunch with dread. *Be alive*, I chant silently.

"Is that..." We are close enough now, my fellow Guardians catch the aroma, and their steps falter. Their training kicks in and they draw their swords, guarding my six as I venture deeper into the woods.

The second I spot the lump covered in leaves, I halt in disbelief, the breath leaving my lungs in a whoosh.

No. My eyes must deceive me. This can't be happening.

Niall breaks rank and rushes past me. I watch as he kneels in the damp leaves to turn the body over, my mind too numb with shock to move.

"Who did this?" Morgan demands, still by my side. His furious voice snaps me out of my stunned state.

Grief moves in like a tidal wave as the numbness fades, crushing my spirit. I stumble over to Niall and collapse on my knees next to him. "H-how?" It's the only word I'm able to formulate, but the Guardian knows precisely what I'm asking.

"Silver dagger through the heart, and it looks like they slit her throat for good measure." The Guardian's hazel eyes are bright with fury, but he's gentle as he slides his massive arms under her and picks the body up before turning to glare at me. "Who did this?" Niall repeats Morgan's earlier question.

I rise with jerky movements, the answer filling my nostrils. "The witch. Abigail," I mutter, staring at the empty shell cradled against his chest, the long braid swinging in the wind.

"Your orders?" Morgan whispers next to me.

Orders? What instructions do they expect me to give? One of our own is dead. Struck down all alone with no backup and by the condition of her body, she fought back. Hard. Abigail must have put a sleep spell on Cel before venturing outside to attack her guard.

My eyes widen, and the sharp nails of terror scrape down my spine as the fog finally lifts. Who the fuck traced back to the castle with Cellica and me?

Son of a bitch. I sensed something was off with Lu, but I just attributed it to her grief.

While I watched over Cellica as she napped and we stood in the living room trying to figure out what was wrong with Moe, Lucretia's ravaged body lay strewn among the leaves.

"Take her to the great dining hall. Gather a dozen of our best and await orders outside the queen's chambers."

Without waiting for their reply, I trace to Nicole's bedroom, my heart in my throat.

Chapter 42

The second I materialize, I ease toward the bed but stop dead at the sight of Nicole holding a tiny, swathed bundle in her arms.

Holy shit. She did it! She fulfilled the prophecy and survived the birth of the next Daywalker king. I blink back the tears of awe and joy, pick my jaw up off the floor and head straight to Logan, standing vigil by his family.

I glance briefly at Abigail, coyly wearing Lu's image, not wanting to play my hand with Nicole and the infant in her crosshairs. Despite the fake grief darkening her expression, a small smile lifts her lips as she gazes at Nicole, and my muscles clench.

I refocus on Logan but keep Abi in my periphery. The mighty warrior looks as exhausted as the queen, but pride puffs his chest, and the green irises shine with love and devotion down at his mate and son.

"Congrats, Logan," I say, clapping him on the shoulder. "You're a fucking daddy."

Without turning, a huge smile spreads across his lips. "Yes. Is he not the most handsome baby in the world?"

Nicole rolls her eyes. "If you start cooing at him like a moron, I will head butt you."

Logan laughs.

This should be such a blessed, auspicious occasion, but all I can concentrate on is the enemy in the room.

'*Nox.*' Darath's voice in my brain startles me, but I try not to react. '*Move around to the other side, closer to Nicole.*'

Nicole glances briefly at Darath with a frown, hearing every mental conversation. Her giddy smile fades, and the gray eyes turn to Lucretia standing at the footboard.

As I move around the huge four-poster bed toward Cellica and Liam, I scrutinize the witch and notice the subtle differences. Lu was always so regal, with her shoulders back and the amber irises watchful and aware.

Abigail knows nothing of Lu, so her posture slumps slightly with her manic focus fixated on Nicole. Her right fist repeatedly clenches like she's fighting an inner battle.

When I reach the other side, I make a show of peering at the baby while easing Cellica behind me. My eyes lock with Nicole's.

'*Do you know what's wrong with Lu?*' she asks mentally, and I offer a barely noticeable nod while presenting a smile.

Logan stiffens, his gaze bouncing between Nicole, Lucretia, and Sebastian. It appears the commander has made Logan aware of the potential danger.

"Where is Viessa?" I ask Liam, noticing for the first time the Oracle isn't among our group.

"She wasn't feeling well earlier and went to lie down in an effort to control the sudden images bombarding her mind," Liam says with a worried frown. "I should go check on her."

"She will come back when she's ready, Liam," Sebastian voices as he subtly shifts Alex to his other side, away from Lucretia. "Give her a moment. Stay and help celebrate."

By now, the entire team hovers around the bed, minus Viessa.

"I wish Kurtis was here to see this," Abigail/Lu whispers, with tears shimmering in her eyes. "He'd be so proud of you, my lady."

Rage thunders through my veins. How dare she act like the grieving widow when it was her magic that destroyed Kurtis? I clench my fist against the desire to tackle the bitch and drive my dagger through her filthy mouth.

The queen nods, sadness darkening her cold expression. "I wish that more than anything, Lu. How are *you* holding up?"

Abigail's gaze bounces around the room, then refocuses on Nicole for a full minute before answering. My hand tightens on the blade at the small of my back. "Did you like the tea? It was Kurtis' favorite."

Logan's skin blanches, and Nicole's breath hitches, her regard swiveling to the cup on her nightstand.

"You gave her tea?" I ask with hushed urgency as Logan grips the hilt of his sword by the bed.

"Yes," Abi answers with a frown, still playing her part. "It always calmed Kurtis when he would get overly stressed."

"Did you drink it?" I question Nicole. When she gives a jerky nod, my heart sinks.

Fuck. Fuck. Fuck.

"Enough of this. Restrain her," the queen orders softly, kissing the sleeping baby's head.

Darath and Sebastian grab Abigail by her arms and force her to her knees. I remain vigilant next to Nicole, ready to defend her with my life.

"Logan, take Lucian, please."

The warrior ignores her, or maybe he doesn't hear her since his sole focus is on Lu, those iridescent emeralds brightening. "This is the second occasion you have played a role in hurting my mate, Lucretia. I spared you the first time because it is what Nicole wished. I will not spare you again."

"Wait… what… what's going on?" Abigail doesn't struggle, plastering a dazed expression on her fake face. Was she hoping to pull off being Lu until she could just stroll out the front door after poisoning our queen?

Viessa suddenly appears, her eyes swollen and red-rimmed. Even though her chin trembles with grief, she strides over to the nightstand and picks up the teacup, already aware of what's happening. She sniffs it and then places her glowing hand over the rim.

After several seconds, the Oracle's gaze slams to Nicole's. The fear in her expression nearly buckles my knees. "Wolf's bane."

"No." Logan's agonized whisper ripples through the room. "How could this happen?"

Wolf's bane. The one poison able to bring a vampire down. It attacks our organs, specifically our hearts. Without the heart, there is no magic, no coming back.

"No." Now the witch struggles. "It's just an herbal tea. It's harmless. Safe. I would do nothing to hurt Nicole."

"Stop the fucking pretense, Abigail," Darath growls. "I know you suppressed Asmodeus and now control Lucretia to gain access to the castle."

"She's not controlling Lu," I say quietly, glancing at the agony in Viessa's expression. The seer must have witnessed her twin's murder in a vision. "I found Lu's body in the woods behind Cellica's cabin. She's... dead."

The collective gasp in the room pierces my gut as all eyes turn to the mirage of Lu restrained on her knees. Viessa climbs up on the bed next to Nicole and begins running her glowing hands over her chest, chanting softly in a strange dialect, tears streaming down her cheeks.

Logan seems frozen, his fingers clenched tight around his sword. I trace into the bathroom and snatch a washcloth off the rack before tracing back and shoving it into Abi's mouth to keep her from casting a magic spell.

"Logan," Nicole growls. "Duct tape. Nightstand."

Her command sets him in motion, and he flings open the drawer behind him and produces a large roll of gray tape. I don't even want to know why they have that in their bedside table.

Within seconds, Logan has it wound around the witch's head, trapping the washcloth in her mouth. Abigail fights in earnest, her authentic form shimmering to life, her palms sparking with magic, and her big blue eyes shoot daggers at Nicole.

Logan crushes one of her hands into a fist, causing Abi to cry out before wrapping it in duct tape to keep it covered and closed. He repeats the process on the other side as Bastian and Darath hold her down.

She screams something behind her gag, but they ignore her as Logan brings down a steel contraption over Abigail's head from the ceiling. Handcuffs dangle from each side. He grabs the witch by her hair, forcing her to stand, and quickly secures her wrists.

Again, I don't care to know why that's in their room, but I think I need one in my bedroom for Cellica and me.

Once Abigail is secure and no longer a threat, I turn to my queen. Sweat dots Nicki's forehead, and the pallor of her skin constricts my chest.

"Alex, take the baby," she commands softly, but the petite valkyrie stares at Nicole with horror, not moving an inch.

"Alexandria!" I shout. The command in my tone snaps her out of the emotions seizing her mind, and she shuffles forward. Nicki kisses little Lucian's head before reluctantly handing off the precious bundle to her best friend.

"Tell me what the fuck happened," my queen demands of me once Alex and the baby are a safe distance from the action. Liam shifts to guard the two, the bright blue eyes of his wolf zeroed in on his grieving mate, still running her glowing hands over Nicole.

"When Cellica and Lu went back to the cabin to retrieve some clothes, Abigail suppressed Moe before he could challenge her and put Cellica into a deep sleep. She then ambushed Lu while she was patrolling the perimeter. Lucretia put up one hell of a fight, but the witch...." I peer over at Viessa before continuing. "She plunged a silver dagger through Lu's heart and slit her throat. I'm assuming she then shifted into Lu, returned to the cabin, and waited for me to notice I couldn't contact Cellica."

"How did we not know she could fucking shape shift?" Logan growls. He's back on the bed with Nicole now that Abigail's shackled to his ceiling and bound in duct tape.

"I knew."

I pivot to face my mate, her confession squeezing my heart in a vice. "Explain," I say quietly, taking in her wide eyes and how she frantically wrings her hands together.

"I vaguely remember Moe talking to my friend Jessica, only he called her Abigail. She must have shifted into Jessica's body."

Which means her friend is dead. According to our history lessons on immortals, a shapeshifter needs to kill the person it wants to morph into, essentially stealing a portion of their soul to sustain their image.

But the bigger question? Why did she keep this from me? We would've been more precautious if we'd known Abigail could shift into anyone. I never would have allowed Lu to guard Cellica alone.

"I'm sorry," she says brokenly. "I didn't remember until now."

"What's done is done, Cellica," Nicole states, rubbing her chest as if it hurts. "This is not your fault."

The queen's right. Moe was in command. He should've fucking told me. I let go of my anger and concentrate on my queen and Viessa. "What can we do?"

"I need a defibrillator and the herb Ma-Huang in raw form," Viessa informs us. "It's only found in Mongolia."

"I will retrieve the herb since I have been to Mongolia before," Sebastian offers. "Nox, can you get your hands on a defibrillator?"

"Yes," I answer, sheathing my dagger.

"Make it quick," Viessa commands.

"How much time?" I ask, needing a timeline.

"Thirty minutes. No more."

Logan leaps from the bed with a roar, picking up the bedside lamp and flinging it against the wall before lifting his sword and marching toward Abigail.

"Logan!" Nicole shouts.

He halts mid-swing, his eyes blinding, his fangs bared. "Do we need her to cure Nicole?" The enraged vampire growls, never taking his blazing focus from the wide-eyed Abigail shaking her head and screaming something behind her gag.

"No. Kill her," Viessa orders, the hard edge in her tone slightly unnerving.

Logan glances over his shoulder at his mate, and she nods, her hatred shining brightly in her feverish gaze.

Abigail yanks on her restraints, her screams amplifying. Fear dominates her expression. Before Logan swings his sword, Darath leans in and whispers something in her ear. Genuine terror darkens her face.

When Darath steps back with a malevolent grin, Logan's blade whooshes through the air with a ring of sound before slicing first through one arm, her neck, and then the other arm.

Abigail's body and head drop silently to the carpet. Blood squirts from her severed arms in a macabre design across her torso and face as they swing by the wrists, still in the handcuffs.

It's done. The fucking witch is finally dead.

Chapter 43

Cellica

Ding dong, the wicked witch is dead.

The freaking song from *The Wizard of Oz* keeps playing over and over in my mind as Darath and Liam remove Abigail's body. The head that hit the floor was all blonde curls streaked with blood and big blue eyes forever frozen open in shock.

Did she honestly believe once the jig was up, she would walk out of this room alive? Well, I guess she's done it twice before, once at the Fae castle and again in the bunker, but this time her luck ran out, and I couldn't be happier about it. I just wish I'd been the one to kill her.

I fetch another glass of water from the bathroom for Nicole, hurrying back to her side. Over the past—I glance at the clock on the bedside table—thirteen minutes and twenty-five seconds, the queen's heart rate has increased to an alarming pace. According to her, her legs have gone numb, her arms tingle, and she feels like she's gonna hurl like the girl in the *Exorcist* movie.

I peer at Logan who is sitting against the headboard, Nicole cradled in his arms, a warm blanket draped over both of them. The male looks like death himself, but he continues to rub his mate's legs and arms to keep the circulation running and murmurs softly in her ear. Dawn is in two hours, but if the boys don't return soon, it won't matter. Nicole will be dead.

'*They will make it back in time. Have faith.*'

The second Abigail's heart stopped beating, the suppression spell on Moe lifted, and he's talked non-stop, begging for my forgiveness for failing to protect me. Of course, I don't blame him. Just like I can't condemn myself for allowing the witch to control us both.

"Logan," Nicole whispers against his neck. "If I die—"

"Then I will follow you into the afterlife." His arms tighten around her. "What did I tell you after you died and returned to me? I've endured your pain. Stroked your soul. Nothing, not God, Heaven, or Hell, this life or the next, will keep us apart. I will find you because you are mine. Now and forever." My chest tightens at the powerful goodbye in his words, and I want to weep for them.

She shakes her head before leaning back to peer into his eyes. "No, Logan. You must raise our son. Teach him to be a great warrior and king. Promise me."

"I cannot. My life holds no meaning without you."

"Do it *for* me then. Stay until he is ready to assume the throne and he no longer needs you. Then join me."

"Nicole...."

"Promise me, my love. Please." Tears leak from her eyes one after the other as Logan stares down at his mate with despair and an everlasting tenderness. Finally, she grips his face between her palms and gently brushes her lips across his. "Please, Logan."

A lone tear leaks from his closed lids as he rests his forehead against hers. I press my hand over my mouth to keep the sob at bay. "I promise." The agonized whisper shatters my soul because I'm not sure I'd be strong enough to make the same vow if Nox asked it of me.

"I want to hold our son," she whispers, and Alex comes forward with the precious bundle.

Logan takes Lucian with one arm and transfers him to settle against their chests. The proud momma smiles when his tiny fingers wrap around Logan's finger.

She kisses his forehead. "You are in great hands, my miracle. Be a good boy for your daddy."

"Fuck, Nicole," Logan breaks. "Do not give up on me. Fight as you always have. Fight to stay with us."

"I will until my dying breath, you know that," she reassures him. "But I also want to say my goodbyes. Just in case."

Oh, God. Where the fuck are Nox and Bastian?

Just as the thought enters my brain, my mate appears with a white metal box with knobs and a small screen. Two ominous paddles attach to either side of the unit.

"Nox is back with the defibrillator, Nicole," I inform her with a huge smile as relief and pride flood through me at the sight of the box and my mate.

"Alex, take the baby," Viessa orders softly.

"Sebastian has located the herb," she informs us as she cradles the next vampire king to her heart. "He should be here any minute."

"Oracle," Darath and Kleora step forward. "What do you need from us?"

"I'm going to require as much power and magic as you can muster. When I tell you, lay your hands upon Nicole. Be warned, when I jump-start her, it will hurt, but don't let go."

He nods and sits on the end of the bed.

"Your touch has always been electrifying, Halfling." He winks at the queen, but his humor doesn't match the serious regard of his crimson gaze.

"Cellica." I start when my sister-in-law calls me over. "I need you to give Asmodeus complete control. We will require his power as well."

"Okay. Like now?" I ask, relieved to feel Nox's heat at my back.

"No. When I tell you."

Every second that passes as we wait for Bastian ramps up the tension in the room. I glance at the clock for the hundredth time. Five minutes left. *Please hurry, Sebastian.*

Alex paces with the baby at the end of the bed.

Viessa continues to run her glowing hands over Nicole while my brother stands as helplessly as I do. His worried gaze bounces between the woman he views as a sister, and his grieving mate with the weight of Nicole's life and the prophecy sitting on her shoulders.

Darath sits soberly with Kleora's hand in his.

What will they all do if we lose the prophesied bringer of peace? What will the immortal world do without the beacon of hope she's become? Will it implode, revert to constant wars and skirmishes for new territory, more power?

When Sebastian appears with two minutes to spare, we sigh with relief. He holds a strange plant in his hand. It almost looks like skinny bamboo shoots with red popcorn up and down the green sticks.

"Mash the berries," Viessa instructs. "Kleora, use your hellfire to dry the stems, but don't burn them. Crush them as well."

Sebastian and Kleora move to a side table to do as instructed.

"Nox, bring me a fresh cup of hot water."

He nods at the Oracle and disappears, returning a few seconds later with a coffee mug. He fills it with steaming water from the pot Alex and Viessa kept boiling during Nicole's labor.

When Bastian and Kleora return with the pulverized ingredients, Viessa dumps them into the steaming water. Immediately, a pungent odor permeates the room, and I wrinkle my nose.

"Damn, that smells disgusting," Liam mumbles his fist under his nose.

"It's going to taste awful as well," the Oracle says as she hands the mug to Logan.

He angles the queen upright since she's too weak to do it herself and places the cup to her lips. "Down the hatch, baby."

"Oh God," Nicole chokes and sputters after downing about half of it. "That's fucking terrible. I'd rather drink motor oil."

"All of it," Viessa commands sternly, and she reluctantly obeys.

Once she's swallowed the last drop, I take the cup and place it on the nightstand out of the way while Nicole keeps making little gagging sounds.

"Remove her shirt and place her flat on her back," the Oracle instructs Logan as she brings the defibrillator next to her and charges it up.

My palms sweat with apprehension, and I wipe them on my jeans. '*You ready for this, Moe?*'

'*Yes. Whatever you need,*' he responds with a confidence I am far from feeling, as usual.

"Darath, lay your hands on her shins and don't let go."

"Never."

"Asmodeus, come forth."

I retreat in an instant, and Moe's power surges forward. "Yes, Oracle?" I hear Moe say through my lips, and I'm glad he didn't shove me so deep I wouldn't be aware of what was happening.

"Still freaky," Alex mutters, eyeing me with a strange expression as she rocks the baby.

"Lay your palms on either side of her head. When you and Darath feel the shock, pound your power back at it and into Nicole. I will do the same. Keep going until I tell you to stop."

"Wait, who is using the fibrillation machine?" Logan asks with a frown, his body bunched with tension as he stands next to the bed, looking helpless.

"The only doctor in the room," she states and looks at Nox.

He swallows but nods, taking the paddles and squirting some gel from a tube hooked to the side of the box onto the plates. Viessa moves farther on the bed to grip Nicole's arm.

"This is gonna fucking suck, isn't it?" she whispers, too weak to keep her eyes open.

"Yes, my lady. Like a motherfucker."

Chapter 44

Nox

I didn't have the heart to tell them I've only used a defibrillator once in my career. It was on a foal in asystole that wasn't responding to chest compression or epinephrine injection. Like a human doctor, I've been trained to use them, but never on my damn queen.

Shit.

"What energy level?" I ask Viessa.

"Highest setting."

I close my eyes, send up a silent prayer that I don't fry Nicole, press the charge button, and place the paddles on her chest. One in the middle of her sternum, the other just below her left breast. The machine lets out a long beep as it charges, and I feel my balls tighten up into my body.

As soon as the pitch of the beep changes and the orange button lights up, I automatically shout, "Clear!" Even though we are going against every safety protocol by making sure the others keep touching her.

Nicole's back bows as the electrical charge enters her body. Logan roars, clutching fistfuls of his hair.

Darath growls against the pain but keeps his fingers wrapped around Nicole's shins. I glance at my wolf gripping the queen's skull, and I'm stunned when Moe's true form shivers over her, his eyes a blinding crimson.

I never thought I'd say this about another dude, but he's fucking incredible. Enormous wings span the wall behind him. Oranges and red dance among the white feathers, making it seem like they are on fire. Thick black hair flows down his perfectly sculpted chest, with delicately pointed ears peeking through, just like the fae. Two massive horns curve upwards from his head on either side into lethal points. His lips are full, his nose straight and flawless, and the ripple of muscles in his naked body stirs something inside me.

Moe was definitely built for sin. No creature subjected to his original form could resist him. Man or woman.

"Again, Nox!" Viessa shouts, and I snap out of ogling the demon and recharge the paddles. "Clear!" I call and watch as Moe absorbs the charge, his image pulsating over Cellica. I grit my teeth against the twitch in my dick and glance at Darath. His proper configuration also shimmers over his body, the gigantic black leather of his wings twice the size of Moe's but not nearly as beautiful.

Only nervous apprehension flutters through my system when I look at Lucifer. His malevolence makes my shoulders bunch. But when I peer at our demon, he causes my muscles to tense for an entirely different reason.

Moe suddenly glances at me as if he senses my scrutiny. Even though he's in obvious pain, the asshole winks at me as if he's perfectly aware of his impact on me.

Son of a bitch.

"One more time," Viessa grits out, her amber magic covering her hands and engulfing Nicole's arm and chest. I glance at Logan as I settle the paddles over the red angry scorch marks I've already inflicted on her skin.

"Please, baby," he pleads as he paces back and forth. "Do not fucking leave me."

By now, Nicole is completely unconscious, not breathing, and the reassuring thump-thump of her heart is absent.

"Clear!" I shout and jolt her again.

"Maintain the charge in her body," Viessa hollers through clenched teeth. "We must burn away the poison."

Moe's form is almost entirely transparent as his muscles bulge with the effort to do as Viessa instructed. The bright ruby glow from both Moe and Darath's eyes washes over Nicole, turning the Oracle's magic into a beautiful red-orange sphere. It undulates over her chest, sparking and pulsating with electricity.

I ease off the bed, dragging the defibrillator with me to place it on the floor by the wall. I watch helplessly with everyone else as Moe—I can't really call him Cellica right now since his image dominates her petite form—Darath, and Viessa fight to save my queen.

As much as I fought and loathed his presence in our lives, I'm grateful he's here. Nicole wouldn't have the fighting chance without his power and strength.

"Push harder, Asmodeus," Darath growls, and I'm stunned when I observe the physical evidence of him redoubling his efforts. A bright flame ignites in his wings, and I blink against the heat undulating from him in waves.

"Kleora, add your fire," Viessa orders, and the Priestess pales but lays a hesitant palm on Nicole's thigh. Her blaze engulfs the queen and everyone touching her. The Oracle screams but doesn't let go, and the image of Liam's beast fluctuates over his body.

"Easy, Liam," Sebastian glares, instructing Alex with a wave of his hand to his side and away from the precarious werewolf.

Darath and Moe's irises brighten to blinding proportions as the inferno licks over them. The Devil and his Prince seem to relish Kleora's hellfire, throwing their heads back as if in ecstasy. With

Moe completely naked, the evidence of his reaction to the blaze is clearly evident, and my eyes widen at his size. His phallus appears ribbed with small nodules at the base.

Jesus. Thank God he's not sentient. I'd never let that thing near Cellica.

"Holy moly," Alex whispers, ogling Moe's dick. Sebastian raises an eyebrow at it but says nothing. Of course, Logan is oblivious, concentrating only on his mate who is grasping for life.

"Everyone, ease your power back slowly," Viessa instructs, looking completely drained.

"Did it work?" Logan demands, moving closer to the bed.

"The poison is gone."

Great, but that wasn't an answer. I tilt my head, weeding out the sound of everyone else's heartbeats in the room, and concentrate on the one I crave to hear more than my next breath. My knees buckle with relief when the first weak thump fills my ears. If Nicole's heart beats in her chest, she will survive.

Moe's image shimmers as he draws his power away. The beautiful fire wings disappear, but before he vanishes back into Cellica, the demon pins me with his lustful gaze, strokes his enormous cock, offering me another wink.

I snort. Cheeky fucker. He will pay for that.

I trace to Cellica's side, catching her before she collapses over Nicole. She snuggles into my embrace, completely drained. "Did it work?" she whispers, lids closed.

"Not sure," I answer.

Liam picks up Viessa and sits down in the chair next to the fireplace. She wraps her arms around his shoulder before striking with her fangs. The werewolf grunts, and his eyes close, but he holds her close as she replenishes her strength with his blood.

Logan gathers Nicole against his chest as before with his back to the headboard. His hand trembles as he tucks her hair behind her ear and caresses her face with little kisses, quietly urging her awake.

King Darath leans against the poster, his eyes closed, while Kleora rests in his lap. "That ranks right up there with my fall from grace. It utterly sucked."

"Moe agrees," Cellica murmurs against my chest.

"Will she need blood, Oracle?" Logan asks.

Liam answers for her. "Yes, when she's conscious."

"Dawn approaches, brother. You must sleep and regain your strength," Bastian states, Alex and the baby tucked against his side. "Alex will take care of our little prince here for the day."

"I'll help," Cellica mumbles, half asleep.

"I've got it, Cel. You need to rest and recharge as well," Alex says. "Your demon is fucking beautiful, by the way."

When she doesn't respond, I glance down. She's out, snuggled against my chest. My heart warms with love at the sight of my female, trusting me enough to be completely vulnerable in my arms.

"Logan, if you don't need me for anything else, I'm gonna take care of my mate and turn in for the day."

"We are good, Nox. Thank you for everything you and Cellica did. We are grateful to Asmodeus for his help."

"I'll be sure to tell him. Good day everyone."

Instead of walking out, I trace us to my room, undress my sleeping wolf and tuck her between the sheets before bending to rekindle the dying fire.

I smile as I recall her little sneaky curiosity when she thought I was unaware. My body and mind tuned in to every twitch of her body even though I couldn't respond.

Per my ritual, I shower before climbing into bed next to her, pulling her body against mine, and resting her head on my chest. As the shutters close to the dawn, the image of Moe plays through my thoughts.

It's difficult to comprehend such an entity lives inside my petite wolf. And with an actual visual of him now, our playtime with Cellica will be twice as erotic.

Can I truly believe the danger is finally over? Abigail is dead. Nicole successfully gave birth to the Daywalker King, and she survived the poison. I feel lighter, like a mighty weight has lifted from my shoulders.

But two things still hang over my head. My punishment by the werewolf families and mending my friendship with Liam.

My arms tighten around my little wolf. I love Liam like a brother, but Cellica is mine now. I will never give her and Moe up. He needs to come to terms with it and accept me as part of the family. For Cellica's sake.

Chapter 45

Cellica

I'm surrounded by warmth, and I burrow deeper against the solid wall I'm cuddled against as my mind slowly awakens.

Holy shit. Nicole almost died, and Moe played a part in saving her. Pride fills my chest. He didn't hesitate, even though the pain was intense. Luckily, I didn't feel the full brunt of the electrical jolts or the combined power flowing between the Oracle, Lucifer, my Prince of Hell, or Kleora's hellfire. And apparently, Moe made quite the impression on Alexandria.

I stretch against the stillness of my vampire and run my fingers over his tattoos. Now that I know he's aware of what I do to him but can't respond, I think it's finally time for me to take a bit of sexual control while my mate is helpless.

'*What a fucking great idea,*' Moe mumbles sleepily. '*I need to recharge after last night.*'

I grin, knowing my demon is always on board for some deviant shenanigans.

The fire died down, but the room is still rather toasty, so I throw off the covers to have full access to my vampire. Even though I've enjoyed him up close and personal, I still gasp at his beauty and the rigid flesh standing at attention, begging for my touch.

'*Damn, his cock is pretty,*' Moe whispers, and I couldn't agree more.

I glance at the clock. Fifteen minutes until the shutters rise, announcing the start of another evening. Time enough to get my mate ramped up before he wakes.

I slide down his body and slip between his legs, spreading them to make room for my shoulders. '*What should I do first, Moe?*'

'*Lick his balls,*' he answers without hesitation.

With the initial swipe of my tongue over the bald flesh of his sack, I moan as the salty goodness perks up my tastebuds. He smells of Cedar and earth, and I want to bathe in his scent.

Nox's cock twitches as I swirl and suck his testicles, and I grin. Oh, my mate is perfectly aware of what I'm doing—seizing advantage of him while he's incapable of responding or taking over. It will probably get me punished when he wakes.

'*But we do love our spankings, don't we, wolf?*' Moe growls with arousal.

'Yes, we *do*,' I respond with a nervous giggle.

'*Lick his anus. He enjoyed that.*'

'*You're so bad,*' I admonish playfully. '*I'm not going there unless he's awake and okay with it.*'

'*Where's your kinky spirit?*' he pouts.

I ignore him as I move up and run my tongue across his shaft, lapping the pre-cum dripping from the slit. Fuck, I love the feel and taste of him. Needing him in my mouth, I rise on my knees between his spread legs, grip the base, and begin loving my mate, bobbing my head as I suck and retreat, my hair caressing his hips and stomach.

I wonder if I can make him come before he's even conscious? With my goal in mind, I set in, taking him down my throat as deep as possible. Moe helps by humming and vibrating the tip. I'm so lost in the enjoyment of sucking my mate, I don't realize his hips lift in time with my bobbing until his hand gathers my hair in a ponytail and fists it to control the thrusts.

"Baby," he moans, fully awake. "I love the way you fuck me with your mouth. And damn, the purring...." He arches his neck as my demon increases the depth of the vibration. "Is that you, Moe?"

'*Yes,*' I reply to him mentally since I refuse to stop sucking him off just to answer.

"Goddamn," he groans.

I reach down and fondle his tight sack, and his legs tremble. Then, feeling bold, I slide a finger coated with my saliva down farther until I press against the puckered opening. Instead of objecting, Nox raises his knees to give me better access, and dampness floods my sex.

"You wish to finger Daddy's ass, baby girl?" he asks, his voice deep with lust, his eyes bright.

'*I want to lick it,*' I respond mentally, watching him intently, shocked by my boldness.

"What a naughty little whore you are, Cellica," he grins before lifting my mouth off his cock. He fists his length, stroking up and down, and for a moment, I'm mesmerized by the sight of Nox pleasuring himself until he wraps his free arm around the back of one knee and lifts it to his chest.

'*Fucking jackpot!*' Moe shouts as I sprawl out on my stomach. I fondle his sack for a bit, loving the texture and feel of it before lowering my mouth to the forbidden.

Fucking hell, this is hot. My juices drench the insides of my thighs, and I rub my mound against the comforter to relieve the pulsating ache in my clit as I swirl and swipe at his anus. It tastes like him. Dark and spicy. I delve my tongue deeper, craving to bring him as much enjoyment as possible.

"Moe," Nox pants. "Make our girl come."

'*With pleasure,*' he rumbles before I feel something hot and wet flick my clit and thick fingers thrust into my sopping opening.

I keen low with bliss and double my efforts, aggressively shoving Nox's knees to his chest as he continues to pump his cock.

"What a talented whore you are, wolf." Nox growls, pumping his stiff length faster.

Within seconds, under Moe's skilled ministrations, and Daddy's degrading words, an orgasm builds rapidly.

Wanting my love to spill down my throat, I swipe my tongue across his sensitive opening one last time before rising up.

Nox's knees drop, as he snatches me by the waist, flipping me around until my pussy is over his face.

"I need to taste my baby girl's beautiful cunt as she comes all over my face."

"Oh, God," I gasp as Nox latches on to my pussy. I try to hover over him, but he's having none of it.

"Sit on my face, baby," he demands, and I obey, lowering until all my weight is on his lips and tongue devouring me.

"Chris... Oh, fuck... yes, don't stop." I shamelessly grind against him as my orgasm fires through me. Nox growls, clamping down on my waist to keep me in position.

'Let's finish him off, little wolf,' Moe orders.

I heed his command, a willing slave to my men, and lower over his body to take him in my mouth once more. Nox continues to lick and suck my pussy, and every time my mate's bulbous head hits the back of my throat, Moe hums with enjoyment as if he's tasting him too and loving it.

'I do taste him, through you,' he admits. *'And our vampire is fucking delicious. Let's make him come together.'*

Nox's strong arms clamp around my waist with one hand buried in my hair, his hips thrusting upward as he fucks my mouth with abandon while licking and sucking me from clit to anus.

"Cellica... fuck..." The muscles in his thighs stiffen, his cock thrusts deep, his hot yumminess shooting down my throat. I swallow, savoring every droplet.

After several minutes, Nox's legs drop open, and his arms fall to the side, completely spent. I grin with satisfaction, taking my time, licking and suckling his beautiful cock, until he's thoroughly clean.

Once it's done to my satisfaction, I spin and collapse on his chest. "Did we please you, Daddy?" I whisper, brushing my lips across the spot above his heart.

He inhales deeply, his arms coming around me to hold me close as he kisses my forehead. "Baby girl, Daddy's never been more pleased in his life."

I sense Moe preen with pride, and I smile. Our threesome may be unorthodox, but based on tonight's sexcapade, we are in for one wild kinky ride I'm eager to explore.

"I wish you could hear Moe in my head." I kiss my way over his peck, taking his pebbled nipple in my mouth and teasing the tip with my tongue.

Nox moans, rubbing my scalp. "It sure would save you from having to be the go-between. I saw him, you know."

I lean up and gaze at him in rapture. "What did he look like?"

"He is quite the specimen," he murmurs, lifting me to straddle his hips, his cock hard once more. "He possessed wings of fire that spanned the wall, long dark hair with pointed ears and horns. He was kneeling, but I think he's about Darath's height with bright ruby eyes."

Nox positions his engorged shaft at my opening and I grip his chest, lowering onto his hardness with a deep moan as the visual he painted of my demon plays in my mind.

"And his cock...."

I glance down when he pauses. My mate watches me with a strange expression. "What? Was there something wrong with it?"

"Besides the fact it was designed to offer immense pleasure, nothing." When Nox is seated inside me, I pause at the delicious stretching. "Fuck, you feel amazing."

"Was it big like yours?" I ask breathlessly, lifting to the tip before slamming back down, getting off on listening to my warrior describing Moe's dick.

Nox arches his neck with a deep groan. "No," he pants, palming my breasts and tweaking the nipples with the perfect pressure to offer me the right amount of pain I crave. "Moe is much bigger, his cock ribbed with raised rings along its length and nodules at the base."

My insides spasm at the image of Moe's phallus filling my anus while I ride Nox.

Reading my thoughts, Moe groans in my ear. *'Ask him if I can fuck your ass while he fucks your tasty cunt?'*

"Oh, Jesus," I whimper.

"What is Moe saying, baby girl?"

"He... he's asking permission to take me from behind at the same time."

Nox's grin is wicked. "Is that what you want, little slut? To be taken by the both of us?"

"Yes, Daddy," I confess and Nox thrusts hard in reward.

"Come here then." He lowers me until my elbows are resting on the pillow under his head.

I bury my face in his neck with a deep breath.

Nox grips my ass, spreading my cheeks, his fingers swirling the puckered opening, preparing me for Moe. As if the demon actually knelt behind me, ready to penetrate me with that enormous cock I visualize in my mind.

"Go slow, Moe. You hurt her unnecessarily, and this is over."

'Yes, Master,' Moe pants eagerly.

"He called you master," I giggle, trying not to tense at the initial sensation of something significant probing my ass.

"Damn straight," Nox growls, holding still inside me, his grip on my hips firm. "Relax, baby girl. Let our boy in."

I try to do as he directs, but the intense stretching has me gasping in pain and clutching the pillow. "Chris," I whimper.

"Look at me," he commands, and I raise my head. Turquoise and blue meet mine. "You are our perfect little slut, aren't you? Eager to do as I command, no matter how dirty."

The name-calling does it, relaxing my muscles even more. "Yes, Daddy. I love everything you say and do to me."

Nox nibbles across my jaw to my ear. "You get off on being treated like a naughty whore, don't you, Cellica?"

"Yes," I moan as Moe inches deeper, the head of his cock finally inside.

'*Open your mind to me, baby. Lower the barrier between Moe and me.*'

I squeeze my lids closed and concentrate on the two voices in my brain, imagining the wall between them crumbling to dust as Moe sinks further.

'*Can you feel me, Master?*' Moe whispers after several seconds. I watch Nox's eyes widen with triumph.

'*Yes, Demon,*' he responds. '*I feel your thick length sliding across mine. When you're fully seated, we will alternate our thrusts.*'

"You doing okay, Cellica?" Nox asks, concern tightening his expression.

"Yes. It hurts a little, but I don't want to stop."

'*Because you are the perfect mate,*' Moe whispers. '*Always eager to satisfy us both.*'

"Moe's right," Nox says, brushing my hair from my face. "We are going to fuck you until you scream for mercy."

"God, yes. Please use and abuse me, Daddy. I need to feel your cocks taking me hard."

"Jesus, Cellica. You are fucking incredible."

Nox pulls back and thrusts deep, and I whimper with pleasure when Moe counteracts his movement in my ass. Even though the stretching and burn are intense, the fullness shuttles in a euphoric peace and I relax further for my men.

For years, I've fantasized about being taken by multiple partners. Never in my wildest dreams did I ever imagine it would come true. And not just any males, but my males. The vampire I love, would lay down my life for, and the demon who captured my heart with his lustful abandon and eagerness to stay with me.

I whimper with pleasure as Moe drives faster, countering Nox's relentless pace. The more they move, the more my muscles expand, allowing Moe to slide in and out with better ease. Those rings Nox talked about caress my inner walls with each thrust, heightening the sensations.

"Can… you feel… him, Chris? Those ridges?" I pant, barely able to speak as an incredible build tightens within me.

"Fuck yes. Between his cock rubbing against mine and your tight cunt, I'm not going to last long."

"Bite me, Christoph. Let me please you in all ways."

When Nox strikes, I gasp his name. The aggressiveness of their taking, combined with my mate's fangs in my flesh, causes tiny explosions in my lower abdomen.

When my climax hits, like a freight train, plowing through my system with the force of a tornado, I scream, undone by the extreme intensity.

Jesus. I've never experienced anything like it in my life. Every muscle in my body quivers, and darkness dances at the edge of my vision. My inner walls pulsate, prolonging the sensations seizing my breath.

Even before the flutters ease, a powerful sting strikes the other side of my neck, and I realize Moe bit me. The delicious pain skyrockets another climax as both of my males fuck me relentlessly, claiming me with their bite and their cocks.

'*We are fucking one,*' Moe growls after dislodging from my flesh. '*I claim you as my Mistress until your last breath.*'

"Yes, Moe," Nox shouts. "Come with me."

At the command, the demon shouts his release, driving deep. I cry out at the exquisite pain and collapse on Nox's chest, loving the fullness of both my mates deep inside me. I could remain here forever, being taken repeatedly in new and inventive ways by my vampire and demon.

A small part of me wishes Moe was sentient so Nox and I could enjoy him together, but I think my mate would object to a *live* threesome.

How did the werewolves put it…? To their swords crossing? Vampires don't share, and the fact he's come to accept Moe as my inner passenger, allowing him to claim me and participate in our relationship, just proves how much Nox truly loves me.

Does my vampire get enjoyment out of Moe joining our intimate moments? Yes, I believe he does. To a point. But if Moe ever crossed the line, my Guardian drew in the sand, I fear he would shut him down and not think twice about it.

Chapter 46

"My queen," I whisper and drop to one knee in front of her and Logan. Shock froze my limbs when I walked into the dining hall to discover her standing at the head of the table, fully recovered, with Lucian in her arms. She and Logan have not stepped foot outside their chambers for the past week, and we were all worried sick. "It is so good to see you up and about."

After the most incredible sex of my life, Cellica and I took a long hot shower where I reveled in tasting her cunt while Moe twisted and pulled her nipples until they both screamed my name.

Every day before dawn and each evening before I start my duties, the three of us have enjoyed enacting Cellica's fantasies. The freaky demon even added a few I would've never thought of.

I have tied her up, teasing and bringing them to the brink for hours, denying them both release until tears ran down her face and she begged and promised me anything. Moe's taken her sweet cunt while I took her from behind. I adorned her with a collar and leash, forced her to hands and knees, and paddled her ass bright red while degrading her with words in just the manner she likes. I've become addicted to waking up every morning with her tongue swirling my anus and her tiny fist pumping my raging erection.

Over the last century, I've been involved in numerous three-somes and orgies. I am a vampire; we have insatiable appetites, but the ménages were always two females and me. Never have I touched a male intimately, nor had any desire to do so.

When I felt Moe's enormous size stretching Cellica with merely a thin wall of tissue separating us, and witnessed the absolute rapture on her face, I let go of my inhibitions and enjoyed the moment with my mate. I'd do anything to drive my wolf insane with lust, to please and pleasure her, and if having Moe as an active participant in our sex life adds to that element, so be it.

But if I ever find him pleasuring her without me, I will sever the connection and force Cellica to shove him deep. She is mine. Mine to touch and tease, taunt and discipline, and lead to climax. Not Moe's. And while I've grown fond of the demon, I'd slay him in a heartbeat, if I could, if he tried to steal my girl.

"Thank you, Nox, for everything you did to bring me back," Nicole responds, laying her hand on my head. "You are a true warrior and friend."

"I would lay down my life for you, my lady."

"Let's fucking hope it never comes to that," she smiles, swaying with the baby in her arms as I rise to my feet.

"Language, my love," Logan admonishes quietly, cupping his son's head.

"Oh, right." Nicki rolls her eyes. "I'm supposed to clean up my foul mouth for my son."

I laugh. "Good luck with that."

"Yeah, and get this, my punishment isn't putting money in a swear jar, `cause Logan looked at me like I was weird when I suggested that. Nope, he threatened me with a lash for every word." She chuckles, and I grin knowingly. "Since I've been deprived for the last couple of months, thanks to this little one," she smiles down at Lucian for a second. "I'm going to be fucking swearing up a goddamn storm."

Logan shakes his head with a smile. "I cannot win."

"Oh, I think that's in the win column, Logan," Cellica chimes in with a wink at Nicole.

"Damn fucking straight it is," she grins back.

When Liam walks in with Viessa at his side, my insides tighten. Only one reason he's at our nightly meeting—my punishment. I hoped we could discuss this in private instead of in front of all my fellow Guardians, but apparently, my shame will be on display for everyone.

Alex bops in and takes the prince from Nicole. "It's auntie Alex's turn with our precious bundle. I'm your favorite aunt, aren't I?" she coos at the baby as she exits the room. Sebastian's grin is tender but strained.

Not too long ago, the valkyrie gave up the possibility of having children to be with Bastian. Unfortunately, the gods decided since she was part shifter and part valkyrie, offspring with a vampire was forbidden. So she either sacrificed her life or the ability to create life.

I'm sure it pains Sebastian to see her so enthralled with little Lucian, knowing he's the reason she will never experience motherhood. But I have no doubt Alex would make the same decision again in a heartbeat. Sebastian and the petite valkyrie have a special bond forged in tragedy and pain and solidified with love and sacrifice. Nothing will ever break it.

When the hundred or so Guardians are finally seated at the long table, Nicole takes her chair with Logan on one side and Sebastian on the other. My place is next to my commander. Liam grabs the seat opposite me with Viessa hovering behind him.

Cellica kisses my cheek. "I'm right here, Christoph. I love you."

I smile to alleviate her worried expression, and she moves back but keeps her fingers wrapped around the top of my chair.

"Maybe you should go help Alex with the baby, Cellica. You shouldn't be here."

"I'm not leaving, brother," she growls, and I grin at her fierce protectiveness of me. It's adorable. I'll have to think of some inventive way to show my appreciation later.

Liam sighs with a glare in my direction, and I shrug. "She's my mate, Liam. Get used to it."

"Okay, can we move past the family drama and get down to it?" Nicole demands, and a hush settles over the table. "Play it out for us, Liam. I want to understand what is going to go down, step by step. And just so you know, I will be there. No one is keeping me from supporting Nox during this bullshit political stunt."

"Tell that to the families left behind, Nicki," Liam responds quietly.

"They slit Cellica's throat, King Scott. Do you not care about the trauma they put your sister through?"

"Of course, I do," he says with a growl. "But Nox struck the first blow. He killed their leader, and they responded in kind."

"By attempting to kill an innocent girl?"

"I'm not saying it's right or wrong, but they paid the ultimate price for it, did they not?"

Nicole grits her teeth. "I fucking hate this. Nox didn't do anything the rest of us wouldn't have done in the same situation."

"You're correct, but that doesn't make it okay."

"My queen," I say, interrupting the stare-off between the two rulers. "As you said, I'm a Guardian. I should have had more control. They taunted me, and I lost it. If this tribunal of sorts brings peace to the families and prevents an uprising, then so be it. I will take my punishment."

Silence prevails as Nicki digests my words until Sebastian speaks up. "My queen, we back whatever decision you make, but this is not just about Nox. If you refuse their demands for retribution, it not only puts King Scott in a precarious spot with his people but with the Vampire Nation as well. Your legacy is about peace, not starting a war over one vampire's actions in the heat of the moment."

"Nox."

"Yes, my queen?"

"Cellica will be at the ready to offer you her blood when it's over." Her eyes ignite with emotion. "We will all be there, and if I determine these families are dragging it out to ensure your death, I *will* stop it, consequences be damned." She directs the statement to Liam, her irises flaring bright to mark her point.

Liam nods. "I agree. Nox is not only my friend but a member of my family now. I will ensure this goes as smoothly as possible."

I inhale a deep breath at his words. It's the first time Liam has acknowledged our mating in a positive way. His gaze shifts to mine, and I nod, warmth blanketing my chest at the acceptance in his eyes.

"Thank you, brother," Cellica says quietly from behind me. I sense her relief at his comments.

"The head of the families set up the competition area at Werewolf Headquarters," Liam begins after a brief smile at his little sister. "It's basically like a gladiator ring, only not as big as the Colosseum in Rome. In the center of the dirt arena, they've built a stand. They will chain Nox's hands above his head and strip him to the waist. The Alpha male of each family will dole out ten lashes with a cat-o'-nine-tails."

"Jesus," Nicole whispers, and I second that sentiment. This is gonna fucking hurt like a mother. The whip will flay the skin from my back, and if they draw out the beatings, I could bleed out and fall into a coma if not replenished quickly enough.

I reach up and squeeze Cellica's hand, sensing her distress. '*It's okay baby*,' I reassure her mentally. '*With all the blood I've ingested from you over the past week, I'll heal in an instant.*'

'*You need my blood,*' Moe growls in my head. '*Allow me to detach from Cellica into my true form for a few minutes and you can drink from me.*'

The mere notion of ingesting the potent Prince of Hell's essence tightens my gut and pools saliva in my mouth. What will he taste like? Intense and spicy the way Cellica described steak. Or will it be sweet and savory like my wolf's?

"Is that even possible?" Nicki challenges with a raised eyebrow, having heard our internal conversation.

'*Yes,*' Moe answers. '*We will need to reconnect in the same manner we did before fairly quickly though.*' Meaning sex and the exchange of blood with my mate. My cock twitches at the thought.

"Will King Darath have to be there for it again?" Cellica asks.

'*No. I won't be possessing Nox, so the transition back to where I'm tethered should be seamless. I just require sex to restore my strength.*' he states, and I sense the devilish grin in his words.

'*Of course you do,*' I mutter.

"For what?" Liam responds to Cellica with a frown. "What's going on?"

"In order to fortify Nox, Asmodeus is suggesting he separate from Cellica for a few minutes so Nox can drink from him. The blood from a powerful Prince of Hell will help heal him faster."

"You can hear him talking to them?" Bastian asks with raised eyebrows.

"I hear all internal conversations," she answers with a shrug. "Make it happen, Nox. I want you juiced up as much as possible."

"When is this taking place?" I ask Liam.

"Tomorrow after sunset."

Shit.

"I need to know who all is coming so I can section off seating."

A Guardian midway down the table, Norrix, stands. "I will be there."

"As will I." Another rises.

One by one, the Guardians come to their feet, announcing their desire to be present and support me. My chest tightens with gratitude. These males are my family. We live together, drink together, and have fought side by side for over a century.

Nicole smiles proudly at the show of loyalty. "Thank you, Guardians. And as much as I'd love to go storming in there with a contingent of my warriors, I think it best if we narrow it down. Say a dozen of our finest?" she directs to Sebastian and he nods. "So our family of seven plus twelve."

"Cellica will sit with me and Josh," Liam states.

"It would be beneficial to have her sit with us," Logan interjects. "Not only as a show of solidarity with the werewolves, but afterward we will not have to hunt her down in the crowd to bring her back here to aid Nox."

I turn to my mate. "Cellica, it's your decision."

She takes a tentative step forward to stand between mine and Bastian's chairs, her hand on my shoulder. "I think it best if I sit with the vampires. They are my family now too, and I want to be available for Christoph."

"I honor your decision. I may not like it since I prefer you by my side, but I respect your choice."

About damn time he started treating her like an adult.

Chapter 47

All night, during the lengthy meeting and as I patrolled the grounds, my mind fretted about drinking from Moe. I'm not sure why I'm so anxious about it. I've consumed from males before when needed. However, they aren't my first choice because the act of partaking from another is intimate and invariably causes arousal. The last thing I need to see again or experience up close and personal is Moe's ribbed member.

Maybe I should have him kneel since he's tall and I can stand behind him. No, then I would witness his erection over his shoulder. But seeing is better than having it pushed against mine, if we were chest to chest.

Fuck. I glance down at my dick pushing against the zipper of my pants with a frown. "What in God's name is wrong with you?" I admonish it. I'm *not* sexually attracted to males. Never have been.

I relish the taste and softness of females—one in particular—and adore the contrast of our size and strength. Even though their emotions and how they think boggles my mind to this day. It's just another aspect of being with a female that I utterly enjoy and am fascinated by.

But the image of Moe repeatedly plays in my brain, and every time it does, my traitorous dick pulses with a need I have no fucking clue what to do with. Is it because he's the demon of lust, built to entice and lure? Maybe I should consult Darath and get his insight into the demon's influence over me.

Mind made up, I take out my phone and shoot a quick text to the king of Hell.

ME: **I need to pick ur brain.**

Darath: **I'm not for sale.** He responds immediately, and I snort.

ME: **Does Moe hold some kind of special allure that draws his victims to him?**

Darath: **Ur not a victim, Nox. Ur a strong, brave little vampire, never doubt that.**

ME: **I'm fucking serious, Jag!**

Darath: **Ur no fun. Yes. Asmodeus' beauty was by design. He exudes sexuality on a carnal level and anyone in his presence, who is not a powerful demon in their own right, falls prey to his appeal. Why? You crave to suck that enormous ringed cock of his? U can tell me. My lips are sealed.**

ME: **Fuck off, Jag**

Darath: **LMAO! Just remember ur his master now, vampire. U and the wolf control what happens, not Asmodeus. His charm may entice u, but whatever arises is on YOU.**

Well, shit. No one to blame but myself, I guess. Although I feel better about what Darath revealed. I now understand why my cock hardens at the thought of him, especially after seeing him in person. It's not because I suddenly crave the fucker. I shudder. No, it's kinda like a succubi's magical temptation. They fill your thoughts with lust, making you believe you can't live without them, that you will die if you don't give them everything they desire when in fact, they are slowly killing you with sex by sucking your soul from you.

Moe's appeal forces my body to respond, even when my mind recoils at the notion of anything sexual between us. I'm okay with Cellica being the focus of our combined sensual deviancy, but it will be a wintry day in Hell before I allow a goddamn thing to happen between Moe and myself.

Here's hoping I can fight his allure when my fangs sink deep into his neck.

"**Y**ou okay, Chris?" Cellica asks for the hundredth time around bites of steak and green beans.

I finished my patrol early, wanting to spend as much time with my mate before the dawn, but I'm antsy. A rumbling fury boils below the surface, making my skin itch, and I struggle with the why.

"Yes. Please stop asking me that." I tap my fingers impatiently on the table, willing her to finish so I can haul her up to our room and fuck her senseless. Without Moe.

"I want tonight to be just you and I. Understood?" My brusque tone jerks her wide-eyed gaze to mine.

"Of course," she replies demurely, and I feel like a complete ass with no way to control it.

"Are you worried about tomorrow?"

"No."

"Okay."

"If you're finished, I'd like to spank the shit out of you."

What in fuck's sake is wrong with me? The slow simmer swells into a boiling fury, and it seems to be directed at Cellica.

Her breath hitches. "W-why? What did I do?"

"You...." *Shut this down, Nox, before you say something you'll regret.*

"Nothing. Forget it." I rise from the table. "I apologize. Finish your meal. I need to speak with Nicole anyway. I'll meet you in our chamber later."

"Nox," she calls out, but I ignore her and stride out of the dining room.

Why the fuck am I taking this out on Cellica? My condition is not her responsibility.

That's not true, my inner voice whispers again. *She's the reason Moe is in our lives. The reason we are soon to be tortured. She put herself in that situation with the wolves. She could have controlled the demon and walked away if she'd been stronger.*

No! Fuck no.

It's not her fault. She was just in the wrong place at the wrong time, and she wasn't even immortal, for fuck's sake. No way she would've had the strength to defy him. So why am I so furious with her?

I should be livid with Moe. Everything that's transpired since that portal opened has been his error. Cellica's possession. His seduction of me, of the wolves. All of it is his fault, but the only thing my intellect can focus on is tossing her over my lap, peeling her jeans and underwear down, and paddling her ass red.

Because it should be Moe, you're disciplining. You should punish him for his crimes, for making your dick hard and craving something abhorrent in your mind.

Yes! That's exactly right. I desire to chasten Moe. Technically, he's the one they should put on the rack and dole out thirty lashes to tomorrow, but since it's impossible, my only other option is to thrash the shit out of the demon through Cellica.

I beeline it for my room to prepare. I require an outlet for my wrath. For the turmoil boiling in my brain, and I know precisely how to accomplish it. Moe has pushed me beyond my limits, and it's time he paid the piper. The demon needs to suffer the consequences of his actions.

My dick strains against my pants as my mind plays out the Prince's long overdue punishment.

Chapter 48

Cellica

'Cellica, *don't go up to the room just yet. Allow Nox time to cool off,'* Moe warns in my mind as I take my plate to the kitchen. I realize they have servants to handle the clean-up, but my dad raised me better, and old habits die hard.

'*Do you know why he's so angry with me?*'

'*Yes.*'

When he doesn't elaborate, I frown. '*Care to share before I get paddled to within an inch of my life?*'

Moe's sigh is heavy, and dread flutters like a hundred butterflies in my gut. As much as I relish getting spanked, something tells me what's coming won't be about my pleasure, but Nox's absolution over whatever I'm not understanding. Fury brightened his gaze at dinner. His whole body thrummed with it, and if I'm the cause, I'd like to identify why so we can talk about it.

'*Nox is pissed at me,*' Moe declares finally, and my eyebrows raise. Why would Nox be furious at him? He helped save Nicole's life and offered his blood to aid tomorrow's healing process.

'*Why? And how do you know?*' I rinse my dishes in the sink and stack them in the dishwasher while carrying on a mental conversation with my demon.

'Because of who I am. The way Lucifer designed me. Anyone who lays eyes on my true form desires me. It's a curse, really.'

'Oh poor you,' I say with an exaggerated eye roll. *'It must be tough to be wanted by everyone.'*

'You have no idea.'

'So why does that anger... Oh, right. Nox saw you.'

'Yes, and now he's pissed for wanting me. I believe he perceives it as a violation of his mind. Or some stupid shit. Tonight will be harsh, love, but understand, it is about punishing me, not you.'

'Great. Sounds delightful.' My ass clenches just thinking about it.

'When we get up there, give me control and I can capture the brunt of the pain.'

'No. Nox already stated he didn't want you involved tonight. I refuse to go against his wishes or trick him, especially in his current mood.'

'Fine. Then let us ask him. If it is me he truly yearns to punish, then he will agree.'

'But I don't want to miss out on a spanking,' I pout, and the demon laughs.

'You will have plenty of opportunities to enjoy suffering the consequences of being a bad girl. I promise. Allow me to suffer this pain for you. It rightfully belongs to me. I have caused you both much misery.'

'Fine,' I relent as I climb the stairs at a snail's pace. *'But only if he agrees.'*

'Deal.'

The second I walk into Nox's chambers, I'm shocked by the transformation. He shoved the enormous bed against the wall, making more room for the chains dangling from hooks in the ceiling. My stomach clenches at the remembered pain and humiliation in the bunker, and I rub my belly where Abigail sliced me open.

Thanks to Nox's blood, the scar diminished, and while Moe took the brunt of the suffering for me, my mind still recoils at the memory.

A warm fire crackles gently in the fireplace, and a thin black belt rests on the bed like a coiled snake ready to strike.

Holy shit. Moe was right... Nox means business tonight. My heart rate doubles and sweat beads my upper lip.

"Take off your clothes," he demands as soon as the door clicks shut.

"Nox, can we talk first?"

"After you're naked. Now, do as I command."

My inner wolf can't deny her Alpha's order, so I lift my t-shirt off, toss it on the chair by the fire, slip out of my tennis shoes, unbutton my jeans, and slide them off to join my shirt.

Once I'm completely exposed, I bite my lip as my muscles tremble with a mixture of fear and desire. "Are you angry with me, Nox?"

"No, baby girl. I'm livid."

I swallow as his eyes brighten and clench my fingers together at my waist. His icy tone scares me more than anything. "Why?"

"You chose him long before he ever bonded to you. It's partially your fault he's in our lives, and I need to take it out on your hide."

"I see. No, wait. I don't see. Be honest with yourself, Nox. You blame me because the vision of Moe gets you aroused, and your dick hardens at the thought of seeing him again." Jesus, why am I pushing him when he's ready to implode?

"Shut the fuck up, Cellica."

My eyes narrow with anger at his snarl. "Do not talk to me that way," I growl back. "This isn't about me at all. Tonight is between you and Moe. He's asking permission to come forward and take the brunt of your wrath. Although personally, I think he should tell you to go fuck yourself."

"I told you, I don't want him engaged until I require his damn blood." Nox clenches his fists at his sides, and the chest muscles bunch and flex with the emotions coursing through him. His fury, his lust, and his shame radiate from his body language and expression like a neon sign.

"But he *is* involved. It's him you truly wish to inflict pain upon. I don't deserve your wrath, Christoph. So unless you agree to grant him control, I will get dressed and leave you to sleep the day by yourself. As much as I enjoy your spankings, I won't allow you to hit me in anger. I deserve better than that." My body trembles with my defiance as one thing becomes finally clear. I am not less than. I am *more* than. "I refuse to allow anyone to strike me in a violent way, especially not the man I love."

Nox stands there bare-chested, barefoot, with his jeans slung low on his hips in silence for several minutes. My comments seem to have stunned him.

"Fuck, Cellica," he groans, and even though guilt radiates from him in waves, I'm dumbfounded when he drops to his knees, his head bowed. "Forgive me. I would never hurt you intentionally. It's just this situation with Moe is fucking with my brain."

With uneasy steps, I close the distance between us. The second my hand grazes his hair, he wraps his arms around my waist and buries his face in my stomach, his chest heaving with the effort to control his emotions. "Chris. The arousal you feel is not your fault. Lucifer cursed Moe to have this effect on anyone who sees his true form."

"Yes, I know. Darath explained things, but it doesn't negate the rage and resentment at being forced to experience desire for him when it's not who I am."

"Would it help if you were able to discipline him, to take your frustrations out on him?"

Nox raises his head, and I witness the violence still simmering in his eyes. "I don't want to hurt you," he whispers. "But I'm fucking pissed as hell, and if my emotions aren't given an outlet soon, I won't be in the right mindset for tomorrow. I need the asshole to experience an iota of what I will endure. He shares in the responsibility for that night."

'You won't harm her,' Moe finally speaks up. *'Cel will only feel the pleasurable burn to heighten her lust. I vow it.'*

Nox rises to his feet and grips my face between his palms. "I love you, baby girl, but if I don't discipline Moe, I'll go postal. I require this control over him. Please tell me you understand and are okay with it."

"I can't lie and say I comprehend what you're feeling, but if this can ease your mind and allow you and Moe to come to some kind of understanding, then I have no choice but to be fine with it. But you two need to work this shit out. Lay down the ground rules and foundation for the three of us to move forward. Moe can't change how he was designed, so you must discover a way to handle your reaction to him."

Nox nods before gently brushing his lips across mine. "I'm sorry I yelled at you. I love you." He moves away from me several steps and I feel the loss in my heart. "Moe. The second I'm done, you retreat. I'm fucking my mate alone. Is that understood?"

I sense my demon tremble at the authority in Nox's tone. *'Yes, Master.'*

Nox inhales at his easy submission, but it seems to only kindle the rage anew. "Come forth, you bastard. I want to see your image hover over Cellica, so I know it's you I'm punishing."

"Yes, Master," Moe says through me as he pushes forward. "I hear and obey."

I study my mate's expression as he takes in what I can only assume is Moe's form looming over mine. I sense the demon's size, his strength hovering over me like a protective bubble, but I'm still aware. When Nox grips my wrist, drawing my arm up into the shackles, it feels like he's grabbing me through thick rubber.

'You will only feel enjoyment, little wolf. I promise.'

In a way, I understood Nox's madness toward Moe for compelling him to experience desire where there is none. Similar to the way I was livid with him for forcing me into the situation with the wolves and then the witch.

However, a part of me wonders if some of Nox's fury isn't directed at himself because of his body's reaction to Moe's presence. I don't doubt Nox's sexual preference for one second. He loves women, but he also enjoys having Moe involved in our sexual escapades. It ramps up his lust knowing that together they propel me to heights of rapture I wouldn't achieve otherwise without the aid of toys.

Nox will never admit it again, but he damn sure loved Moe's tongue swirling around his ass while he fucked me on our mating night.

In my mind, right or wrong, our situation is unique. Different from an actual physical threesome. Moe is merely an entity living inside me with the ability to offer pleasure to his host. He doesn't manifest as a real sentient immortal, just a shimmering apparition over my body when circumstances demand it. Like tonight.

Nox's bitterness, guilt, and wrath fuels this punishment directed at himself and Moe. Add in the fact he condemns the demon for putting me in the situation with the wolves in the first place, and it's a volatile scene I'm relieved to be shielded against.

I sincerely hope this eradicates my mate's rage, and the three of us can move past it and continue to enjoy each other. Because if Nox can't get beyond his emotions, I fear he will demand I shove Moe deep and banish him from our lives.

As much as I love the Prince, and it would break my heart to not feel his presence inside me, I choose Nox. The vampire owns me. Heart. Mind. Soul. Now and forever.

Chapter 49

The second Moe's wrists are secure, I step back and take a deep breath. In my century and a half, I've never felt so out of control, my emotions ready to rip me in two. I hope this session purges my guilt and resentment toward the demon. It's a dark cloud hovering and expanding over Cellica and me. If I don't eradicate it, it will consume me and destroy us, but I must remain in control.

"Asmodeus, do you understand why I am whipping you?" I shove away his nickname. Tonight is about dominating the Prince of Hell and bringing him to heal, so he understands I will not tolerate any bullshit moving forward. If we move forward.

"Yes, Master," he replies quietly. "I deserve to be punished for the things I did to Cellica and for what my actions forced you to do."

"I'm giving you the exact number of lashings I'll receive tomorrow. Cry out if you need to, but I will show no mercy."

"I deserve none. Don't hold back, vampire. Give me your rage." The demon's hands grip the chains in readiness and a cold smile lifts my lips. I'm going to fucking enjoy striping his ass red.

I move into position, ignoring how my cock strains against the zipper of my jeans. Or the sexual images flitting through my mind as I raise my arm, the belt dangling from my fist.

At the first strike across his muscular ass, Asmodeus jerks but doesn't utter a peep, and the rage burning a hole in my gut spreads.

I take my time, wanting to draw out his suffering for as long as possible. By hit ten, red welts crisscross his athletic cheeks, but he still refuses to make a sound. A sick, depraved part of me craves to hear him whimper or shout out, and the fucker damn well knows it.

"You nearly got my mate killed." *Crack.* "Didn't you?" *Crack.*

"Yes, Master," Asmodeus groans and my cock shoves against my zipper.

"You forced her to orgasm with the witch." Another two hits, the melody of leather slapping flesh fills the room and hardens my cock to painful proportions. "Didn't you?" *Crack.*

"Y... Yes, Master."

At the halfway point, I pause. "Why, Asmodeus?"

"Because I'm a deviant son of a bitch who requires daily sexual release," he grits out between clenched teeth. "You refused to fuck her, so I took matters into my own hands."

I squeeze my eyes shut as rage washes over me like molten lava, threatening to consume me. I raise the belt and strike him four times in a row with enough force; the demon finally roars, clenching his butt cheeks.

"You son of a bitch," I snarl. *Crack.* "You will never touch my mate again without my permission." *Crack.* "Is that understood?"

"Yes, Master," he pants out, his knuckles white on the chains. "I hear and obey."

Crack. Crack. Crack. Crack.

Asmodeus shouts, locking his knees to keep from dangling from the shackles around his wrists, and when I step to the side for a better angle, I freeze with my arm in the air.

The demon is rock hard. Pre-cum drips from the bulbous tip as it jerks with pleasure.

What the fuck? He's getting off on the agony. He wasn't locking his knees to remain standing against the pain. He's fucking ready to detonate, which means Cellica is as well.

The image of my mate's pussy glistening with her desire has me squeezing my cock for a second to relieve the pressure.

"Five more hits, Asmodeus. When the last hit strikes your ass, I want you to come. Let me see you shoot your load clear across the room."

What in holy hell am I doing? This was supposed to be about doling out punishment, not giving him an orgasm. But I can't seem to stop myself. I crave to witness Moe's enormous cock explode from the pain I'm inflicting. It's fucked up and beyond deviant, but the second I realized he was finding pleasure in his beating, I could think of nothing else.

The demon's hips buck at my command. "Yes, Master."

"Count with me, Asmodeus." I rear back and strike him with vampire strength.

"One!" he roars, and his dick jumps.

Crack.

"Two. Fuck!"

"If you come before five, I will lock you down for a week. Do you understand?" A week without sexual release would be *real* torture for the demon of lust.

"Yes, I understand."

"Who controls you, Asmodeus?"

"You do, Master."

"Say my fucking name!"

"Nox. You control me, Nox."

Crack.

"Three!"

"You will never touch Cellica without my permission."

"No! I hear and obey, Nox."

Crack.

"Four!" His hips pump in earnest now, and the massive thighs tremble with the need for release.

I stride closer, delaying the final blow, and rub his blazing red ass. The demon pushes against my palm, no doubt relishing the burn.

"If you behave like a good little demon, I will whip you into an orgasm regularly, but if you defy me," I grip his hair and jerk his head back, showcasing my bright eyes and fangs. "I will deny you the ability to participate in our sex life or any release for as long as I see fit. Are we clear?"

"Yes, Master. Crystal. Please let us come."

I shove his head forward and step back. "Come, my little wolf and demon."

The second the leather slaps his sore, heated flesh, Moe arches his neck with a roar, and I step up behind him, shove his head to the side and sink my fangs deep into his neck as he explodes.

While I gulp down his powerful essence, I watch over his shoulder as stream after stream of cum shoots from his massive length. His ass shoves against my harness with every thrust of his hips until his orgasm wanes. But when I clamp down harder, sucking down his potent blood, Moe sighs, resting his head on my shoulder.

I reward him for his offering by running my palm across his torso, down the impressive washboard of his abs, until I grip the base of his cock. He groans in pleasure, bucking into my palm. And even though he just orgasmed, the demon's dick is still rock hard.

It's strange to hold another male's engorged member in my fist. I don't stroke him. I merely support him as he pumps his hips and thrusts into my hand while I swallow down gulp after gulp of the essence that will allow me to heal at lightning speed tomorrow.

I can't stop my body's response when I take nourishment directly from the vein, and it's no different with Moe. My inner vampire reverts to pure instinct, craving sex as much as the blood.

Within seconds, Moe's legs stiffen, his momentum becoming frantic. Christoph, the man in me, is repulsed by what's happening. I'm practically giving a demon a hand job. But the vampire in me is totally aroused and intrigued by the idea of bringing off such a powerful being.

'Do not come, Asmodeus,' I command in his mind, needing to bring a semblance of control back. His body freezes. The thrusts cease. *'Your next orgasm will be through Cellica. As your reward for obeying and taking your discipline well, we will fuck her together.'*

"Yes, Master," he whispers with a shudder when I clamp down hard on the base of his cock as a warning.

"Did you mean what you said about offering me punishment on a regular basis?" he asks tentatively.

'Yes, Moe.'

"Can I make a request, Master?"

'You may.'

"Will you use a whip or something that will score my flesh next time?"

Jesus. He requires extreme measures. But I'm more than happy to offer him that level of pain. It grants the demon release, but it also eases the turmoil in my mind.

I would never inflict something so harsh on my delicate mate, but with Moe, I crave doling out pain to him as much as he relishes receiving. It satisfies a deep dark part of my soul I never knew existed until the Prince of Hell came into our lives.

'I'll see what I can do.' I mentally grin at the excitement pouring from him at my words.

Moe's blood stimulates my lust, for my demon, but primarily for my mate. By the time I remove my fangs from his neck, my stomach is pleasantly full. I've taken more from him than I would dare from Cellica, and a buzz of power hums through my system.

"Thank you for your offering, Moe. Your blood will sustain me through what's coming."

"My pleasure. I would take tomorrow from you if I could, Master."

"No doubt. Retreat," I command, and his image immediately fluctuates and alters until my naked mate is dangling from the chains, her toes two feet off the floor.

Anxious I might have hurt her, I stroll around and brush her hair behind her ear. Her chin rests on her chest. "Baby girl? Are you okay?"

Dark lashes flutter. "Jesus," she whispers, and my heart plummets.

"Fuck, Cel. I'm so sorry." I frantically work the shackles with one hand while holding her body against mine with my other arm wrapped around her tiny waist.

When her wrists are free, she collapses weakly against me, and I run my palms over her ass, searching for the welts that marred Moe's flesh. When I find nothing, I grip a fist full of her hair and tilt her head back so I can study her face. The corners of her lips lift as those whiskey irises, that burned through my walls into my soul, gaze up at me with satisfaction and relaxed bliss.

"That was fucking incredible, Christoph. The emotions and lust igniting through Moe with every strike were beyond anything I've ever experienced." Her smile widens. "Our demon is an extremely complicated being."

"So, I didn't hurt you?"

"God no. I didn't think it was possible to orgasm from a spanking, but holy crap, when he came, so did I and then again when you gripped him."

I grin. "Well, hang on, baby girl. The night is still young."

Chapter 50

Cellica

I squint against the stadium lights shining down on the raised platform in the center of the dirt arena, my leg bouncing with anxiousness and my thumbnail torn and jagged from chewing on it. I'm about to explode out of my skin. My wolf hovers below the surface, apprehension and fear clouding her mind.

'*Easy, little one,*' Moe murmurs. '*Our boy has my blood running through his veins. He will heal quickly.*'

'*It's still gonna hurt, Moe. Like really bad.*'

'*Yes, but he's a warrior, Cellica. A battle-hardened soldier. He will get through this fine.*'

"He's right, you know," the vampire queen sitting to my right whispers in my ear, making me jump. I forget she hears all telepathic conversations. "Nox is tough as nails."

Logan sits on my left, and the heat from his naked torso warms my side. "My queen speaks the truth. Nox is a resilient son of a bitch and with a Prince of Hell's blood in his system, it will be a distant memory in no time."

"One I will help him forget," I vow quietly.

"Atta girl," Nicole grins, but I notice her words don't diminish the rage in her bright gray eyes. The queen is clearly pissed her

Guardian must suffer through this in the first place, and I couldn't agree more.

I fidget on the hard seating, glaring at my brothers seated at the head of the arena, surrounded by the families of the fallen. Liam leans back on his throne casually, with one ankle resting on the opposite knee. Still, the rigidity of his jaw is painfully apparent even from this distance.

Viessa perches next to him in a smaller chair with Josh on the other side. Besides the dozen Guardians behind me, the stone seating surrounding the spectacle about to take place below over-flows with werewolves eager to witness vampire blood spilled.

This is all my fault. I should be the one being punished tonight, not Nox. If I'd had a better handle on my demon, none of this would be necessary. Instead, my mate will experience excruciating pain because of me.

'*And me,*' Moe pipes in, always in tune with my thoughts and emotions.

My body tenses when two buff werewolves bring a chained, shirtless Nox out onto the arena. His eyes scan the stands, searching, and when those beautiful irises land on me, his shoulders appear to relax.

"You are his lifeline through this, young wolf," Logan murmurs. "Be strong for him."

I nod and force myself to smile down at my mate. '*I love you, Christoph. And when this bullshit is all over, I'm going to show you just how much.*'

His eyes brighten at my words as the wolves shackle his wrists to the stanchion, his arms spread wide, and my gut clenches. Jesus. I don't know if I can watch this. How will I keep my wolf calm while our mate is being tortured in front of us? It will be a miracle I don't morph out at the first strike and knock all the Guardians on their asses.

'*Give me strength, Moe. Keep my wolf at bay.*'

'*I've got your back, Cellica,*' he vows.

I inhale a deep breath and let it out slowly just as a large male strides into the stadium, a vicious-looking whip clutched in his fist.

Dave's father, Dalton, marches up behind Nox but turns to his king to await the go-ahead. Before Liam can say anything, Nicole stands. She's dressed in black dress pants, a silk button-down shirt the color of lilacs, with a dark blazer over the top. You would never know she just survived a poisoning and childbirth a mere week ago.

"I would like to speak if I may, King Scott," she announces in a loud, commanding voice, and a hush falls over the crowd. My brother's eyes narrow, but he offers a nod. "The Vampire Nation grieves with you over the loss of Dave Hill, Mike Grim, and Luke Loneclaw. As a new mother, I can't imagine the enduring pain you feel losing a child, no matter their age. And no one understands the need for retribution or revenge more than I do. But my Guardian's actions were that of a bonded male who felt his female was being threatened. Would any of you react first and question later if your mate was in danger?

"I have allowed this tribunal out of respect for your king and because, as a Guardian, mated or not, Christoph Nox should have shown more restraint and control. But understand this; After tonight, the Vampire Nation will never again allow you to harm one of our own, no matter the circumstances. I seek peace with every pack in the Werewolf Provence, but I protect my own first and foremost. As will my son, Lucian Moretti, when it comes time for him to assume the throne."

Murmurs wave through the crowd as Nicole resumes her seat and offers me a wink. She's so calm in the face of thousands of wolves, some still filled with hate toward the vampires. Even outnumbered a hundred to one, not one of the Guardians twitch or seem fazed in the least.

My brother stands, and his wolves quiet. "First off, congratulations on the birth of the Daywalker vampire, your next king, my lady. You have fulfilled the ancient prophecy, bringing truth to the words of the gods. As we all know, vampires and werewolves have been at war for centuries and we have lost numerous lives on both sides. Fathers, sons, brothers, and husbands. The Werewolf Provence does not long for the bloodshed of old. We desire peace as much as you do, Queen Giordano, but one of your own murdered three of mine. And such a heinous crime cannot go unpunished. But understand this. It is out of respect for our friendship and the promise of truce for my people I am not allowing the grieving families to take his head. I too protect my own first and foremost."

Wide-eyed stares swivel back toward the vampire queen, and the tension in the arena presses in on my chest. I feel like I should say something, explain to the crowd how my actions forced Nox to do what he did and that the deaths are my burden to bear, not his. But Liam ordered me to keep my mouth shut.

My gaze zeros in on Nox, and our eyes lock.

'*I command you to remain silent,*' Nox orders mentally, no doubt sensing my chaotic emotions and exerting his Alpha role over me. My scrutiny bounces between Liam, Nox, and Nicole. What should I do? I want to defend my mate. Shout at these people to cease this insanity, but will anything I say make a bit of difference? Will it stop the tribunal?

Doubtful, but I have to try. Before I can leap to my feet and argue in defense of my mate, Nicole latches onto my wrist, holding me with ease in my seat.

'*Obey your mate, Cellica. Nothing you do can halt this and all you'll do is turn your people against you. Is that what you want?*'

'*No,*' I admit grudgingly to Moe, so the queen can hear me since I can't speak to her directly. '*But maybe my words will force them to think about what they are doing and go easy on him.*'

'Everything that needs to be said has been said. All we can do now is support Nox through this.'

"Dalton Hill," my brother barks, and I flinch. "You may begin your ten lashes in the name of your slain son, Dave Hill."

Nicole's grip on my wrist tightens briefly before she releases me and faces forward, her bright gray eyes remain focused on Nox.

I must be strong like Nicole, for Christoph's sake. I chant the mantra repeatedly as I follow her lead and focus on my mate as the first lash of the cat-o-nine strikes his back. I nearly cry out when Nox bows slightly, but he doesn't utter a sound, and his concentration never waivers from mine.

I school my features and offer him a slight nod and smile. 'I love you,' I mouth.

A rebellious tear slides down my cheek as Mr. Hill continues to dole out his ten lashes. Yet, through it all, Nox stands strong. The only indication he's in pain is his fists and jaw clenching.

I'm glad I can't see the damage to his back. I'd probably lose it, leap down into the arena, and rip Mr. Hill apart.

'Yeah,' Moe growls low. *'That sounds like a great idea.'* I sense the demon working to suppress his agitation and fury for my benefit. *'Right now, I wish I still possessed Nox so I could take this punishment for him.'*

'This was my fuck up. Mine alone,' Nox mutters to Moe.

'No, it wasn't,' he argues. *'I'm the one who forced Cellica on those wolves.'*

'As interesting as this threesome is, can we concentrate on the matter at hand, please?' Nicole interrupts with an irritated sigh, and we all clam up as Mike's father stomps into the arena, his own whip in his hands.

When the two fathers pass each other, they nod, and my gut tightens.

I squint at the lash in Mr. Grim's hand. The wicked barbs along the leather strips look bigger than Mr. Hill's whip. Why aren't they using the same one?

Liam stands and strolls down a couple of steps to the railing, his knuckles white as he grips the metal. He has a clear view of the damage to Nox, where he's positioned.

"Connel Grim, you may begin your ten lashes in the name of your slain son, Mike Grim."

The first hit buckles Nox's knees, and I slap a hand over my mouth to keep the strangled cry at bay. My fearless Guardian somehow rallies and locks his legs for the next strike. The brightness of his eyes showcases the pain more clearly than if he'd cried out.

Fuck.

'*I'm here, baby. Concentrate on me,*' I whisper, and his head lifts, the brilliant orbs, filled with agony, find me in the stands.

By the end of Mr. Grim's ten lashes, Nox struggles to remain upright, and scarlet blood pools at his feet. So much blood. Jesus, how much more can he lose and still remain conscious?

"Jeremiah Loneclaw," my brother calls out, and I realize they saved the worst for last. Jeremiah is a barrel of a man with the strength of three wolves. His rage clearly shines in his expression as he takes up position with his back to his king, not even acknowledging him.

Before I comprehend what's happening, Nicole traced into the arena and has Jeremiah by the throat. Logan and Sebastian are at her side in a heartbeat.

I leap to my feet and sprint down the steps just as my brother vaults over the railing, landing with a loud thud before calmly strolling over to the group.

"What is the meaning of this, Nicole?" Liam demands as I hop over the balustrade and race to Nox.

The second I reach him, I lift his head and kiss his dry lips. He's no longer standing on his own. The chains are the only thing keeping him upright. '*I'm here, Chris. Stay with me.*'

"I agreed to a fair tribunal, Liam, not a crucifixion." She grabs the whip out of Jeremiah's fist as he struggles against the fingers clamped around his throat. "The barbs on asshole number two's whip were larger than the first, and now this piece of shit's lance is bigger yet and laced with salt. What the fuck, Liam?"

Salt? Holy shit. They meant to scar him for life.

"He beheaded my son," the werewolf chokes out, gasping for air.

"You're about to suffer the same fate, Jeremiah," my brother snarls after examining the whip and turning to Nicole. "Release him." When she does, he takes her place. "You defied my direct order," the king growls low, and Jeremiah has the intelligence to swallow in fear.

"He needs to be reminded of what he did for the rest of his miserable existence. Fucking vampires have no regard for life. They kill and destroy everything they touch."

"That may have been true during King Dimitri's reign, but Queen Giordano has only wanted peace."

"You're pathetic and weak if you believe that, *my king,*" he sneers before spitting on the ground next to Liam's foot. I inhale sharply at his audacity.

My brother passes the whip over to Josh without turning his scrutiny from the wolf challenging him. "If you think you can be a better ruler than me, Jeremiah, you know what must be done."

"I don't *think*, Liam Scott. I *know*," he snarls back. "I'll gladly fight you to the death, and when I'm finished, every blood-sucking vampire in this place will be next. Including your bitch of a mate."

Chapter 51

Blue fire ignites in Liam's eyes, and before Logan can finish freeing Nox and get out of the way, Liam and Jeremiah lock in mortal conflict. No ceremony, no nothing.

I have no fear for my brother, even though Jeremiah has more combat experience. Liam is fierce and deadly, and after the wolf's stupid remark about Viessa, Liam will enjoy slitting his throat.

Once Nox is loose, Logan lays him over his shoulder with gentle care, and I get my first look at the damage done to Nox's back. The barbs flayed open his skin, ripping through muscles and tendons. The tips of his scapula peek through, as well as several broken ribs and his spine.

Christ almighty.

Bile threatens the back of my throat, but I swallow it down and follow Nicole and Logan to the side of the arena, away from the wolves trying to kill each other. A mighty roar rips through the air, and I peer over my shoulder to see Liam fling the bulky werewolf into the stanchion, his enormous body smashing it to smithereens. Good. I never want to lay eyes on the fucking thing again.

The watching crowd cheers their king on, chanting his name and stomping their feet. I smirk. Jeremiah never held the support of the people against my brother. He just couldn't see past his own grief and anger.

Viessa stands with regal poise off to the side, her bright amber scrutiny never deviating from her mate as he pounds his fists into Jeremiah's face repeatedly until the wolf no longer has the strength to defend himself. Then and only then does Liam swipe his claws through Jeremiah's throat, deep enough to sever his head from his body.

The crowd goes crazy, jumping to their feet, screaming and hollering as if their favorite football team just won the Super bowl.

The king's grief at slaying an old friend plays across his face, and my heart bleeds for him. My brother didn't want to destroy one of our own. Jeremiah gave him no choice.

He signals several wolves to come and collect the body before he spins in a circle to the salivating crowd with his arms outstretched. Blood drips from his fingertips, and his people settle.

"Are there any others who feel they can beat me, who crave my throne?"

Crickets.

Liam nods. His shoulders relax. "The Werewolf Provence served justice here today. We avenged our lost. Go home with the knowledge your king protects and cares for each one of you." He turns to Viessa as she passes him a cloth to wipe Jeremiah from his hands before they sprint over to us.

"How is he?" he asks.

"We need to get him back to the castle and more of Cellica's blood down his gullet," Sebastian states.

"It looks like it's mending already," Alex says with a grimace as she peers at the wounds.

My vampire is still unconscious over Logan's shoulder, and the worry over him not waking creases my forehead.

"Settle your affairs here, Liam, while Cellica gets Nox healed up," Nicole urges. "Then meet us at the castle for Kurtis's and Lu's burial rituals."

He nods. "You got it." He steps up close and grabs her hand. "Hey. We good?"

She grins. "You mean before? That was merely a little power play fun. We are always okay."

My brother's shoulders sag with relief before he turns to me. "See you in a few. Get our boy up and moving. He and I need to have a chat."

When we materialize in Nox's bedroom, Logan lays my vampire on his belly on top of the bedspread and leaves, saying nothing.

"Man of few words," I mumble as I tug off his huge shitkickers and remove the pillow under his cheek to make him more comfortable.

The muscles have started the healing process, covering the shocking white of his bones, but it has a way to go.

"I thought you said your blood would heal him instantly?" I question Moe aloud since the only other person in the room sprawls across the bed, passed out cold.

'*His injuries are severe. Without my lifeblood, it would take weeks to repair the damage.*'

"Should I try to wake him, to provide him my blood?"

'*Yes, let's rouse our boy.*'

I brush my fingers over the side of his face with tender care, loving how young and vulnerable he appears. I want to wrap him in my arms, but my gut churns at causing him more pain.

"Nox. Can you hear me?" He doesn't even twitch. "Christoph," I repeat a little louder. "Wake up. You need to feed."

'*Lick his anus. That will light him up,*' the demon chuckles.

"Seriously, Moe?"

'*What? What did I say?*'

Ignoring my naughty demon, I break the skin on my wrist with my canines and rub the blood across Nox's lips, hoping the scent will rouse him enough so he can drink. When he doesn't even twitch, my wolf whimpers in distress.

'*Roll him over,*' Moe offers.

"No. I don't want to impair his healing or hurt him further." I tilt his chin up and pry open his mouth, making sure several drops of blood land on his tongue.

'*Be prepared. He's going to...*' Before Moe can finish his warning, Nox rears up into a seated position, throws me across his lap, and plunges his fangs deep into my neck. '*...be ravenous,*' the demon finishes with a moan as if Nox's enormous canines sank into his dick.

I cradle the back of my mate's head, careful to stay away from the muscles and skin knitting closed, and murmur words of encouragement. Now is not an ideal time to experience the churning burn of desire, but I can't control it when my vampire is taking nourishment from me. It's like a string connects from his bite to my clit, tugging with each pull on my vein.

I shift, pressing my thighs together to ease the throbbing, but the action ignites a deeper fire.

'*Help me, Moe,*' I moan with selfish need, demanding relief from the ache. '*Please.*'

'*No,*' he responds with an agonized groan.

My body stills. '*What? Why?*'

'*I'm forbidden to touch you without Nox's consent.*'

'*Are you shitting me?*' What the hell? '*Do you want to touch me?*'

'*More than anything.*'

'Then as your Mistress, demon, I'm granting you permission.'

'I... you... fuck,' he growls. *'Sorry, love. You may be my vessel and Mistress, but Nox is my Master and I must obey if I want more.'*

This piques my interest, distracting me somewhat from my denied horniness. *'More of what?'* I ask.

'More of his delicious discipline, and if I'm a really good demon, more involvement in your sexual activity.'

Holy cripes. Nox's harsh commands flash through my brain. At the time I was in such a lust-filled euphoria I didn't really pay attention to what was being said, only the magnificent sensations bombarding my body.

It appears Nox laid down the law with Moe without even consulting me? I'm the fucking vessel. Don't I get a say? Anger and resentment churn with lust as my vampire continues to draw sustenance from my vein, causing my sex to pulse with need.

I'm so sick of the men in my world trying to rule over me like I'm a damn child who can't decide for herself.

But wouldn't you feel the same if the roles were reversed and a female demon possessed your mate? Would you want her touching him without you?

Fuck no. But I ignore the logical thought process and allow my sex drive to dictate my next comments. If he can strike a bargain without consulting me, so can I.

'Moe, if I'm not enjoying your talented fingers circling my clit in the next five seconds, it's not Nox you have to worry about. It's me. I will shove you deep, with no release in sight for weeks. Do you feel me?'

'Not fair, wolf. If I disobey Nox, he'll deny me. If I defy you, you'll deny me. I'm fucked either way and not in a pleasurable fashion.'

'You'll get off right now though. Isn't that what you seek above all else?'

'No,' he pouts. *'I crave to be included, not used as a tool.'*

I laugh. *'Stop pouting, Moe. You fucking love being our sex tool. It's your entire purpose in life, but you must realize you mean more to me.'*

'*I'm the third wheel Nox tolerates and uses for your enjoyment or when you need something from me.*'

Jesus. I hate that he's right. Shame grips my heart.

'*I don't know what to say, except I didn't choose to be possessed by the demon of lust. Nox certainly didn't ask for a mate with an entity ruled by his desires inside her. I realize you had no intention of staying with me forever, but here we are. I'm not sure what the solution to our problem is, Moe, but I can promise you I will work every day to make you feel more included and not just commanded.*'

'*And Nox?*'

'*I can't speak for him.*'

Strong arms grip me tighter as the lethal fangs ease from my neck, lapping at the punctures to seal them. I peek over his shoulder and am relieved to see not even a pink mark mars his perfect flesh.

I'm about to lean back when I'm unexpectedly flipped over on my stomach across his thighs with a surprised yelp. He shoves my jeans and underwear below my ass, and before I can object, Nox's big palm comes down on my cheek with a loud slap. I gasp at the painful sting.

Son of a bitch. This is the thanks I get for nourishing my mate? What the hell.

Chapter 52

Cellica

"That's for tempting Moe to touch you without my permission," he growls. Before I can defend myself, he offers up two more slaps on either cheek.

"Oww! What were those for?" I whimper.

"Those were for Moe, standing strong and being a good little demon. As are these." He delivers five more strikes, and Moe purrs with pleasure while I grip the comforter to keep from crying out.

Tensing for more, I am surprised when Nox shoves me to my knees between his spread thighs.

"Now, I remember you telling me you were going to show me how much you love me, little wolf." He unbuckles his pants, and my eyes widen.

'Oh fuck, yes!' Moe shouts, and I fight to control the exaggerated eye roll at his enthusiasm.

'Back off, big boy. You'll get your turn.'

Nox smirks. "Take out my cock, baby girl. Show me how exceptional of a little slut you are."

"Yes, Daddy." I ease down the zipper and reach inside for his rock-hard length. Nox lifts his hips so I can slide his bloodied jeans and boxer briefs off and toss them in a corner.

Saliva pools in my mouth at the beautiful specimen before me. So rigid, with the right amount of girth to offer me the painful but delicious stretch I covet.

Without needing further direction, I set in, running my tongue over the slit and down the shaft before taking him down my throat. I grip his balls with one hand and pump his length with the other in rhythm with my bobbing mouth.

"Fuck, baby. I love your naughty mouth on my cock." Nox gathers my hair into a ponytail and uses it as leverage to control the momentum. Sometimes he yanks up, forcing me to hover over the tip while he dives in with quick shallow thrusts, and other times he shoves my head down, urging me to take him to the back of my throat. I gag and tears leak out my eyes, but I love every second.

"Let me feel you hum, Moe," he commands, and the demon eagerly complies. "Christ. Swallow me down, my filthy little sluts."

Jesus. I could almost orgasm from his dirty talk. I need more. Crave more. More spankings. More wicked talk. More name-calling. I fucking love it all. When I reach a finger down to circle his puckered opening, Nox jerks in response.

"Only vulgar little whores lick ass." He shoves deep, and Moe hums low and hard. "Are you Daddy's dirty whore, Cellica?"

He lifts me off his dick with a pop, and I peer up at the male I would do anything for. "Yes, Daddy. Always."

Nox stands, his thighs knocking me back. "Strip," he orders, and I shiver at the cold command in his tone.

While I undress, Nox disappears into the bathroom. When I hear the shower start, I kneel back on the carpet and await his return. No doubt he wishes to rinse the blood and night off his skin. It soaked the back of his jeans.

My heart rate spikes when the shower cuts off and my mate strolls back out unashamedly nude, his erection jutting up proud and strong. Instead of striding to me, he disappears into his closet before returning with something clutched in his hand. He walks over to the chair by the fireplace, and I admire his perfect ass until he plants it on the cushion, hiding it from view.

"Crawl to me," he commands.

My insides clench, and my clit pulsates painfully. This is one of my recurring fantasies, crawling on my hands and knees at Nox's directive. Kneeling at his feet, collared and leashed. My degradation knows no bounds. I fucking want everything with my mate.

I plant my palms on the carpet and slowly make my way over to him. His bright irises watch me with such intensity, it's like a heated caress everywhere they land. By the time I'm between his spread legs, the evidence of my lust glistens between my thighs. My heart nearly pounds out of my chest. My skin crawls with the need for more pain, more pleasure. More everything.

"You are so fucking beautiful," he murmurs before gripping my chin. "Do you trust me?"

"Yes, of course."

"Good girl." He opens his palm, and I finally get a proper look at what he had coiled in the center. There is a black leather collar with a slim metal plate in the middle and several small rings on either side. I peer up at him in confusion. I was expecting a sex toy or something.

"Look at the engraving," he invites, and I glance back down at the choker.

Etched in intricate cursive, centered in the plate, is one word. *Daddy's.* My eyes widen in understanding as I run my finger across the title.

"Daddy's," I whisper in awe.

"That's right, baby girl, you belong to me and anytime we are alone or at play, you will wear my collar."

"What if I want to wear it all the time?" I murmur.

I'm not ashamed of our relationship. On the contrary, I'm addicted to the way Nox makes me come alive. He and Moe brought

me out of my insecure shell and fulfilled every desire, every im-
proper, naughty thought in my head.

"You would honor me, but maybe not in front of your brother.
No need to antagonize the beast," he grins.

I chuckle. "Are you afraid of my brother, mate?"

"Of Liam? No. Of his beast? No vampire in their right mind
wouldn't be, love. Now lift your hair and turn around."

The second the cool leather encircles my neck, a sense of peace
and belonging settles in my chest. I brush my fingers over the
etching on the plate as Nox secures it, and tears blur my vision.

I have many dreams and aspirations for my future, and I plan on
working hard to bring them to fruition. Still, my one constant, the
thing driving me to be better, succeed, and let go of my inhibitions
and my insecurities, is Nox.

He brings my heart and soul alive just by being in the same room
with him. I'm proud to be his female. His mate. And since he's
a vampire and his claiming bite doesn't display on my skin for
everyone to see as mine does on his, this collar is the next best
thing. It proclaims me as his. Loud and clear.

'*Hellfire*,' Moe exclaims. '*Is the collar branding me as well?*'

"Yes, Moe," Nox answers, and I gaze up at my generous mate.
"Darath spelled the metal, so you belong to me as well. You are a
part of us and I wanted you to be included."

'*I... I don't know what to say.*' From the first moment Moe came
barreling into our lives, he's speechless, his emotions all over the
map. '*Thank you, Master,*' he replies, stunned by Nox's generosity.

"It also means I can summon you out of Cellica for brief periods
so we can pleasure our girl together."

I gasp. "Like as an actual person?"

"Yes," he grins. "Would you like that, baby girl?"

"Oh yes. I would love to see Moe."

"Asmodeus, come forth."

The collar heats for several seconds as Moe's essence expands away from mine, and I suck in a lungful of air at the odd sensation. It's not unpleasant, but it feels as if a part of me is stretching in half, beyond its limits.

"Turn around, Cellica," Nox whispers, his heated regard lifted behind me and I rotate on my knees.

The second I behold my demon, the breath seizes in my lungs. My jaw drops, and I stare wide-eyed at the most beautiful creature I've ever seen. Asmodeus' seven-foot frame is absolute perfection. The pointed horns spark my imagination, and I bite my lip as I visualize gripping them as he devours my pussy. The spectacular beauty of his fiery wings entrances me for several minutes. The enormous feathers undulate with orange and red flames.

Moe grins down at me, and my insides clench in response. Jesus. Nox was right. Asmodeus was built to draw you in. The sexual energy radiating from him in waves would bring me to my knees if I wasn't already on them.

It takes great effort to peel my gaze from his captivating ruby irises and continue exploring his masculine perfection. I ogle the sculpted flawlessness of his torso and abs, but when I get to the apex of his lean hips, my eyes nearly pop out of my skull.

Jutting up from his hairless groin is the biggest damn cock I've ever encountered. Not that I've seen many in my brief life, but still. Fuck me, I thought Nox was huge. Raised ridges wrap his girth down the length of his shaft as if rings burrow under the skin. The thick bulbous head drips pre-cum, jerking at my scrutiny and my insides clench at the enhanced nodules nestled at the base.

"Moe," I breathe in awe. "You're beautiful."

The demon smirks with wicked intent, and my sex flutters. He grabs the other chair and moves it out of the way to kneel before Nox. "Thank you, Master. How may I be of service?"

"Don't turn that fucking glamour on to me, demon," Nox growls, even as his dick jerks in response to Moe's overpowering sexual magnetism.

I pivot to my mate. "How can we please you together, Daddy?" I ask to alleviate the tension radiating between my males. One is lustful and eager, the other fighting his lust with anger.

Nox tears his glare from Moe, kneeling behind me and fists my hair. "Suck my cock, while Moe fucks your eager cunt. Would my little slut like to be taken from both ends?"

"Oh yes, Daddy."

Nox leans back in the chair, glaring at Moe. "Fuck her hard, Moe," he commands, and the demon's scorching heat envelops my spine. I grip my mate's thick member and lick and suckle Nox's balls before running my tongue up the shaft. My body pulsates with need and eager anticipation, but a part of me fears Moe's size impaling me.

The demon's searing skin slides along the outside of my thighs, one foot planted by the chair for better leverage. I moan at the image we must make, and my insides gush with desire, helping to pave the way for Moe's massive girth. When his cock nudges my entrance, he runs the head through my juices before probing inside.

Holy fuck. The stretching from just the head is too much and I let go of Nox's cock to evade the burn. Nox grips my hair tighter, and Moe's enormous hands clamp down on my hips. "Slap her ass, Moe. I didn't tell our little whore to stop sucking my cock."

The instant warmth from Moe's palm smacking my ass spreads straight to my stretched core, tightening around his head. The demon groans low, and I renew my efforts on Nox.

"So fucking tight," Moe mutters as inch by painful inch, he stuffs his length inside me, and I force my muscles to relax. The spread is immense, but I am ready to shatter from the delicious pain, and he hasn't started fucking me yet.

"Does his cock feel good, baby girl?"

I moan in response, bobbing up and down on his delicious hardness.

"Fuck her, Moe. Our little girl is hungry for it."

Nox leans back in the chair, his ass on the edge and his thighs stretched out next to my body. The second Moe retreats and plunges deep. I shatter, gripping Nox's hips as my orgasm washes through me like a flash flood.

"Allow me, Master," Moe requests before replacing Nox's fist in my hair. Pain tingles across my scalp as Moe guides my mouth up and down Nox's length while he pounds into me, the ridges on his cock bouncing across that sweet spot with every thrust.

"That's it, Moe. Punish her hard. Make her come again."

Out of the corner of my eye, I see Nox's fingers digging into Moe's thick thigh planted by the chair, and I want to cry at its beauty. My mate wants nothing more than to grant me every pleasure I can imagine—including some I can't. Even though he bucked his presence from the beginning, he accepted our situation and embraced Moe as his. For me.

He went one step further to brand him *Daddy's* right alongside me, and I couldn't be more thrilled. These males are my life, and I will wear Nox's collar with pride.

"Fuck, Cellica," Nox groans. His head rests on the back of the chair, his hooded gaze pinned on both of us while he sits back like a king and enjoys the show—the demon forcing me to suck him with abandon. All the while his fingers dig into Moe's knee with a punishing grip. "Come with me, Cellica. You too Moe. Fill her sweet cunt with your cum."

Daddy orders, and we obey.

My sex convulses as Moe's hot cum lashes my insides, and Nox's salty goodness shoots down my throat as Moe pushes my head to swallow him down.

Fucking. Utter. Bliss.

As Moe's thrusts slow and his grip on my hair moves to my hips, I clean up every last drop from my mate. I'm so satiated and relaxed I can hardly move. My demon's hold keeps me from collapsing at Nox's feet.

My energy sapped, I rest my cheek on my vampire's thigh, slowly caressing his hardness that hasn't diminished in the slightest.

Moe's warmth folds over my spine, his wings blocking the light as he drops a kiss on my shoulder. "Thank you, Mistress," he murmurs. "I couldn't have asked for a better pairing than the two of you." He brushes his lips over Nox's fingers, still clutching his knee. "I am forever yours, Master, but this has weakened me. I must return."

I'm shocked when Nox lifts his hand and runs it over one of Moe's horns. A shudder passes through the demon, and his cock twitches inside me. Moe worships Nox. Craves any iota of attention the vampire offers him. I know the feeling.

"Until next time, Asmodeus. You did well."

"Thank you, Master." Moe grins. "I hope one day you will allow me to pleasure you as well."

Nox frowns, and I bite my lip to keep from grinning. That's my demon. He loves to push the limits.

"Don't test me, Asmodeus," Nox admonishes gruffly. "Retreat."

The second we are physically alone, the vampire lifts me onto his lap, and I shiver against the coldness in the room. "How about a hot shower before joining the others for the burial ritual?"

"That sounds lovely," I murmur, snuggling into the warmth of his chest. "Thank you for this," I say, grazing my fingers over the collar. "And for tonight, Christoph. It was perfect."

"My goal in life is to make you happy, Cellica, to pleasure you, spoil you, and give you everything you desire."

I sit up to stare into the eyes of the creature who pushed me away for the longest time, afraid his affections for me would destroy his friendship with my brother.

While Liam and Nox still need to have a heart to heart, or whatever you call it, when men grunt out their emotions, the obstacles to our future are gone. He's accepted my passenger, even collared him as our own.

"Thank you for including Moe in this," I murmur, unable to stop caressing my new jewelry. "In us."

"He's a part of you. It may have taken me a bit to accept a third entity in our relationship, but I didn't understand his devotion to you or yours to him. His time with you made me jealous and angry. I'm a possessive vampire. I abhorred the thought of having to share. It's the reason I forbade Moe from touching you without my permission. I own your pleasure, Cellica. Your body belongs to me and me alone."

"Yes, Daddy," I whisper, brushing my lips across his in confirmation.

Chapter 53

A heaviness settles over my leather-clad chest as Cellica and I walk into the great dining hall. Despite having spent the last hour and a half in carnal bliss with both my mates.

I snort. Never in a million years would I have imagined the fates would pair me with a petite, submissive werewolf, whose sexual needs match my own, but also a damn demon of lust. None other than a Prince of Hell who worships at my feet. Life is strange, and I'm excited to explore more with both of them.

We stride in solemn silence to join our family, her small hand gripped in mine. Nicole stands with regal grace at the head of the table, dressed for battle. The leather hugs her lean body, her favorite guns strapped to her thighs and a short sword adorns her back. Grief darkens her expression as she gazes down at her best friend, his mate positioned next to him. Their fingers intertwine as if they were simply napping on the enormous table.

The Shifter Territory performed the first half of their ceremony for their king and queen already, allowing us time to say our goodbyes. After, they will burn their bodies as per their custom.

If Lu were a Guardian, we would spend the next two days celebrating her life before placing her remains on a pyre and sending her spirit to the gods. But since she was the shifter queen, the burial rites transfer to them.

I wonder who is next in line to take over the crown. Unfortunately, neither Kurtis nor Lu had any offspring. I shrug. A worry for another day.

Nicole holds up her hand and the room, packed full of Guardians and friends dressed for battle as per our custom, quiets. "We all express grief in different ways. Sadness, guilt, despair, anxiety, fear, hopelessness, longing, anger, and frustration will likely run through your mind. And while I sometimes have difficulty expressing my emotions, in times like these, your feelings need to be expressed. What is it about crying we are afraid of? They say it helps you heal. Yet we fight it with everything we have. They teach us that tears reveal weakness."

Her sad smile clenches my jaw as the thought of never seeing Kurtis and Lu again burns the back of my eyes. I've shared so many memories with Lucretia. We fought, trained, drank, and patrolled together for over a century. Her death, how she died alone, haunts me. If I'd been there, she might still be alive. Instead, I will live with my mistake for the rest of my days.

"When I was little," Nicole continues. "My mom took me to church once, and to this day I remember what the pastor said about grief. Weeping may stay for the night, but rejoicing comes in the morning. At the time, I didn't understand what it meant. How could you possibly recover from the death of a loved one so quickly? But it's not about getting over the loss and moving on, it's about celebrating their lives and rejoicing in the fact you were blessed to have them in your life, no matter how brief or long. Kurtis was a loyal friend with a big heart. A hard but fair king. A devoted mate to Lucretia."

"A terrible poker player," Sebastian pipes in with a sad smile, and several chuckles rebound around the room.

"With the worst taste in beer," Liam adds, his smile strained as he grips Viessa's hand.

"A fierce warrior," Darath interjects. "With a body built for...."

"Okay, Jag," Nicki interrupts with a tolerant grin.

"What?" he responds with an innocent shrug, and I snort. I see where Moe gets it.

"The point is," my queen continues. "It's fine to grieve. Talk with others about your loss and pain. Kurtis demanded the hidden emotions in us all. He brought out the best in Lu and vice versa. Share your precious memories of them. It keeps their spirits in our hearts and minds. Forever. Even though Lu and I had a rocky start, she proved her worth time and time again."

Logan steps forward in full battle gear, his huge broadswords jutting up over his shoulders. "I will never forget the day Bastian and I received Lucretia's application to become a Guardian. We were stunned at her resume, her accomplishments, and not once did it ever enter our minds to disregard her because she was a female. Her achievements spoke for themselves. She trained harder than any male here, eager to prove herself. And even though circumstances forced the queen to excommunicate her from vampire society, she never left our hearts and was always welcome in our home. Kurtis and Lucretia will forever be members of this family. We grieve their loss, but rejoice in their lives. They touched each one of us in one way or another and they live on in our hearts and minds."

Sebastian moves to the other side of his queen, his mate tucked to his side, and I take my place with Cellica next to them. Liam and Viessa move in next to Logan with Darath and Kleora.

"We have survived so much together over the last few years," the queen states as her scrutiny scans her friends and Guardians. "And fulfilled the prophecy. Together, we defeated my father. Achieved peace among the majority of the immortal world. And your next king rests in the other room. His life will bring forth a new era of vampires."

A whoop rises from the Guardians, echoing off the stone walls, and a chill runs down my spine. She did it. Nicole Giordano, the first human-vampire hybrid, achieved everything Icarus said she would. And even though her beginning scarred her soul, she overcame, sacrificed, and fought for Logan and our people.

Since the day we discovered she existed, I have guarded and watched over her. Witnessed firsthand her courage, loyalty, and unwavering devotion to Logan in the face of impossible odds. She's more than earned my piety and love, and I would follow her to the ends of the earth and back, willingly forfeit my life to preserve hers and the new king.

"Our new task is to find the human females and their destined mates," she continues when the warriors settle once more. "We no longer fear extinction." Another whoop floods the room. "So let us celebrate Kurtis and Lucretia's sacrifice. Their life."

The hundred-plus warriors gathered to honor Kurtis and Lucretia, pound their fists to their chests in answer, and bow their heads to our fallen. I glance down at my mate, her little fist clenched over her heart, her blue hair cascading around her shoulders, and my chest swells.

When her chin lifts to gaze up at me, I look at her beautiful face. I look at her beautiful eyes. I think of all the ways this little wolf has proven herself to be so much more than I ever imagined, and how undeserving I am of the love shining from her gaze.

Moe will play a huge part in the coming search for the precious human females to ensure our continued survival, and I couldn't be prouder to call the deviant fucker my mate. He will no doubt test my patience and control, but I wouldn't have it any other way. One thing is for certain—our lives will never be boring.

I contemplate my friends honoring our dead, and more emotions clog my throat. Nicole's right, we have endured much to get to this point. Lost precious lives. Jimmy Scott, Cellica's father. Icarus, our Oracle. And now Kurtis and Lucretia. Our lives have been a tsunami of ups and downs, twists, and turns, but we endured. Together we endured.

No matter the outcome of the coming years in our search for the breeder females, and continued peace among our kind, our final storm will never be forgotten.

THE END

Also By

A.R. Vagnetti

<u>Storm Series Complete Set</u>
Forsaken Storm Prequel
Forgotten Storm
Forbidden Storm
Fiery Storm
Fractured Storm
Fatal Storm
Final Storm... The Conclusion
<u>Coming Soon</u>
Immortal Breeder Series—A Spin-off Paranormal Romance Series
Gemma's Fate
Calista's Destiny
Willow's Doom
Layla's Future
<u>Coming Soon</u>
Keystone Series—A Paranormal Fantasy Romance Series
Diamond Key
Emerald Key
Sapphire Key
Ruby Key

Acknowledgments

First and foremost, I want to thank my husband for his patience during the writing process as I sequestered myself in the office for hours upon hours and barked at him if he dared to open the door.

To my amazing cover designer, Les at German Creative, you are the bomb and your artistic talent literally explodes on the cover! It's like you reach into my mind and make a reality exactly what I envision.

To Haley Willens, my lovely and brilliant editor, thank you for all your hard work and ingenuity to make this book the best it can be. You turn my ramblings into a cohesive stream of words.

To my intuitive beta readers: Dawn, Paul, Mia, and Jodi. Your perspective shines a light on the forest I can't see through the trees, giving the story and characters more depth. You guys rock!

To my Street Team. You are the last eyes before publication, catching what the rest of us missed, and your honest reviews mean the world to me. Reviews are the bread and butter of any book.

To every reader, thank you so much for picking up this book, for sticking with me on this journey through the Storm series. For your constant praise and words of encouragement. I hope we meet again in the next adventure.

Until next time,

A. R. Vagnetti

About Author

A.R. Vagnetti

A.R. Vagnetti is an American writer of Adult Paranormal Romance. She grew up in the scalding Tucson desert and does her best writing while camping, traveling, and on the beautiful shores of Lake Huron where she is now blessed to spend her summers away from the Arizona heat. A.R. loves to transport readers into a fantastical world of paranormal romance where bold Alpha males will sacrifice anything for the strong, deeply scared, kick-ass females they love.

Thank you, dear readers, for continuing to love the Storm Series! Stay tuned for the **Immortal Breeder Series**, a paranormal romance spin-off from the Storm series!

If you loved **Final Storm... The Conclusion** or any of the books in the Storm Series, please consider reviewing it or recommending it to a friend—your reviews help indie authors so much.

Let's Connect:
Join the Stormster Club! You will get exclusive previews, spicy book recommendations, giveaways, and news on upcoming releases. A.R. loves to connect with her readers.
Email: ar@arvagnetti.com

Please Follow A.R. on:

BookBub—Goodreads–Instagram—Facebook—TikTok—Pinterest

Check out her website:

www.arvagnetti.com

www.ingramcontent.com/pod-product-compliance
Lightning Source LLC
Chambersburg PA
CBHW020915110726
47900CB00001B/152